RED ROMEO

Peter Bernhardt

For Agnes and Rolf

In Loving Memory

I want to express my gratitude to the members of the Sedona Writers Critique Group, the Internet Writing Workshop, and my beta reader for their constructive criticism and valuable feedback that improved this novel beyond measure.

I especially thank Marilyn for her keen insights that inspire me to do better, for being a thoughtful sounding board as each chapter was born, and for her unwavering support.

Glossary

Main Characters

Sabine Maier, Agent, Federal Intelligence Service, West Germany.
Stefan Malik, East German journalist/writer, recruited as a Stasi Romeo. Cover: Günter Freund, writer for *Gemeinschaft Unbegrenzt*, a fictitious Vienna peace organization.
Werner Heinrich, Lieutenant General, Stasi spymaster.
Monika Fuchs, Executive Secretary to Chief of the West German Chancellery.
Horst Kögler, former intelligence agent turned computer consultant.
Helga Schröder, General Heinrich's secretary.
Traude Malik, Stefan's daughter.
Bernd Dorfmann, Sabine's boss.
Gisela Sturm, Executive Secretary to the West German Foreign Minister.
Hans Mertens, Agent, Office for the Protection of the Constitution, West Germany.

Organizations

STASI: Ministerium für Staatssicherheit, East German Secret Police, East Berlin.
HVA: Hauptverwaltung Aufklärung, Stasi Foreign Intelligence Service, East Berlin.
BND: Bundesnachrichtendienst, Federal Intelligence Service, West Germany, Pullach, Bavaria; reports to West German Chancellor.
BfV: Bundesamt für Verfassungsschutz, Office for the Protection of the Constitution, Cologne. West Germany's domestic intelligence service that reports to the Bundestag (lower house of parliament).

ASBw: Amt für die Sicherheit der Bundeswehr, Office of Security, Federal Armed Forces, Cologne; 1956-1984. Since 1984: MAD: Militärischer Abschirmdienst, Military Counterintelligence Service, Cologne.

BKA: Bundeskriminalamt, Federal Criminal Investigation Bureau a/k/a Federal Criminal Police Agency, Wiesbaden, West Germany; reports to the Federal Ministry of the Interior.

RAF: Rote Armee Fraktion, Red Army Faction terrorist group.

GDR: German Democratic Republic; in German: DDR: Deutsche Demokratische Republik (official and euphemistic name for communist East Germany).

Definitions

mole: 2. a spy who becomes part of and works from within the ranks of an enemy governmental staff or intelligence agency.

double agent: 1. a person who spies on a country while pretending to spy for it.
2. a spy in the service of two rival countries, companies, etc.

www.dictionary.com

Chapter One

The Choice

Rummelsburg Prison, East Berlin, Friday afternoon, 15 July 1977

The guard shoved Stefan Malik across the threshold and slammed the cell door. The scraping of the giant key sliding the deadbolt into place bore the sound of permanence. A stench from the toilet at the far wall, its splintered seat hanging off to one side, pervaded the damp cell, but the foul smell was the least of his problems. His apprehension turned to alarm at the sight of three prisoners staring him down. Two lurked behind a burly redhead, the obvious ruler of this space.

An ugly smirk spread across the stout man's fleshy face, barely visible in the faint light spilling through a small, iron-barred window high on the wall. "What's the matter, pretty boy, never smelled shit before?"

His two cellmates, leaning against one of the bunk beds, cackled—the forced laugh of subordinates at a superior's bad joke.

The redhead asked, "What's your name?"

"Stefan."

"We are your new best friends. I'm Emil." He turned to his left, "Anton," then to his right, "Hans."

Both gave slight nods at the mention of their names. But Stefan kept his eyes on Emil, who appeared to be listening to the sound of the guard's boots striking the cement floor in the hall.

When the sound faded, Emil turned to his cellmates. "Don't you think Stefan has a nice ass? What say, boys, we get better acquainted with him?" He leered at Stefan. "Lots better."

Stefan took a step back. He'd heard about Rummelsburg housing homosexuals, branded social deviants by the state, and now perhaps he'd fallen in with three of them. Gays or not, they had rape on their minds. Before he could react, Hans and Anton had circled behind him. One twisted his right arm against his back while the other pushed him onto his knees. He struggled against excruciating pain. It felt as if his arm were coming out of its socket.

"Just relax, pretty boy." Emil lowered the trousers of his striped prison uniform. "Do as you're told and we'll get along fine."

Stefan stared at the bulge in the man's gray boxer shorts. The next few seconds would determine his fate. Sweat popped onto his forehead. Raped in prison? If he succumbed now, there'd be no end to it. Yelling for the guards was pointless. Even if they heard, they probably wouldn't care. He was on his own.

Stefan quit straining against the hold the two guys had on him. "You want a blow job?" He feigned a smile. "Why didn't you just say so?"

Emil wasn't so easily duped. "Anton, bring him over here. Hans, don't let go."

Stefan forced his eyes from the yellow stains on Emil's shorts and made his body go limp. The ploy worked. When the grips loosened the slightest bit, Stefan jerked himself free. He jumped to his feet and thrust his right shoe into Emil's groin, hard.

The bully stumbled backward. He snarled through clenched teeth, "You'll pay for this. Grab him, guys!"

Stefan pivoted to face Emil's minions, but not in time to fend off a violent kick to his right leg. He collapsed, scraping his knee on the cement floor. He tried to roll off to the side, but one of the convicts straddled him, keeping him pinned while the other pressed his face against the floor. He strained to breathe.

Emil's angry voice rang in Stefan's ears. "Big mistake, boy. I'll show you who's boss."

Stefan winced at a violent jerk that forced his head back and upward at a sharp angle. His eyes transfixed by the boxer shorts moving toward him, Stefan fought panic. He would not give in. If he had to, he'd bite the brute's cock off. But wait, why was Emil retreating?

The sound of the deadbolt sliding back provided the answer. Emil yanked his pants up from around his ankles. The cell door flew open and two guards rushed in.

One pulled Stefan to his feet. "Starting a fight on your first day?"

"These perverts—"

The guard yanked him from the cell. "Save your excuses for the boss."

He pushed Stefan down the hall, while the other guard locked the cell. There was no point in trying to explain. The whole thing stank. The guards had appeared so fast, as if they'd expected the brawl.

When the police had picked him up at his apartment less than an hour ago, they'd told him it was just to clear something up. Of course, he hadn't believed them. He'd heard of too many citizens being swept up in the dragnet of the secret police. The Stasi was the most feared institution in all of East Germany for a reason. To clear something up was a euphemism for harsh interrogation, torture, long prison sentences, or worse. Was his name about to be added to the growing list of missing East Germans?

During the ride in the unmarked van through the city streets, he'd mentally reviewed the article he'd submitted for publication earlier this week. Always careful to toe the party line, he couldn't think of anything that could have gone against official doctrine. Still, one never knew when the winds in a totalitarian state might shift. Perhaps he'd unwittingly offended one of the party bosses.

The guard shuttled him through the cellblock gate toward the administrative offices. Stefan wondered what disciplinary action he'd face. The thought of being locked up with rapists was unbearable. He slowed when they reached the prison director's office, but the guard pushed him past toward an unmarked door and knocked.

"*Herein,*" a deep voice bellowed.

The guard eased the door open and pushed Stefan onto the tattered linoleum floor of a small room. Flaking olive-green paint on bare walls made for a drab place. Behind a large imitation teak desk sat a man in gray uniform, black hair neatly parted. Dark eyes peered at Stefan through wire-rimmed glasses.

Gone was the guard's officious attitude. He addressed the man, who looked to be in his fifties, in a deferential manner. "*Generalleutnant,* prisoner Stefan Malik."

The officer leaned forward, affording Stefan a glimpse of the two-star insignia of a lieutenant general on his shoulder. "Guard, close the door behind you and wait in the hall."

While the guard complied, the general pointed to an angular metal chair that proved to be as uncomfortable as it looked. But more important things occupied Stefan's mind. This was no ordinary army general, but a Stasi officer. What could he possibly want from him? Whatever it was, nothing good ever came from run-ins with the secret police.

♫ ♫ ♫

Lieutenant General Werner Heinrich watched the prisoner take the chair. So far his plan was working. He liked what he saw. Malik appeared cautious, but not obsequious like the guard. The task he needed to recruit him for demanded boldness. It was not for the demure or faint of heart. Malik's eyes spoke of intelligence, and most important, he was as handsome as his file had promised. Who could resist the open face that suggested sincerity, the black hair combed straight back, the athletic build?

First pleasantries, then pressure. "May I call you Stefan?" At the silent nod, Heinrich continued, "I'm Lieutenant General Heinrich. You may address me as General."

No response.

Heinrich opened the large manila folder on the desk. "If you're as smart as this says you are, you've figured out by now that I'm a Stasi officer."

No reaction.

"But you don't know why you're here."

Stefan shifted in his chair.

"It's not your writing. Your articles are entertaining and stick to the party line or *Neues Deutschland* wouldn't publish them."

Heinrich looked for signs of anxiety or fear. If Stefan felt either, he hid it well. Perfect. A poker player mentality was ideal.

Almost time to start the recruitment, but first a little more praise. "You're here because you're good at something we can use."

Stefan arched his eyebrows but said nothing.

Heinrich made a show of flipping through the folder on his desk. "You're a regular Don Juan, aren't you?" He looked up. Still no reaction. "We know of at least a dozen women who . . . to put this delicately . . . who've succumbed to your charms."

"Having sex is not illegal, is it?" Stefan's baritone rang measured but firm through the small office.

Another plus.

"Illegal? Not usually." Heinrich paused for emphasis. "Except for a couple of things." He stared at Stefan. "One, several of the women you seduced are married. Two, you bilked them out of money, because you can't live on your writing. And three, our state does not look kindly on freeloaders who don't contribute to society."

"That's why you had me thrown into a cell with a bunch of queers?"

"I'm asking the questions here." Heinrich leaned forward. Time to apply pressure. "I hoped we could clear all this up with a friendly chat. Regrettably, you attacked your cellmates."

"I didn't start it."

"So you say. Unfortunately for you, it's your word against that of two guards and three prisoners." After a pause to let his message sink in, Heinrich continued, "Well, there is a way to get yourself out of this. Put those charms of yours in service of the state."

"An informer for the Stasi?"

"Something more important, more difficult, more challenging, and more fun."

Heinrich relished the quizzical expression spreading across the prisoner's face. "If you're as good at seduction as this file indicates, you can get laid and serve your country. It pays well enough so you won't have to hit up your lady friends for money."

"Are you asking me to become a Stasi spy?"

"We call it 'ficken fürs Vaterland.' Fucking for your country is a nice privilege, don't you agree? You're uniquely qualified for the romance part, and we'll teach you the tradecraft."

"General, I have no interest in spying for you, fringe benefits or not."

Heinrich shot up from his chair, moved around the desk, and towered over the seated prisoner. "Let me put this in plain language, Stefan. Either you join us and serve your country or you languish in this prison. You just got a taste of what that might be like. An easy choice, don't you think?"

Stefan twitched in his chair, possibly weighing whether to challenge the accusation of starting the fight with his cellmates. But he held his tongue, clearly sharp enough to realize that protest was futile; the court would hand out whatever sentence the Stasi dictated. Heinrich returned to his chair, all the while keeping an eye on the prisoner.

Stefan met his gaze. "What do I have to do?"

"I knew you'd make the right decision," Heinrich said, as if the prisoner ever had a real choice.

He rose, stepped around the desk and shook Stefan's hand. "*Willkommen.* Report to me at Stasi headquarters at nine Monday morning. And not a word to anyone. Is that clear?"

"Yes, sir."

"There's a car waiting to take you to your apartment."

Heinrich escorted Stefan into the hall and instructed the guard to have him discharged. Long after they had disappeared around a corner, the image of one of his most attractive recruits remained with Heinrich. Stefan Malik was handsome indeed. He would no doubt make a seductive Romeo.

Chapter Two

The Assignment

Bundesnachrichtendienst [BND], Federal Intelligence Service, Pullach, West Germany, Friday afternoon, 15 July 1977

Sabine Maier drove her VW past the blue-lettered *Bundesnachrichtendienst* sign, anchored to the ground in front of a massive concrete wall engraved with an oversized depiction of the Federal Eagle—the emblem of all things official in West Germany like the national flag, banknotes and coins, and federal buildings. She waved at the young guard who stood by the open gate. He raised his hands in a questioning gesture, a not-so-subtle reminder of his repeated invitations for an after-hours drink.

For a moment, she thought about encouraging him. A few more years and she'd hit the big four-oh. How much longer would men find her attractive? Still, she cherished her independence too much to risk getting stuck in a ho-hum relationship. She shook her head and smiled sweetly. The guard grimaced and motioned her through.

The dashboard clock showed two p.m., the time she was supposed to be back from lunch. She parked in her assigned slot and pulled the Beetle's convertible top over her head just as the first raindrops fell from dark clouds. It had been muggy all day and now the skies opened up. She couldn't decide whether to welcome the cooler temperatures or dread the prospect of another gray, rainy weekend. Whatever had possessed her to buy a convertible? German summer—an oxymoron.

She fastened the clamps securing the top, snatched her purse from the passenger seat, extricated herself from the cramped space, and locked the car. Careful to dodge deepening puddles, she made a dash for the building across the lot through the downpour, swiped her card, and almost ran into the glass door that swished open too slowly.

She bypassed the elevator, climbing the staircase two steps at a time to the second floor. Breathing hard, she rushed down the hall past the secretary cubicles, rounded the corner to her office, and stopped. The door stood open, affording her a view of her boss sitting in a visitor's chair.

The gray-haired fifty-something in a blue suit, white shirt, and striped tie turned to face her. "Caught in the downpour?"

Self-conscious, Sabine dabbed at her damp auburn curls, tugged at her red blouse, which clung to her body, and smoothed her black skirt. Realizing the futility of attempting to make herself look more professional, she dropped the purse on the desk and sank into the leather swivel chair. "Sorry—"

Bernd Dorfmann cut short her apology with a wave of the hand. "Another rainy weekend. Perfect for working, don't you think?"

She studied his face for signs he was kidding. He often joked, but not this time.

"You don't have any plans that can't be put off?" he said.

She shook her head at the rhetorical question, not volunteering she had promised to take her mother to the opera Saturday evening. No way would she miss *Don Giovanni*, sold out like most Munich Opera Festival performances. She hadn't stood in line for hours to give up their seats now. Her opera evenings were sacred. If he made her work, she'd manage to squeeze it in, even if it meant pulling an all-nighter.

"Good." Dorfmann leaned forward. "I'm giving you a new assignment."

"But—"

"I know I'm working you too hard, but that's the price you pay for doing such a great job."

"Except for finding the mole in our midst."

"Don't blame yourself, Frau Maier. If there is a mole, you will expose him."

She knew if her boss had any qualms about her performance, he would tell her. Still, she couldn't help searching his face for signs of insincerity.

He continued, "We need a change in direction."

She sat up.

"What do you know about *Rasterfahndung?*" he asked.

"Not much. It's used to create profiles of likely terrorists. A kind of dragnet investigation."

"Right. It's painstaking detail work that has paid off for the *Bundeskriminalamt* in catching Red Army Faction members."

"You're not assigning me to hunt down RAF terrorists?"

He made a dismissive gesture. "Heavens no. In five years, you've caught more spies than anybody. You make the BND proud. But in spite of all your arrests, we're still being overrun by Stasi agents. We're under pressure from the chancellor to use Rasterfahndung to stop this deluge."

She hesitated, unsure whether to raise her concern. Since he'd always encouraged her to voice her opinions, she spoke up. "There've been rumblings about the legality of such a data-mining approach, profiling individuals through computer searches."

Once again, he waved her off. "Never mind that. Until the constitutional court in Karlsruhe tells us otherwise, we're not going to forgo using this method."

Puzzled, she stared at him. "How does this relate to my spy-catching?"

"Good question. I want you to shift your focus. We thought the arrest of the chancellor's right-hand man meant the end of Stasi spies infiltrating our ministries. Were we ever wrong!"

"Günter Guillaume," Sabine said, her tone hushed, as she recalled how the unmasking of the chancellor's trusted assistant as a long-time Stasi spy had caused Willy Brandt's downfall three years ago.

"But now it's pretty clear that the communists are still stealing our most guarded secrets. It's as if they're reading the ministers' mail and sitting in on cabinet meetings." Dorfmann clenched his fist. "I want you to put an end to this."

"And you think Rasterfahndung can accomplish that?"

"Look, I'm going to be honest with you. I have my doubts, but I'm under orders to determine whether it's feasible."

"You mean you'll have me work on the weekend learning about something we both know won't work?"

Dorfmann raised a hand. "Don't jump to conclusions. I don't know that and neither do you."

"You do realize I just told you all I know about it."

He tapped a thick folder lying on the desk she hadn't noticed before. "Nothing like a rainy weekend to remedy that." His stern gaze relaxed the slightest bit. "By next week, you'll be the expert."

She searched his face for a smile that wasn't there. She sighed. "You're serious. All right, tell me what I'm looking for. Stasi agents in general or something more specific?"

He shrugged. "I wish we had more to go on."

"Which agencies do you suspect have been infiltrated?"

Dorfmann leaned back and studied her as if deciding what to reveal. After a long pause, he said, "We can't rule out any. But the type of secrets that have made their way east point to the Federal Foreign Office, the Chancellery, and the intelligence services, even our own BND."

"A big job for one person," was all she could say.

"Look at the rewards. You break the Stasi spy network wide open, and I'll see to it that you get a healthy raise." Now he did smile. "High time you traded that Volkswagen for a car large enough to keep you from twisting yourself into a pretzel to get in."

"A silver Mercedes or a red BMW would be nice." She laughed. "That prospect really makes me want to work all weekend."

"That's the spirit." He turned serious. "Study that file and get up to speed on Rasterfahndung. I hope you prove us both wrong. But if you do find that we can't catch spies that way, give me solid reasons why not. And if that's what you conclude, you need to think of an approach that will work. The chancellor doesn't like to be told no."

Dorfmann stood. "First thing Monday, I want to hear your brilliant ideas for putting these Stasi operatives out of business." He strode to the door and stepped into the hall.

Sabine turned the file right side up. It looked every bit of five centimeters thick. Better get started if she hoped to spend Saturday evening at the opera and still be prepared by Monday morning.

Chapter Three

The Divorce

Bonn, West Germany, Friday evening, 15 July 1977

With a burst of energy she hadn't felt in months, Monika Fuchs climbed the steps of the *Stadtbahn* station escalator. She clutched her umbrella, ready to defend against the rain that had been pelting Bonn all afternoon. While most women might consider rain fitting for a day of divorce, she did not.

She emerged from the station to a balmy evening. The rain had stopped, as if the weather had decided to match her buoyant mood on this day she'd regained her freedom. She restrained her impulse to skip down the sidewalk, hopping over puddles instead. A few hundred meters and she stood in front of Café Diplomat. A silly name for a restaurant, which would be out of place in any town but this one. Its international cuisine catered to the plethora of diplomats assigned to West Germany's capital.

Monika almost chided herself for not modifying "capital" with "temporary" or "provisional," which any West German politician hoping to get reelected was obliged to recite at every opportunity. Neither her colleagues nor the higher-ups at the Chancellery really believed they'd see Germany united during their lifetime. Bonn, not Berlin, would remain the seat of West Germany's government for a long time, perhaps forever.

But why think politics on this day of her rebirth? Determined to let nothing sour her mood, she pushed the door hard, almost knocking down an elderly gentleman. He exited before she could apologize.

If the hostess had noticed, she didn't let on, asking Monika whether she had a reservation.

"It's under 'Sturm.'"

"Your party is already seated. This way, please."

Monika followed red stiletto heels and a swinging bottom that stretched the teal miniskirt to its limits. The long-legged hostess pointed to a table in the far corner. Gisela rose. Reddish-brown hair in a pageboy cut framed her round face. They hugged.

"Congratulations. You're finally rid of that brute." After a kiss on each cheek, Gisela let go and they sat.

Monika pointed to the half-empty glass of red wine on the table. "Am I late?"

"No. I got off work early."

"How did you manage that? I thought you told me the Foreign Office was a sweatshop."

"Yeah, well. It usually is. But the minister left late afternoon, and I cleared out right after that. He works me hard enough when he's there, I figured I deserve a break now and then."

"Good rationalization." Monika glanced at the wine glass. "What are you drinking?"

"Beaujolais. Your favorite." She waved over the waiter hovering near the table. "One for my friend and another for me, please."

After the waiter withdrew, Gisela said, "I can't wait to hear how it went. Did Jochen make trouble?"

"I thought he might after all the haggling he and his lawyer did for weeks on end. But he was surprisingly civil."

"You're telling me the bastard behaved himself?"

"Hard to believe, I know. It was rather anticlimactic, if you ask me. A few perfunctory questions and the judge signed the divorce decree. You can't believe how liberating this feels. Time to celebrate."

As if on cue, the waiter set down their drinks. They clinked their glasses. Monika took a long, slow sip, reveling in the sensation of smooth French wine spreading relaxation into every cell.

They studied the menu. After the attentive waiter had taken their dinner orders, Gisela raised her glass. "Here's to you and romantic adventures coming your way."

During the toast, Monika studied her friend. Expertly applied makeup smoothing out wrinkles of forty-year-old skin, blouse and skirt accentuating her voluptuous figure while deemphasizing the few extra pounds Monika knew were there—in short, Gisela was not beautiful but reasonably attractive.

Monika set down her glass. "Romantic adventures? I'd take your sexy husband anytime you want to trade lives."

Gisela laughed. "Not a chance. You keep your mitts off."

Monika raised her hands, palms toward her friend. "Understood, of course, but Klaus is a great catch, and you must be very proud of your son."

A frown passed over Gisela's face. "Rainer is almost a teenager, and it shows. I'm not looking forward to the next few years." The frown disappeared. "But let's talk about you. Aren't there any eligible bachelors at the Chancellery?"

Monika scoffed. "A choice between married fuddy-duddies, most of them bald with beer bellies, or overly ambitious climbers who're in love with politics, certainly not women."

"Yeah, it's the same in the Foreign Office. Not that I'm looking." Gisela reached across the table and squeezed Monika's hand. "You're young and attractive. With that great figure of yours you'll have to fend off admirers. Just choose better next time."

"You can count on that." Monika returned the squeeze, then withdrew her hand as the waiter brought their meals and more wine.

Midway through her pasta dish, Gisela said, "Don't tell me you're going right back to the daily grind. You need some fun in your life."

Monika swallowed a bite of salmon, washed it down with Beaujolais, and tried for her best mysterious smile. "Matter of fact, I do have plans."

"I knew it." Gisela pointed her fork, her eyes playful. "Do tell."

"I'm on vacation for two weeks. Leaving tomorrow."

"And . . . where are you going?"

"Viareggio. It's on the Italian Riviera, close to Lucca and Florence. I can only lie on the beach so long and not get bored."

"Sounds wonderful. Wish I could go with you. Watch out for those dark-haired gigolos pinching you. They do like blondes."

"Maybe I'll leave the bikini at home."

"Don't you dare! A holiday romance is what the doctor ordered."

Monika shook her head. "I'm not sure I'm ready for that."

"What's the matter? You look disappointed."

"You know me too well. I tried to get a ticket for *Aïda* at the Arena di Verona. It's my favorite opera, and the open-air production on the giant stage is supposed to be spectacular. But it's sold out."

Gisela again squeezed her hand. "I'm sorry. Maybe someone will turn in their tickets."

Monika sighed. "If not, I'll go to the Puccini Summer Festival in Torre del Lago."

"You haven't told me the name of your hotel," Gisela said. "Come on, don't make me drag everything out of you."

"Why do you want to know? Sending a good-looking bachelor my way?"

Gisela hesitated. "Right." She laughed.

There was something in her laugh, the way she'd hesitated, that gave Monika pause. But Gisela was a friend. There was no harm in telling her. "Pensione Garibaldi."

Gisela nodded. "Can't wait to hear about your adventures when you get back."

They finished their meal amidst more small talk.

As she descended the steps to the underground Stadtbahn station, Monika wondered once more why Gisela had expressed so much interest in her Italian sojourn. Maybe it was her way of being supportive, except she'd never been that curious before.

Chapter Four

The Training

Stasi Headquarters, Berlin-Lichtenberg, Monday morning, 18 July 1977

Stefan exited the underground station and squinted against the morning sun. It took him a moment to orient himself. He knew the Stasi headquarters were on Normannenstraße, but he'd never gone near the state's most feared institution. Now he had no choice. Once in the cross hairs of the secret police, there was no way out.

A man in his thirties hurried down the sidewalk. His gray uniform, his imitation-leather briefcase that spoke of government issue, and his purposeful stride surely meant he was headed for Stasi headquarters. Stefan fell in behind him. The uniform led the way down Normannenstraße toward a massive building complex.

To combat tiredness from the weekend's insomnia, Stefan took deep breaths. He'd fretted endlessly over what he'd done to attract the general's attention. What reason could there be, other than having published in the state's official newspaper? That had to be it, unless—he'd sat straight up in bed when the thought formed—unless one of his lovers had tattled to the Stasi. But he hadn't mistreated any of them. Matter of fact, they'd been all too happy to help a poor writer with expenses, hadn't they? If those thoughts hadn't been enough to keep him awake, worries about being returned to prison if he didn't perform had kept him chasing elusive sleep the entire weekend.

The man ahead disappeared into a covered entryway jutting out from a brown-brick eight-story structure and Stefan followed him into the dreary building. The man flashed a picture ID at two armed guards sitting behind a metal table. They waved him through.

The shorter of the two guards rose and stepped in front of Stefan. "May we help you?"

"I'm here to report to Lieutenant General Heinrich."

"Your name?"

"Stefan Malik."

The guard held up a hand. "One moment." He about-faced and entered an office behind the table.

Stefan could make out sounds of a rotary phone dial and a muffled voice. Within a minute, the guard reappeared. "Raise your arms."

Stefan complied.

After a thorough pat-down, the guard said, "Wait here. Someone's on the way to take you to HVA in Building 15."

"What's HVA?"

The guard shot him a quizzical look, no doubt astonished that anyone could not know. Whether he liked Stefan's looks or was simply bored with standing around and waiting, he deigned to give an explanation. "*Hauptverwaltung Aufklärung.*" With that, he returned to his seat behind the table.

So Heinrich was a lieutenant general in the Stasi's foreign intelligence service. He should have guessed.

A low voice interrupted Stefan's thoughts. "Herr Malik?"

He turned to face a guard, who looked to be retirement-age. "Yes."

"Follow me."

With a pronounced limp, the guard led Stefan through a labyrinth of hallways, the pistol in his holster swinging with every step. The slow pace tested Stefan's patience. He grew anxious at the sight of a wall clock that was a few ticks away from straight up nine. When the old man climbed a flight of stairs by dragging his bad leg up to his good one on each step, Stefan felt like running ahead. The general would not look kindly on his being late for their first appointment.

The clickety-clack of typewriter keys ceased when the guard lumbered to the top of the staircase. Stefan pulled up beside him, and they crossed the tile floor of a reception area.

A thirty-something woman sitting at a small desk regarded him, her eyes showing signs of curiosity. "Herr Malik?"

Stefan nodded while taking in her features—well endowed, short-cut brown hair, high cheekbones. As the guard withdrew, she spoke Stefan's last name in a hushed tone into the receiver of a yellow desk telephone.

She terminated the call, got up and beckoned him to a door across the way, which he hadn't noticed until now, its ochre shade almost indistinguishable from the surrounding drab wall paint. A plate at eye level displayed the general's name and title in stark black lettering. She knocked, and at the sound of a deep voice, opened the door. Keeping an eye on Heinrich seated behind a large desk, Stefan took a few hesitant steps onto a thin carpet. As the door latch clicked into place, the general looked up and pointed to a small table with four chairs by a window. Stefan settled in a chair below the portraits of Socialist Party leader, Erich Honecker, and Stasi chief, Erich Mielke.

While the general shuffled papers on his desk, Stefan noted the absence of family portraits. Either Heinrich wasn't married or he chose not to put his personal life on display. Stefan took a quick look around. Though larger and better furnished than the one at the prison, this office did not match Stefan's image of a Stasi lieutenant general's quarters. The blond imitation wood paneling clashed both with the dark-brown wooden desk and the olive-hued carpeting. A framed depiction of the Stasi emblem, a hand clutching a rifle with a bayonet, encircled by the words, *Ministerium für Staatssicherheit,* hung from the wall behind Heinrich. Large enough to hide a wall safe?

Stefan quit speculating when Heinrich grabbed a file off the desk and carried it to the table. He pulled out the chair across from Stefan, sat and placed the file on the glass tabletop.

He stared at Stefan. "I said nine o'clock."

Stefan glanced at the clock above the door. Five minutes past the hour. "I didn't know which building—"

"I didn't ask you why you were late, comrade." He slammed the file with his fist. "I will accept no excuses. You will always be on time. Understood?"

"Yes, sir." Stefan suppressed the urge to point out he'd been at the office for several minutes already.

"First lesson—disobey instructions or flout procedures and you'll blow your cover. Never forget that."

Stefan nodded.

"Did you tell anyone about coming here?"

Surprised by the question, Stefan hesitated. "No, I . . . I didn't."

"That sounds like you had to think about it. You're sure?"

"Yes." Stefan held the general's gaze.

"No one outside the agency is to know where you work. Is that clear?"

"Yes, sir."

Heinrich pulled a paper from the file, slid it across the table, and handed him a pen from his coat pocket. "It's spelled out in our standard contract."

Stefan was scanning the first paragraph, when the general barked, "Turn it over and sign. You can read your copy later."

This time, the general didn't make any pretense of choice. Stefan complied and handed the signed original back. Heaven only knew what all he'd agreed to.

"During the next few weeks you'll be learning tradecraft from the best in the business." The general's face gleamed with pride.

"Are you teaching—?"

"No. The training is in Golm. It's west of Potsdam, about forty kilometers."

"But—"

"You don't have a car, I know. A driver will pick you up at your apartment after lunch. Pack for a few weeks' stay. It's all arranged. Questions?"

Stefan shook his head.

"You'll be trained in the essential tools of the spy trade. But that's just the beginning. I'm going to teach you to be a Stasi Romeo."

Heinrich flipped through the open file. "Here it is." He stabbed a finger at a paper. "This will give you expert advice on how to approach West German secretaries, how to court them, how to establish a relationship, how to get them to trust you, how to get them to fall in love with you, how to persuade them to turn over state secrets."

Stefan fought conflicting emotions. While he enjoyed romance and sex, he always picked attractive women for his flings. Sure, he'd borrowed money from some, but he never faked love to manipulate them. The general was grooming him for something entirely different. Could he woo a dumpy-looking secretary, sleep with her, and pretend to love her, all so she'd spy for the Stasi?

Heinrich resumed his instructions. "I'm just going to cover a few points this morning. Take this file with you and study it. When you come back from Golm, I'll expect you to know every last detail."

"Yes, sir."

Heinrich regarded him for a long moment, then returned his gaze to the place in the file he'd marked with his thumb. "We're interested in secretaries in the Chancellery, in government ministries, and other West German institutions for several reasons. They know more than you'd think, and many have access to sensitive, often secret, materials. Managers and ministers come and go. Secretaries stay. They are therefore an excellent investment for the long haul." Heinrich looked up. "You're with me so far?"

"Yes, General."

"We focus on secretaries who are single or divorced, which is not too difficult. Believe it or not, about thirty percent of the secretaries in Bonn who work for the government and the parties fall into those categories." Heinrich sounded triumphant.

The man's smugness grated on Stefan, but he managed to blurt, "That's great, General."

"I'd say fertile hunting ground for you." Heinrich leaned forward. "The easiest targets are lonely women who have trouble making friends. And if they happen to be looking for a husband, so much the better."

The general shut the file with a thump and slid it across the table. "That's enough for today. You study the rest. Questions?"

"No, sir."

Heinrich stood. "My secretary will take you downstairs to get your picture ID. Then go home and pack. Be ready at one o'clock sharp."

"I will be, General." Stefan picked up the file and walked to the door.

"Don't forget. Tell no one what you're doing, where you're going, or who you work for."

Stefan turned to face Heinrich. "I won't."

"And that includes Traude. You wouldn't want to do anything to harm her, would you?"

"No, of course not."

The mention of his daughter's name and the threat it implied brought Stefan up short. He wanted nothing more than to charge the bastard and drag him across the huge desk. But he couldn't, or he'd find himself back in prison. He grasped the door handle so hard that his fingers slipped. With his second attempt, he undid the latch and stepped out.

As he approached the secretary, he pondered Heinrich's veiled threat. What would he do to Traude if her father didn't do the general's bidding?

Chapter Five

Rasterfahndung

Federal Intelligence Service [BND], Pullach, West Germany, Monday morning, 18 July 1977

Coffee cup in one hand, file in the other, Sabine was about to exit her office when her boss crossed the threshold. He too held a cup. "Stay put. We'll talk here."

She made a U-turn, almost spilling her coffee as she slid into her chair behind the desk.

Settled in a visitor's chair, Dorfmann gave her a wry smile. "This weekend was your chance to make yourself the expert on Rasterfahndung, but you don't look sleep deprived."

"Very funny, boss." She tapped the file. "I may not be an expert, but I know everything that's in here and I can tell you this: when it comes to finding Stasi spies, Rasterfahndung is a dead end."

His smile gone, Dorfmann leaned forward, putting his hands on the desktop. "Don't tell me that."

She shrugged. "It won't work."

"What makes you so sure?"

"The fact that it was designed to catch leftist terrorists, and even there, it's proven successful only in a few instances."

"Explain why you think it won't help us catch spies."

Sabine gazed at a spot high on the far wall, focusing on how best to support her opinion. Taking a deep breath, she returned her attention to Dorfmann. "For it to work, we must identify individuals who belong to a group of perpetrators so that we can establish certain characteristics common to its members. In other words, we create a profile. Then we run a computer search that compares this profile with data we've gathered from domicile registrations, police records, health insurance records, public utility payments, apartment rentals, telephone records, and so on."

Dorfmann scooted to the edge of his chair. "Wait a minute. Are you telling me all that information is necessary?"

"I am."

"That takes a lot of manpower. More than we have."

"Even if we had the personnel, the method wouldn't work for us."

Dorfmann raised an eyebrow. "Because?"

"Because unlike leftist terrorists, Stasi agents don't fit neatly into a certain profile. We simply don't have the information to feed into a computer that would give us any meaningful results." She set her jaw, holding her boss's gaze. "You've heard what the Americans say?" She paused for effect. "Garbage in, garbage out."

His stern demeanor softened. She could have sworn he suppressed a chuckle. Still looking her in the eye, he said, "All right. You've confirmed our doubts about Rasterfahndung. It won't help us catch spies. But that doesn't solve our problem, does it?"

"Guess not."

"The chancellor is getting more impatient by the day. He wants us to put these Stasi spies out of business now. Did you come up with a new approach?"

She shook her head. "I'm afraid I spent the entire weekend trying to make Rasterfahndung work for us." Suppressing thoughts of the opera evening, she said, "I ran out of time to consider anything else."

An impish expression crossed his face.

"You've got something in mind, boss, and I have a feeling I won't like it."

"I expect to be summoned to Bonn any day now. And who better to explain to the chancellor why we're not using Rasterfahndung than our new expert on the subject?"

In a mocking gesture, Sabine wagged a finger at him. "I've often suspected you have a mean streak."

Dorfmann grinned. "Touché. But I'm serious about you accompanying me to Bonn. And we wouldn't want to arrive without a proposal for a new method to catch Stasi spies. You're creative. I know you'll think of something that'll work."

Sabine held his gaze. He was counting on her, and she had to deliver. "Okay. I'll think of nothing but Stasi spies during all my waking hours, and a few sleeping ones, too."

Dorfmann stood and pointed at the file. "This goes back to Records." He grabbed his cup and made for the door. Once there, he turned around. "Just keep thinking about that silver Mercedes."

Chapter Six

The Mission

Hauptverwaltung Aufklärung [HVA], Foreign Intelligence Service, Stasi Headquarters, East Berlin, Monday morning, 18 July 1977

The way Stefan Malik had fumbled with the door handle at the mention of his daughter's name left Heinrich with mixed feelings. Good that Malik had gotten the message his daughter would suffer if he screwed up; not so good that he'd let it show how much the threat had rattled him. Had he made a mistake in recruiting a novice? Maybe he'd let himself be swayed by Malik's obvious attributes. Brushing away his doubts, he put the signed agreement in the file on his desk. Rome was not built in a day, nor did one morning session a spy make.

He swiveled in his chair toward the rear wall and reached with both hands for the bottom edge of the low-hanging Stasi emblem. A slight push upward dislodged the frame from its hook. He lowered the piece onto the carpet, exposing a small wall safe. Heinrich stood to spin the wheel with the numbers that filled him with pride and anticipation: 5-4-7-4. Pride over his promotion to lieutenant general on 5 April 1974, anticipation of the next big spy coup that would land him the rank of colonel general.

When the safe swung open, he added Malik's file to the other Romeo spy folders he kept inside the compartment. Some might call him paranoid for not storing them in the secure records department downstairs, but he slept easier this way.

About to close the safe, he stopped at the sound of his secretary's voice on the intercom. "Lieutenant Gruber just dropped off an envelope. He said it was urgent."

"Bring it in."

She entered and handed him a sealed envelope addressed to him and stamped TOP SECRET. Ignoring the letter opener in her outstretched hand, he ripped into the envelope and pulled out a sheet of paper. He unfolded it and read the short note. Blood rushed to his face. His patience was finally being rewarded.

He dropped the note and envelope on the desk. "Have Colonel Borst report to me immediately. And bring me the Monika Fuchs file from Records."

She nodded and left. He stepped to the open safe and flipped through the stack of folders until he found the one labeled Uli Borst. He tossed it onto the desk, closed the safe, and replaced the framed Stasi emblem. Too excited to sit, he paced the office. Things were finally falling into place. He stopped in front of the portraits of Honecker and Mielke. They'd surely promote him to colonel general after he pulled this off. He resumed his trek back and forth over the threadbare carpet. Where in the devil was Borst? What was taking him so long?

A faint knock tore him from his thoughts. He strode to the door and pulled it open. As his eyes fell on Colonel Uli Borst, Heinrich wondered, as he had so many times before, what women saw in this man. Midthirties, no taller than one meter seventy-five, brown hair that showed signs of thinning, and the hint of a paunch the uniform couldn't hide. But there was no arguing with the colonel's success. One of their star Romeos, his romancing of lonely West German secretaries had yielded countless secrets over the years.

He motioned for Borst to take a chair. The colonel's expression showed curiosity, but like a good Stasi subordinate, he knew better than to ask questions.

"Colonel, we can finally zero in on the target we've been watching all these months."

"Monika Fuchs?"

"Yes. I just got word she's on a two-week holiday in Italy after her divorce. That means you're leaving for Viareggio tomorrow."

Borst gave him a blank stare.

"A beach resort on the Riviera, near Florence. You've heard of Florence, Colonel?"

"Yes, of course, General."

From the corner of the desk, Heinrich grabbed a pad and a pen, and wrote Pensione Garibaldi, Viareggio. He tore off the sheet and handed it to Borst. "Here is where she's staying."

His secretary knocked and entered. "The file you requested, sir." She laid it on the desk.

When she had left the room, he turned to Borst. "Do you need to study the Fuchs file again to refresh your memory?"

"I don't think so, sir." The colonel hesitated. "Unless there's new information since the last time I looked at it."

"That was last week?"

Borst nodded.

"Nothing new. Any questions then, Colonel?"

"No."

Heinrich stood. "I'll have my secretary make the travel arrangements. Go home and pack. Wait for her call."

Borst rose and walked to the door, but turned around when Heinrich called after him.

"You do realize how extremely valuable Fuchs is to us?"

"Yes, General."

"You've done good work with the others, Colonel, but this is your most important assignment. You must succeed."

"Yes, sir." He drew the door closed behind him.

On his way to instruct his secretary, Heinrich assured himself he'd picked the best Romeo for this task—one who couldn't fail.

Chapter Seven

Don Giovanni

Munich, Monday evening, 18 July 1977

Cradling a bursting grocery bag in one arm, Sabine Meier stabbed the key at the keyhole in her apartment door—a task made difficult by the dingy hallway lighting. Maybe she'd spend the extra money from the first paycheck after the promised raise not on a Mercedes but on a nicer apartment. What raise? She'd racked her brain all day at the office without coming up with even one idea for the new approach her boss demanded.

The key finally found the hole. She entered, shoved the door shut with her heel, and set the bag on the kitchen counter. On her way to the bedroom, she unbuttoned her blouse and loosened her skirt. She dropped the clothes onto the bed, kicked off her pumps, and grabbed a T-shirt and jeans from the dresser. She slipped them on, half hoping the change in wardrobe would somehow wash away the day's frustration.

A few barefoot steps along the short hallway carried her back to the small kitchen. Thoughts of the day's travails again pushed to the forefront, but remembering what her mother had taught her many years ago when she'd fretted about difficult homework, she batted the thoughts away. The harder you try to think of a solution to a problem, the less likely you will find it. Relax, occupy your mind with other things, and sooner or later, inspiration will provide the answer. And what better way to distract herself than to prepare a nice pasta dinner while drinking some wine?

After putting a pot of water on the stove burner's high gas flame, she took the half-full bottle of *Spätburgunder* from the counter and poured a generous portion of its contents into the crystal *Viertele* glass still standing on the drying rack by the sink. Not a wine snob, she found the red wine just as delicious as she had during her weekend study of the Rasterfahndung file.

Fifteen minutes later, fettuccine covered with marinara sauce and grated parmesan graced her dining room table. She poured the last of the wine into her glass and sat. About to dig in, she stopped. Something was missing. Of course, an Italian dinner demanded Italian music—a perfect opportunity to sample the *Don Giovanni* record she'd purchased at the opera shop during the intermission at Saturday evening's performance.

All thoughts of the day's frustration disappeared, erased by Mozart's glorious music, the red wine, the pasta. Halfway through the sumptuous meal and with the wine glass verging on empty, one of Sabine's favorite pieces filled the room. She leaned back to enjoy the catalogue aria, in which the servant, Leporello, recites the lengthy list of women seduced by the Don all over Europe. The baritone's mocking song rang out, "*Ma in Ispagna, son già mille et tre.*" The tally of one-thousand-and-three conquests in Spain always made her chuckle.

She drained her glass. While she debated whether to uncork another bottle, inspiration hit: Don Giovanni, who seduced women with promise of marriage. The image of the Bonn secretary convicted of espionage this spring flashed into her mind. The woman had succumbed to the charms of an East German spy. Thanks to Mozart, she might have happened on the Stasi's method of stealing West Germany's secrets.

This called for opening another bottle. After finishing the now lukewarm fettuccine, she raised her glass, but set it down again. Understanding how the Stasi infiltrated the West German government was one thing, but tracing the operatives was quite another. Experts in tradecraft, they covered their tracks. Still, they had to leave a trail, however faint.

She took a swallow of Spätburgunder, then another, savoring the dry wine. As if it had been biding its time until her senses were occupied with something other than chasing spies, an idea stole into her mind. What if she focused not on the spies, but on their likely targets? This could be the new approach she'd been searching for: ferret out vulnerable women and watch them closely.

If she could put together a profile of women who had access to government secrets and examine their characteristics, she just might pick up some common factors that would put her on the scent of Stasi agents. What might these women have in common? They probably were single or divorced. While married women certainly weren't immune to affairs, she'd rule them out for now. The Stasi spymaster, whose appearance was still unknown in the West, would be too smart to risk having one of his Romeos exposed by a jilted husband.

Surely, scores of women in government service were unmarried. There had to be a way to narrow it down, and not through Rasterfahndung. She swallowed the rest of her drink. Then she remembered the case of a secretary in Cologne who also fell for a Stasi spy. There must be others. No telling how many were copying documents to hand over to their lovers.

First thing in the morning, she'd dig up the information on women charged with espionage. There had to be a common thread.

Chapter Eight

The Accident

Foreign Intelligence Service [HVA], Stasi Headquarters, East Berlin, Tuesday morning, 19 July 1977

Deep in thought about the mission he'd set in motion yesterday, Heinrich mumbled a hasty good morning to his secretary. Uli Borst would be boarding his flight to Milan about now.

"General." There was an edge to her voice.

He spun around. "What is it, Frau Schröder?"

"General, I need to tell you—"

"What's wrong? Out with it!"

"Colonel Borst was in an accident last night."

"What?" He assumed the worst from her expression. "Is he—?"

"He didn't die, but he's in intensive care."

"*Verdammt!*" He stared at her. "What kind of accident?"

"All I know is the police pulled him from his car at two thirty in the morning. He must have lost control and driven into a ditch."

Heinrich recalled rumors of Borst's drinking. He'd dismissed them since there'd been nothing to indicate it interfered with his work. Just one of the boys cutting loose once in a while after a job was done. Maybe he should have heeded the rumors. Angry at Borst and himself, Heinrich was about to curse again, but his secretary's sad expression stopped him.

He asked, "What do the doctors say?"

"Well, you know how doctors are. They wouldn't commit to anything other than it's going to be a long recovery process."

Heinrich stood there, thoughts swirling in his head. The Monika Fuchs mission all shot to hell. His secretary's questioning gaze reminded him he needed to give instructions.

"As soon as the colonel is allowed visitors, take him flowers." He turned to walk to his office, but stopped partway there. "And Frau Schröder, notify his relatives if the hospital hasn't done so already. I only know of a brother in Leipzig."

She nodded and picked up the telephone. Heinrich closed the office door behind him and stomped to his desk. "Son of a bitch," he said over and over, not caring whether Schröder heard. He slumped into his chair. Damage control. He had to get a replacement and fast. At the thought, he sprang from his chair, removed the Stasi emblem from the wall, and opened the safe. He took out the stack of folders, piled them on the desk, and flipped through them at a feverish pace to find someone he could tap for the job on short notice. All his Romeos were on assignment in the West. *Verdammte Scheiße!* There had to be someone he could pry loose.

He went through the folders again, this time more methodically. Toward the bottom of the pile, he came upon Major Dietmar Kurz's file. His latest report from Cologne promised success in wooing a secretary with access to NATO correspondence. He'd bedded her over the weekend. A few more weeks of romance, and he might be able to recruit her. Getting their hands on North Atlantic Alliance documents was tempting, but not as much of a coup as infiltrating the West German Chancellery through Monika Fuchs.

Heinrich gazed at the far wall, trying to focus. If there was even the smallest chance of gaining access to the chancellor's mail, he had to take it. As much as he hated to abort a promising mission, he decided to pull Kurz off the job. Monika Fuchs took precedence. Her sojourn to Italy might be the only chance they had to make contact.

Determined not to miss this opportunity, Heinrich grabbed a notepad and pencil. After a moment's thought, he wrote the prearranged message instructing the agent to return to headquarters immediately, "*Heimat Sofort.*"

He checked the file and muttered "*Scheiße.*" The message couldn't go until the time of day he'd set for Major Kurz to receive transmissions—five in the afternoon.

Heinrich scribbled *17:00 Uhr* on the paper and pressed the intercom. "Frau Schröder, please come in."

When she entered, he ripped the sheet off the pad and gave it to her. "Take this to Radio Intelligence and have them transmit to Major Kurz at seventeen hundred hours sharp."

"Right away, sir."

When she was gone, Heinrich returned the folders to the safe. He tried to take solace in the fact that Borst's accident would only cost them two days. Major Kurz would arrive tomorrow to receive his instructions and be on his way to Italy on Thursday. Still, he couldn't suppress the niggling feeling that this might not be soon enough. He imagined an Italian beach populated by German blondes and Italian gigolos on the prowl. A freshly divorced Monika Fuchs might just be in the mood for a holiday fling with one of those dark-haired Casanovas, relegating Major Kurz to the role of a spectator. Much could happen in two days—none of it good.

He gazed at the portraits of party functionaries that hung on the wall. What would Mielke or Honecker do? He was sure of only one thing: if they found out he'd missed a chance to turn a Chancellery secretary with the highest access into a spy, they'd not only not promote him, but might very well demote him. The winds in a totalitarian state could shift in a heartbeat, and he needed to keep them at his back at all times.

Heinrich leaned back in his chair and stared at the ceiling. If only he could have Kurz there sooner. Maybe he should skip the orientation session here and send him from Cologne straight to Viareggio. Not ideal, since the major might not be experienced enough to improvise.

Pen poised above the notepad, Heinrich tried to formulate a message clear enough for Kurz to understand without alerting West German intelligence, which he knew monitored radio chatter from the East. Nothing came to him. Perhaps the radio intelligence guys could help. A note in a dead drop location would be the best, but there was no time for that.

Then he thought of something that might inoculate Fuchs against advances from the gigolos until Kurz got there. A simple solution. And he knew exactly the person who could make the arrangement. Heinrich buzzed his secretary, hoping she was back.

When she answered, he said, "Radio Intelligence all set for the transmission I gave you?"

"Yes, sir. It'll go right at five."

"Good. Now get Signore Amato Conti in Milan on the line."

"Yes, General."

While he waited for the call to go through, Heinrich thought about what to tell their Milan contact. He could always depend on Conti to arrange whatever he wanted done in Italy. The generous payments from the Stasi guaranteed that.

Chapter Nine

Common Traits

Federal Intelligence Service [BND], Pullach, West Germany, Tuesday, 19 July 1977

Sabine Maier strode down the first-floor hallway, silently repeating the name that had come to her when she woke up this morning. She pushed open the glass door to the records department. At the sound of the buzzer, Heinz Riedel emerged from a narrow corridor between file racks. His wrinkled face broke out in a smile, causing his mustache to curl up.

"*Guten Morgen,* Frau Maier. What brings you to these lowly quarters so early?"

She returned his greeting, chuckling at his self-deprecating humor. His beige polyester suit, shiny at the elbows, and a narrow clip-on tie hanging askew from a limp, white collar smudged at the edges were typical of old German men who no longer cared for their appearance. Or could his mode of dress be a reflection of a meager salary, despite his having capably managed the records department—a crucial function of intelligence work—since the inception of the BND twenty-one years ago?

"Lowly? You're the most important person here, Herr Riedel, and you know it."

"Tell that to the higher-ups." He wagged a finger at her. "You must want something out of the ordinary."

"Actually, I was wondering whether you have a file on the Bonn secretary convicted this spring of spying for the East German government. I believe her last name is Vogel."

"Yes, of course." Riedel turned and hurried down an aisle. He was remarkably agile for a man who had to be approaching seventy.

He returned in less than a minute and slapped a file next to a thick book that lay open on the Formica counter. "Dagmar Vogel."

He made an entry in the register and turned it toward her. She signed beside the file name and number.

Then she looked at him with the most innocent expression she could muster. "There is something else I need your help with."

"Ah, here comes the reason for the flattery. Which regulations would you have me flout? Which rules would you have me break?"

"No, nothing like that. I just need to call on your institutional memory. If anyone would know, it's you."

"All right. Enough buttering up. What is it you're looking for?"

"The name of the Cologne secretary convicted of spying a year or two ago. We should have something on her as well."

Riedel stroked his chin. "Hmm. Offhand, I don't recall the name, but if we have a file, I will find it for you. I'll bring it to your office."

When she didn't leave, he said, "That's not all you want, is it?"

"I was hoping you could locate records on other women who've been accused, convicted, or even suspected of spying for the Stasi over the years."

"You want me to recall spies caught over the last twenty years? Not only that, but it's got to be women?"

"This is really important, Herr Riedel. Would you please try?"

He mumbled something under his breath, then gazed at her. "If it were anyone else, I'd tell them to go to hell. But for you, Frau Maier, I'll see what I can do."

She grabbed the folder. "You're a sweetheart."

As the door swished closed behind her, she barely heard, "*Ja, ja.* I make no promises, Frau Maier."

♫ ♫ ♫

Sabine leaned back in her chair and rubbed her weary eyes. Riedel had brought three additional folders, one about the Cologne secretary she'd asked him for and two concerning cases unfamiliar to her. From the materials, she'd compiled two lists. The first contained specific information about each woman; the second, their common traits.

A quick glance at the wall clock confirmed it was near quitting time. A full day of work hadn't yielded much. Though she'd probably attain better results analyzing the data with fresh eyes in the morning, she'd give it one final push before leaving the office. Perhaps another look would reveal a connection she'd missed. If nothing else, cementing the details in her mind might lead to an insight while listening to Mozart at home this evening.

She studied what she'd scribbled on the sheets of paper.

Monika Fischer, 33, never married, secretary at the Federal Ministry of the Interior, Bonn, for seven years, convicted this spring of delivering state secrets to a Stasi agent, sentenced to five years in prison. She said she spied for love.

Brigitte Koch, 37, divorced, secretary at the Armed Forces Security Office, Cologne, for five years, mother of a five-year-old son. Last fall she was sentenced to a three-year prison term for handing copies of NATO teletypes to her lover, an East German posing as a Danish diplomat. She thought she was helping a NATO ally.

Dagmar Vogel, 27, single, secretary at the Ministry of Defense, Bonn, for three years, gave intelligence regarding West

Germany's military strategy to the East German government in exchange for a promise of leniency for her mother living in East Germany. She was sentenced to three years' probation.

Ursula Klein, 29, divorced, secretary for six years at the Office for the Protection of the Constitution, Cologne, supplied secret documents from Germany's domestic spy agency to a Stasi agent. She told the court she knew she was doing wrong, but was desperate to keep her lover from leaving her. She received a five-year prison term in 1972.

Sabine gazed at the second sheet of sparse notes. The common traits she'd identified so far: all four were secretaries, worked for the government, had access to sensitive information, were either single or divorced. Three spied for love, one to gain leniency for a relative in East Germany. One didn't know the boyfriend was a Stasi agent, the others did.

Sabine gathered her thoughts. The files were woefully short of personal information about the women. She needed psychological profiles. Were they attractive or homely? Outgoing, or shy and introverted? Confident or insecure? What were their personal habits? Weaknesses and vices? Her questions were endless, and the agency's records answered none of them. She'd have to order trial transcripts and scrutinize the prosecution files.

When the clock showed five, she locked the four files in a side desk drawer. Taking them home was against policy. Not so her notes, which she put in her briefcase. As she left the office, it dawned on her that she hadn't seen her boss all day. She'd expected him to be camped out on her doorstep this morning, demanding a new approach to catching Stasi spies.

Before she could gain the staircase, Bernd Dorfmann stepped from the interrogation room at the end of the hall. "Glad I caught you, Frau Maier. I need to talk to you."

Once they were seated in his office, door closed, he said, "I've been debriefing a Stasi defector most of the day. He's Captain Manfred Ruhland. Forty-three, has been a Stasi officer for ten years. Crossed over to West Berlin last night with a fake ID."

"Alone?"

"Yes. He's divorced, no children."

"And he's not worried about his ex?"

"No. Nasty divorce. He'd like nothing better than the Stasi putting the screws to her."

She studied his expression for signs of skepticism about the defector's assertions, but saw none. "Makes things less messy, if you believe him."

"What he told us about three Stasi moles embedded in the West has checked out so far. He couldn't give names, but from what he said, we've managed to identify two Stasi collaborators: a pastor in Bad Godesberg and a journalist in Hamburg."

"And the third?" Sabine asked.

"That one is dating a secretary at one of the Cologne agencies. Ruhland doesn't know which office, or the secretary's name. I'm hoping you can help me zero in on them."

"You want me to interrogate the defector?"

Dorfmann raised a hand. "Absolutely not. I don't want him to see you."

"You think he could be a plant?"

"No, I believe he's legit, but I don't want to take a chance on your name making the rounds, especially since we've gone to great lengths not to publicize the scores of arrests you've made." He hesitated. "Of course, if the Stasi spymaster is as good as his reputation suggests, he may already know about you."

She furrowed her brow. "A chilling thought."

"Not to worry. So far, you're probably flying under his radar. I want to keep it that way. The defector is not to lay eyes on you. Besides, I'm satisfied I got out of him all he knows about the third spy."

She thought for a moment. "You said an agency in Cologne. That's got to be either Domestic Intelligence or Armed Forces Security."

He nodded. "I've got an idea which one it is, but I want you to come to your own conclusion after you hear what I have to tell you. If we agree, we'll track down the secretary."

Sabine raised an eyebrow. "And the secretary will lead us to her beau."

"That's right."

Dorfmann leafed through a spiral notebook. "Ruhland couldn't give me much on the secretary." He stabbed a finger at a page. "His information is sketchy, but I'm hoping it's enough."

She squirmed in her seat, fighting the urge to tell her boss to get on with it. As if to make sure she was paying attention, Dorfmann looked at her. Patience was not one of her virtues, but she did manage to hold her tongue.

Finally, he read from his notes. "As a captain, he didn't have access to top-secret spy reports."

Sabine interjected, "Does that sound right to you?"

Dorfmann shrugged. "I don't really know, but I can't see any reason for him to lie about it. The better the goods he delivers, the better his chances for a comfortable setup here in the West. He did pass the polygraph, and the intelligence he gave did lead us to the two Stasi collaborators."

"So what did he say about the spy in Cologne?"

"He overheard two colleagues at a birthday party for one of the generals. Off to the side, they were cutting up, gossiping about one of their own 'ficken fürs Vaterland.' Ruhland couldn't make out the spy's name. Only what I already told you: the man was dating a secretary in an agency in Cologne."

"That's it?" Sabine couldn't hide her disappointment. How in the world was she supposed to identify a mole from that?

"Not quite. They were talking about how lucky the guy was. Screwing a hot divorcee."

"A divorced secretary. Well, that narrows it down."

"Don't give up. I saved the best for last. The two Stasi officers were boasting they'd soon be reading Harold Brown's mail."

She scooted to the edge of her chair. "You mean—"

"The U.S. Secretary of Defense. None other." Dorfmann gazed at her. "Does that give you a clue as to where our secretary is working?"

"Armed Forces Security Office," Sabine blurted. "She's got access to NATO correspondence."

"Exactly." He closed the notebook. "First thing in the morning you leave for Cologne. Check out every divorced secretary with potential access, and be quick about it. You'll have a day at most to find the spy. The Stasi won't take any chances. If they suspect the defector knows about their man in Cologne, they'll pull him back to East Germany in a flash."

Chapter Ten

Blown Cover

Foreign Intelligence Service [HVA], Stasi Headquarters, East Berlin, Wednesday, 20 July 1977

"Major Kurz reporting for duty."

Heinrich's spirits rose at the sight of the young officer he'd chosen to replace the injured Borst. The gray uniform fit his trim figure as though custom-made. His good looks made up for what he lacked in experience. Blue eyes, high cheekbones dominating a broad face, and thick, dark hair were sure to melt even the coldest female heart. Yes, indeed, he would do as a substitute for Borst.

"Good morning, Major. Have a seat. Any trouble making it home?"

"No, sir." Kurz slid his long frame into the closest chair. "I got your message just in time to catch the night train to Berlin."

"Well done, Major." When Kurz blinked hard several times, Heinrich said, "You've not had much sleep. Coffee?"

"No thank you, General. I had half a pot at home already."

"Very well." Eager to implement the next phase of the plan to ensnare Monika Fuchs, Heinrich continued, "I'm assigning you the most important task of your career. The success of this mission is crucial. I can't have you nodding off. You tell me if you need more caffeine. Understood?"

Kurz straightened. "Yes, General."

Heinrich slid the file in front of him across the desk. "This contains the profile of your next conquest: Monika Fuchs. Secretary in the West German Chancellery with security clearance. She's on holiday in Italy, where you will make contact."

"When—?"

"You're on a morning flight to Milan. Rental car and hotel have all been arranged."

"Where—?"

Impatient, Heinrich raised a hand. "Frau Schröder will give you the travel papers. Now take this folder to your office, learn the material and return in an hour. I will give you further instructions then."

Kurz grabbed the file and left the office. Heinrich reached for his cup, but put it down hard at Frau Schröder's excited voice on the intercom. "General, Lieutenant Gruber is here with an urgent message."

"Send him in."

Without knocking, the stocky Gruber charged into the room. "General, I have some bad news."

"Just what I need."

Gruber remained standing. "We suspect Captain Ruhland has defected."

"Rubbish." Heinrich leapt to his feet. "You'd better have some evidence."

"He didn't report for work yesterday. His secretary is on vacation, so no one thought to check on him. I wasn't notified of his absence until early this morning."

"*Verdammt nochmal!* Is everyone sleepwalking around here?"

Gruber shifted from one leg to the other. "I immediately called his home phone. When he didn't answer, I sent Sergeant Beck to his apartment."

"And?"

"He just called me from there. The janitor let him in. The place is a mess. Clothes strewn over the bed. Suits in the closet pushed to one side. Cupboards open. No suitcase anywhere."

"Son of a bitch! Do we have any idea when he might have left?"

"The janitor saw him come home from work on Monday. I assume Ruhland absconded later that evening."

Heinrich slumped into his chair. "How long has Ruhland been with us?"

"About ten years."

"How much does he know about our assets in the West?"

"At his rank, he shouldn't—"

Heinrich slammed his fist on the desk. "No guesswork. I must know for sure—"

He broke off when Frau Schröder ran into the office. "Excuse me, General, but I was told to give this to you right away."

He snatched a sealed envelope from her outstretched hand and tore into it, obliterating the top secret stamp. In disbelief, he read the message, then flung the paper and envelope onto the desk. "Here is our answer. Two of our top West German informants were arrested last night. That traitor must have fingered them."

Heinrich motioned for his secretary to leave. When the door closed behind her, he turned to Gruber. "Tell me about Ruhland's family. Is he married? Children?"

"Divorced. No children."

"What about parents, brothers, sisters, other relatives?"

"I'll have to check his file, General."

"Do that now." He waved his hand at Gruber. "Go." Before the lieutenant could slip out the door, Heinrich called after him, "And bring in his ex. I want to have a talk with her."

"Yes, sir."

Once alone, Heinrich leaned back in his chair and stared at the far wall. Two veteran Stasi informants exposed by the deserter. As a captain, Ruhland shouldn't have had access to information about the Stasi spy network in the West, but that didn't guarantee the man hadn't picked up intelligence he wasn't entitled to see or hear. Losing informants was bad enough, but could the snitch also have compromised Stasi spies embedded in West Germany? At the thought, Heinrich buzzed his secretary. "Have Major Kurz come to my office immediately."

Folder in hand, Kurz entered a few minutes later. "I'm sorry, General, but I've not finished reading—"

Heinrich waved him off. "Never mind that. Give me the file."

Kurz laid the file on the desk. "I don't understand."

"You're off the assignment, Major. We have a defector, and he may have blown your cover."

Kurz grimaced.

"Just be glad you left last night, Major. I'll have something else for you in a few days."

"But what about Monika Fuchs? I'm willing to chance it, General."

Heinrich made a sweeping hand gesture. "Out of the question. Return to your office and wait for my instructions. As for Fuchs, I'll think of something."

While Major Kurz let himself out, Heinrich leaned forward on the desktop. Yesterday he'd lost Borst, today Kurz. Two Romeos out of commission in as many days. Monika Fuchs was about to slip from his grasp. He could not let that happen.

As he sat back in his chair, an idea came. What if he . . . ? No, too risky. He hadn't gotten to be head of Stasi's Foreign Intelligence Service by taking unnecessary chances. Still, he'd run out of options, and Monika Fuchs was a prize worth taking a risk for.

He reached for the telephone.

Chapter Eleven

Deceived

Amt für die Sicherheit der Bundeswehr [ASBw], Office of Security, Federal Armed Forces, Cologne, West Germany, Wednesday, 20 July 1977

By the time Ingrid Müller left the visitor's office, Sabine had crossed the brunette off the list of the dozen divorcees who had access to sensitive documents at the Federal Armed Forces Office of Security. On the rebound from an unhappy marriage, Müller had consoled herself with a boyfriend who had moved in with her at the beginning of the year. She kicked him out last month after she caught him two-timing her.

Sabine pecked her pencil on the desk. Since the Stasi spy had been actively wooing his victim as recently as a few days ago—if the defector had told it straight—she could eliminate Müller's boyfriend. Besides, she couldn't imagine a professional spy jeopardizing a prospect by taking up with another woman.

Seven down, five to go. The intercom buzzed. "Frau Schneider is here," the receptionist's high-pitched voice announced.

"Send her in." Sabine glanced at the next name on the list. Renate Schneider, eight years with the office, promoted to executive secretary five years ago. Sabine did a double take at her age—twenty-eight. Put in a high position at the tender age of twenty-three and after only three years of service. A top performer, or did she know someone?

The door, left ajar by Müller, opened wide and in strode a woman exuding confidence. Long dark curls cascaded over a red blouse that revealed considerable cleavage. A tight black skirt accentuated the woman's curves. Full makeup, mascara, eyeliner—Renate Schneider believed in advertising the whole package of her considerable charms. According to defector Ruhland, his colleagues had bragged about one of their own screwing a hot divorcee. This woman certainly qualified.

Without waiting for an invitation, Schneider took a chair facing the desk. After introductions, Sabine began the interview with general questions about the woman's career, to which she already knew the answers. She'd learned the hard way that asking personal questions too early often resulted in the interviewee shutting down. She needn't have bothered about this one.

Schneider drummed her long, red nails on the desk surface. "You're not here to chat about my job, are you?"

Sabine leaned forward. "You're very perceptive. Actually, I need to ask—"

"My life's an open book. Ask me anything you want."

No sense wasting more time with preliminaries. "You've been divorced five years?"

A nod.

"Tell me about your relationships since your divorce."

Schneider broke out in riotous laughter, as if Sabine had told the funniest joke she'd ever heard. "Have you got all day?"

"You mean—?"

"I've never had so much fun as after I divorced that boring husband of mine." She gazed at Sabine, a conspiratorial smile in her eyes. "I play the field, and I don't get involved."

Though she suspected what the answer would be, Sabine nevertheless had to ask the question. "So you're not in a steady relationship now?"

Schneider rolled her eyes. "No way. I learned my lesson. When a guy gets possessive, he's history."

"But you're seeing someone now?"

"No, broke it off last week."

"Any of the men ever ask you about your job?"

"I see where you're headed. Not to worry. When someone asks, I tell them I work for the government, and I can't talk about it." Schneider gave her a quizzical look. "I know one of our secretaries got caught spying for East Germany last year. Do you suspect we have another mole?"

"You know I can't tell you that. I do ask you not to gossip about it. Will you promise me that?"

"Sure thing." She rose. "You're through with me, I take it?"

"Yes. And thank you for being so forthright."

Before Schneider slipped out the door, she said, "Good luck finding the snitch."

Sabine leaned back in her chair. While she didn't share Schneider's philosophy, she had to admire the woman's confidence and honesty. A firm line drawn through the name on the list meant that after eight interviews she was no closer to tracking down the compromised secretary and her beau than when she'd started. She steeled herself, trying not to think what she'd do if she hit a dead end with the last four secretaries as well.

A timid knock drew Sabine's attention. At the threshold stood secretary number nine, a questioning look in her eyes. Sabine waved her inside. Unlike the previous visitor who needed no encouragement to sit, this one was the shy type. Only after Sabine pointed to a chair did Gabi Schulz lower herself onto it, as if she were afraid she'd break the damn thing. But if anything was going to break, it would be the woman's doll-like figure, not the chair.

During the introductions, Sabine assessed the secretary. Curly brown hair, expressive eyes, a floral cotton dress hanging loosely on her small frame. She wasn't sexy like Schneider, but men who liked their women slim and demure would certainly find her attractive.

As she'd done with Schneider, Sabine began with simple background questions. Schulz didn't interrupt her, but dutifully gave the information Sabine already possessed. After finishing secondary school, Schulz had entered the office's apprentice program while still a teenager. Her long and faithful service had been rewarded last year when, at age thirty-one, she was assigned as secretary to a department head. She'd passed all background checks, the latest coming last spring before her promotion.

When she'd succeeded in getting Schulz to make more and more eye contact, Sabine sat back, trying to relax so she could deliver what came next in as casual a tone as possible. "Frau Schulz, I'm here on a rather delicate mission, which necessitates my asking you some personal questions. Are you all right with that?"

After a nervous gulp, Schulz said, "Yes, of course."

The tension in the woman's voice put Sabine on full alert, but she forced herself to follow up with easy questions, lest she alarm her, put her on the defensive. "You were married right after school?"

Schulz nodded.

"How long—?"

"He . . . we divorced last year."

"If you don't mind my asking, what was the reason for the divorce?"

Schulz squirmed in her seat and studied the carpet. Not wanting to push, Sabine waited. Finally, Schulz looked up. "He found someone else."

"I'm sorry."

Schulz met Sabine's gaze. "Thank you."

"You must have gone through a difficult time." The empathetic tone came with ease. She really felt sorry for the woman. Still, she had to broach the crucial subject. "It's hard to keep your faith in men after something like what you've been through. But there are good men out there."

"Oh, I know," Schulz gushed. "I've met a wonderful man."

Sabine's pulse quickened. Slow, she admonished herself. "That's great news. I'd like to hear about him."

Schulz drew back in her chair and eyed Sabine with suspicion. Perhaps it had dawned on her that the true focus of this BND agent's visit was her private life. Sure enough, she clammed up. "There is really nothing much to tell. We've been dating for a few weeks." She stopped. "Is there anything else you need to ask me about the job?"

Nice try, Sabine thought. "Frau Schulz, I'm afraid I need to ask you more about your relationship. You said you've been dating for a few weeks. How did the two of you meet?"

The secretary squirmed some more. "It was during rush hour. The street car was packed. This nice man got up and offered me his seat. Next thing you know, we were making conversation."

"And you started seeing each other?"

She nodded.

"What's his name?"

"Brian McGregor."

"British?"

"Yes, he's a correspondent for a London paper."

"How's his German?"

"Perfect."

"No accent?"

She shook her head.

"Hard to believe," Sabine said. In fact she didn't believe it, having yet to encounter a Brit or a Yank who spoke German without some trace of an accent. Time to press.

"Have you made any plans together?"

"You mean—?"

"A future together."

"Well, he's told me he loves me. But he's in the middle of a divorce."

A Brit with no accent and the old pending divorce story. Was this woman really that gullible? Sensing she was on the trail of something, Sabine probed, "Has your boyfriend ever asked you what you do?"

"Of course." Schulz jerked forward as the full import of the question hit her. "Why are you . . . You don't mean to imply that—?"

"Frau Schulz, it is extremely important that you answer my questions. What conversations have you had pertaining to your job?"

"He knows where I work."

"Does he know you have access to highly confidential materials?"

"Well, I may have let something slip."

"Has he ever asked you what specific documents you get to handle?"

Schulz withdrew into her chair, as though that would stop the barrage of probing questions. "He may have. I don't recall. You know how it is when you make small talk." Her eyes sought Sabine's as if in search of confirmation or approval.

No, I don't know how you would make small talk about secret government documents, Sabine thought. "Do you recall any specific conversation?"

Schulz shook her head.

"Has Mr. McGregor ever expressed an interest in looking at any of the documents that cross your desk?"

Another headshake.

Realizing she wouldn't get any more out of Schulz on this subject, Sabine asked, "Where does Mr. McGregor live?"

"He keeps an apartment at Gasthof Rheinland. That's a residential hotel downtown. He's often gone to Bonn for several days and stays in a hotel there."

"When's the last time you were together?"

"This weekend. We had an early dinner date yesterday, but he didn't show."

"Has he stood you up like that before?"

"Never. I called his hotel. He wasn't in. So I left a message. When I hadn't heard back by late evening, I called again and was told he had checked out. Maybe something's wrong and he had to return to England."

Something was wrong all right, but if he went anywhere, it most likely wasn't to England. Sabine didn't share these thoughts. Instead, she asked, "He didn't leave a message?"

"No."

"You wouldn't happen to have a photo?"

An impish expression appeared on the secretary's face. "Brian forbade me to take his picture, but I sneaked a snapshot in the park when he wasn't looking."

"Do you have it with you?"

Schulz pulled a small color photo from her purse and laid it on the desk. It showed the profile of a trim, dark-haired man on a park bench, his hand in a paper sack, pigeons crowding around his feet.

"Do you mind if I take this for a moment?"

The secretary nodded reluctantly. "Go ahead."

"Be right back."

Sabine rushed down the hall and showed the picture to the receptionist. "Can you have this faxed to my office?"

The woman pulled a cover sheet from a drawer. "Photo will take a while and it won't be in color."

Sabine grabbed a pen off the desk, wrote down Dorfmann's fax number, her own name and a note requesting the man's identity.

She handed the sheet and photo to the receptionist. "Please let me know right away if you get a response from Pullach."

She turned and hurried back to the interview room.

Schulz didn't seem surprised when Sabine returned without her photo. "Do you think Brian McGregor is a . . . spy?"

"I have my suspicions. I should know as soon as I hear back from my office."

"I've done nothing wrong. He's never asked me to do anything and I wouldn't have if he had."

Though she'd seen other lonely secretaries betray their country for love, Sabine didn't voice that fact. If McGregor turned out to be a spy, she didn't envy Schulz the vetting she'd have to endure. But if she'd told the truth about not having compromised the agency, she might escape the ordeal unscathed.

The receptionist burst in, holding a fax. Sabine tore it from her hand and read. "Ruhland identified the man in the photo as Dietmar Kurz, a Stasi officer. We are checking all routes to East Germany."

After the receptionist had left, Sabine turned to Schulz. "I'm afraid I have bad news. Your boyfriend is a Stasi spy."

Schulz broke into tears. Sabine walked around the desk and put an arm around her shoulder. "I'm so sorry."

When the sobbing didn't stop, Sabine stepped back and reflected what she had to do. There remained little doubt that the arrest of the two collaborators after Ruhland's defection had spooked the Stasi. Figuring Kurz's cover had been blown, they'd pulled him back to the East. With the Pullach office on the manhunt along the entire Eastern border, there was nothing for her to do but check on his hotel. Perhaps in a hurry, he'd left a clue.

The sobs had given way to soft cries. Sabine laid a gentle hand on Schulz's arm. "Pull yourself together now. I need you to come with me to Gasthof Rheinland."

She helped Schulz up from the chair and guided her out the door.

Chapter Twelve

Italian Sojourn

Viareggio, Italy, Thursday, 21 July 1977

Monika stirred in half-slumber on her beach towel when the sun against her eyelids turned to shadow. Funny, the Mediterranean sky had been cloudless all morning.

"Excuse me, Miss. You are British?"

She opened her eyes wide at the Italian-accented English. A corpulent middle-aged man, his belly flopping over the top of his swimming trunks, stood at the edge of her towel. Shuffling his bare feet in the sand, he stared down at her. When his gaze traveled the length of her bikini-clad torso, Monika sat up and self-consciously crossed her arms and legs.

"No." She hoped her curt response would move this meddler along. Definitely not the type of handsome Italian she'd envisioned meeting on the beach.

Instead of leaving, he pointed to the paperback propped open on the towel, the cover facing up. "But you read E.M. Forster in English?"

She'd brought *A Room with a View* to sharpen her English language skills—a necessity at the Chancellery position—and the story took place in Florence, making it a perfect companion for her Italian holiday.

What's it to you, she almost blurted. But she said, "I've read it in German already. It's one of my favorite books." Why was she explaining herself? None of his business what she read or where she was from.

"Ah, *tedesco.*" An ugly grin spread over his fleshy face. "We like German blondes on our beaches. My German not good. Better in English. You speak Italian?"

She shook her head. How could she get rid of this pest?

"You like nightlife? I show you a good time."

I know the good time you have in mind, she thought. "I'm here to relax."

He kept staring at her. God, just what she needed—another bully after she just got rid of an abusive husband. What was the matter with her that she attracted bossy men? Still seeking the approval of a domineering father?

She'd better leave now. "*Scusi.* I've got to get back." She dropped the book in her handbag, pulled the towel around her waist, and trotted off in her sandals. Once she reached the seafront promenade, she tossed a furtive glance over her shoulder. No sign of the man on the beach.

She dashed across the boulevard, causing a red convertible Fiat to screech to a halt. A horn blasted, arms shot up in the air, teenagers hurled expletives in Italian she couldn't quite make out. Ignoring the commotion, she ran down the side street toward Pensione Garibaldi. The last thing she needed was for a repulsive guy on the make to find out where she was staying.

♫ ♫ ♫

An hour later, her skin tingling from a slight sunburn and a long shower, Monika strolled along the beachside boulevard, dodging the throng of tourists crowding the sidewalk. Stretching her limbs felt good, but a predinner drink would feel even better. Animated conversations in English, German and Italian flowed from the half-dozen sidewalk cafés she passed.

When she spotted a couple leaving a small table next to the sidewalk, she made a dash for it, barely beating out two women who retreated while grumbling in German. So unlike her to be assertive, but she'd learned that a shrinking violet got nowhere in this tourist town. Still, it had taken her several days to screw up the courage to elbow her way into places.

She turned to people-watching, guessing the nationalities of the crowd passing by. The Northern Europeans were easy to spot. Bereft of the dark hair and the olive complexions of the natives, they were either suffering from various stages of sunburn or their skin was still whiter than Feta cheese. She had fun picking out the Germans by their rigid posture, firm gait, and the shoulder-padded polyester jackets only elderly German men would consider fashionable. The Brit's dress tended to be on the formal side, and she easily recognized the few Americans by their relaxed stroll in often sloppy clothes.

"Signorina?"

The waiter's question tore her from her reverie. She thought for a moment, then decided on the Italian cocktail that had grown on her during the past few days. "*Negroni, per favore.*"

"*Kommt sofort.*"

She suppressed a snicker at his recognition of her German origin. But then, even at his young age, he'd surely served thousands of her countrymen. At least he'd considered her young enough to address her as signorina.

True to his word, he reappeared in no time with the concoction of vermouth rosso, bitter Campari, and dry gin. Sliding the orange slice and lemon peel garnish along the glass rim, she took a sip and leaned back. The alcohol intensified the pleasant tiredness she felt from the day's sunbathing. She'd spent the last five days recovering from the office grind and the stresses of the divorce. Time to explore Tuscany. While she weighed where to go sightseeing tomorrow, a figure in the crowd caught her attention. The man from the beach.

She turned her face away, holding her breath and praying he'd fail to see her. No such luck.

"*Buonasera, signorina.*"

Dressed in khakis and an open-collared sport shirt that exposed too much of a flabby chest, he approached her table and took the chair opposite her. Protest caught in her throat.

As if in cahoots with the intruder, the waiter appeared promptly at his side.

"*Birra alla spina.*"

As the waiter hurried off, the man turned to her. "*Perdonno.* Don't want to offend. Alfonso Rossi." He extended a hand, which she ignored. Unfazed, he continued, "I'm from Lucca. You like to see Toscana, I can show you."

She clenched her jaw, trying to summon the courage to tell him to get lost. Either she was overly defensive or the recurrent theme of her life—her inability to stand up for herself—was playing out once more. He was unattractive, but that didn't make him a bad person, just a pushy Italian. Not unusual in beach resorts.

The waiter lowered his tray and plunked down a tall glass, beer foam cascading over the sides and puddling on the table cloth. Alfonso took a huge gulp, investing further in his considerable beer belly. Not the stereotypical Italian wine drinker.

"As I told you earlier, I'm here to relax, not sightsee."

"*Ma Toscana, è magnifica.*" He raised his hands. "You must see. I take you, no?"

His eyes seemed full of genuine enthusiasm, almost enough to make her give in before she caught herself. How to get rid of him? "Do you have a card?"

After a slight hesitation, he produced one from his shirt pocket and handed it to her. Without reading it, she put it in her purse. "If I want a tour of Tuscany, I'll call you."

She swallowed the rest of her cocktail and fled the table in search of the waiter to pay her bill. Surely, this time the man had gotten the message.

Chapter Thirteen

The Consultant

Federal Intelligence Service [BND], Pullach, West Germany, Thursday, 21 July 1977

No sooner had Sabine entered her office and seated herself behind her desk than Bernd Dorfmann strolled in through the open door. He mumbled *"Guten Morgen"* and dropped three folders onto the desk.

Eager to learn what task he was dumping on her now, she barely remembered to reciprocate his good-morning greeting. While he settled in a chair, she stole a glance at the folders.

Her curiosity did not escape his notice. "We'll get to these in a minute. But first things first. Any luck at the spy's hotel?"

"Not really. I did check his room."

"How'd you manage that? You didn't use your credentials, I hope."

"Of course not. Doubt it would've done any good."

"They let you in the room just like that?"

Sabine took a second to revel in the amazement, maybe even admiration, reflected in her boss's tone, before responding. "I had the jilted secretary with me. She was a complete mess. But by the time we got to the hotel, she'd calmed down enough to follow my instructions."

"Which were? Come on, don't make me drag everything out of you, Frau Maier."

"She pretended to have lost her earrings. Would they please let her check the room? Luckily, they hadn't rented it, and the staff knew her from prior visits."

"Find anything?"

"I went through every drawer, searched the entire place. The guy left nothing behind. No socks, no underwear, no toothpaste, *gar nichts.*"

Dorfmann nodded. "No surprise there. The Stasi trains their agents well."

"And he left in a hurry. The desk clerk seemed to feel sorry for the secretary, probably thinking the guy had ditched her. He told us how Mr. McGregor came running into the hotel at six Wednesday evening, demanding his bill and requesting a taxi for six-thirty."

"Did he give a reason for his abrupt departure?" Dorfmann asked.

"An emergency back home." She chuckled. "I guess a defector blowing his cover qualifies as an emergency."

A hint of a smile played on Dorfmann's lips for just an instant. "So he only had half an hour to pack and sweep the room."

"And still, he left the place as if no one had ever stayed there. Six-thirty sharp, he settled his bill and climbed into a waiting taxi, which took him to the Hauptbahnhof Köln. We know, because the clerk couldn't order a taxi without giving the company the destination."

"That fits with what we learned," Dorfmann said. "Wednesday evening, a man matching his description caught the seven-thirty train to Berlin at the Cologne main station." He clenched his jaw. "The Stasi seems always a step ahead of us. We've got to improve our methods."

"I—"

"I'm not blaming you, Frau Maier. You did a great job nailing down the secretary in just one day. But what we've been doing is obviously not working."

Sabine tried to think of something to suggest, but nothing came to her.

Dorfmann pointed at the folders. "These are copies of the prosecutors' files on the three women convicted of espionage. I had to get the chief involved before those self-important lawyers would deign to even let us have copies."

"That's what I asked for, but now I'm not sure how much help they will be for catching spies who are stealing our secrets as we speak. I need to know about every single or divorced secretary working for the intelligence agencies, the Chancellery, the Foreign Office, and the Interior and Defense Ministries. Remember, it was personnel records that led me to Gabi Schulz's Romeo."

"You should have at least some of them in the morning."

She looked for signs that he was kidding. "You mean—?"

"The chief approved my request for them on Tuesday; he even designated it as urgent."

"I don't believe it. You're reading my mind."

"Well, we've worked together long enough." His quick smile morphed into a peculiar expression. "But aren't you forgetting something?"

"I don't understand—"

"Combing through the personnel records won't do you much good without having a compass, will it?"

"A compass?"

"What we talked about before—common traits among the women who fell for the charms of a Stasi Romeo. Only with that information will you be able to zero in on current and potential victims."

"You're not resurrecting Rasterfahndung? I thought you agreed it's a dead end."

"That's not what I'm referring to." He glanced at his wristwatch. "You've got a couple of hours to go through those folders. Come to my office at eleven thirty. We're meeting someone for lunch."

"We?"

"Yes. It's on the firm."

"Who—?"

"No one you know." He stood and slipped out the door.

♫ ♫ ♫

Relaxing into the black leather seat of Dorfmann's silver Mercedes sedan, Sabine mulled over what she'd gleaned from the folders he'd left with her. Her extensive note-taking had mired her in so much detail, she couldn't detect an overall pattern, if one even existed.

When her boss passed up the usual lunch spots in Pullach and drove north on B11, she wondered why they were going all the way to Munich. Before she could ask, he said, "Did you finish going over the folders?"

"Not by a long shot. It's going to take a while to cross-reference that information with our files. And once you get me all the personnel records—"

"Overwhelming, isn't it?"

"For sure."

"Frau Maier, you work harder than just about anyone in the agency." He stared straight ahead, presumably concentrating on the thick traffic. Still, the long pause reeked of intentionality. "As dedicated as you are, you can't possibly make sense of the mountain of information in the short time we have to catch these spies."

She had an inkling where he was headed. Before she could voice her suspicion, he went on, "Even with your stellar work in sniffing out the secretary and her beau in record time, we were still too late."

He gunned the engine to pass a tourist bus. She waited until he eased back into the right-hand lane to ask, "So you're assigning another body to share the task?"

Dorfmann glanced over, then returned his gaze to the road. "Well, not exactly. It'll be clearer once you meet him."

Who the hell was this guy, and why did her boss find it necessary that she share responsibility for a task that should be hers alone? And why on earth were they meeting over lunch instead of at the agency? She was still groping for answers when Dorfmann pulled the Mercedes into the parking lot of *Trattoria Bel Canto*—a favorite Schwabing restaurant of hers.

As they exited the car, he said, "You've told me about this place. Good food, great atmosphere. But I made sure the student-waiters from the conservatory only sing at dinnertime." He held open the front door for her. "The company pays us to solve problems, not to listen to opera. And we have much to discuss."

When Dorfmann gave the college-age hostess his name, she grabbed two menus from a pile on a side table and asked them to follow. She led them through a bustling dining area to a small side room with half a dozen tables. At a few minutes past noon, most were unoccupied. She steered toward a round table at the far corner. When they approached, a man casually dressed in khakis and an open-collared plaid shirt, put down his menu and rose.

The hostess laid her menus on the white tablecloth and left. While the two men shook hands and exchanged greetings, Sabine took in the stranger's features. Dark hair, olive complexion, maybe early forties, a few centimeters taller than she—it all added up to a handsome Mediterranean type. She almost fell over when her boss introduced him as Horst Kögler. About as German a name as there was.

When Kögler turned his attention her way, a bright smile lit up his broad face and played in his dark eyes. "Good to meet you, Frau Maier."

No trace of an accent. So much for Mediterranean type. As they sat, she reminded herself this was a business meeting. Otherwise, she would have thought her boss was trying to set her up with a blind date.

Dorfmann explained, "Herr Kögler has been consulting with several intelligence agencies, including ours, for a number of years. He runs a computer business here in Munich."

She was about to ask how a private person could be working with intelligence agencies, when Kögler spoke up. "You're wondering about my having access to secret materials. Before starting my own company a few years ago, I was an agent with the Cologne intelligence agency."

Digesting this information, Sabine glanced at the menu. The two men followed her lead. A waitress appeared a few moments later and took their orders for three different pasta dishes and mineral water all around.

After she was gone, Kögler resumed his explanation. "When I left the Cologne office, I didn't expect to do intelligence work ever again, but it seems our government is behind when it comes to computers. So I've been asked to consult on occasion. And each time, they update my security clearance. So you see, you can share all your secrets with me."

Sabine hoped to God she wasn't blushing at his flippant remark. "I'm actually leading a pretty boring life, Herr Kögler, but if I have any exciting secrets to tell, you'll be the first to know."

"Touché."

"I see you two will get along just fine," Dorfmann chimed in. "Sharp wits, bordering on smart ass."

"And what exactly will we be working on together?" Sabine tried to keep annoyance from creeping into her voice. Sharing intelligence work with a civilian—who'd ever heard of such a thing?

"As soon as you get the personnel records, I want you to consult with Herr Kögler about how best to look for patterns," Dorfmann said.

Sabine shrugged. "Sounds like Rasterfahndung to me."

"Not exactly," Kögler said. "I had some exposure to Rasterfahndung when the federal criminal police used it to track down terrorists. From what Herr Dorfmann has told me, we'll be looking for patterns identifying likely targets of Stasi spies. I know how to use computers to enable you to do just that. In no time, I'll have you exposing spies before they can escape to the East."

She couldn't decide whether he sounded self-confident or arrogant. Maybe a bit of both, but at least he'd referred to her as the one tracking spies. She might be able to work with him after all.

When the waitress brought their entrees, all conversation ceased. The pesto sauce on her pasta primavera was not as messy as the marinara sauce on the men's pasta. Dorfmann got a few red spots on his white shirt, but Kögler seemed quite adept at handling his spaghetti and sauce. There must be a drop of Italian blood in his veins. He certainly didn't look like a computer geek. She felt his occasional glance, but she kept her eyes on her plate.

What the hell. Why not ask? "You've got me baffled, Herr Kögler. Are you German or—"

"You're not the first to try to square my German name and speech with my looks." Unfazed by her probing, Kögler explained, "My father was German, my mother Italian. As you can see, her genes were stronger than his. I grew up in Germany, but I learned enough Italian from her to get by." He looked her in the eye. "I gather you're purebred German."

She held his gaze. "As far as I know. If my mother dallied with the milkman, she's not told me."

Both men chuckled. Dorfmann pushed back his empty plate. "Let's talk logistics. Do you need to do your research at your place, Herr Kögler?"

"Yes. Be too much trouble to move my computers to your office."

Dorfmann stroked his chin. "Hmm. I'll have to set up a protocol for Frau Maier to bring the records to your office. And I need to inspect your setup. Make sure it's secure enough. Can we do that after lunch?"

"Of course."

"And I may ask Frau Maier to stay with the files while you work with them."

"That's certainly no hardship."

Sabine wasn't sure how she felt about Kögler's complimentary remark. He was definitely her type, but nothing good ever came of a romantic entanglement at work. She laid her fork on her unfinished pasta.

Chapter Fourteen

Third Choice

Golm, East Germany, Friday, 22 July 1977

Fascinated by the various methods the Stasi employed to transmit clandestine information, Stefan didn't notice the man in gray uniform standing at the classroom door until the instructor stopped talking midsentence.

All heads turned toward the intruder, who pointed at Stefan. "Herr Malik. Step outside, please."

Stefan fumbled with his notepad and pen. This sounded ominous, but he'd done nothing wrong. Maybe a ploy to see how he'd react when faced with something unexpected.

"Don't just sit there. Get a move on."

In his haste, Stefan dropped the pen, which bounced off the desk and rolled along the floor. He started to bend down, but stopped at the officer's command, "Leave it."

Clutching the notepad, Stefan stepped into the hall. Why would he be pulled from class? If he'd learned one thing during the first week at Golm, it was not to ask the Stasi the reasons for its orders.

"Pack all your things and be downstairs in ten minutes."

Stefan hurried to his room. While he threw his few possessions into a suitcase, he kept wondering why he was being dismissed two weeks before finishing the course. He'd paid attention, studied, and participated in class. Had they decided he didn't have what it took to be a spy? If so, could he get on with his life, or were they sending him back to prison?

When he entered the lobby, a guard pointed to a black Wartburg sedan idling out front. He was stepping through the exhaust spewing from the car's tailpipe when a chauffeur jumped out, took his suitcase and opened the rear door for him. Stefan climbed in while the chauffeur stashed the case in the trunk. Hmm, almost the royal treatment. He must not be going back to Rummelsburg Prison. Maybe home, to his private life.

As the car pulled away from the curb, Stefan leaned forward. "Where are we going?"

No response.

He knew the answer when the Wartburg entered Normannenstraße. The driver stopped in front of Building 15, which housed the foreign intelligence service, retrieved the suitcase and set it on the sidewalk next to Stefan. He offered the first proof he was not mute. "General Heinrich is expecting you."

He climbed into the driver's seat and engaged the clutch, causing the car's engine to sputter. To avoid breathing exhaust fumes the Wartburg left in its wake, Stefan grabbed the suitcase and turned toward the building entrance. An officer emerged from the revolving glass door, looked at him askance, and hurried past him down the sidewalk. Stefan took a hesitant step forward, but stopped at the revolving door still turning from the officer's exit. Even if the Stasi had concluded he didn't measure up, how naïve of him to think they'd just send him home. Once entangled in the Stasi's web, he wouldn't extricate himself easily, if ever. The revolving door beckoned, as if eager to suck him inside.

Get a grip. He entered the slowing door and pushed his way into the building. The lobby guard insisted on storing the suitcase. Stefan removed the file Heinrich had given him and headed up the stairs to the second-floor reception. Climbing two steps at a time, he told himself that if Heinrich intended to throw him back in the slammer, he'd be there by now. The general had to have a different reason for summoning him in such a rush, something that would tighten the Stasi's grip on him even more.

When Stefan reached the top of the staircase, Heinrich's secretary stopped typing and pointed to the open door. "Go on in."

At the sight of the general studying a folder, Stefan stopped at the threshold and cleared his throat.

Heinrich looked up. "There you are. Come in and close the door."

Stefan complied and took the nearest chair, resting the file on his lap.

"I'll take that file." While Stefan handed it over, Heinrich asked, "What did you learn this week?"

"You mean in Golm or from the file?"

Heinrich made a dismissive hand gesture. "In class, of course. I'll get to the file in a minute."

Surprised by the question, Stefan hesitated, unsure of what to say.

"Tell me what subjects they covered." Heinrich's voice carried impatience.

Stefan regained his composure. "They showed us how to use a minicamera that fits in a matchbox or a cigarette pack."

"What else?"

"How to conceal microfilm in pens, cans, coins, hollowed-out pencils."

"They teach you about dead drops?"

"Yes."

"Good. You've got the basics at least." After a slight pause, the general said, "I've heard good things about you from Golm."

A compliment from the general? Before it fully sank in, Heinrich went on. "Don't let it go to your head. You're still pretty green. There's a lot you don't know about tradecraft, but we'll catch you up later."

The general clenched his jaw, as if wrestling with a difficult decision. "Right now, I need you for a job that cannot wait."

So much for getting back to private life.

Heinrich leaned forward. "Now let's talk about the file. You studied it?"

"Yes, sir."

"Could you make sense of it?"

"I think so, General."

"Well then, tell me what you've learned."

The sheer volume of information contained in the file flooded Stefan's mind. He took a deep breath to help him organize his thoughts. "The methods of wooing a woman so she falls in love with the Romeo."

"So, how do you lay the scent for a woman?"

"Building a relationship of personal trust that can withstand great stresses."

Heinrich raised an eyebrow. "That sounds good, but how do you put it into practice?"

Stefan swallowed. He'd been asking himself the same thing when he'd read the abstract ideas and theories. "Well, as I understand it, there is a prerequisite. For this to work, we must deal with a particular kind of woman."

"Such as?"

"We target women who are timid, reclusive, weak, easily influenced, have trouble making friends—"

"And withdrawn, gullible, introverted, unsociable," Heinrich interjected. "Yes, yes. You've retained most of it. What else might the Romeo have to do once he gains the woman's trust?"

"He has to convince her he's in love with her, to dangle the prospect of marriage."

Heinrich's face brightened the tiniest bit. "Excellent. The instructors in Golm were right. You are a quick study." The general turned serious. "Know that I'm taking a risk by giving you an important assignment so soon. Failure is not an option. You understand?"

Once more Stefan swallowed hard, wondering what tough task awaited him. "Yes, General."

"You're on an afternoon flight to Milan."

"Italy?" Stefan burst out before he could stop himself. Where else would Milan be?

"You're good in geography too, I see."

"What will I be doing in Italy?"

"Romancing a good-looking blonde on the beach. Monika Fuchs. A key secretary in the West German Chancellery. Put your charms to work on her."

The way the general eyed him made Stefan uneasy.

After a slight pause, Heinrich said, "Do whatever it takes to get her to fall for you. Is that clear?"

Stefan nodded. Faking love. Could he do it?

"There is an office across the hall." Heinrich slid a folder across the desk. "Take this and go through it carefully. I expect you back in no more than an hour for final instructions." Heinrich dismissed him with a wave of the hand.

Stefan grabbed the file and left the office. He approached the secretary, who kept typing. Thinking she'd finish up a sentence or paragraph, Stefan waited. He glanced at the white plastic nameplate that displayed *Frau Schröder* in stark, black letters, befitting her stern demeanor.

When the clickety-clack didn't cease, Stefan spoke up. "Frau Schröder."

She typed another word or two before looking up. "What is it, Herr Malik?"

Before he could stop himself, he quipped, "The general is lucky to have an efficient typist like you." When she didn't react, Stefan added, "The general told me to go to an office . . ."

She pointed to a wooden door across the way. "It's open."

Stefan ignored her gruffness, forcing a *"Dankeschön"* from his lips. A few seconds later, he closed the office door on the noise of the typewriter. Brown linoleum floor and bare gray walls made for a drab atmosphere. Two visitor chairs in front of a small imitation-wood desk, one chair on rollers behind it. No other furnishings. He turned toward an insistent ticking sound and spied a white wall clock with black numerals above the door.

He lowered himself onto the roller chair. Before he could settle himself and gain traction, the chair started to roll on the slick linoleum. He grasped the seat, barely keeping his backside from sliding off. The file flew from his hand and landed with a thud on the floor, scattering papers everywhere. Chagrined, he gathered the errant pages and dropped them along with the file onto the desk. He expected Frau Schröder to charge into the office at any moment, but the muted sound of typewriter keys assured him he'd be spared the embarrassment.

He pulled the chair close to the desk, keeping his feet hooked around the front rollers. Couldn't they at least put a chair mat in this damn place? He leafed through the loose pages. They were all out of order. Just what he needed—having to take extra time to reassemble the file, time he didn't have. Thinking he'd rearrange the pages later, he shoved them off to the side and opened the file. Stapled to the upper left of the inside cover was a color photo of a blonde in a tight red pullover that stretched over ample breasts. Hmm. Nice long hair, pretty face, expressive eyes. Would the rest of her live up to what this upper-body shot promised? One could never tell from this kind of partial photo. For all he knew, she had tree trunks for legs and a flabby ass. Still, he wouldn't mind gazing into those eyes while having a drink at a poolside bar under palm trees gently swaying in a Mediterranean breeze.

He forced his gaze away from the photo and quit daydreaming. One hour was all he had to learn about this woman. He started with the last page on the right-hand side and worked his way forward. After having read the most recent entry on the top sheet, he glanced at the clock above the door. Ten minutes until he had to see Heinrich.

Leaning back, his feet still securely anchored behind the front casters of the chair, he reviewed the essentials. Monika's early years pointed to a lonely childhood without a close friend. A strict upbringing by her father, a Lutheran minister, and a compliant mother, a housewife. No siblings.

Monika married young, perhaps to get away from home, but as so often happens—Stefan shook his head contemplating the irony—she chose a partner much like her dominant father. Add verbal and occasional physical abuse to that. Divorced last Friday. On a two-week holiday in—Stefan squinted at the name of a town he hadn't seen before—Viareggio, Italy. So that's where he was going.

Stefan checked her age. Thirty-five, just a few years behind him. Young enough for romance and old enough for conversation. If Heinrich quizzed him, it would be about her job. She was executive secretary to the chief of the West German Chancellery, who reported directly to the chancellor. Monika possessed top security clearance, giving her access to highly classified information. No wonder Heinrich was so eager to turn her into an informant.

What else did he need to know? Something jumped out at him: Monika liked opera. Probably not of any significance, but it might come in handy during his stay in the country where opera was born and still revered. Although he couldn't fathom why people paid good money to sit through melodramatic opera plots, he was willing to do whatever he could to support his daughter's dream of studying voice. And it couldn't hurt to do a little research to see if there were performances in the Viareggio area while he was courting Monika. Catering to a woman's passion was a sure way to her heart, and if that meant taking Monika to an opera, so be it.

He needed to read the loose pages, but one glance at the clock told him he'd run out of time. He stuck the papers into the center of the file where they might escape notice. With his luck, they contained a crucial detail Heinrich would ask about, but better to take the chance than risk the general's wrath for being late a second time.

A few minutes later, he once again sat in a chair facing Heinrich, who held out a hand for the file.

After Stefan complied, the general said, "She's a looker, don't you think?"

"Quite attractive."

"I told you how much fun you'd have seducing women in service of the state. Makes the job easier when the subject is gorgeous."

Heinrich seemed to expect a response, so Stefan suppressed his scruples against faking love and said in as sincere a tone as he could manage, "I appreciate you're assigning me to a beauty."

The general stabbed a finger at the file on the desk. "Did you see anything in Monika Fuchs' background that fits the profile of vulnerable women we talked about earlier?"

Stefan gathered his thoughts, hoping the pages he'd skipped didn't hold the information the general was after. "She has some of those traits: a lonely childhood, a domineering father, and later an abusive husband." He paused, trying to think of something else. "She seems to have trouble making friends, and—"

"Good enough."

Stefan relaxed. He apparently hadn't missed anything important.

"Any questions?" Heinrich asked.

"No, sir."

"You saw in the file that you're going to Viareggio."

"Yes."

"A Signore Amato Conti will meet your plane in Milan. He'll help you with the rental car and give you directions to Viareggio. I asked him to keep things on track until you get there. He'll fill in the details for you."

Stefan wanted to ask what keeping things on track referred to, but held his tongue. If the general wanted him to know, he would have told him.

"You will introduce yourself to Monika as Günter Freund, a writer who works for *Gemeinschaft Unbegrenzt*, a peace organization in Vienna, Austria. 'Fellowship Unlimited' has a certain ring to it, don't you agree? And best of all, it's not listed in the Vienna phone directory. If she asks why she can't find it, just tell her it's a startup. We can arrange to have an office set up on a temporary basis, if things get that far."

"What about a Vienna apartment?"

"Hmm, you're thinking ahead, Malik. That's good. Yes, of course, there will be a furnished apartment for your use."

While Stefan was digesting the rare praise, Heinrich continued, "After we're done here, go down to the equipment room. They expect you. Did Golm teach you how to operate the radio we use for communication?"

"No."

"Well, the guys downstairs will give you a crash course." He leaned forward. "I expect you back here at the end of Monika's vacation. Depending on where things stand, I may send you to Bonn or Vienna to meet up with her. Just make sure you've got her hooked so she's eager to see you again."

"I'll give it my best, General."

"Your *best*? Wasn't I clear? You will give it your all."

"I will, General."

Heinrich studied him for a long moment. Seemingly satisfied, he said, "Frau Schröder has travel papers and money in three currencies for you."

Stefan could hardly wait to interact with Frau Congeniality again.

"Before I let you go, I need to make something very clear. You are on a delicate mission for the German Democratic Republic. Do whatever is necessary to seduce Monika Fuchs, but never forget who you're working for."

Stefan wondered where this was headed.

"And don't get too enamored with the Western lifestyle. I don't need to tell you how we deal with traitors." Heinrich narrowed his eyes. "I understand your daughter has applied to the *Hochschule für Musik* in Weimar."

Stefan's gut clenched. "Yes, she dreams of becoming an opera singer."

"An ambitious goal. If she has the voice, we will do everything to see her succeed." Heinrich gave him a meaningful look. No need to specify what would happen to Traude and her dream if her father screwed up.

Heinrich extended a hand. "Good luck, Günter Freund. I'm counting on you."

Stefan shook the general's hand, turned and walked out the door.

This time Frau Schröder stopped typing as he approached and handed him a bulky manila envelope. "Your travel papers. Please count the money."

Stefan emptied the contents onto the desk. After a quick glance at airline tickets, and car and hotel reservations, he went through each of three small envelopes: 500 East marks, 1,000 West marks, and 1 million Italian lire. He knew about the marks, but had no idea how much the lire were worth.

Schröder opened a spiral notebook and slid it across the desk. "Sign here."

He checked the amounts in the ledger. They matched his count, and he signed. While she closed the notebook and put it in a desk drawer, Stefan stuffed the money and papers back in the large envelope. He should be leaving but hesitated.

Schröder must have noticed. "Did you have a question, Herr Malik?"

"I do actually. Thank you for asking." He hoped he wasn't laying it on too thick.

"What can I help you with?"

"Do you happen to know what a million lire are worth?"

"Don't hold me to it, but I think it's a little over a thousand West marks."

"Thanks. Italy is expensive."

A hint of a smile graced her face, giving the first indication she might be human after all. "Yes, you can spend a bundle there, especially when you're more than a tourist."

Stefan held her gaze, wondering how much she knew about his Italy assignment. For sure that Heinrich was sending him to seduce a West German secretary. But what else did she know? Had she read his file?

As her smile faded, he asked, "What if a million lire isn't enough?"

"Your travel documents have instructions on how to get more if you need it." Her stern demeanor returned. "The General requires a full accounting of all your expenses."

"Of course."

"They're expecting you in the equipment department."

Stefan nodded. "Thank you, Frau Schröder. I really appreciate your help." A little honey never hurts, he thought.

Her voice followed him down the stairs. "Good luck, Herr Malik."

Well, well, maybe she did have a woman's heart hidden away somewhere. He would find it and stay on its good side. As he was bounding down the steps, his thoughts turned to what he needed to accomplish before catching the plane in the morning. He hoped the radio instructions wouldn't take too long.

Despite Heinrich's admonition to keep the mission a secret, he had to let his daughter know about his foreign travel. Of course, Traude might not even want to see him. He hadn't been a model father when still married to her mother, nor since the divorce. At least being on the Stasi's payroll meant he'd be able to offer financial support for her musical studies. But if he messed up, no amount of support could save her career. He had no choice but to do the general's bidding.

Chapter Fifteen

Soprano

East Berlin, Friday, 22 July 1977

Stuck on a bus that crawled along Unter den Linden in rush-hour traffic, Stefan ogled the attractive brunette standing by the exit door. If he weren't on his way to Italy, he'd try his luck. To take his mind off running late, he pondered what kind of approach might work on her. He'd never had any success with the old line of having seen her somewhere before. But she might respond to a comment about the pleasant weather or the linden trees that lent the boulevard its name. He'd learned over the years that success hinged not so much on what he said but how he said it. Sincerity was the key. If you could fake sincerity, you had it made.

Brakes squealed, the bus veered to the curb, and the exit doors swung open. Stefan squeezed by the brunette, who turned sideways to let him pass. He carried the image of her splendid figure with him as he jumped onto the curb and weaved his way through the pedestrians crowding the sidewalk. Luckily, the equipment guys hadn't loaded him down with the radio they'd demonstrated. If he needed one, he'd be contacted. Travel documents and money ensconced in the large inside pocket of his jacket, Stefan covered the several hundred meters to Café Franken in a few minutes. His mind churned. Would Traude still be there, and if so, what could he tell her? She'd sounded upbeat on the phone, eager to see him.

Still groping for a plan, he pulled open the heavy entrance door and stepped inside the café. Warm, stale air greeted him. Sweating from the brisk walk, he wiped his brow. Smoke hovered over the several dozen tables in the dimly lit dining room. While the hostess busied herself with an elderly couple, Stefan sneaked by.

Patrons lingered beyond the usual afternoon coffee hour. He squinted against the haze. A movement caught his eye. Traude stepped from a corner booth and waved. His heart lurched. In his haste, he snagged a tablecloth with his jacket, sending cups and saucers dancing on a large table. Ignoring stares, he moved past. Before he could follow his impulse to hug her, Traude lowered her runner's body onto the bench seat. Strands of her red, curly hair lay over the collar of her white blouse. He never could fathom how that small frame of hers could support such a gorgeous soprano voice. Stefan folded his long body into the booth.

She was nursing a half cup of coffee and a slice of almond torte, which so far had only suffered a bite or two.

"I went ahead and ordered," she said matter-of-factly.

"Sorry I'm late."

"Female trouble?" This time her tone carried disdain.

Stefan took a deep breath, swallowing the defensiveness arising in him. "No, nothing like that." He waited until she looked at him. "I know I've not been a very good father . . . or husband to your mother. But—"

Traude raised a hand. "Sorry. I've got no right to judge you."

"You've got every right to be disappointed. But I want to talk to you about something else."

A waitress appeared and took his order of coffee and *apfelkuchen*.

"What's so important for you to want to meet on the spur of the moment?" Traude asked as the waitress disappeared.

Where to start? "I'm going to be traveling for a week or two."

She raised her eyebrows as if to say so what?

"Outside the country."

Her quizzical expression remained.

"In the West," he said.

That got her attention. "How on earth did you swing that? No one gets to travel to the West, unless they're working for . . ."

Stefan nodded ever so slightly.

"*Vati*, you're putting me on."

Stefan's blood pulsed in his ears. He couldn't recall the last time his daughter had addressed him as Dad. "I'm serious."

"What are you—?"

"Traude, I can't tell you. But what I can say is this: for the first time in my life, I have a steady income. That means I can help you with your music studies." He paused. "You're going to study voice at Weimar, aren't you?"

She shrugged. "Well, I applied. Chances of my getting in are pretty slim, as you know."

"I know no such thing. You will be admitted."

Traude stared at him "How can you say that? There are dozens of applicants for every slot." She lowered her voice. "And you know how things work around here."

The waitress approached and plunked down Stefan's coffee and apple pie with a dab of whipped cream he hadn't ordered.

Once she was gone, Traude continued in a low voice, "You and Mother aren't exactly well-connected. It's not just talent, but who's in favor with the party bosses."

"I know all that, Traude. But things are different now."

"Are you trying to tell me you're a big shot all of a sudden?"

"No, that's not what I'm saying. Please trust me. As long as I don't screw up, you'll be attending the *Musik Hochschule* in Weimar."

Traude studied him for a long while. He doctored his coffee with cream and sugar, and took a bite of apple pie. While he drank some coffee, she said, "I hope you're right. I'd give anything to get into their opera program."

He put down his cup. "I know. And you've got the talent and the passion." He added in a whisper, "And it's your ticket to get out of this drab existence."

While it wasn't wise to discuss politics in East Germany with anyone, including spouses and children, who might well be informants for the Stasi, he knew Traude felt as much trapped under the thumb of the autocratic socialist state as he did. He'd trust her with his life. Still, one could never be sure who was listening, even in the *gemütlich* atmosphere of Café Franken.

Traude checked the neighboring tables before returning her attention to him. She took a bird-size bite of her almond torte.

"Has your voice teacher said anything about your weight?" Stefan asked.

She furrowed her brow. "You mean has she suggested that I strive to fit the stereotype of the hefty soprano?"

"No, that's not what I mean at all. I'm certainly no expert, but don't you need a solid foundation, a strong body to sustain the kind of singing opera demands?"

"Oh, Dad. You're so old school. And you're showing your prejudice. To make it in opera today requires more than a beautiful voice. Nowadays, you have to be able to act, and if you can look the part of a consumptive courtesan, so much the better."

Stefan shrugged. "I'll never understand what attracts people to opera, but it's good to see you so passionate. I will do whatever I can." He had a terrible thought. Why hadn't he insisted that Heinrich make arrangements guaranteeing Traude's education if anything should happen to him during his mission?

"What's the matter?"

Her question brought him back. "Oh, I just remembered something I need to take care of. I want to make sure your music studies are covered in case—"

"In case of what? Are you doing something dangerous?"

Stefan looked into her eyes. What was he doing worrying her? "Never mind. I'm just a babbling old fool."

"I don't think thirty-eight qualifies as old, Dad." The corners of her mouth turned upward, lending her freckled face an impish expression. "No comment as to the fool."

He joined in her laughter. While they nibbled on the pastry, Stefan pondered what he could do to safeguard Traude and her studies. Since he was leaving for Italy in the morning, arrangements would have to await his return. He'd just have to be careful not to do anything that might jeopardize her dream.

Chapter Sixteen

The Hunt

Schorfheide, East Germany, Saturday, 23 July 1977

With his Trabant rattling as if it would fall apart at any moment, Lieutenant General Heinrich downshifted and slowed his speed on the bumpy forest road. To allow for the possibility he might get lost, he'd set out half an hour early this morning on the fifty-kilometer drive from Berlin to the *Schorfheide*. One of the largest continuous forests in Germany, featuring pines, oaks and several lakes, Schorfheide took its name from its heathlands. He envied the party bosses' short jaunt of twenty kilometers from Wandlitz, proximity probably one reason socialist party chief Honecker established these woodlands as the state hunting grounds. As a Stasi lieutenant general, Heinrich had no chance of being awarded a villa in the exclusive Wandlitz enclave.

The muddy road stretched on. Just when he thought he'd taken a wrong turn, Heinrich spotted a guard station ahead. He slowed, stopping a meter in front of a barrier arm blocking the road. When a young man in uniform stepped out, Heinrich rolled down the driver's window and inhaled the damp, cool morning air. Not in uniform, he flashed his credentials.

The guard saluted. "Good morning, General. They're expecting you at *Jagdschloss Hubertusstock*. Do you know the way?"

Heinrich slid the ID into the inside pocket of his anorak. He'd only been there once, in the early seventies when the building dating to the mid-nineteenth century had been razed and rebuilt in the style of an old Bavarian hunting lodge. He pointed ahead. "As I recall, I follow the road for a few hundred meters and take the first right."

The guard nodded and raised the barricade. "You'll see a bronze statue of a stag along the lane to the hunting castle."

While easing the Trabi over the ruts in the road to minimize the rattles, Heinrich pictured what a weekend of hunting with the party chief might be like. He'd have to be careful. One wrong word while in the company of the man governing East Germany could doom his career. The higher-up politicos wouldn't normally invite someone of his rank to partake in privileged social activities like their hunt.

Down with the flu, Mielke had called him last night. "You're taking my place on a hunt with Honecker. He requires a full report on what we're doing to limit the damage done by the defector. You're expected at the Schorfheide at eight-thirty in the morning."

Refusing the Stasi chief's order was not an option, so Heinrich found himself passing the bronze of a stag bugling a rutting call. He pulled the car in front of a hunting lodge that looked nothing like a *schloss*. It hadn't been named for any castle-like appearance but for having been built by a king, Friedrich Wilhelm IV.

Before Heinrich could exit the car, a middle-aged man in uniform rushed from the building. "General Heinrich?"

"Yes."

The man pointed toward a row of bungalows erected as part of the renovations in the early seventies. "You're in building four. It's the one at the far end. The general secretary is expecting you at eight-thirty in the lodge." He checked his watch. "In half an hour."

Officious bureaucrat. Heinrich didn't voice his thought. He drove to building four. Finding the front door unlocked, he did a quick tour of the two-story bungalow. In the downstairs sitting room, two armchairs faced a small table, on which sat a black rotary-dial phone. A fireplace took up a good portion of one side. A small television was mounted on the far wall. Wooden stairs led to an upstairs bedroom with a small commode, a nightstand with a radio alarm, and a bed that could sleep two people in a pinch. The tiny bathroom and its shower were not for the claustrophobe. It was probably for places like this that the word rustic had been coined.

Heinrich returned to the car, retrieved his duffel bag and carried it upstairs. Unsure what to wear for a hunting party, this morning he'd put on his anorak with leather gloves in an outside pocket, just in case the day turned cold. Nylon pants and ankle-high hiking boots completed his outfit. He'd locked his pistol in the car's glove box. Mielke had assured him he'd be given a proper hunting rifle. Heinrich hoped he meant a firearm that made hitting a target easier for someone whose marksmanship-skills were a bit rusty. He now regretted having passed up the last annual refresher training at the shooting range. With fifteen minutes to spare, he headed for the main lodge.

The man who'd greeted Heinrich earlier led him to a group of half a dozen men sitting around a table eating breakfast. Heinrich recognized Honecker by his trademark horn-rimmed glasses and gray hair going on white.

Before he could introduce himself, Honecker announced to the others, "Lieutenant General Heinrich is joining us this morning. He's here for General Mielke who's battling the flu." He shook Heinrich's hand, then pointed to the spread of crusty rolls, butter, marmalade, ham, sausages, and sliced bread. "Say hello to the others and grab some breakfast. Hunting's no good on an empty stomach."

Heinrich walked around the table and shook hands. All but one of the men garbed in hunting clothes sported gray hair.

He retained only one name, that of the secretary in charge of the economy, Günter Mittag. Judging from the lifestyle of the party bosses, Mittag did his job well. Of course, citizens standing in long lines to buy necessities might have a different opinion, which the smart ones among them would keep to themselves.

Suppressing these subversive thoughts, Heinrich grabbed a roll, on which he spread butter and strawberry marmalade. He poured himself a cup of coffee and headed for the only empty chair, but stopped when Honecker pointed to a small table in the corner.

"Take your food over there."

Did the politicos not want him at their table while they discussed matters of state? He'd hardly finished the thought, when Honecker joined him at the corner table. "Go ahead and eat while we talk."

As he took a bite from his roll, Heinrich noticed for the first time a burly man in civilian clothes who stood off to the side. His eyes swept the room, glancing in their direction every so often. The general secretary's bodyguard, ever observant, kept his distance.

Heinrich shook off the distraction and focused on the upcoming conversation. Good thing Mielke had warned him the party chief would ask about the defector. Not so good that Mielke had not offered any guidelines on what to say. Heinrich had settled on the strategy of delineating the amount of damage done and the arrest of two informants, but not giving the general secretary any cause to question whether the Stasi spy network in the West had been compromised.

Sure enough, Honecker demanded a full account of who the defector was, what access he had, and whether he'd blown the cover of any Stasi spies operating in the West.

Between bites, Heinrich answered the party chief's questions and gave him the bad news that the West Germans had arrested two Stasi informants.

"But you said this Captain Ruhland didn't have access to information about our spy network in the West."

"That's right, General Secretary. Maybe he overheard something, or maybe—"

"I'm not interested in your speculations, General. You don't know, do you?"

Heinrich held Honecker's stare. "No, I don't."

"So what guarantee is there that he won't betray others?"

He had to concede the point. "There's no guarantee, but I have taken precautions."

"Such as?"

Heinrich swallowed the last of his roll while contemplating how to respond. "Our officer in Cologne seemed vulnerable. So I had him return to Berlin." Heinrich saw no point in enlightening the party chief that he'd recalled the Romeo for the Fuchs mission.

Honecker fiddled with his glasses. "What about our other assets? Can you be sure this traitor hasn't fingered them?"

Time to stick his neck out. "Captain Ruhland defected Monday. He's been debriefed by West German intelligence, probably the Bundesnachrichtendienst in Pullach. Besides our two informants, the West Germans haven't arrested anyone. If the traitor knew of our other assets, he would have given them up by now."

The whole time Heinrich had been speaking, he'd maintained eye contact. Honecker held his gaze, then stroked his chin. "Well, I hope you're right. Have General Mielke keep me informed of any developments."

"Of course."

Honecker checked his watch. "Time to get started. You've not hunted with us before?"

"No."

"You'll love it."

"I don't have your marksmanship, and I didn't bring a rifle."

Honecker stood. "Never mind that. We'll get you one." He strode across the room and shouted, "Let's go hunt, gentlemen."

The men followed Honecker out the door, Heinrich trailing behind.

♫ ♫ ♫

A forest ranger led the group down a wide path. Honecker, shadowed by his bodyguard, marched at the front. Rifle slung over his shoulder, Heinrich walked alongside the two hunters who brought up the rear. Low voices carrying anticipation drifted back. Dodging an occasional puddle left by recent rains, Heinrich breathed in the fresh morning air, smelled the forest and, between conversations, listened to birdcalls.

After a brisk fifteen-minute walk, they marched single-file as the trail narrowed and meandered around a bog. When they reached a dense growth of pines on the other side, the forest ranger raised a hand. Fingers to his lips, Honecker faced the group. He slipped his rifle from his shoulder and the rest of them followed suit. His excitement building, Heinrich gripped his weapon. Firearms at the ready, the hunters crept along the path as it led up a gentle slope, gradually widening. When Heinrich gained the crest, he found the others kneeling, pointing their rifles. The excitement Heinrich had felt vanished in an instant at the sight of a feeding station populated by a large herd of deer and stags. So much for taking part in a sportsmanlike hunt.

Someone jostled his elbow. None other than the general secretary himself motioned for him to kneel and aim. Fighting disgust, Heinrich complied. The crosshairs in his scope showed a magnificent stag. The majestic animal raised its head, sniffed the air, perked its ears, and peered his way. Heinrich's finger on the trigger stiffened. He started to curl his index finger but stopped. Just then the rifle next to him fired. The stag's head jerked back. Blood spurted from the animal's throat. After a stagger that seemed interminable to Heinrich, the stag dropped to the forest floor, twitched, and then lay still.

Heinrich lowered his firearm. Gunfire erupted all around him. In a frenzy of bloodlust, Honecker at his side shot incessantly. The herd galloped away, leaving several stags sprawled on the ground behind. His eyes wild, Honecker rushed over to the dead animals, laying claim to three of seven bodies.

He waved Heinrich over and pointed to the stag with the largest antlers. "You could have had this one."

To keep his feelings from showing, Heinrich lowered his head. "I thought you had him in your aim first, General Secretary."

Honecker tapped him on the shoulder. "Mighty sporting of you."

Several forest rangers appeared on the scene and loaded the dead animals on a wagon they pulled along a wide path, which apparently led back to the lodge. The hunters returned the same way they'd come. Heinrich fell in with the man in his forties striding at the rear of the pack.

"Did you get one?" the hunter asked.

"No, I'm a little out of practice."

The image of a citizen being gunned down while trying to climb over the Wall flashed unbidden into Heinrich's mind. That was different, he told himself. The border guards were following orders, doing their duty to prevent enemies of the state from escaping to the West.

The image faded at his companion's voice. "You'll have better luck tomorrow. There's plenty of game here."

"The hunting doesn't deplete the stock?"

"Not to worry. Honecker has the rangers import stags from Hungary." He lowered his voice. "And they can't escape."

"You mean the Schorfheide is fenced in?"

The man nodded.

Shaking off mounting revulsion, Heinrich changed the subject. "Where are they taking the . . . trophies?" He almost stumbled over the word.

"To the game hall where they'll be measured and photographed, and everything will be recorded. Honecker insists on the ritual."

When they reached the lodge, Heinrich tried to slink away, but the young hunter led him to a large hall. Somehow, the wagon crew had beaten them there. Giddy with joy, Honecker surveyed the stags spread on the concrete floor.

How could he be so proud of shooting fenced-in animals at a feeding station? No real hunter would revel in such a slaughter. As much as Heinrich tried though, he couldn't think of a valid excuse to quit the weekend hunt.

Chapter Seventeen

The Altercation

Viareggio, Italy, Sunday, 24 July 1977

Monika shivered at the sudden late-afternoon breeze that swept sand across the beach and onto her towel. She put down her paperback, its spine broken from continual thumbing back and forth to capture the meaning of unfamiliar words from context. Reading *A Room with a View* in English proved to be more challenging than she'd imagined, especially since she'd left the dictionary in her hotel room.

Tomorrow she might do some sightseeing. The thought brought the insistent Italian tour guide to mind. Fat chance she'd hire him. He seemed to be everywhere—in town, on the promenade, at the Fountain of the Four Seasons, on the beach—no matter where she went, she'd feel his piercing stare. His lurking unnerved her. So today she sunbathed on the public beach farther down the cove, picking a spot hidden in a cluster of chairs, parasols, and canopies. It worked. No sign of him.

Amid the lengthening shadows cast by a low western sun, Monika slipped into her shirt, dropped her book and sunglasses into her bag, and started to roll up her towel when an all-too familiar voice stopped her.

"Buonasera, signorina."

She cringed at the sight of the obnoxious Italian's grin.

"I have marvelous tour for you."

"I'm not interested." She hated how timid her voice sounded.

Rossi took a step toward her. "Ma, signorina."

She pointed a shaking finger at him and yelled, "*Hau ab!*"

Instantly, she realized she'd told him to beat it in German. Still, the shrillness of her voice made him back up.

Then out of nowhere came another voice. "Is this man bothering you?"

She turned. A man about her age stood a few meters away. Dark hair, open brow, friendly eyes set in an angular face, short-sleeve shirt unbuttoned at the top exposing curly chest hair.

Rossi turned around. "Mind your own business, *Kraut.*"

The handsome stranger stepped between her and Rossi. "Did I misunderstand?" he asked her. "Are you having an argument, or are you trying to get rid of this man?"

She couldn't believe his composure, letting such an insult pass. "I want him to leave me alone. He's been stalking me for days."

The German nodded and told Rossi, "You heard the signorina. You'd best leave."

"And you'd best butt out, *Heinie.*"

The stranger frowned. "Ah, I see. We're dealing with the sophisticated, intellectual type here."

Rossi pointed a finger at the German. "Keep your Teutonic arrogance to yourself. I'm the signorina's *cicerone.*"

"That's a lie," Monika exclaimed. "He's the last person I'd have for a tour guide."

Her countryman nodded at her protest. "I can understand that. Hurling insults at Germans is a funny way of trying to get a German customer." He said to Rossi, "If name calling is your forte, shall we have a little contest, *Dago*? Or do you like *wop* better?"

Monika could have sworn Rossi's olive complexion turned pale. He advanced toward the stranger, who put up his fists to ward off the threat. Just when she thought there'd be a fight, Rossi stopped.

"Go to hell, both of you!" He turned and slunk away, parting the gathering throng of curious sunbathers.

The German called after him, "Don't ever bother the lady again." He then turned toward her, "I'm sorry—"

"No, *I* am sorry for your trouble," Monika said. "I don't know how to thank you. He was a real pest."

"I don't think he'll bother you again. But just to be sure, I'd be glad to walk you back to your hotel."

She hesitated.

"Oh, I beg your pardon. Where are my manners? I'm Günter Freund."

"Monika Fuchs."

His handshake was firm but not overly so. She held on a second longer than decorum dictated.

Not giving any indication he'd noticed, he asked, "Where are you from?"

"Bonn. And you?"

"I live in Vienna."

"You don't sound Austrian."

"I'm originally from Berlin." He pointed to her belongings. "If you're ready to leave, it would be my privilege to escort you."

"I'd like that," she said, with more enthusiasm than she intended.

He rolled up her towel and tucked it under his arm. She picked up her bag and took a step down the beach. "My hotel is that way."

As he strode beside her, he asked, "How long have you been here?"

"A week. And you?"

"I just arrived yesterday." After a slight pause, he said, "Do you know a good place for dinner?"

Her heart jumped. "Several, I like to try different restaurants. What are vacations for if not culinary adventures?"

Her sandal slipped in the sand as she tried to step onto the boardwalk. He steadied her with a firm grip on her elbow, only letting go after she gained a foothold on the wooden planks.

On their way toward the promenade, he said, "If you don't mind my asking, are you here by yourself like me?"

"Yes."

"Then, if you don't have plans, I'd like it if you joined me for dinner this evening."

Not wanting to appear too eager to accept, she held her tongue while they crossed the busy beachside boulevard. She waited until they reached Via Bellini to respond. "All right, but dinner is on me."

"But—"

"I'm in your debt, Herr Freund. It's the least I can do."

"Fair enough," he said.

"Where are you staying?"

"Hotel Busoni. It's just a few minutes away."

When they reached Pensione Garibaldi, he handed her the beach towel. "What time should I come for you?"

"I'll need an hour to get ready."

He checked his watch. "Eight?"

She nodded and entered the lobby before she could change her mind about accepting a dinner invitation from a man she just met.

While taking a shower, fixing her hair, and applying makeup, Monika kept telling herself this was not a date, just a friendly dinner with a nice man who'd come to her rescue. Attractive men like him were rarely single, though he probably wouldn't be here by himself if he weren't. Maybe separated or divorced.

She was still speculating when she entered the lobby and found him waiting, dressed in khakis, a long sleeve shirt, and a wool pullover tied casually over his shoulders.

His gaze lingered on her curve-hugging dress for just an instant before finding her eyes. "You look lovely."

"Thank you." She tried to suppress a blush.

They strolled through side streets making small talk about what there was to see and do in Viareggio. When they reached the beachside boulevard, they joined the crowd on the sidewalk engaged in the Italian tradition of *passeggiata*. And the ritual of promenading through town was especially popular on Sunday evenings. Monika plunged right in. Unlike the tourists in their shorts and T-shirts, Günter in his khakis and she in her dress fit in more with the Italians who liked to dress up for the occasion. If not for her blonde hair, she might have passed for a native. The sidewalk restaurants were even more crowded than during the week. After a few hundred meters' walk in the pleasant evening air, she spotted a sign announcing in curved blue letters *A Due Fratelli*. On impulse, she walked across the patio and looked over the menu posted next to the entrance.

"Looks nice," Freund said, glancing over her shoulder. "How's the food?"

She turned toward him. "I've not been here before. I'm game if you are."

He pointed to an empty table bordering the sidewalk. She nodded and claimed it before someone else could.

Within minutes, an attentive waiter brought a glass of Pinot Grigio for her and a glass of Valpolicella for him. Monika welcomed the silence between them while they studied the menu, hoping it would calm the anxiety she felt being out with a man other than her ex-husband for the first time in years. And having drinks and dinner with someone so good-looking only made her more nervous. Clearly, she was out of practice.

After they ordered, salmon for her, pasta for him, she raised her glass. "Thank you again, Herr Freund, for coming to my rescue."

They clinked glasses, but he kept his raised. "Please call me Günter. On vacation in Italy, we can dispense with the German formalities, don't you agree, Monika?"

Though she thought it a bit early for first names, she found herself saying, "Agreed."

They drank and set down their glasses.

"So Monika, what do you do in Bonn?" Her first name rolled off his tongue as if they'd been lifelong friends. It would take more effort on her part to dispense with the formality.

She ran her fingers along the stem of her glass while deciding how much to tell him. "Like just about everyone in the capital, I work for the federal government."

That's as far as she wanted to go, having been instructed numerous times not to volunteer her exact position. Just then the waiter served their entrees.

During the meal, she asked, "What do you do in Vienna?"

"I write press releases and articles for a peace organization."

"Sounds interesting. Which one?"

"Gemeinschaft Unbegrenzt."

"Hmm. I've not heard of it."

"It's fairly new. I just started there this year." He paused as if trying to decide whether to say more.

When he didn't, she asked, "Do you miss Berlin?"

Now it was his turn to play with the stem of his wineglass. "I don't want to bother you with personal details. Let's just say I needed to get away."

"No bother. If it's not too personal, what was so bad in Berlin?"

He took a hefty gulp of his wine. "Nasty divorce."

"Looks like we've got something in common. I just got divorced last week."

"Really?" He looked her in the eye. "You'll probably think me strange, but it strikes me that there may be a reason we met at this juncture in our lives, vacationing in the same beach resort."

She lowered her gaze and pierced a piece of broccoli with her fork, uncomfortable with what he seemed to be insinuating. "Well, Herr . . . Günter." There, she'd said it. "There is such a thing as coincidence. I wouldn't read too much into it." She chewed the broccoli. "Divorced people meet in vacation spots all the time. And we Germans do like Italy. But tell me what you do in Vienna when you're not working."

"Vienna is a wonderful place. It's impossible to get bored there. When I'm not feeding my sweet tooth with the delicious pastries, I try to take in a bit of history and culture. Palaces, concerts—"

"Do you ever go to the Wiener Staatsoper?"

"Every chance I get. Do you like opera, Monika?"

"No, I don't like opera. I love opera."

"So do I."

"*Nicht zu glauben*," she muttered to herself, hardly believing this handsome man shared her passion for opera. Before she could stop herself, she blurted, "Maybe there is something to your notion."

Blood rushed to her face. What was she saying—that their meeting was preordained, not a coincidence? To cover her embarrassment, she quickly said, "You know about the Puccini Festival?"

"In Torre del Lago, just down the coast?"

She nodded. "I was thinking about attending *La Bohème* tomorrow night."

"Can you still get tickets?"

"Oh yes. The Puccini Festival is not as popular as the famous Arena di Verona. I would love to go and see *Aïda* there."

"Why don't you?"

"The only seats left are on the stone steps, and I'm not sure how much you can see and hear from there. The place is huge."

"They don't mike the singers?" he asked.

"No." She played with her paper napkin. "Maybe I'll take a chance and go."

"When is the performance?"

"This Thursday. It's on again later, but I'll be back in Bonn by then."

He stroked his chin, making her wonder what he was contemplating. His next words clued her in. "Have you bought a ticket for *La Bohème* already?"

"No, I was going to get one this evening. They're selling them at the hotel."

"I hope you don't think me forward, but I would love to take you there." Perhaps to forestall an immediate refusal, he went on, "We could visit Puccini's villa first."

Needing time to think over his invitation, she drank some wine. She'd seen *La Bohème* several times, but to watch it in a theater that Puccini frequented, in the town where he composed most of his operas—that was an experience not to be missed. And what better way to enjoy it than in the company of a fellow opera lover? Still, she didn't really know Günter.

She set down her glass, contemplating her response, when he spoke again. "If you'll allow me, I'll treat you to tomorrow's performance."

"You will do no such thing, Günter." Her resolute tone and the way she liked saying his name surprised her. Seeing his quizzical expression, she quickly added, "You can get the tickets, but I will pay for my own."

"Only if you absolutely insist, Monika."

"I do insist, but thanks for your offer." She raised her glass to his. "To a wonderful evening at Torre del Lago."

As they drank, she couldn't help but wonder whether this was the holiday fling her friend had so adamantly advocated. Gisela would die if she knew the handsome prospect was not Italian, but a fellow German. Stop speculating, she admonished herself. You just met this man. He could be a drunk or a bully like your ex. Better to take it slow and be on guard.

Chapter Eighteen

Tickets

Viareggio, Monday, 25 July 1977

Sunshine and fresh morning air laden with the fragrance of a briny sea breeze greeted Stefan when he exited Hotel Busoni. He hurried down Via Catalani, stealing an occasional glance over his shoulder. He cut a sharp corner into a side street, then ducked into a shady alley that reeked of spoiled fish.

The squawking of a seagull reverberated off the walls of century-old houses that crowded a passageway so narrow neighbors could lean from opposite windows and shake hands. Stefan squeezed through a tight spot as claustrophobia, intensified by the harrowing sound, assailed him. Was the bird mocking him, or sending him some kind of message? He dismissed the silly thoughts. Picking up his pace, he nearly tripped over a black cat that jumped from a dark entryway, hissed, and slunk away. The alley spilled into a busy two-lane street. He crossed against traffic and entered the lobby of Hotel Modena.

Sunbeams filtered through glass panels atop the three-story atrium. Dark-paneled wood graced the reception area and a side bar surrounded by small tables, armchairs and chaise lounges. Gold-plated balustrades spoke of opulence. Definitely upscale from Stefan's plain lodgings. Did Heinrich have an inkling of the luxurious accommodations his Milan contact, Amato, had arranged for Rossi? The thought of the hefty bill awaiting the general assuaged Stefan's feelings of envy.

On his way to the reception desk to ask for Alfonso Rossi's room number, Stefan stopped when the Italian called from the bar area, "Signore Freund."

He wove around the lobby furniture toward Rossi, who remained seated in an armchair and indicated a chair next to a small side table, which held a drink.

Rossi must have noticed Stefan's questioning look. He pointed to his drink. "You want?"

"No thanks. It's a bit early for me."

"The signorina fall for our act?"

Stefan sank into his chair. "I think so."

"So you have luck with the lady?"

Stefan ignored the man's intimation. "She's grateful I got rid of you."

"Ready for romance?"

"Not quite. I must ask you to do something else."

"I deliver sexy Fräulein and you want more?"

"I must have two seats, and good ones, for Thursday's opera at the Arena di Verona." When Rossi gave him a quizzical look, Stefan added, "There are no decent tickets available, and I can't have her sit on the stone steps."

"You're difficult, Herr Freund. You want tickets that do not exist."

"But you can arrange it?"

"Maybe."

"How much?"

"*Cinquecentomila.*"

"Are you saying five hundred thousand lire?"

"Si."

Stefan did a quick calculation. "Five hundred West marks—that's a lot for two tickets."

"Not easy, signore. I must ask—"

"Scalpers?"

Rossi hesitated. "Scalpers?"

"Yes, people who buy tickets and then resell them to make a big profit," Stefan said, though he suspected the man understood perfectly well. "And if that fails?"

"Then must make donation to *teatro*."

"But the good seats are gone, remember?"

Rossi grinned. "Gone for public. Not for generous donor."

"And generous means five hundred thousand lire?"

"Si, signore, maybe more."

Stefan wondered what percentage Rossi planned to keep for himself, but did not ask. Instead he focused on how to get the money. He couldn't use his stash, since he was under strict orders to pay cash for everything, including his hotel. He had to get a message to Heinrich through Amato, and the request had to make it clear there was no better way to romance Monika than to fulfill her dream of attending *Aïda* at Verona. Only then would the general authorize such a large sum.

Stefan said, "I don't have that kind of cash. Find tickets and get the money from Signore Amato."

"I try."

The lackadaisical response grated on Stefan. He needed to impress on Rossi how crucial those tickets were. This called for a little exaggeration.

He leaned forward. "I must take the signorina to the opera, or my mission will fail. Make sure Amato understands this."

"I will tell him." Rossi raised his glass. "To your success."

Stefan stood. "There's no time to waste. Get on this right away."

He left the hotel wondering whether Rossi could be relied upon to follow through. Heinrich was sure to throw a fit, but he seemed so obsessed with netting Monika Fuchs that he might just spring for the tickets.

Chapter Nineteen

Systems Solutions

Munich, Monday, 25 July 1977

Sabine parked her yellow Beetle in Horst Kögler's cobblestoned courtyard. She jammed the gearshift into first, killed the engine, let out the clutch, and yanked the emergency brake hard. She removed her scarf, shook her head and ran her fingers through her windblown hair. One look at the blue sky convinced her to leave the convertible top down. If only her mood matched the sunshine.

She'd been stewing during the entire half-hour drive from Pullach, rehashing the argument at the office this morning. Having spent all of Friday and most of the weekend combing through the personnel records Dorfmann had dumped on her, she had to admit to slow progress. Ignoring her protest, he'd insisted she enlist Kögler's help. That's why she found herself outside the computer geek's business on this Monday afternoon. An inauspicious start to the last week in July.

Sabine stepped from the car and slammed the driver's door. Why was she so frustrated? The reason had to be the sheer amount of data and her inability to make any sense of it. Add to that her boss making her share responsibility with a businessman. But she had to admit to being mad at herself for being irrational. After all, what could it hurt to consult a computer expert?

Determined to swallow her wounded pride, she strode across the lot toward a one-story brown-brick structure that jutted out from a two-story gray-mortared building, which she knew from last week's inspection was Kögler's residence. A sign above the front door said "Systems Solutions," in black capital letters, and in small script beneath, *Kreative Lösungen für die Zukunft.*"

She hadn't noticed the German slogan during last Thursday's visit. It was all well and good to claim creative solutions for the future, but she needed to catch Stasi spies now. She pushed on the door. Locked, unlike last week. Good, Kögler seemed to be heeding Dorfmann's security instructions.

Before she could ring the bell, the door opened. A smiling Kögler stood on the threshold and offered the typical southern German greeting, *"Grüß Gott,* Frau Maier. Herr Dorfmann phoned and told me to expect you." His gaze traveled from her face down her blouse and skirt to her empty hands. "Didn't you bring—?"

"The records are in the car."

He followed her to the Volkswagen and after she released the latch, he pulled the front hood up and propped it open on its rod. The two boxes she'd brought had slid all the way to the rear of the luggage compartment. She must have taken out her frustration on the accelerator pedal.

Kögler reached in and pulled the boxes to the front. "That's all you've got?"

It took her a moment to catch on. "Don't worry. There'll be more to keep you busy. These are just the records from the intelligence agencies plus three government ministries. I'm still waiting for the Chancellery records. From the way you talked the other day, you'll have the names of potential Stasi collaborators for me by the end of the afternoon."

He laughed. "You've got a wicked sense of humor. Looks like we'll be spending a good part of this week together." He didn't sound displeased.

She fought conflicting emotions. Maybe this week would be less unpleasant if she relaxed a little and shelved her suspicions.

He picked up a box and took a heavy step back. "I'll come back for the other."

"Nonsense." She steadied herself against the front bumper and heaved the second one from the car.

While they carried their loads toward the building, she asked, "Why is your firm name in English and your slogan in German?"

"You know how we Germans are. English expressions are cool these days. And anything having to do with technology—especially computers—has to sound American. We haven't even bothered to come up with a German word for computer. But just to be sure our native customers have an idea about what we're doing, I added the German slogan. You like it?"

"I'd like it more if it promised creative solutions for the present instead of the future."

He stopped at the front door. "What do you . . . ? Oh, I get it. Not to worry. We'll smoke out the likely spies for you in no time."

They entered a small room with two chairs and a metal desk, behind which sat a woman who'd not been there when Kögler had given them a tour of the facility.

After they set the boxes on the desk, he introduced his receptionist, Erika Braun. "I'll close your car hood and be right back," he said, slipping out the door.

Engaging in small talk had never been one of Sabine's strong suits, so she was glad that Frau Braun started to peck away at the typewriter. Her two-finger method, her fluffed-up platinum-blonde hair, a low-cut blouse revealing ample cleavage, and long, red fingernails made Sabine wonder whether she was more than a receptionist. None of your business, she admonished herself.

Just then Kögler returned. They carried the records down a corridor that led to a long and narrow room lit by fluorescent bulbs hanging from a ceiling of acoustic tiles. A row of tables held half a dozen computers, all unused except for the one at the far end.

Having parked the boxes on the closest table, Kögler led her toward a young man he introduced as his part-time assistant, Martin Klinger. If ever there was a stereotypical computer geek, he was it: unruly red hair, pale complexion, beanpole-figure that bordered on emaciated. He studied her through lenses the thickness of magnifying glasses, and after a limp handshake resumed staring at the computer screen.

She and Kögler went back to the first table. She pointed at the materials and said in a low voice, "You know you're the only one here with permission to work on these."

"Yes, Dorfmann made that clear." Kögler pulled up a chair on rollers for her and took one for himself. "So tell me what you brought me."

"Prosecutor files for three secretaries convicted of spying for the Stasi. Personnel files from the Foreign and Defense Ministries, and the intelligence services—mine, your old outfit, and the Army."

"Surely not *all* the personnel files."

"Of course not."

"Then what?"

For the first time, she detected a hint of impatience. Kögler had shifted from easygoing into business mode.

"Personnel records of all the single or divorced females with security clearance in those agencies."

He stared at the boxes. "Are you telling me there are that many unattached females in the federal government?"

"Single or divorced, but not necessarily unattached."

"Of course," he said. "That's the big question, isn't it? Are they attached to someone we need to keep an eye on?"

"Precisely."

"Have you established any criteria indicating females who might be susceptible to advances by East German agents?"

"Yes, I have."

He touched the keyboard in front of him and the computer sprang to life. A few keystrokes later, a table appeared on the screen. After typing 'single' and divorced' into separate boxes, he said, "All right, give me some key phrases."

"Introverted, not sociable, difficulty making friends—"

"One at a time, please."

When he was caught up, she continued, waiting after each phrase for his nod indicating he was ready for the next one. "Shy, reserved, reclusive, distant, withdrawn, aloof, timid, weak, gullible, easily influenced, trouble standing up for herself, dominant parent."

After he'd entered the last one, she said, "That's all I've come up with so far."

"That's quite a list." He turned toward her. "Something tells me you've been putting a bunch of hours in on this."

"And it's cut into my sleep, you can be sure of that. But I don't see how the computer is going to come up with anything more than we can on our own. Don't you still have to go through all the records looking for any of those traits and put them into the computer?"

"Good question."

His response smacked of platitude, but he'd said it without a hint of condescension. "So what's the answer?" she said.

"I've developed a program that searches for relevant phrases like the ones I just entered. We input the personnel records, and the computer will flag the secretaries who are likely targets."

"I still don't see any advantage to using a computer. Won't it take just as long?"

"Initially, yes. But once we've input the information, it'll be much more efficient." A wistful expression played on his face. "I wish scanners were more advanced so we could scan all of those documents straight into the computer. In a few years maybe."

"So we're just gaining efficiency?"

"No, much more. We're getting accuracy, reliability, and most important, selectivity."

"Selectivity?"

"That's right," he said. "With my program we can select which traits we want the computer to look for. Some of them, all of them, or even just one. The computer will search through the information we put in and generate a report according to the criteria we specify."

Kögler's voice had risen and his speech accelerated. While he didn't look the part of a computer geek, maybe he was one after all.

"So you see, speed is not the crucial factor here," he went on. "Still, if everything goes according to plan, we should have what we need in a few days."

"If everything goes according to plan," she repeated. "Meaning the computer program might not work?"

"I know it works, but nothing's perfect. I might have to fix an occasional hitch." He checked his watch. "I have a commitment at five. That gives us about an hour, unless you want to wait till morning to get started."

"Let's go ahead."

"All right. Where do you want to start?"

"Might as well begin with our sister spy agency in Cologne. It'll give you a taste of all the eligible females you've been missing out on since you left." She couldn't believe she'd said that. "I'm sorry, that was presumptuous of me."

"Don't apologize. I like your sense of humor, and I appreciate the challenge of keeping up with you."

"Are you always this direct?" she asked, trying to cover her embarrassment.

"Too often, probably. Got me in plenty of trouble with the bureaucrats when I was still with the agency, but like you, I prefer to speak my mind."

Lacking a good comeback, she handed him one of the personnel files from the Cologne intelligence agency. He pointed to the computer on the table in front of her. "We can use several machines at the same time. The information is stored on my network and can be accessed on all of my computers."

While she grabbed the next file, he performed a few keystrokes on her computer. "Before you ask, all my machines are password protected, as is my network."

She glanced down the row of tables and asked in a low voice, "What about your assistant?"

"I give him a temporary password for the computer I have him work on, but he can't access the network." After a few more keystrokes, Kögler had a blank document up on her screen. "Let's use a separate document for each file and title them with the person's name."

He rolled his chair over to his machine, and positioned his fingers on the keyboard, but before he even started typing, she asked, "What kind of information are we entering?"

"Everything."

"No matter how trivial?"

"Absolutely. You may think it a waste of time, but I want every last detail in the computer, no matter how unimportant it seems."

She shrugged. "You're the expert."

They worked in silence until he stopped to stretch his back. "I'm curious how you came up with that elaborate list of traits for likely Stasi targets."

"I delved into the backgrounds of all the females convicted, accused or even suspected of spying. And thanks to a defector, we got our hands on a document that reads like it's from a Stasi playbook for enticing secretaries to spy for them."

"But most of the spies caught in the West were Stasi agents or collaborators like journalists, intelligence agents, and business executives. What made you think of government secretaries?"

"I suppose the seed was planted when I studied the case files of several secretaries who'd fallen for Stasi Romeos. To expose the spies before they could do most of their damage and abscond to the East, I had to focus on their likely targets: vulnerable females in sensitive government positions."

"Let the victims lead you to the perpetrators," he said. "Makes sense, but what made you think of that?"

"I know this is going to sound strange, but it came to me while listening to a recording of *Don Giovanni*. You know the opera?"

"Only that Mozart composed it. I've heard of Don Juan, the legendary seducer, of course. But I still don't understand how listening to the opera would have—"

"In the famous "catalogue aria," the Don's servant recounts all of his master's conquests, including no less than one thousand three women in Spain alone. Listening to that gave me the idea to switch my focus from the Stasi Romeos to the women they targeted."

Kögler shook his head. "Over a thousand! Makes you wonder what the Don had going for him." He continued in a more serious vein. "Whether you call it strange or not, I applaud your creative thinking. An intelligence agent has to keep an open mind."

"Well, it was no great insight, but when you focus so hard on one thing you tend to overlook the obvious."

"Don't sell yourself short, Frau Maier. Like any good operative, you were receptive to a new approach." He rubbed his chin. "But opera being the catalyst? That is kind of weird. I take it you're quite a fan?"

"You could say that. What about you, Herr Kögler?"

"No. I've only been to one opera in my life. Something by Wagner. It went on forever, and I fell asleep."

"You were saying at lunch last week how your Italian mother's genes were stronger than your German father's." She gave an exaggerated headshake. "And for your first opera you pick Wagner—not a wise choice for a novice."

"Bad move, I know. I'm afraid I've been damaged for life. Shrill singing, fat sopranos, the whole bit. Credit my mom for my dark hair and complexion, but her genes apparently weren't strong enough to impart her appreciation of opera to me."

"Maybe all is not lost." Sabine wondered whether she should say more, having learned long ago that trying to explain the magic of opera was a waste of her breath and the listener's time. Against her better judgment, she went on, "You're supposed to start with the Italian repertoire. I'll tell you this, Herr Kögler, if you've never seen an opera by Verdi or Puccini, or even Donizetti or Bellini, then you haven't lived."

No sooner had the words left her lips than she regretted them. "I'm sorry, how arrogant of me. Talking opera, I get carried away sometimes."

"Not at all. I love your passion." He grinned. "You, supposedly a full-blooded German—though I wish you'd ask your mom about the milkman—you love Italian opera, and I, with Italian blood running through my veins, I listen to jazz and rock music, and then let Wagner turn me off. How ironic is that?"

After joining in his laughter, she checked her watch. "Let's keep going. It's getting close to five."

They finished inputting the two files with a few minutes to spare. While she returned the folders to their box, he said, "You recall that Dorfmann okayed storing the materials in the safe so you wouldn't have to transport them back and forth."

"I do," she said.

Kögler looked at her. "I'll be glad to put in a few more hours this evening, after I'm through with my appointment."

His offer sounded tempting, but she couldn't let him do it. "My boss said I need to be here when you're working on the files."

"Yes, I know, but it doesn't make much sense, does it? What good is my security clearance if the agency doesn't trust me with personnel records?"

He had a point, but before she could respond, he said, "Don't get me wrong. It's not that I don't enjoy your company."

"I appreciate that, Herr Kögler, but I'll tell you what. Let's lock these up and call it quits for tonight. I'll check with Dorfmann."

"If he's in as much of a hurry as you are, Frau Maier, he'd better okay my working after hours. I know you don't get paid overtime, but if you're willing to put in extra time, I can certainly accommodate you here."

"I'll let you know tomorrow what the boss decides. He might even lend us a typist or two, if it would speed things up."

They locked the materials in Kögler's sizable safe, and he escorted her to the car.

She climbed into the Volkswagen. "What time do you want to start in the morning?"

"As soon as you get here."

She started the engine. "See you around nine."

Sabine put the car in reverse, backed up, and pulled from the courtyard into the street. As much as she hated to admit it, she was rather looking forward to another day at Systems Solutions. It certainly beat paper shuffling at the Pullach office, though she knew that wasn't the only reason.

Chapter Twenty

Money Talks

Foreign Intelligence Service, Stasi Headquarters, East Berlin, Monday 25 July 1977

"Five hundred thousand lire?" Lieutenant General Heinrich screamed into the phone. "Are you out of your mind?"

"*Scusi—*"

"You take me for a *dummkopf,* Signor? I know what opera tickets cost, and it's no five hundred thousand lire."

Heinrich breathed so hard, he barely heard Amato Conti's voice cutting through the static of the lousy connection from a Milan public phone booth. "Good seats are all gone. My man was very lucky to find two tickets close to the stage. He must buy them now."

"Out of the question."

"As you wish, General. I tell Herr Freund—"

"Wait. Where is the opera?"

"Arena di Verona."

Heinrich had a vague recollection. "The amphitheater?"

"Sì."

"No cheaper seats?"

"Maybe on stone steps."

Heinrich pictured hard, uneven steps in a huge Roman amphitheater. Not conducive to impressing Monika Fuchs, to say nothing of romancing her. But what was so damn important about this opera? "What did Herr Freund tell you?"

"He says, to do job he must have tickets—"

"Where is your man getting them?"

"Private seller."

"Scalper," Heinrich mumbled to himself.

"*Non capisco.*"

Heinrich shouted into the static. "When is the performance?"

"Thursday."

Though he expected a good part of the cash to end up in the pockets of Amato and his minion, Heinrich said through clenched teeth, "You'll have your money. Get the tickets."

Amato's profuse *grazie* only strengthened Heinrich's suspicion that the scalper wasn't the only one reaping a healthy profit.

He slammed down the phone and gazed at the posters on the wall. A Honecker younger than the one on the weekend hunt stared back at him. If the state could spend millions on the party boss's exclusive hunting grounds despite a flagging economy that had people lining up for necessities, then by God, he could wager a few hundred marks on netting a West German Chancellery secretary with expensive opera tickets.

Honecker's portrait brought back memories of the disgusting slaughter Heinrich had witnessed over the weekend. Even though he'd had clear shots at several stags, he hadn't bagged one trophy. When asked about his lack of success, he'd cited rustiness as an excuse. The higher-ups surely thought him such a bad shot they'd never invite him back.

Heinrich took off his wire-rimmed glasses, rendering Honecker a fuzzy image. Time to put the hunt behind him and concentrate on what he had to do. He wished he could quiz

Malik about his plan, but the man was soaking up Mediterranean sun thirteen hundred kilometers away. As much as he hated to, he'd have to trust his newest Romeo. For now, he'd do his part and arrange for the money.

He put on his glasses and buzzed his secretary. "Frau Schröder, have five hundred thousand lire wired to Amato Conti right away."

"Yes, General."

He was about to cut the line when she added, "Someone from Radio Intelligence just dropped off a message for you."

"Bring it in."

Seconds later he ripped into a sealed envelope, extracting a typewritten page while his secretary stepped out. He read the cryptic message from the agent who went by Kurt Rabe. "Alert: Romeo Hunter Sabine Maier BND."

Heinrich flung his glasses onto the desk. He rubbed his temples. Great, just what he needed, a West German intelligence agent on the trail of his Romeos. Who in the hell was this Sabine Maier? He intended to find out. Heinrich grabbed his glasses and stormed from the office. As he passed his secretary, he said, "I'll be down in Records. Don't call me unless it's urgent."

Chapter Twenty-One

Puccini

Torre del Lago, Monday, 25 July 1977

Stefan and Monika had barely settled in their tenth-row seats in the theater by Lago Massaciuccoli, when the house lights dimmed. While starving artists in a freezing Parisian garret diverted their landlord yet again from collecting their overdue rent in the opening scenes of *La Bohème*, Stefan's mind drifted.

As far as he knew, he hadn't made any missteps. He'd picked up Monika in his small Fiat rental car after lunch. After a short visit to Villa Borbone, they'd arrived at Villa Puccini, the composer's former-residence-turned-museum, only to discover it was closed on Mondays. Stefan promised Monika he'd bring her back for a guided tour later in the week.

As they strolled along the placid lake, Monika related how this area Puccini had called paradise inspired him to create enduring operatic masterpieces. They found a cozy restaurant for an early dinner. The server persuaded them to try the local specialty—*cacciucco,* a traditional fish stew. Monika declared it her most delicious meal of the week.

"How did you acquire your taste for opera?" she asked him.

"It's my daughter's passion. She hopes to study voice."

He feared Monika would ask where his daughter intended to study, a question he couldn't answer without lying. Mentioning the premier opera school in Weimar would give him away as East German. During the first week of spy training, he'd been admonished repeatedly never to resort to a lie unless absolutely necessary—lying about inconsequential things had undone many a spy—so he steered their chat to Monika's background.

After describing her dominant father, she played with the stem of her wine glass, as if contemplating whether to say more. He gave her an encouraging nod.

"I thought I'd married the most charming, considerate man. Was I ever wrong! But let's not spoil this beautiful day by talking about abusive ex-husbands." She took a healthy swig of Chianti. "Aside from a daughter who aspires to opera stardom, what other excitement is there in your life?"

He'd anticipated the question and rattled off imaginary parties, visits to concerts, museums and operas, in Berlin – West, of course - and then in Vienna. He rationalized those lies were necessary. Then he turned the conversation back to her. She became quite talkative, perhaps releasing the pent-up emotions of a woman recently liberated from an oppressive marriage. Stefan listened attentively, an easy task as her narratives never were boring. She did not talk about her job, and Stefan didn't ask. That had to wait until much later.

A sexy Fräulein, as Rossi had called her, and a good conversationalist as well. Stefan couldn't recall the last time he'd met a woman with both qualities. She expressed how, for the first time in her life, she felt free. Stefan had looked in vain for shyness, social ineptitude, or any of the other traits of likely Romeo targets. Still, despite her vivaciousness, her lonely childhood and domineering men must have left their marks.

The tenor's aria drew Stefan's attention to the stage. Puccini had composed some catchy tunes to close out the first act. Thunderous applause filled the brief pause between acts. Monika's face beamed as she joined in. A strange sensation came over him. He'd joked with Heinrich about assigning him to a good-looking prospect, but now he almost wished Monika weren't so appealing—not only because of her looks, but her wit, intelligence and vitality. He'd feel better faking feelings for a less attractive woman. But his task was to seduce. He'd been sent to do a job, to conduct a cold business transaction. He had to comply, or both he and Traude would suffer the consequences. When Monika looked at him, he averted his eyes, grateful when the curtain rose.

The second act went by in a blur. He couldn't stop his mind from churning. During intermission, he joined the long queue at the concession stand, glad for time alone to regain his composure. With only a few minutes to spare before the chimes would call the audience back to their seats, he rejoined Monika on the plaza, carrying two glasses of Pinot Grigio.

For a while, they sipped in silence while watching the lights surrounding the dark waters of Lago Massaciuccoli.

Then, Monika turned to him. "What do you think of the performance?"

"Very good." As soon as the words left his mouth, he realized how lame they sounded, so he commented on the only piece he remembered, "I especially liked the tenor's aria."

"*Che gelida manina?*"

Though he didn't know the title, he nodded. He could only hope she wasn't testing his almost nonexistent knowledge of opera.

"Yes, the tenor sang it well, but I liked the soprano even better. I never tire of Puccini's glorious music."

Her enthusiasm was infectious. He resisted the impulse to put his arm around her waist.

The chimes sounded, and they finished their drinks. As much as he tried to engross himself in the music and drama of the final two acts, Stefan couldn't shake his misgivings about this assignment. They drove most of the way back in silence. Monika seemed far away, perhaps savoring what must have been a moving experience for her. Not wanting to intrude on her thoughts, he remained quiet.

When they reached the outskirts of Viareggio, she said, "I have a good friend whose mother listened to opera all the time. My friend told me how, as a little girl, she'd ask her mom why she always cried, even though she already knew the sad ending."

He chuckled. "I thought I saw your eyes getting a little moist, Monika."

"I admit it." She poked him in the side. "And you're not fooling me, Günter. You looked like you were fighting tears."

His qualms about the mission must have shown, except that she'd read his serious expression as a reaction to the opera. He could make use of that. "You caught this sentimental old fool."

"I like a man who's not afraid to show emotion. My ex never shed a tear. That should have been a warning. But tell me, how old a fool *are* you?"

"I'm thirty-eight." He looked at her expectantly, but did not give voice to the question hanging between them.

Her response matched what he recalled from her file. "I'm thirty-five."

A woman who didn't lie about her age. She'd just climbed another notch in his estimation. He turned onto Via Bellini and peered down the street for a place to park near her hotel.

"It's late," she said. "You can drop me here." He stopped the car, and she turned toward him. "Thank you for a wonderful evening."

"I had a great time, Monika. May I call you tomorrow?"

"I'd like that."

She reached for the door handle but lingered. An invitation for a kiss? Perhaps, but he couldn't be sure. Too early. Don't rush things. Better to be certain she was ready for romance rather than move prematurely and turn her off. He covered her hand on the seat with his. She smiled at him, then withdrew her hand, and so the moment passed.

"Talk to you tomorrow, Günter." She opened the door. "*Buona notte.*"

"*Buona notte*, Monika."

She stepped from the car and crossed Via Bellini. The image of her slender figure entering Pensione Garibaldi stayed with him long after he put the car in gear and eased his way past the parked vehicles crowding the narrow street. He'd made progress. She seemed enthusiastic about seeing him again. Still, when it came to women, it paid not to be overconfident.

Chapter Twenty-Two

In the Wee Hours of the Morning

Munich, Tuesday, 26 July 1977

Otherwise a sound sleeper, Horst Kögler was like a mother with a newborn when it came to Sara. A tiny nudge of the Great Dane's wet, cold muzzle, and he'd wake from a deep sleep. So when her tongue slobbered across his face, he peered through half-open eyelids at the dog's large head hovering over him. He turned to look at the clock's lighted dial: barely two thirty.

"*Menschenskind*, Sara! Don't tell me you need to go again."

He shut his eyes, but before he could turn over an insistent poke into his ribs made him sit up.

"All right, all right, I get the message." He threw off his cover, swung his feet onto the wood floor, and stepped to the patio door. "Out you go."

He slid the glass door back, but instead of dashing outside, Sara stood at the entrance to the hallway, growling. Horst shut the patio door and grabbed his Walther PPK from the top drawer of the nightstand. Safety released, he opened the bedroom door. As if catapulted from a slingshot, Sara bolted from the room. Barefoot, Horst moved down the hallway by the faint glow of a nightlight. Between steps, he listened into the dark. Nothing.

He'd almost reached the turn into the kitchen when a shadow played on the wall. Pistol in hand, he peered around the corner. No movement in the kitchen. When shadows thrust and parried anew, he spotted the source: the branches of the giant beech tree outside the bay window were swaying in a breeze, a three-quarter moon projecting the image onto the wall.

Sara's deep growls guided him through the dark kitchen toward the entrance hall, where he found her pointing at the door to the shop. Her growl morphed into the type of ferocious Great Dane bark that struck terror into even the bravest of hearts. Horst shushed her and put his ear to the door. Muffled voices, footsteps, a door slamming. He threw back the deadbolt, pulled the door open, pointed the pistol, and flipped the light switch. Sara jumped into the shop. The familiar buzzing of ballasts, then the harsh light from overhead fluorescents flooded the room. He squinted, looking for movement. Nothing. Eyes adjusted to the bright lights, he stepped into the shop. No one there.

Sara's barks drew him to the entrance hall. The computer at the far end was on. No time to check it now. Quick steps carried him through the reception area to Sara, still barking and trying to nudge open the front door. A car engine sprang to life. Tires squealed. Horst tore the door open. A car with no lights sped from the yard. Too dark to read the license plate, even if Sara hadn't obstructed his view. He ran after her into the street. With no streetlights this time of night, all he could see was a black sedan disappearing around the corner. Almost to the end of the block, Sara stopped and trotted back at his command, "*Komm!*"

He peered up and down the block. It occurred to him he shouldn't be seen standing there barefoot, in his pajamas, brandishing a gun he wasn't supposed to have. He ushered Sara inside, ready to survey the damage. First check the safe. Still intact. The intruders either hadn't spotted it or had planned on cracking it open last. Then to the computers. All were in place, turned off as he'd left them, except for the one he'd noticed earlier.

About to sit down and type the command for accessing the network, he stopped. On the off-chance that the intruders were amateurs simply out to steal his computers, they might have left fingerprints. More likely, they were professionals who'd been after information, not equipment. Still, he decided not to touch the keyboard.

He moved to the next computer, turned it on and accessed his network. No sign that it had been compromised. Sara must have detected the intruders early on. He shut down the unit, checked the other computers, and inspected the entire shop. He found the door locks undamaged. Another sign pointing to professionals. Nothing seemed to be missing. He turned off the lights, locked up, and shepherded Sara back to the bedroom. After reengaging the safety, he returned the Walther PPK to the nightstand top drawer.

He'd have to notify Dorfmann of the break-in, but not in the middle of the night and certainly not until after he rechecked his network in the morning to make sure the burglars hadn't managed to gain access. If there had been a security breach, his BND consulting days might be over. He'd hate to lose this project, which was not only lucrative but exciting, providing a welcome break from the routine computer tasks most clients saddled him with. And he'd certainly miss interacting with Sabine.

Since he couldn't accomplish anything until morning, he crawled back into bed. While the adrenalin rush began to subside, he couldn't stop his mind from churning. No doubt the intruders had sought information about his work for the BND. But who had sent them and how had they found out about this project? The questions kept him awake the rest of the night.

♫ ♫ ♫

When she steered her VW into System Solutions' courtyard a few minutes before nine, Sabine stepped on the brake at the sight of two parked cars. Did Kögler have clients this morning? How silly of her to assume he'd be dedicating his time exclusively to her project. He was a businessman who needed to make a profit. She pulled into the remaining parking place and got out. Funny, both cars were white Opel sedans with plain hubcaps and black-wall tires. They looked just like the agency's fleet . . . Before she could finish the thought, two men exited the building.

"*Guten Morgen,* Frau Maier," they said in unison.

"*Guten* . . ." The good-morning greeting stuck in her throat when she recognized the agency's technicians. "What in the devil are you two doing here?"

As they got into one of the cars, the driver said, "Looking for fingerprints and bugs after an early morning break-in." He shut the door and started the engine, but rolled down his window when Sabine stepped up to the car.

She leaned in. "What happened?"

"Ask Herr Kögler."

"Is he all right?"

"Appears to be."

She was wasting time trying to pry details out of these tight-lipped technicians, but asked nevertheless, "Any prints or bugs?"

"No." The driver put the car in reverse, and rolled up his window.

Better find Kögler. She whirled around and saw him standing at the threshold. "You okay?"

He gave her a mischievous grin. "*Unkraut vergeht nicht.*"

"You've not lost your sense of humor, I see." The Germans had a lot of strange sayings, but 'weeds endure' ranked among the most self-effacing.

"Come inside and I'll fill you in."

He ushered her past the receptionist and led her into the shop. When she caught sight of four women at his computers, Sabine stopped so abruptly that he bumped into her.

He put a hand against her back, steadying himself. "Pardon."

"How in the world—"

"I called your boss early this morning to tell him about the break-in. He asked me to finish the project as soon as possible. So I told him we needed several typists to speed up the input." Kögler turned and pointed toward the women. "And voilà."

"That sneak. That's why he was so noncommittal when I asked him for two secretaries."

"You see, I've got leverage with your boss. He gave me four." He turned serious. "But you want to know about the break-in."

"Damn right, I do. You didn't catch anyone, I take it?"

"No. Didn't even get a look. Just the image of the rear end of a black sedan racing from the yard and disappearing around a corner."

"License?"

He shook his head. "Two thirty in the morning. No street lights."

"Anything missing?"

"No."

"What were they after?"

"They turned on the computer over there." He pointed to the machine closest to the hallway. "I checked and they did not access my network. I think we caught them right after they broke in."

"We? I thought you lived by yourself."

The hint of a smile played in his eyes. "Sara woke me right at two thirty. I grabbed my . . ." He cleared his throat. "I mean, when we approached the shop, they ran. It sounded like two of them."

So he had a girlfriend, maybe even a wife. "And who is Sara?"

"I don't know what I'd do without her. Would you like to meet her?"

He was going to introduce her? Well, she'd asked. "Why not?"

He led her through the shop and into the house. Upon entering the kitchen, he said, "She's probably sleeping." Then he yelled, "Sara, *komm!*"

A few seconds later, she thought she heard a pony on the wood hallway floor. She wasn't too far off—the largest dog she'd ever laid eyes on galloped around the corner and ran up to her. She wasn't usually afraid of dogs, but this one made her take a step back.

"She's friendly, Sabine."

He'd called her by her first name. She let it pass for now. While the dog licked her outstretched hand, she admired the smooth fawn coat, the huge head, the soulful eyes. "Great Dane?"

"Yes."

"Beautiful. Look at those giant paws."

"You should feel honored. She normally prefers men." He pointed a hand, palm down. "Sara, down!"

Sara plunked herself onto the floor, rested her head on her front legs with a sigh, and ogled him.

Sabine turned to Kögler. Time to let him know she'd noticed him calling her by her first name. "Now that you've introduced me to your girlfriend, does that mean we're on a first-name basis, Horst?"

He grinned. "Caught. But since we're going to spend a lot of time together, I'd like that, if you're okay with it."

"Well then, Horst. Shall we go see what progress the secretaries are making? But first, tell me what you meant earlier when you said you grabbed something."

"Nothing escapes your notice, Ms. Secret Agent." Having skirted her question, he led the way to the shop.

He obviously wanted to keep secret whatever his slip of the tongue referred to. This was not the time to press him, but she'd worm the answer out of him eventually.

Chapter Twenty-Three

Happy Birthday

Munich, Wednesday, 27 July 1977

Sabine rang System Solutions' doorbell and listened. A minute that felt like an hour passed. She rang again and again, pressing the white button for several seconds each time. Six thirty was a bit early, but what she had to do couldn't wait. Her index finger poised to push the doorbell once more, she dropped her hand at the darkening of the peephole.

The door flew open. Horst Kögler stood on the threshold, hair disheveled, blue pajama legs protruding from a brightly-patterned bathrobe. "What in the—?"

"Good morning, Horst. Sorry to interrupt your sleep, but this is urgent."

He rubbed his eyes and motioned her to step inside. On their way to the shop, he said, "What's so important you had to yank me out of bed?"

"Dorfmann called me at five this morning. We picked up something in the radio chatter from the East he thinks bears investigating." She continued in a light-hearted tone. "You see, you're not the only one who's been pulled out of bed. So don't expect any sympathy from me."

"Fair enough." He shuffled in his slippers toward the residence.

She ran after him and jogged his elbow. "We need to get on this right now. Your program is ready, isn't it?"

He turned and faced her. "Sabine, I don't do anything without my morning caffeine. You start the coffeemaker while I get dressed, then you can tell me over that first cup what's so pressing your boss won't let us have a decent night's rest." He headed for the door. "And yes, the program is ready. Thanks to the typists Dorfmann gave us, everything we know about vulnerable secretaries is in the system."

Following him into the kitchen, she said, "We're still missing the Chancellery records. They're dragging their feet."

He pointed toward the coffeemaker. "It's all set. Just push the button. I'll only be a minute."

Sara galloped in from the hallway. Sabine caught the dog's muzzle in time to deflect her intrusive sniffing.

"Sorry about that," Horst said. "Sara, down!"

With an exasperated sigh, the Great Dane complied.

"Why didn't she bark when I leaned on the doorbell?" Sabine asked.

"She only barks at suspicious noises, not the doorbell. Don't ask me why. I could claim it's how I trained her, but I'd be lying." He disappeared into the hallway.

While the coffee brewed, Sabine stroked Sara's large head and long, floppy ears, eliciting a satisfied grunt.

Horst reappeared in a sweatshirt and jeans, his hair neatly combed and parted. With his rumpled look, he'd been even sexier, a man she could imagine waking up to. The hissing coffeemaker cut off her salacious thoughts.

A minute later, they carried two cups of steaming coffee to the kitchen table and drank.

"So what's the nugget your agent picked out of the radio chatter from the East?" Horst asked.

"Alles Gute zum Geburtstag. Großartige Leistung. Zukunft liegt in Ihren Händen."

Horst set down his cup. "That's it? Birthday wishes, congratulations on doing a great job, and a reminder that the future is in the hands of whomever this was sent to?" His eyes lit up. "It's the birthday message that's got Dorfmann all excited, isn't it?"

"Exactly. Can your program—?"

"Not a problem." He picked up his cup. "Let's go."

She followed him into the shop, leaving Sara behind.

After he'd fired up the closest computer, he turned to her. "When was the message sent?"

"Five minutes past eight last night."

"Hmm." He stroked his stubbled chin. "Early or belated birthday wishes?"

"That's the question," Sabine said. "From what we know, Stasi spies transmit at a certain time of day, and then only for a few minutes. So the wishes could be for yesterday or today." She shrugged. "Impossible to tell."

Horst began to type.

"What are you inputting?" she asked.

"Single and divorced females with birthdays on July 26 or 27."

"But we don't know who the message was intended for. Could be a Stasi agent, a mole in any number of agencies, or a secretary who's spying for the East Germans."

He stopped typing. "Good point, but all I can do here is search what's already in my program."

"Which only covers single and divorced secretaries." She stared at him. "I guess we might as well start with that. If nothing comes of it, I'll have to request that a number of agencies and ministries give me the names of all their employees with birthdays on either of those dates."

"Let's just hope the message was for one I already have in my database." After a few more keystrokes, he pressed the "enter" key.

Sabine stared at the screen. The computer made straining noises that reminded her of the static pervading a bad overseas telephone connection.

She looked at Horst. "Well?"

"Patience. This will take a few minutes. I wish I could afford one of those new supercomputers that do this kind of search in seconds."

To occupy herself, she sipped her coffee. Horst leaned back, seemingly unconcerned about the laboring machine.

"It's not—" The chart appearing on the screen stopped her. She leaned in. "What does it say?"

"It's a list of names," Horst replied. He performed a few keys strokes and the printer in front of her made a whirring noise, but nothing seemed to be happening.

She shot him a questioning look.

"Sorry, but the dot matrix is slow. Maybe I'll spend some of the generous consulting fee the BND is paying me on a laser printer."

She responded to his deadpan remark with one of her own. "Judging by what they pay me, I'd say you better find a used one."

At last, the machine advanced a sheet. She tore it off at the perforation. "Five names. Three with birthdays on the 26th, two on the 27th."

"Which agencies?"

"Two in Defense, one in Foreign Office, one at my outfit, and one where you used to work."

She stood.

"Where are you going?"

"Back to the office."

"Why don't you fax the list to your boss so he can start the investigations right away?"

"I wish I could, but your fax isn't secure. I'll have the employees in Bonn and Cologne checked out while I take a look at the woman in my shop."

When she reached the hallway, she turned back. "I'll be in touch. Be sure to pet Sara for me, and don't you dare go back to bed while I'm working my butt off."

Chapter Twenty-Four

Tuscany

Florence, Wednesday, 27 July 1977

In a manner that struck Monika as fancy for the trattoria she and Günter had chosen for dinner, the waiter presented the bill on a silver tray. Ignoring Günter's protest, she snatched it and after a quick glance deposited it along with a handful of lire notes on the tray still in the waiter's hand. He turned and headed for the cash register.

"But—"

"My way of saying thanks for your showing me so much of Tuscany today," she said. "The hill towns, the museums here in Florence." After a slight hesitation, she added, "You're a wonderful . . ." She almost blurted "man," but settled for "tour guide" instead.

He reached across the table and touched her hand. "Tuscany is beautiful, and being your tour guide made today special for me too."

Her cheeks flushed. Hoping the soft light emanating from the candle on the table obscured her blush, she squeezed his hand, then withdrew hers. "What a nice compliment, Günter."

"I mean it, Monika."

She held his gaze. A handsome man who knew just what to say to a woman. He seemed sincere, but could she trust him? Could she ever trust another man?

When the waiter reappeared with her change, she waved him off.

He mumbled "Grazie" and left.

"What else would you like to do before we head back?" Günter asked.

"If it's not getting too late, let's stroll along the Ponte Vecchio."

After a few minutes, they reached the bridge spanning the Arno. Günter now and then placed a hand on her shoulder to guide her past clusters of tourists gawking through windows at displays of jewelry and leather. She luxuriated in his gentle touch and considered placing her hand over his to prevent its withdrawal. But her rational mind counseled against it.

To distract herself, she said, "I've heard you can get gold jewelry here at less than half what you'd pay back home. And it's 18 karat."

"Are you interested?" he asked.

"No, just window shopping. How about you?"

He shook his head. "Call me conservative, but I think jewelry is for women not men. I can certainly see you in one of those gold necklaces."

"Thanks, but jewelry is not my thing."

As they neared the end of the bridge, a fresh breeze came up from the Arno, causing her to shiver.

Günter took her hand. "If you've seen enough, let's head back."

Leaving the throng of tourists behind on the Ponte Vecchio, they entered a side street. He loosened his grip slightly, but kept her hand in his until they reached the parking garage.

During the hour-long drive, they reminisced about all they'd seen. While each had favorites—she the walled town of San Gimignano; he the Palazzo Pitti in Florence—they agreed on one thing: Tuscany was magical.

At the outskirts of Viareggio, she became wistful. "Tomorrow is Thursday already."

He glanced over. "You leave Saturday?"

She nodded.

"Me too," he said. "What do you say we make the most of the time we have left here?"

She was almost afraid to ask, but did anyway, "What do you have in mind?"

After a moment's hesitation, he said, "Can you be ready around ten in the morning for another outing?"

"Where to?"

"I thought we'd visit the Leaning Tower of Pisa and then explore Lucca—"

"Puccini's birthplace," she exclaimed. "That sounds fabulous."

When he pulled over and brought the Fiat to a stop in front of Pensione Garibaldi, she leaned toward him for a kiss on the cheek, but he turned his face and met her lips with his. She hesitated at first but then responded with a long kiss.

She pulled away. Three more days and the holiday fling would be over. Or could this be more than that? Her spinning thoughts stopped when he caressed her cheek. She rested her head on his chest. After a moment, she drew back and reached for the door handle.

Before she could open the door, he said, "Be sure to bring something warm to wear in the evening." He hesitated, then added, "And some overnight things in case it gets too late for driving back."

Unsure what to make of his comment, she faced him. "What do you have planned for tomorrow evening?"

"I'd rather not say." He gave her a mysterious smile. "I'm sure you'll like it."

"I love surprises, Günter, but I need more of a hint. Are we going somewhere fancy?"

"I'm sorry. I should have thought of that. Nothing formal, but dressier than shorts or jeans. Does that help you?"

"Somewhat. If that's as much as you will say, then I'll make it work. I wouldn't want to spoil your surprise." She gave him a quick kiss on the cheek and opened the door. "Till ten in the morning. Sleep tight." She stepped into the narrow street.

His good night wishes followed her into the hotel, but what lingered were the memory of his kiss and the anticipation of what tomorrow might bring.

Chapter Twenty-Five

Pseudo-Date

Pullach and Munich, Thursday, 28 July 1977

Sabine slammed down the phone. Two days of investigating the birthday girls at the agencies in Bonn and Cologne hadn't yielded anything worth pursuing. One had never married, while the other three were divorced. The single secretary appeared to have a close, possibly intimate, relationship with a woman at her workplace, and no boyfriend. Two divorcees had boyfriends with nothing suspicious in their backgrounds. The other one hadn't been in a relationship since her divorce a few months ago.

Not that Sabine was doing any better with the secretary in her own agency. Katrin Jung, twenty-four as of yesterday, single, three years with the BND, secretary to an assistant manager in Department 5. Unclear how much exposure she had to sensitive information, but even if minimal, the Stasi was known to cultivate prospects for years, expecting them to attain top security clearance eventually. Jung might well be a sleeper the East

Germans were grooming to gain access to government secrets in the future.

The photo in her personnel folder depicting a brunette with a pug nose did not do her justice. She was cuter in person. Even though they worked on different floors, Sabine had passed her in the hall a few times, catching a whiff of the popular 4711 Eau de Cologne, and she'd seen her at Christmas parties. She'd followed her after work yesterday, hoping to get a glimpse of a boyfriend. If Jung had one, she'd surely celebrate her birthday with him. But Jung had driven straight to her Munich apartment and stayed in all evening, at least until ten when Sabine had given up and dragged herself home to a late snack and a glass of wine.

A young, attractive female like her without a boyfriend? Not likely. Maybe he was traveling or they planned to celebrate her birthday on the weekend. Sabine sighed at the thought of spending a second evening camped outside the secretary's apartment and perhaps having to tail her on the weekend. Quit feeling sorry for yourself. That's what you get for wanting to be a spy hunter.

A glance at the wall clock caused her to spring into action. She'd better hurry if she hoped to catch Jung leaving the office. Sabine locked the folder in her desk drawer and headed downstairs. A few minutes after five, Jung drove her lime-green Ford Taunus from the lot, returning the guard's wave. When Sabine rolled up to the exit, he barely nodded in her direction. He seemed to have finally gotten the message that she was not interested in going out with him.

She drove through the open gate and followed the Taunus down the street, but hung back, as the Ford's loud color could be easily spotted from a safe distance. They soon were traveling on B11, heading for Munich. Half an hour later, she found herself driving by the Taunus parked on the street near Jung's apartment building. Sabine circled the block and pulled into an open space by the curb about ten cars away. This time she'd come prepared, having brought a sandwich, mineral water, and a book—though reading while keeping an eye out for Jung could prove challenging.

Sabine had hardly finished her sandwich when Jung hurried from the building. She'd exchanged her business attire of a white buttoned-up blouse and a black skirt for a low-cut red top and blue jeans. Sabine tossed her open book onto the passenger seat and started the engine, but waited for the Ford to make it halfway down the block before she pulled away from the curb. Judging from Jung's attire, she most likely didn't have a mundane trip to the grocery store in mind. Sure enough, the Taunus drove past a supermarket, promising something more exciting in the offing.

Since she didn't know where the secretary was going, Sabine had to take a chance and follow more closely. Jung would remember her, but probably wouldn't recognize her yellow VW convertible. She had to push through one traffic light changing to red, luckily not eliciting any angry horn blasts that might have drawn Jung's attention. After a several-minute drive through mostly residential streets, the Taunus pulled into the lot of *Zum Hopfen,* a beer garden popular with the young Munich crowd.

When Jung disappeared into the restaurant, Sabine drove into the lot and parked at the far end. She entered the building and passed the approaching hostess, telling her she was looking for a friend. Dodging waiters buzzing back and forth between the kitchen and glass doors leading outside, Sabine stepped to one of the many empty tables that afforded a view of the garden. Due to the muted indoor lighting, she'd be hard to spot from the outdoors. She peered out at the lively crowd of beer-guzzling patrons. Finally, she spotted the red top. Jung appeared to be talking to someone sitting across from her, but her body shielded the person from Sabine's view. Sabine moved to the side to gain a better vantage point. The companion was definitely male.

Sabine retreated toward the front of the dining room. An acquaintance, a relative, or a boyfriend? How could she find out? Approaching them was out of the question, unless . . . yes, it was worth a shot. She headed for the restroom. Predictably, she found two public telephones in the hall, one of which was free. Dropping a coin into the slot, she dialed the number from memory.

Three rings, four. He was probably out. On the fifth ring, he answered, "Kögler."

She hesitated, not quite knowing what to say.

"Hello, anyone there?"

Sensing he was about to hang up, she said, "Horst, it's Sabine."

"Don't tell me you're still at the office."

"No, I've got a favor to ask you."

"What's that background noise? Are you at a bar?"

"Not exactly. I'm about ten minutes from you at the beer garden Zum Hopfen."

A pause, then a deep inhale. "You're inviting me to have a beer with you?"

"Well, yes. I need you as cover. I've followed the BND secretary here. She's with someone and I need to find out who he is."

"Ah, and I thought this was personal."

Blood rushed to her head. "Look, Horst, I'm sorry if I've—"

His laugh stopped her. "I'm messing with you, Sabine. Don't go away. I'll be there in ten."

The line went dead. She hung up, went to the bathroom, then out to her car. True to his word, he arrived in ten minutes' time. She waved his blue BMW next to her VW. He climbed out, clad in blue jeans and a plaid open-collared sports shirt.

She explained her plan. He listened, then nodded. "I understand, but we're going to look funny for a couple supposedly on a date—I'm in jeans and you're still in your office garb."

She took him by the hand. "All the more reason to pretend we really like each other."

"That shouldn't be too difficult," he remarked as she led him inside.

"We're joining friends outside," she told the hostess.

As soon as they set foot in the garden, she searched for the red top. Good, it hadn't moved. Still holding Horst's hand,

Sabine guided him past several tables until they reached Jung, but she was alone. Dumbfounded, Sabine stopped.

Just then Jung turned around. "Frau Maier. What a surprise."

"*Guten Abend,* Frau Jung. This is my friend Horst Kögler." She turned to Horst. "Katrin Jung."

Horst asked, "May we join you or are you with someone?"

Good probe, Sabine thought.

"My boyfriend will be right back. And yes, please join us." She pointed toward the building. "There he is now."

Sabine turned and barely stifled a gasp. Jung's boyfriend was none other than the young guard. What an awkward evening this would be. And she could cross Jung off the list of those being wooed by suspicious males. Oh well, a beer or two should get her through the evening.

Chapter Twenty-Six

Aïda

Verona, Thursday, 28 July 1977

Monika stretched her tired limbs as far as the Fiat's small passenger compartment would permit. She stifled a yawn.

Günter shifted into fourth gear as they left the walled city of Lucca behind. He glanced over. "Tired?"

"Worn out from walking in the hot sun all day. I feel like we explored every nook and cranny of Pisa and Lucca. The pasta dinner and Chianti did the rest."

"Lean back and relax. We've got a two-and-a-half hour drive ahead of us."

"And where are we going?"

"Nice try, Monika. It's a surprise, remember?"

"I thought you would tell me by now."

"No such luck." He kept his eyes on the road.

"All right, Mr. Secretive." She fumbled for the passenger seatback release. "Can you stay awake while I'm napping?"

"No problem."

She pulled the lever and reclined. Her thoughts drifted from the day's explorations to what possible adventure was awaiting her this evening. Whenever doubts cropped up about trusting a man she'd only known for five days, she pushed them aside. Maybe she was a fool, but she thought him honorable. She closed her eyes to the golden light of the late afternoon sun and the rhythmic singsong of the radial tires.

♫ ♫ ♫

The Fiat's engine, whining from a sudden downshift, snapped her awake. She pulled up her seatback and rubbed her eyes. A glance out the window showed her a sign displaying *Centro*. They were stuck in traffic. Pedestrians crowded sidewalks on both sides of a *strada* lined with shops, restaurants and hotels.

"Where are we?"

Günter swung the car around a delivery van jutting into the road and accelerated to catch up to a limousine ahead. "You'll see. We should be there any moment."

"Surely you can tell me what town this . . ." She spotted the sign, *Arena*, on a covered parking lot. "Arena as in Arena di Verona?"

"So it is," he said as he steered toward the entrance.

So flabbergasted was she that she hardly noticed him dealing with the parking attendant and entering the garage. He pulled into a spot, killed the engine, and faced her. "If we hurry, we'll have time for a stroll and a cappuccino, maybe."

"You have tickets to *Aïda?*"

He nodded.

"But it's sold out, except for . . . how silly of me to let sitting on stone steps dissuade me from experiencing Verdi's masterpiece in this spectacular setting."

Once again he gave her a mysterious smile, but said nothing.

"Oh Günter! You know how much this means to me." She kissed him on the cheek.

He drew her to him, but before he could steal a real kiss, the shift knob poked into her side, and she pulled away. He patted her arm. "Come on."

He looked suave in his blue sports shirt, tan slacks, and navy sweater tied around his waist. Glad she'd opted for a blouse and skirt, she draped the charcoal shawl she'd brought for a cool evening over her shoulders. They exited the garage and headed toward the picturesque *Piazza Brà* adjoining the arena. He took her arm, and she snuggled against him.

She had no idea how long they'd been strolling along the square when Günter gently led her toward the arena. "I'm afraid the cappuccinos will have to wait until after the performance."

Though bereft of most of its outer wall and its decorative marble façade, the arena was far from a ruin, but an impressive Roman amphitheater that according to Monika's guidebook was built in 30 AD as a stadium for games.

Unable to contain her enthusiasm, she told Günter that the first operas were performed there in 1913. When he didn't respond, she asked, "Do you know which opera and why they picked that year?"

"No."

Surprised that an opera aficionado like him wouldn't know, she said, "*Aïda*, and 1913 in celebration of the centennial of the birth of Giuseppe Verdi."

"Then it's extra special to see the same opera this evening."

She was about to follow a stream of patrons headed for the gates to the upper sections when he nudged her elbow and pointed to a nearby tree. "Please wait for me over there. Be right back." He disappeared in the crowd.

She soaked in the atmosphere, the plaza bathed in the rays of the setting sun, the lively throng of patrons, some decked out in formal attire, others in jeans and shorts, but worries overshadowed her enjoyment of people-watching. Did he have tickets on order, or was he banking on cheap seats still being available? Then the thought hit her he might be paying an exorbitant amount to a scalper. She had to dissuade him, or she'd feel forever guilty.

Before she could take a step, he reappeared holding up two tickets and led her onto a red carpet at a gate decorated with fancy red curtains. He couldn't possibly have reserved seats on the expensive floor section. But sure enough, an usher in a blue blazer studied the tickets in Günter's hand and said, "*Poltronissimi.*"

Not only reserved seats, but the most expensive ones in the center close to the stage. He must have paid a scalper. Befuddled, she let Günter guide her into the giant stadium and to fourth-row seats.

She regained her composure and the words tumbled out of her. "How in the world did you manage to get these seats? They were sold out weeks ago. These tickets must have cost a fortune. I can't let you pay."

He laid a hand on her forearm. "Let me explain, Monika. When I called my boss a few days ago I let it slip how disappointed I was that I couldn't take a beautiful German lady I'd met to this evening's performance. I just about dropped the phone when he told me there'd be two tickets waiting for me at the box office. He said they'd been donated to our peace organization."

"They are free?"

"Exactly. So you see, you're not obligated—"

"I didn't mean it that way." She covered his hand on her forearm with hers. "But still I'd feel guilty if you'd paid the exorbitant price these tickets must sell for."

He squeezed her hand. "So let's enjoy this grand opera guilt-free."

She looked around. "In the early years, patrons brought candles to the operas, because there was no electricity here. And there is talk of reinstituting the tradition of having viewers on the stone steps light candles."

He followed her gaze. "I can imagine the romantic ambience of candlelight."

As darkness engulfed the arena, the performance began. On stage only a few minutes, Radames sang the famous "Celeste Aïda." The arena's superb acoustics carried the hauntingly beautiful melody. Because Verdi had inserted the aria so early in the score, it presented a formidable challenge even for accomplished tenors. This evening's rendition earned sustained applause but no calls for a repeat.

Monika became so engrossed in the glorious melodies, the drama, the spectacle of live animals parading across the stage during the second-act triumphal march, she almost forgot the man at her side until they were mingling with the crowd during intermission.

Günter asked if she wanted a glass of wine, but one look at the long line dissuaded her. "Let's just stroll." She took his arm. "So what did you like the best so far?"

"The victory march. Spectacular."

She nodded. "That's probably everyone's favorite part, but mine is yet to come."

"Which one?"

"The tomb scene in Act IV."

"Oh yes."

Surprised by the lack of enthusiasm in his voice, she studied his expression. He'd sounded as if he weren't familiar with the scene—impossible if he loved opera as he'd claimed. She was about to quiz him, but thought better of it, chiding herself for being so suspicious. They turned back toward the theater at the sound of chimes calling them to their seats.

As the fourth act began, she eagerly anticipated the final scene. She'd worn out her recording with Zinka Milanov and Jussi Björling by listening over and over to the lovers bidding farewell to the world. She admonished herself to banish those voices from her memory, lest she be disappointed this evening. No matter how good these artists sounded, and they had beautiful voices, to her, Milanov and Björling would forever remain unequaled as Aïda and Radames.

From the corner of her eye she caught Günter looking up at the sky. Clouds had gathered over the arena. If it rained, the performance would stop, and there'd be no refund. Determined not to let worry distract her from enjoying the opera, she returned her attention to the stage.

Midway through the final act Monika felt a raindrop on her arm, then another. She shook her head. No, it can't rain.

Günter gave her a reassuring look. A few more drops, then the sprinkle stopped. But no sooner had Radames sung the first few notes of the tomb scene than lightening flashed across the stage followed by a crash of thunder that reverberated throughout the arena. The heavens opened up and what she had feared most, occurred: the musicians quit playing and scrambled to carry their instruments to safety from the downpour; the singers fled the stage, and the audience rushed toward the exits.

Günter took her by the hand. "Let's get out of here."

In a trance she stood, waiting for the patrons to vacate their row. By the time they reached the square, they were both drenched. Her blonde hair hung limp, pasted against her cheeks, and her wet clothes clung to her skin—all outward signs of the misery she felt inside.

She shivered in the cool night air. Günter led her into a small bar they'd discovered during their earlier stroll. As they made their way past occupied tables to a couple of stools at the bar, she drew stares. Her wet teal blouse hugged her braless breasts. She covered herself with her damp shawl, causing her to shiver even more. Günter must have noticed. He unknotted the sweater still around his waist and offered it to her. Rolled up, it had remained relatively dry.

She slipped it on over her blouse, grateful for his consideration, yet feeling a tiny tinge of regret that he hadn't so much as glanced at her revealing condition. He's a gentleman who doesn't stare, she told herself. The steaming cups of cappuccino the bartender set in front of them cut short her speculations. The hot brew warmed her insides, and she quit shivering.

Günter set down his cup. "I'm sorry you had to miss the ending."

The foam gracing his upper lip tore her from feeling sorry for herself. She chuckled.

"What's so funny?"

"You look cute in your milk mustache." She wiped the foam off with a finger, tracing his upper lip for longer than was necessary. "Like a baby."

Before she could withdraw her finger, he took hold of her wrist and pressed her fingers against his lips. "I hope you enjoyed your surprise, even if it was cut short."

She sought his eyes. "Ending or not, it's the best present I have ever received." She longed to kiss him, but not in a bar. "Thank you for your thoughtfulness."

They finished their cappuccinos. "Another?" he asked.

"I'm okay, but if you need the caffeine to stay awake during the drive back, I'll join you in a second one."

He studied his empty cup for a moment, then faced her. "We got out a little earlier than planned, but it's still almost midnight." After a slight hesitation, he continued, "What would you think of spending the night in Verona? As if afraid of her answer, he quickly added, "We could do a little sightseeing tomorrow and then drive leisurely back."

She held his gaze. The desire she saw in his eyes dispelled her earlier doubts when he didn't seem to have noticed how much her damp blouse had revealed. To gain time to think, she said, "I bet the hotels are full with the opera crowd and tourists on the trail of Romeo and Juliet."

He seemed to flinch at her mention of the famous star-crossed lovers. She couldn't fathom why. Maybe she'd imagined it. But there was no misreading the impish expression on his face.

"I thought it might get really late so I made a reservation in a small hotel. That's why I asked you to bring some overnight stuff, just in case. And I saw that you did."

Monika looked away. He'd given her fair notice last night. Not only had she not objected, but signaled her willingness to spend the night. No point kidding him or herself.

Before she thought of what to say, he spoke again. "We have adjoining rooms with a connecting door, if that makes you feel more comfortable."

She fished several lire notes from her tiny purse, laid them on the bar, and led Günter outside. The rain had stopped. They walked hand in hand. When they passed an alcove, she pulled him into the dark space, and kissed him. He pressed his body into hers and caressed her face.

She felt him stiffen against her and drew back. "Now where is that little hotel of yours?"

Chapter Twenty-Seven

A Wider Net

Pullach, Friday, 29 July 1977

As soon as she made it into work, Sabine headed straight to Dorfmann's office. He often arrived ahead of her in the mornings, but he lived only ten minutes away while she had a half-hour commute from Munich. His door stood open. She stopped when she caught a glimpse of him on the telephone. Not wanting to intrude, she hesitated.

"Frau Maier. Come on in."

With one hand covering the telephone, he pointed to a chair. Feigning disinterest in his phone conversation, she took in the familiar surroundings. Portraits of the chancellor and the president of the Federal Republic hung on the muted ochre walls behind Dorfmann. A painting depicting the Zugspitze in the German Alps adorned the sidewall opposite the windows. The obligatory wall clock ticked away behind her. Faint traffic noise drifted in through the open windows.

"I'll expect the records early next week then. *Auf Wiederhören.*"

Dorfmann slammed down the phone, and Sabine turned her attention to her boss. He jerked his red polka-dot tie off to the side and undid the top button of his white shirt.

He let out a sigh. "These Bonn bureaucrats. This is the third time I've called to ask for the personnel records you requested."

"The Chancellery?"

"Yes. The way they treat us, you'd think we're working for a different government. Looks like I finally convinced them to send everything you asked for." He studied her. "Well, don't fall all over yourself for joy. What's the matter? You don't believe they'll actually—?"

"It's not that. I appreciate your getting those records for me." She hesitated. How to formulate what she needed to say without annoying him further. "It's just—"

"What? Come on. Spit it out."

"I . . ." Not wanting to shoulder all the blame, she quickly continued, "Horst . . . Kögler and I have hit a dead end."

If he'd noticed her using Kögler's first name, Dorfmann didn't let on. "Well, don't give up before you input these Chancellery records."

"Oh, I'm not, but I suspect they won't give us what we're after."

Dorfmann leaned across his desk. "And what leads you to that conclusion, or shall we say assumption?"

Sabine swallowed hard. She hadn't seen him so annoyed in some time. That Chancellery bureaucrat must have really grated on him. But it was too late to back off now. "Remember how excited you were when we intercepted those birthday greetings?"

"Yes."

"Kögler and I agree that you're onto something there." She congratulated herself on phrasing the words so they complimented him.

"Frau Maier, just tell me what it is you want."

He'd seen through her. She took a deep breath. "We need from the Chancellery, the Foreign Office, Interior and Defense Ministries, and the intelligence services the personnel records of all employees with top-security clearance, plus those with birthdays on July 26 and 27."

He stared at her. "You're not serious."

She didn't flinch. "I am."

"Care to enlighten me on why, for heaven's sake, you need this massive amount of data?"

"I know it's a lot to ask, but as I said, we have to follow up on the intercepted birthday wishes. They're the first and only lead we have."

"But if I heard you right, you're not limiting the records to those who got a year older this week."

"Everyone with top-security clearance needs to be checked out." When Dorfmann raised his eyebrows, she quickly added, "Only assistants and support staff, not ministers and agency heads, of course."

"Is this your idea or Kögler's?"

She didn't hesitate. "Well, it's my call, but Kögler agrees with me one hundred percent."

"And what do you hope to gain by going through all these records?"

"We need to cast a wider net. What we've done so far obviously hasn't proved adequate. There is an employee somewhere with access to classified materials who has a reason to betray us. And if that person happens to have celebrated a birthday this week, that would cinch it."

Dorfmann cupped his chin and stared at her. "You realize what a long shot this is?"

"Maybe it is." His skeptical expression caused her to speak louder and faster. "But no matter how long the odds or how enormous the task, we simply must pursue this. We can't afford to do nothing, boss."

Dorfmann leaned back and studied the ceiling for a long while. Finally, he returned his attention to her. "Do you have any idea what's involved here? And I'm not just talking sheer volume, but recalcitrant bureaucrats protecting their turf, and red tape from here to Timbuktu."

She didn't know what to say that wouldn't annoy him further, so she held her tongue.

"You and Kögler are out of your blooming minds. And just so you know, Kögler is a free spirit. It got him into trouble with the higher-ups at his former outfit in Cologne. Not that anyone would ever accuse them of having a sense of humor."

"What do you mean?"

"That's all I can say. Just be careful."

She wished he'd fill her in, but she knew that prodding would get her nowhere, so she focused on what she'd come for.

Perhaps a little lightheartedness would work. "You may well be right to be skeptical about the value of these extra records. But if you really want me to trade in my VW for that Mercedes . . ."

He laughed. "You're good, Frau Maier." He threw up his hands. "Maybe I'm the one who's nuts. I'll see what I can do. Now get out of here before I come to my senses."

Trying her best to hide her grin, she hurried from his office.

Chapter Twenty-Eight

Meet Me in Vienna

Verona, Friday, 29 July 1977

By the time Günter and Monika returned to their Fiat in the Arena parking garage most of the cars had cleared out. Günter pulled a map from the side pocket of the driver's door and studied it by the dim garage light.

"Is it far to the hotel?" Monika asked.

He folded the map and stuck it back in its cubbyhole. "No, we should be able to find a parking space downtown and walk there. Too bad we can't leave the car here overnight."

He started the engine, backed out, and pulled up to the guard station. He paid and passed below the raised bar. After negotiating his way through city-center traffic, light at this late hour, he drove down a side street lined with cars parked bumper to bumper, leaving barely enough space for a pedestrian to squeeze through. No place on the next street either, or the three or four after that.

"I haven't seen a sign for public parking, have you?" he asked her with an even voice.

She wondered how he could sound so calm. He didn't seem as eager as she was. She wanted to get to the hotel now. Didn't he have the same desire?

An engine roared, interrupting her thoughts. Headlights down the street sprang to life; a midsize sedan pulled out into the road and accelerated past them. Günter drove to the spot, made a U-turn, and maneuvered the Fiat into the empty space. "We're in luck. The hotel is just one street over." He turned off the motor.

She grabbed her small overnight bag from the rear seat and waited for him on the sidewalk. The straps of his bag slipped off his shoulder while he fumbled with the key. Were the streetlights too dim, or was he as nervous as she was? After he finally succeeded in locking the car, he extended a hand. She wiped her clammy palm on her skirt before interlacing her fingers with his. He led her down the sidewalk, his grip firm.

Within a few minutes, they stood in front of a three-story building. An illuminated copper sign on the wall next to a tall door read *Albergo Tulipano*. Monika reached for the door handle.

"They told me the door is locked at midnight," Günter said.

He pushed a white button on the wall. The faint sound of the doorbell sifted into the street, then died away. Maybe the hotel was shut down until the morning. While they waited in silence, she began to have qualms. Günter fidgeted from one leg to the other. He reached for the bell, but before he could ring, the door creaked open. A middle-aged man with dark, disheveled hair, clad in a robe tied haphazardly over striped pajamas, studied her, then Günter. "Signor Freund?"

"Si."

Without introducing himself, the night clerk opened the door wide and beckoned them inside. "*Entrate, prego.*"

Monika stood off to the side in the small lobby while Günter filled out a registration form at the reception desk. With no elevator in sight, they walked up a broad staircase to the second floor.

They entered Room 247 and dropped their bags onto the carpeted floor. She stepped past the double bed and checked out the adjacent room, which was so small the single bed did not leave much space to maneuver around. It had its own little bathroom with a shower. Günter came up behind her, encircling her waist with his arms. She leaned back into him. Feeling him stiffen again, she slowly turned, pressed her body into his, and kissed him hard.

With steady fingers, he unbuttoned her damp blouse and caressed her cold nipples. She clutched at his shirt buttons, her fingers trembling. With his help, his shirt soon tumbled to the carpet on top of her blouse. He took her hand and led her to the double bed. Her skirt joined his slacks at the foot of the bed. Eager now, she stripped off her panties while he did the same with his boxers.

His smooth skin against hers, his knowing hand, the long kisses, his exploring tongue—she lost control and wanted more. "Please, now."

He gave her a questioning look.

"It's all right."

He understood. She shuddered as he entered her, riding the waves of deep pleasure from his thrusts, gentle at first, then growing more intense. When she sensed he was near climax, she contracted her pelvis muscles, causing him to withdraw slightly. Her teasing only increased his desire, as she'd intended. She toyed with him until she could hold him off no longer. With a feral grunt he clutched her buttocks to him and they joined in rhythmic thrusts, ever deeper and faster. Climaxing seconds after him, she heard herself scream as her release came in wave after ecstatic wave.

♫ ♫ ♫

They lay side by side, hips touching. Günter ran his fingertips lightly over Monika's pale skin. Her shiver of delight told him he'd succeeded in accentuating her afterglow. As she played with the curly hair on his chest, he stared at the ceiling. Monika had surprised him. Not so much her passion, which must have been stored for months, or even years, during a loveless marriage, but her expert lovemaking, how she'd teased him, toyed with him, increasing his desire to a level he'd rarely known. The sensation in release had been overwhelming. Moreover, she'd immediately understood his questioning glance about birth control. She definitely did not fit the Stasi playbook profile of the lonely, withdrawn secretary, desperate to land a lover who could become a husband.

Get yourself together. You can't afford to get attached. He reminded himself that his freedom and Traude's future hinged on the successful performance of this mission.

Monika must have noticed his disquiet. "Something wrong?"

He stroked her side. "No, I'm just marveling how special this was."

He propped himself up on an elbow to gaze at her body. She shivered again, this time probably more from lying naked on top of the bedspread. He rolled to one side and lifted the covers, first for her, then for himself, as he felt sleep coming on.

♫ ♫ ♫

The morning sun played on his eyelids and he felt a weight on his chest. Günter opened his eyes. Monika's arm was draped across him. When he turned toward her, she greeted him with smiling eyes.

"Good morning. Do you always conk out so fast right after making love?" she teased.

"Only after a tsunami-like climax."

She punched his side.

"Ouch. How about some breakfast before we explore Verona?"

"Breakfast can wait." She caressed his chest, her fingers dancing down his torso ever so slowly.

Aroused by her kiss and exploring hand, he gave himself over to her ministrations.

♫ ♫ ♫

While devouring his continental breakfast in the small dining area, Günter cast an occasional glance at the yellow tulips arranged in a vase on the table, from which Albergo Tulipano apparently derived its name. Monika's wistful expression made him ask, "What's the matter?"

"Just thinking about this being our last day."

He took her hand. "It doesn't have to be, Monika. I know we're leaving Italy tomorrow, but I hope this is more than a holiday fling. I really want to see you again. Do you feel the same way?"

"Oh, I do. But you're in Vienna and I'm in Bonn. I'm not sure about a long-distance relationship."

"We will make it work." He squeezed her hand. "I want you to come to Vienna, soon. How about next weekend?"

She held his gaze. "You're serious."

"I am."

She withdrew her hand, hesitating. "Well, I'll have to be sure I'm clear at the office."

Not good enough. Get her to commit. "Give me your number so I can call you this week."

"I'd like that," she said.

"Good. Now let's enjoy our day in Verona. And, Monika, I can't wait to show you Vienna. I know you'll love it."

"But the Vienna State Opera is on summer break," she said, the corners of her mouth turning upward.

"What do you want to bet we'll find ways to occupy ourselves?"

She smiled and stood. He congratulated himself on his progress and then followed her out of the breakfast room. He already looked forward to spending the weekend with Monika in Vienna, to lay the groundwork for completing his assignment. He dimly suspected there was more to it than that though.

Chapter Twenty-Nine

Roter Morgen

Oberursel, Taunus Mountain Range, West Germany, Saturday, 30 July 1977

Shortly after five in the afternoon, the intercom in the Ponto villa buzzed and the bank president's private secretary announced Susanne Albrecht and two companions. Jürgen Ponto hesitated. When Susanne's parents had called, they'd not mentioned she'd bring company. She would have to come today of all days—only a few hours before he and his wife planned to board a plane to Rio de Janeiro, a much-needed respite for him from the rigors of running Dresdner Bank.

But no matter how inconvenient, he'd never decline to receive the daughter of the close friend he'd known since grammar school. He thought of the unbreakable bond between their families. He was godfather to Susanne's younger sister Julia, and his own daughter Corinna was the godchild of his friend. Though they were not related, Susanne had always called him *Onkel Jürgen.*

Ponto spoke into the intercom. "Susanne? Yes, let them in."

His wife came into the living room, leaving the door ajar. "I don't like this, Jürgen. She's bringing strangers into our home. I can't imagine what she wants."

"I grant you, it's a little strange." Ponto got up from the sofa. "Probably nothing more than three friends on their way to a movie or a party."

"I hope you're right. Keep it short. You still need to finish packing."

Ponto nodded, but said nothing. No need to worry Ignes by signaling he shared her misgivings.

After a few moments, Susanne stepped through the doorway, followed by a young woman with brown hair falling to her shoulders. Her round face projected a friendly disposition—a sharp contrast to the angular features of the lanky man who took a hesitant step onto the carpet. His unruly dark hair refused to submit to a neat center part. With a smile on her freckled face that seemed forced, Susanne handed Ignes a bouquet of long-stemmed, slightly wilted roses. She then introduced her friends, Brigitte Mohnhaupt and Christian Klar.

The young man's clammy handshake and his piercing eyes that darted around the room as if guarding against some unknown danger gave Jürgen an uneasy feeling. While Ignes left the room in search of a vase, Klar began to fidget, shifting from one leg to the other, and he wouldn't meet Jürgen's gaze. Why was he so nervous?

At that moment, Klar drew a pistol fitted with a silencer from his leather jacket. "Red Army Faction, Commando Red Morning, Herr Ponto. You're coming with us, *now!*"

Mohnhaupt, too, pointed a shaky gun at him.

Ponto stepped toward them. "You must be crazy."

Their bullets slammed into him. Pain, blood, a crash to the ground, a deafening roar in his ears, then darkness.

Chapter Thirty

Red Army Faction

Munich, Saturday Evening, 30 July 1977

Stunned, Sabine turned off the radio. Unbelievable—
Jürgen Ponto shot dead in his villa by the Red Army Faction.

She carried her dinner dishes to the kitchen, dropped
them into the sink full of soapy water, and began to scrub them.
The sharp sound of a plate clanging against a bowl startled her.
No telling how long she'd been working her frustration and anger
out on these dishes. Lucky she hadn't cut herself on the knife
submerged in the water. The rinsing and drying could wait until
she was in a better frame of mind.

She returned to her seat at the dining room table, filled
her wineglass to the brim, took a hefty swallow, then another.
The *Spätburgunder* seemed to have lost its flavor. She set down the
glass. You'd think the federal police would have offered
protection to Jürgen Ponto, one of the most prominent public
figures in all of West Germany, who not only was president of
one of Germany's largest banks, but economic advisor to

Chancellor Helmut Schmidt as well. An obvious target for the Red Army Faction terrorists.

Sabine knew he was a huge supporter of the arts. With Herbert von Karajan, Ponto established a foundation at the Dresdner Bank for the support of musical talent. Perhaps he was motivated by his daughter who was studying to become an opera singer. Sabine started to question whether her single-minded focus on tracking down Stasi spies deserved the importance she and Dorfmann gave it when there were threats to the very fabric of West German society by the Red Army Faction. These home-grown left-wing terrorists were systematically murdering public officials, businessmen and any prominent figures they considered representatives of capitalism.

The ringing phone tore her from her thoughts. Saturday evening; it had to be her mother wanting to commiserate over the dreadful news. She swallowed the rest of her drink, carried the glass to the kitchen, and picked up the wall phone on the fifth ring. "Maier."

"Sabine?"

It took her a moment to recognize the hesitant male voice. "Horst?"

"Yes, it's me. Sorry to bother you at home, but I needed to talk to someone. You've heard about Jürgen Ponto's murder?"

"Yes. It's sad and depressing."

"You know, Sabine, it got me thinking. Maybe we're spinning our wheels going after the wrong bad guys while the RAF continues its killing spree. Are the police and the intelligence agencies asleep at the switch? They can't seem to nab these terrorists, and I'm afraid it's only going to get worse."

Strange, but hearing him express doubts similar to her own about going after Stasi spies somehow made her feel better. "I was thinking the same thing, Horst. But there is a connection. Many of the terrorists have been trained in East Germany, and when they're on the run, the Stasi shelters them, gives them new identities. I'd say let's put those commie spies behind bars, and maybe we'll pick up the scent of a few RAF terrorists along the way."

"Hmm. Maybe you're right. Speaking of hunting down spies, how'd you do with Dorfmann? Is he getting the additional records you want?"

"He didn't like it, but I persuaded him."

"Any idea when we can input them?"

"Early next week, I hope."

"I'll be waiting." After a pause, he added, "I know it's getting late, but if you're up for a repeat visit to the beer garden without using me as a cover, I can meet you there in fifteen minutes."

Her immediate thought was to say no. Mixing professional and personal affairs was not a good idea. Or was she too strict? After all, Horst wasn't a coworker, but a consultant. There'd be no harm in socializing. Still, she had a buzz from several glasses of wine.

"Sabine, you still there?"

"I'm here. I'd love to another time, but not tonight. I've got a few glasses of wine under my belt already. Will you give me a rain check?"

"Of course. Talk to you early in the week."

She hung up. On her way to have one final glass of wine, she had to admit that she liked the disappointment in his voice.

Chapter Thirty-One

Doubts

Bonn, Sunday, 31 July 1977

Her travel clothes washed and put away, Monika settled on the sofa with a glass of Riesling. She reached for the TV remote, but thought better of it. The last thing she wanted was to watch yet another report of the heinous murder of Jürgen Ponto. The RAF terrorists were growing bolder by the day and law enforcement always seemed to be a step behind. She thought of her boss. As chief of the Chancellery, he might well be the next RAF target. The terrorists surely had him in their sights.

Resolved to quell her worries, she let her thoughts drift back to last week. She'd never dreamed of meeting a handsome, considerate fellow German on the beach in Italy. And he'd seemed sincere about making the romance last beyond a holiday fling. She leaned back, trying to imagine what Günter might be doing at this moment in Vienna when the phone on the end table rang. Could that be him? She scooted to the edge of the couch and picked up on the second ring, unable to keep anticipation from her voice. "Fuchs."

"Monika, it's Gisela."

"*Hallo.*" Gone was the enthusiasm.

"Well, don't sound so disappointed. You didn't expect Plácido Domingo, did you?"

Monika forced a laugh. "No, you just surprised me, and I'm a bit tired from cleaning up after the trip."

"Your vacation—that's why I'm calling. I can't wait to hear about all the sexy Italians who must have hit on you. You did take your bikini, didn't you?"

This time Monika's laugh was genuine. "So I did, since you insisted."

"And? Come on, spill the beans. Holiday fling or not?"

Monika fought irritation. Somehow Gisela's question cheapened her feelings about the liaison with Günter. "You won't believe this, but I met a fellow German."

"Don't tell me you went all the way to Italy and hooked up with a countryman. And it's more than a fling, isn't it?"

"What makes you say that?"

"The excitement in your voice."

Monika felt herself blush. "I don't know what to think. He wants me to visit him in Vienna this weekend." As soon as the words left her mouth, she regretted them. Even though Gisela was a friend, Günter's invitation was a private matter. So she backtracked. "But I doubt I'll go."

"Why on earth not?"

Not wanting to discuss this further on the phone, she said, "I tell you what, Gisela. Let's have lunch this week and I'll fill you in."

"How about tomorrow?"

"I'll have to let you know. I may not see any daylight until midweek. I'll call you." For some reason, her thoughts circled back to the news. "You've heard about the Ponto murder?"

After a long pause, Gisela said, "Yes, what about it?"

Monika stared at the receiver, as if it had distorted her friend's voice, which held a twinge of "so what?" in it. "The Dresdner Bank president."

"Yeah, it's been all over the news."

"Fifty-three, leaves a wife and two children. Aren't you upset about it?"

"Yes, of course. It's just that I find the news depressing, so I try not to pay too much attention."

Somehow Gisela didn't sound genuine. Monika pressed. "You know both of our bosses are likely RAF targets."

"You're probably right."

Time to sign off. "I'll call you and let you know when I can get away for a long lunch."

"The sooner the better. I'm dying of curiosity. *Tschüs.*"

Monika replaced the receiver, wondering why she'd resisted telling her friend more about Günter. Maybe Gisela's holiday-fling remark had put her off. She drank some wine as her thoughts returned to her passionate lover. Maybe he was too good to be true.

She mused about their day exploring Verona and doubts began to creep in. Even though she knew the Juliet's House was a put-up job for tourists, she had still wanted to see the famous balcony for the romance it would conjure up, but Günter had adamantly refused. What was the big deal about giving in to fantasies about Shakespeare's famous lovers? Then there was his apparent lack of knowledge of Verdi's anniversary and unfamiliarity with the tomb scene in *Aïda*, things any professed opera fan would know about.

She shrugged. Maybe there was more to Günter than met the eye, but wasn't that true about every member of the human race? With that she drained her glass, admonishing herself to keep an open mind about seeing him in Vienna this weekend. If she were honest, she'd admit she could hardly wait to feel his body against hers.

Chapter Thirty-Two

The Report

Stasi Headquarters, East Berlin, Monday, 1 August 1977

"How's the executive secretary on this fine morning?" Stefan said in his best upbeat tone.

Helga Schröder made a show of closing a file before looking up, but she didn't fool him. She'd been watching him from the moment he'd crested the staircase leading to the reception area.

"Well, if it isn't the money man. You got some of those five hundred thousand lire still in your pocket?"

This was a changed Schröder from the humorless stickler who'd instructed him on the minute details for his trip to Italy. He found her teasing disarming, but she worked for the Stasi, where one could not trust anyone. He had to assume that whatever he said to her would reach Heinrich's ears.

"I'm afraid I spent it all in one place. But it was for a good cause and I got a dose of culture along the way."

"Oh?"

Sensing a genuine curiosity, Stefan saw no harm in telling her what Heinrich apparently hadn't. "The money went for expensive opera tickets. Do you like opera, Frau Schröder?"

"Never been to one in my life, and am not likely to go anytime soon if tickets are that much."

Time to do a little probing. "You can get good seats at the Staatsoper for what you'd pay at a fancy restaurant. You ought to have your husband take you sometime."

She gazed at him. "I'm not married, Herr Malik . . . haven't been for years."

Well, well, maybe there was a way to get in her good graces. It couldn't hurt to have the general's secretary on his side—perhaps get some dirt on Heinrich. For that, he'd even sit through another opera.

"I'm sorry, I didn't mean to pry."

Her slight smile told him she knew otherwise and didn't seem to mind.

He followed up. "If you'd like to see for yourself what opera is like, I'd be happy to spring for a couple of tickets when something good is on."

"And what would that be?" she asked.

Encouraging sign; she hadn't turned him down. Now he had to come up with some names, not easy for a non-operagoer. So he said the first thing he could think of, "Can't go wrong with Mozart."

"I suppose that notorious opera Romeo *Don Giovanni* would fit nicely with your line of work, but I'd prefer *Magic Flute* or *Marriage of Figaro*."

He studied her face for signs of disapproval, but saw only impishness. "How do you know about these operas when you've never been to the theater?"

"They play a lot of Mozart on the radio."

Stefan nodded. "If you'd like, I'll check the Staatsoper and—"

"You do that." The serious Schröder had returned. She pointed to the door across the way. "The general is expecting you, but knock."

"Enjoyed our little chat, Frau Schröder." Stefan tried to gauge whether his words had the desired effect of softening her up even further, but she'd already returned her attention to the folder on her desk.

He knocked on the closed door. He thought he heard the general's voice and so he entered, but Heinrich's consternation as he shoved a magazine into a file drawer told him he must have imagined it.

"I'm sorry, General. I thought you asked me to come in."

"Never mind," Heinrich said, his voice gruff. "Have a seat. I'm ready for your full report."

Stefan took a chair and proceeded to relate the details of his Italian adventures, emphasizing his confidence that he'd managed to hook Monika Fuchs. Heinrich frequently interrupted with questions. Stefan could hardly stomach the self-satisfied expression on the general's face at the description of his altercation with the fake pursuer he'd arranged. Stefan had to admit it worked, but for some reason Heinrich's gloating grated.

He was still puzzling over why, when the general said, "You say you've got her hooked, but do you think she'll come . . . I mean, did you tell her you wanted to see her again?"

The way Heinrich had stumbled over his words gave Stefan a sense that the general already knew about the planned tryst in Vienna. Stefan watched him closely while recounting his invitation to Monika for the weekend but couldn't pick up anything concrete. Still, the general's enthusiasm and surprise upon hearing of Vienna struck Stefan as somewhat feigned.

"Are you listening to me?" Heinrich's harsh voice cut Stefan's speculation short.

"I'm sorry, General, I was trying to think how to pull off the rendezvous," he lied.

"Then pay attention. I told you about the Vienna apartment last week. It has a phone connected to an answering machine with a generic message. I prefer that you call her, but if Monika asks for your phone number, you can give her that one. Get it from Frau Schröder."

"What about setting up a temporary office as you suggested?"

Heinrich leaned back in his chair. A few moments later, he straightened up. "You call her to make sure she's coming. Report back to me. If she commits, then I'll arrange for a place you can show her. But do everything you can to dissuade her from wanting to meet you there."

"What if she asks for the office phone number?"

Heinrich stared at him. "I was just coming to that. Tell her you're not allowed to receive personal calls except in an emergency. Do you remember what to say if she can't find Gemeinschaft Unbegrenzt in the phone book?"

"The Vienna offices are too new to be listed."

"Good. At least, you were paying attention last week."

Stefan held the general's stare, trying not to react to the rebuke.

"Are you clear?" Heinrich continued, his tone softening.

"Yes, General."

"If you manage to recruit Monika, we'll have Gemeinschaft Unbegrenzt transfer you from Vienna to Bonn. Start thinking about a good explanation to give her, in case she asks." Heinrich grinned, in apparent appreciation of having thought up the pretext of a transfer. He continued, "For a novice, you've done a good job, Malik. You do well in Vienna, and there'll be a promotion waiting for you."

"You mean—"

"Captain in the Stasi for starters. Continue to perform, and you'll be richly rewarded in rank and pay."

Stefan fought conflicting emotions about a career as a Stasi officer. It promised a steady income enabling him to foster his daughter's dream. Traude's studies would be secure so long as he performed to Heinrich's satisfaction. But at what price? He'd be ensnared further in the secret police's machinations. The longer he did the general's bidding, the less likely would he be able to disentangle himself from the Stasi. For now, he had little choice but to go along; he certainly had no taste for being thrown back in with the queers at a Rummelsburg prison cell. Still, he'd keep his eyes open for a way to extricate himself from the Stasi's grip without jeopardizing his daughter's future. If there was a way out, he had to find it.

Since Heinrich was pleased with him, this seemed an opportune time to bring up Traude. "I appreciate the promotion, General, but there is something I meant to raise with you before I went to Italy, and that is my daughter's—"

"Don't you worry about her. She will be admitted to the Weimar Opera School."

"Thank you, General, but—"

"What else do you want, Malik?"

"I'd like assurance that she'll be allowed to finish her studies."

"A guarantee is out of the question. Whether she will graduate is up to her and to you. As long as she progresses and as long as you carry out your assignments, she will remain at Weimar. If either one of you fails, she won't. It's as simple as that."

Summoning his courage, Stefan asked. "And if something happens to me?"

"You mean what if you get caught in the West?"

Stefan nodded, though that wasn't the worst scenario he could imagine.

"We stand by our agents. Unless you disgrace our state, your daughter will be taken care of. I promise you that."

"Thank you, General."

"That's it for now. Frau Schröder will show you to your office down the hall. You'll find instruction materials from the training in Golm you missed. Study them. Let me know as soon as Monika Fuchs commits to come to Vienna. Questions?"

"No, General." Stefan stood. Before he drew the door closed on his way out, he noticed Heinrich retrieving the magazine from the drawer where he had so hurriedly stashed it earlier.

"Ready to see your fancy office?" Schröder's mocking tone told him he'd likely been assigned a cubicle fit for a dwarf, but he swallowed a wisecrack about not having brought a shoehorn.

He followed her down the hallway. While admiring her tight, undulating skirt, he pondered his earlier suspicion that Heinrich might have been tipped off about the Vienna rendezvous. Even with his slew of spies and informants in the West, how could the man have possibly learned of it? Stefan thought back to his conversation with Monika over breakfast at their Verona hotel when he asked her to come to Vienna. He'd been so focused on persuading her that he'd paid no attention to patrons at neighboring tables. A seasoned spy he was not. Heinrich could well have tasked Armato with having them shadowed. Or had Monika told someone?

Helga Schröder opened the door to a tiny office. "Here you are."

On the downside: confined quarters rivaling the crammed prison cell at Rummelsburg; on the upside: he'd only have to contend with navigating around cheap furniture instead of fending off three queers.

He shrugged. "The good news is there's not much chance I'll get lost in here."

That elicited a smile from Schröder. She lingered in the doorway, as if she had something on her mind. Finally, she said, "Good luck to your daughter on her studies at Weimar."

"Thank you, but she's not heard from the school."

"Oh, she'll be accepted. The general will see to that." Schröder stepped into the hallway, then turned back. "And as long as you please him . . ." She spun on her heel and strode down the hall.

Heinrich's secretary was definitely informed about his private life; she'd probably read his entire file. But what did she know about Heinrich? Inviting Helga Schröder to the Staatsoper seemed more and more like an excellent idea. He had to find out whether someone had leaked information or was playing a double game, and she just might know who could have informed Heinrich of Monika's plans for coming to Vienna.

Chapter Thirty-Three

Foreign Office

Munich, Tuesday, 2 August 1977

Sabine drummed her fingers on the desk while counting the telephone rings. Three . . . four. The wall clock above her office door showed ten after five. Had Horst quit for the day already? Six . . . seven.

"System Solutions." Horst's businesslike voice came over the line.

"Good, you're still there. Sabine here."

"Hi, Sabine. What's up?"

"We have a new lead I need to talk to you about. Do you have dinner plans?"

The slight pause told her she'd caught him by surprise, but he recovered quickly. "Well, I could be persuaded to forgo my usual evening feast of cold cuts, bread and a *Löwenbräu.*"

She laughed. "Did you like *Trattoria Bel Canto* where we met for lunch, or do you have a favorite Italian restaurant you consider more authentic?"

"Assuming you didn't have a drive across the Alps in mind, *Bel Canto* will do nicely. I can meet you there in an hour."

"No, you can't."

"Why do you—?"

"Because, I want you first to run your program with different criteria and bring the results with you."

After another pause, longer this time, he said, "Tell me what you need."

Surprised by his curt tone, Sabine took a deep breath. "Look, Horst. One of these days we'll make time for a personal dinner, but—"

"No explanation necessary. I understand you've got to pursue the new lead right away. So please tell me what you want me to wrestle from the computer this time."

"Two searches, limited to the Foreign Office. One, single and divorced support personnel whose birthdays fall on the July dates we established, and a second search without regard to birthdays."

"Consider it done."

"Any idea how long—?"

"Minutes. I'll do it right now. Meet you at *Bel Canto* at six thirty?"

"Okay. Scratch your girlfriend's ears for me."

"She'll want more than a scratch. She's high maintenance. First, I have to feed her, after which she insists I take her for a walk. *Ciao.*" With that, he hung up.

♫ ♫ ♫

Despite making a detour to her apartment to shed her office garb in exchange for something casual—Horst hadn't seen her in anything but staid business attire—Sabine arrived at the restaurant a few minutes early.

The hostess, recognizing her as a regular patron, greeted her, "*Guten Abend*, Frau Maier. Your party is seated already." She guided her to a table for two in the far corner.

Horst, clad in crisp khakis and an open-collared navy shirt, stood and shook her extended hand. "Good to see you out of office clothes."

While his remark carried a suggestive tone, his innocent smile told her he'd meant it as a compliment. She pulled out the cushioned chair before Horst could and sat. "Just so you know, I wasn't born in dresses and pantsuits."

"Never thought you were." He slid two sheets across the table. "Here are the reports you wanted."

Before she could take a look, a waitress appeared. Since Horst had already studied the menu and Sabine knew it by heart, they ordered their entrees along with a bottle of Valpolicella.

Sabine picked up the printouts. The first one listed a secretary with a birthday on July 26. Sabine searched her memory. "I think that's the same person . . ."

Horst nodded. "She was on the earlier list, and you cleared her already."

She laid the paper aside and studied the second one, which in addition to that secretary contained three new names she did not recognize. She looked up. "You ran this one without regard to birthdays?"

"Yes."

While she resumed her study, the waitress brought the bottle of wine and two glasses. The ritual taste test and Horst's approval accomplished, she poured the wine and left.

Sabine laid down the paper and took a moment to inhale the red wine's distinctive bouquet before raising her glass in a salute. "Thanks for doing this so quickly."

"Of course."

After they clinked glasses and drank, he asked, "Anything useful?"

"Three divorced secretaries with security clearance."

"What made you zero in on the Foreign Office?"

She looked around. Although the closest tables seemed out of earshot, she said in a low voice, "Another Stasi officer defected last night. After debriefing him all day, Dorfmann told me to focus on the Foreign Office. Apparently, the defector possesses intelligence that points to a leak there."

"So you'll be off to Bonn?"

"First thing in the morning."

"Any chance you need me to come along as a consultant?" Horst's eyes sparkled.

"I'm sorry I have to say no. Besides, you'll be busy here."

"Oh?"

"I don't know how he did it, but the boss has already gotten the records I requested, except, of course, the ones from the Chancellery. They're making things difficult, as usual." She stabbed a finger at the list in front of her. "I'll take the files of these three with me. Dorfmann will have the four secretaries who helped last week bring you the rest in the morning."

"So we get to drown ourselves in papers and computer work while you're being a real detective, interrogating potential moles in the capital?"

"Serves you right for quitting your job as an agent," she said, hoping he wouldn't take her comment the wrong way.

He raised his glass. "I'll console myself with drink and my girlfriend."

As they drank, the waitress brought their entrees. Conversation ceased while they ate. Midway through his meal, Horst picked up his wine glass. "Here's to a successful hunt in Bonn." His face took on a wistful expression. "I wish I could go with you. Promise me you'll be careful."

Surprised, she put down her glass without drinking. "Thank you, but I don't see this as a particularly dangerous—"

"Famous last words." He furrowed his brow. "You're after Stasi spies, and who knows, you might stir up some Red Army Faction terrorists along the way. After Jürgen Ponto's murder . . ."

She was touched by his comments, which seemed to signal more than concern for a fellow professional. "Okay. I'll keep my guard up. But you've got to promise me something as well."

"What's that?"

"Ride herd on the secretarial team and have all those records in your system by the time I return."

"Slave driver."

The piano across the dining room almost drowned out his words. Then a female voice started to sing in Italian.

Horst raised his eyebrows.

"I forgot to tell you they have students from the conservatory perform at dinner time."

"You haven't given up hope of turning this philistine into an opera lover, have you?" Ignoring his half-finished pasta dish, Horst leaned back and listened.

Chapter Thirty-Four

Going?

Bonn, Tuesday, 2 August 1977

Nearly out her apartment door, Monika stopped when the phone rang. She would have ignored it, but the ring pattern indicated an international call. She dropped her purse, ran inside, and picked up the receiver. "Fuchs."

"Hello, Monika. I'm glad I caught you."

Her heart rate spiked. "Günter—so good to hear from you."

"Is this a bad time?"

"Actually, I'm on my way to work, and I've got about ten minutes to catch the Stadtbahn."

"Oh, in that case, I'll make it quick. I'm calling to make sure you're coming to Vienna this weekend."

"I'm sorry, but I've been so busy with work, I haven't had time to think about it." Would he see through her obfuscation?

"Will you please? I miss you terribly, Monika."

Blood rushed to her face. She so much wanted to say yes, but she hesitated. Was Günter for real or just another Jochen? The nearby church bell sounded the Westminster chime. "I'm sorry, Günter, but I have to go. I can't be late to the office. I'm still playing catch-up." She hated the excuse, so she followed it up with, "Where can I reach you to let you know?"

"Call me at—"

"Wait." She grabbed a pen from the plastic cube on the end table. "Okay. What's the number?"

"01 7625490."

She scribbled the figures on the notepad by the phone and tore off the top sheet. "Got it. Sorry, but I've got to run. I'll call you." She hung up before he could respond and bolted from the apartment.

♫ ♫ ♫

Late for her lunch appointment, Monika crossed the street against a red light. Her boss had run her ragged all morning, and she was conflicted about whether to lament the lack of time to think about Günter's invitation, or to be grateful she'd been too busy to mull it over. Truth be told, she wasn't ready to make a decision.

As she'd expected, Gisela was pacing the sidewalk in front of Cafeteria Pikant in her spike heels. "There you are."

"Sorry, but—"

"I know, that slave driver boss of yours." Gisela grabbed her by the arm. "Come on, before it gets too crowded."

They joined the line going through the self-serve salad bar. Gisela's heavy makeup and long, bright red fingernails made her stand out from the other women, her conservative charcoal business suit the only clue that she worked in an office. After paying at the cash register, they climbed onto a couple of stools at a small, round table.

"I know you're pressed for time," Gisela said. "But I want to hear all about your Italian romance."

Monika felt herself blush. "Not much to tell. A handsome fellow German. I guess you could say we hit it off. But whether anything more—"

"Oh, come on. He's already invited you to see him this weekend."

"But I'm not sure I should go."

"Why on earth not? What better place for a romantic getaway than Vienna."

Monika took a bite of lettuce, not so much to quell her hunger, but to buy time to ponder her friend's words. "Vienna is enticing, and it's not like I have a rousing weekend planned in good old provincial Bonn."

"Tell me about this good-looking man."

Monika gave her friend an accurate, but restrained description of Günter. Even if she had come to grips with her feelings, which she hadn't, sharing them with Gisela didn't feel right just yet.

When Monika stopped talking, Gisela shook her head. "You meet an eligible man who's handsome *and* considerate. For the life of me, I can't understand why you're hesitating even for a second."

Monika gestured with her fork. Gone was her earlier trepidation at laying bare her feelings. "I'll tell you why. I fell for my ex because he was all those things: good-looking, charming and considerate. He'd open my car door—bring exotic flowers. He always seemed to know the right things to say, made me feel so desirable when we made love. But we were barely back from our honeymoon when the real Jochen emerged. He picked at the way I folded the laundry—ironed his shirts. At first I wrote off his constant criticism to a perfectionism streak. Before long, he began to belittle me when we were with friends. Don't you remember him telling you how he had to take care of everything, how he couldn't trust me not to screw up?"

Gisela nodded.

"Then the name-calling started. I was stupid—clumsy. I couldn't do anything right. I spent his hard-earned money on frivolous things. Jochen turned out to be the exact opposite of the 'considerate' man I married. I don't know how I endured the verbal abuse for so many years. The day I divorced him, I swore I'd never go through that kind of ordeal again." She paused and caught her breath. "You ask why I'm hesitating. I don't ever want to hurt like that again. That's why."

Gisela reached across the table and squeezed Monika's hand. "I'm sorry for what you went through. But you've got to learn to trust sometime. Just because Jochen turned out to be a shit, doesn't mean your new love interest isn't genuine." Gisela withdrew her hand. "But you'll never find out by hiding away in fear. Give the relationship a chance, Monika. You're not the naïve girl who married Jochen anymore."

Monika held her friend's gaze. "Maybe you're right."

"You know I am." Gisela waggled a teasing finger. "I can tell you're smitten. Go to Vienna, for God's sake. If you don't, you'll never forgive yourself for passing up this opportunity. What have you got to lose?"

Surprised by her friend's fervor, Monika picked at her salad. How could Gisela, who'd never even met the man, be so convinced that seeing Günter was the right thing to do? But she had a point. If Monika didn't take a chance, she might regret it for the rest of her life. Handsome, considerate men didn't come along very often. They certainly were an endangered species in Germany's capital, overpopulated as it was with single and divorced females. Still, was she willing to risk another romantic disaster?

"Thanks, Gisela, I'd really like to go, but I want to be sure. I'll sleep on it." She placed her fork across the half-finished salad and slid from the stool. "Sorry, but I have to get back to the office. I'll let you know what I decide."

Before her friend could protest, Monika rushed out the door.

Chapter Thirty-Five

BND Snoop

Bonn and East Berlin, Wednesday, 3 August 1977

Sabine showed her ID to one of the uniformed Foreign Office lobby guards. "I have a nine-thirty appointment with the personnel director."

The young man, sitting behind a metal desk, took the ID and held it against the open page of a thick ledger. He scrolled down to a name written above a crossed-out entry.

Sabine couldn't read the name upside down. "Is there a problem?"

He glanced from the ID back to her. Apparently satisfied the photo matched the woman standing before him, he handed the card back and pointed to a row of chairs. "Someone will be with you shortly."

So much for answering her question. She slipped the ID into a jacket pocket and carried her briefcase to the nearest chair. While she sat and waited, she couldn't keep from speculating as to what the crossed-out name might mean. Had her request for interviews aroused suspicion? Maybe the personnel director had referred the matter to internal security. Nobody liked having an intelligence agent snoop around, and federal agency bureaucrats were no exception. She'd endured being given the runaround a few times in her career. Would this be another instance? Perhaps she was reading too much into it.

According to the huge black-and-white wall clock above the guard station, she was still a few minutes early. Her thoughts turned to the type of questions she needed to ask the three divorcees. She'd resisted making an outline, having learned long ago it was more important to study body language and rely on her instincts. Being wedded to a script could cause her to miss clues that demanded follow-up.

A hard-edged female voice intruded on her cogitation. "Frau Maier?"

Sabine chided herself for not paying attention. Not good for a supposedly observant intelligence officer. She rose and nodded at a woman in a charcoal pantsuit. Short hair, dyed reddish-brown, and heavy makeup spoke of a woman trying hard to look younger.

"Yes, I'm Sabine Maier." She shook the woman's outstretched hand.

"Gisela Sturm."

A strong handshake, a firm chin, and probing eyes attested to a self-assured woman.

"This way please."

The guards let her pass without questioning what she might be carrying in her briefcase, let alone inspecting it. She followed Sturm to a bank of elevators. During the ride up Sabine pondered the guards' nonchalance. These automatons apparently had no clue as to the resourcefulness of the RAF terrorists, who in Sabine's view were certainly inventive enough to produce a fake intelligence agency ID. No wonder there seemed no end to the growing number of bank presidents, corporate CEOs, and politicians being murdered by the left-wing assassins.

With a ding, the elevator doors opened on the fourth floor. Sturm led the way along a narrow hallway, her high heels clicking on the linoleum. They passed a row of interior windows that showed a sizable room with an oval table surrounded by some dozen chairs. When Sturm opened the door, Sabine stepped onto the plush brown carpet and glanced around the room. Portraits of the president and the chancellor of West Germany hung on the sidewall. The far end featured a serving area and a movie screen, as well as a large television set mounted high in a corner.

The sound of the door closing drew Sabine's attention back to Sturm, who strode to the leather swivel chair at the head of the table, sat and pointed to the chair next to hers. A power move to show she was in charge. Sabine took the indicated chair, which proved surprisingly comfortable. She laid her government-issue briefcase on the table, its faded patent leather looking shabby against the polished dark wood surface.

"I'm the foreign minister's personal secretary. This is his private conference room."

While speaking, Sturm had been watching her, as if waiting for a reaction. Hmm, that's what the crossed-out entry meant. Personnel had kicked her interview requests upstairs.

When Sabine didn't respond, Sturm continued, "The personnel director referred your request to interview three of our employees to the minister, and he asked me to find out what exactly you are looking for."

None of your business, was the response that came to mind, but if she wanted to accomplish what she'd come for, Sabine couldn't afford to alienate this gatekeeper. So she said, "As you know, I'm an intelligence officer with the BND. I'm working on a highly classified project, the nature of which I can't reveal."

She paused, hoping she'd sounded sufficiently self-important, something this woman would certainly understand. Still, she had to throw her a bone, since Sturm seemed to have it in her power to bar access to the employees. "What I can tell you is that this relates to a matter of national security, and the director of the BND has tasked me with conducting these interviews as soon as possible."

She suppressed a chuckle at the thought that she'd just promoted Dorfmann to the head of the BND. The skeptical expression on Sturm's face meant she had to offer something else.

So she improvised some more. "Please rest assured that we do not suspect these employees of any wrongdoing. Nor do we believe there is a problem at the Foreign Office. But we have picked up intelligence that seems to indicate one or more of these women might be able to help us connect some dots, if you know what I mean."

Not bad for made-up bureaucracy-speak that sounded important without saying anything. Sabine held Sturm's gaze. Would she buy the pompous drivel?

"Well, you haven't really told me anything, but we want to cooperate, of course. If you don't mind, I'd like to sit in."

Time to put this woman in her place, but not too harshly. Instead of saying out of the question, Sabine forced a smile and said, "I wish that were possible, but the classified nature of the project prohibits that. I'm sure you understand."

Sturm's set jaw spelled no, but then it softened. "Of course, I completely understand." She pointed to the briefcase sullying the elegant table. "You have the copies of the personnel folders we made for you?"

"Yes."

"In that case, I'll send the first of two employees in for you."

"Two?"

"I'm sorry, but the third one is off today. If you want to talk to her, you will have to come back tomorrow."

Sturm's smug tone belied her protestation of regret. Sabine wanted to ask why they hadn't insisted the employee come to work, but thought better of it. She needed to get back to Munich to follow up on Horst's latest findings instead of spending another night in a Bonn hotel.

But she had no choice, so she said, "Can you have her here at nine in the morning?"

Sturm nodded, stood and walked to the door. "I'll send in Frau Pohl."

♫ ♫ ♫

When his secretary burst into his office, Heinrich snapped shut the magazine he'd been perusing. "What happened to knocking, Frau Schröder?"

"*Entschuldigung, Herr General,* but the messenger from the radio department said this was extremely urgent."

She laid a sealed envelope addressed to him on top of the men's magazine he hadn't quite managed to shove under a stack of files. If the sight surprised her, she gave no sign. Too late now anyway. Before he could ask, she handed him the silver letter opener from the tray on the corner of his desk. No question Schröder was efficient, but was she discreet?

"Wonder what's so damn urgent," he muttered as he slit open the envelope and pulled out a sheet. He read the message written in block letters. *BND Agent Sabine Maier – interrogating 3 secretaries at Foreign Office – strongly suspect in search of Romeo targets.*

"*Verdammte Scheiße!*"

On her way to the door, Helga Schröder stopped and turned around. "Do you need to send a reply, Herr General?" Her voice was even; she'd long ago grown used to his swearing.

"No."

After she'd left his office, he tossed the paper on the desk. He fingered the magazine, but he was no longer in the mood to gaze at pictures of muscular young men. That BND snoop was getting too close. He had to do something about her. If she caught the scent of his well-placed mole, she might wreak havoc on his elaborate plan to recruit Monika Fuchs. He could not allow that. The party functionaries staring back at him from the sidewall would demand action, and Heinrich had a strong hunch what kind.

He retrieved a folder from his wall safe and leafed through a list of the valuable assets he'd established in West Germany over the years. He flipped back and forth, looking for someone suited for the task he had in mind. The delicate mission required the services of a consummate professional who not only could assure success, but who would leave no clues that could be traced to the Stasi. He'd certainly not use the amateurs who'd bungled the break-in at the computer consultant's business. There! Halfway down the fourth page, he stabbed a finger at the name of the perfect man for the job.

Chapter Thirty-Six

Weimar

Stasi Headquarters, East Berlin, Thursday, 4 August 1977

Eyes strained from reading all day, Stefan leaned back in the vinyl-covered swivel chair and surveyed his tiny office. A small imitation-wood desk and a wooden chair no visitor would want to endure were crammed into the confined quarters, leaving barely enough space to move around. A black desk telephone covered a spot where the laminate was peeling, probably from the prior occupant's beverages.

Stefan wondered what happened to his predecessor, only because it could provide a clue to how long he might have to suffer this place. Good thing he wasn't claustrophobic. Gray walls, bare except for a clock above the door, made for a depressing atmosphere. Whoever was in charge of furnishing offices had deigned to set a wooden coatrack in the corner. At least that was something. Only an hour till quitting time. His mood brightened.

He'd been studying the training manual all week. If he had to do the Stasi's dirty work, he'd better learn all he could about tradecraft. Even the most skillful secret agents lived with the constant threat of exposure. The list of things that could undo a spy seemed endless: a careless word, botched surveillance, failure to shake a tail, a too-lengthy transmission intercepted, sheer coincidence, or bad luck. To compensate for his lack of experience he would have to prepare extra well. No sense increasing his odds of capture in the West by operating as a blundering spy.

He leaned back in his chair, fantasizing about returning to private life where he, and not the Stasi, decided which woman he should pursue. Would he ever again have the choice of taking a woman out to dinner, romancing her, making love to her, solely because he desired her? Not as long as the Stasi had him in its grip, selecting his female targets. Monika's image flashed through his mind. Why did she have to be so attractive? He seemed to have fallen for her, as Heinrich had sensed.

Stefan shook his head, trying to ban illusionary thoughts of a life untouched by the Stasi. He wouldn't be regaining his liberty anytime soon, if ever, so he'd better concentrate on the task at hand. He rubbed his eyes, scooted forward and refocused on the manual lying open before him, intent on finishing his second read-through by the end of the day. Before he could turn the page, the door flew open and General Heinrich stepped onto the thin carpet.

Knocking before entering apparently applied to underlings only. Not that Stefan would have dared to express the thought.

Heinrich eyed the visitor's chair, but obviously knew better than to test its hard seat. "Good God. I had no idea you were stuck in this dinky closet. You keep performing, Stefan, and I'll see that you get a real office before long."

The general leaned on the desk. Astonishingly, it did not collapse under his weight. "We just picked up a message on the answering machine in the Vienna apartment."

"Monika?"

"None other." Heinrich grinned. "She wants you to call her this evening."

"Did she say anything about this weekend?"

"No, but we need to plan for Vienna. Give her an hour or so to make it home before you call."

"What if she won't come?"

"She will." Heinrich stared down at him. "Remember what I recruited you for. I want to see that self-confident seducer whose escapades are plastered all over your file."

"Yes, General."

"That's better." Heinrich stepped back from the desk. "I received word that your daughter has been admitted to Weimar on a full scholarship. If she performs as expected, she won't have to worry about tuition, books, or even living expenses."

"That's wonderful." Though overjoyed at the news, Stefan had no illusions. It was his performance, not Traude's, that mattered.

"You don't sound very enthusiastic, Stefan."

"I'm sorry, General. I'm a little overwhelmed by the great news."

"Well, you'll have plenty of opportunity to show your gratitude." Before closing the door behind him, Heinrich said, "I'll give you your marching orders for Vienna in the morning. My office. Eight thirty. Sharp."

As the general's heavy footsteps grew faint, Stefan marked his place with a slip of scratch paper and shut the thick manual with a thump. His thoughts turned to this evening's phone conversation. Would Monika say yes as Heinrich had predicted? More than predicted—he seemed almost sure, as if he already knew what her answer would be.

But what if Heinrich was wrong? It could mean an early—if inglorious—end to Stefan's Romeo career. He fancied returning to his private life, enjoying the limited freedoms that could be had in the East German police state. But he was deceiving himself. Not only would he let Traude down, but he'd likely find himself back in the slammer. He shuddered at the thought of languishing in a Stasi prison. Stefan slumped in his chair. No matter what Monika decided, he was stuck.

Chapter Thirty-Seven

False Lead

Systems Solutions, Munich, Friday afternoon, 5 August 1977

Sabine's auburn curls bounced off the collar of her teal blouse as Horst led her past the row of computers to a corner table. "How did the interviews go at the Foreign Office?"

She grimaced. "Not well."

"No clues? No suspects?"

"None."

"I'm not sure this will help." He slid a printout across the table. "Here's the report I ran this morning after we input the latest records."

She picked up the paper and read. A moment later, she tossed it onto the table. "Crap!"

"What's wrong?"

"We're going in circles." She stabbed a finger at the sheet. "These are the same names you had on your other reports. Five of them from the birthday search and the last three from the Foreign Office. Vetted and cleared, every last one of them." She shoved the paper across the table with so much force that it slid off and fluttered to the floor.

Horst took a deep breath. Was she just frustrated about their lack of progress or was she questioning his work? Don't defend yourself. She needs to vent.

Sabine plucked the paper off the floor and laid it on the table. "I'm so frustrated. The computer searches are getting us nowhere, and the Foreign Office interrogations were a complete waste of time."

"I'm sorry I haven't been able give you what you need."

Sabine touched his forearm resting on the table. "I didn't mean to blame—"

"I know. But what we've been doing isn't working. Time to think of a new approach." He covered her hand still on his arm. "How about we brainstorm over a nice dinner somewhere?"

She withdrew her hand. "I'd like to, but I promised this evening to my mother. Maybe if we take our minds off this project over the weekend a solution will present itself."

Horst swallowed his disappointment. "Don't force things, you mean."

"Exactly." She checked her watch. "I need to go."

They stood and left the office, an awkward silence hanging between them. Sabine filled the void as they passed the empty reception area. "What happened to Frau Braun?"

"Oh, she's part-time only. You won't find her here on a Friday afternoon."

He walked Sabine to her car. She climbed into the Volkswagen, rolled down the driver's window, and started the engine. "Talk to you Monday."

She backed from the parking space and started to drive forward, but then stopped.

Had she changed her mind? Horst stepped to the driver's door. "Did you—?"

"I said Monday, but if something comes to you before then, call me." She let out the clutch and sped from the yard.

On his way through the shop, he admonished himself to tone down his hopes. They were working together, that was all.

Maybe once they finished this project. For now, keep things on a professional level.

At the sight of Sara wagging her tail in anticipation of her afternoon walk, his spirits lifted. "Looks like you and I will have ourselves a fine weekend, old girl. Women—who needs them?"

♫ ♫ ♫

Horst put down the book he'd been struggling to read. It was no use. The novel couldn't hold his interest, though he didn't blame the author. He kept thinking about the BND project. Sara's limbs and eyelids were twitching in a wild chase dream. For a moment, Horst considered turning on the television, but Saturday evening programs were abysmal.

His mind churned. An idea came. What if he ran a search with the July birthday dates and security clearances as the sole criteria? He'd start with that and then enter an additional trait one at a time in subsequent searches. A lot of work, but it beat sitting around doing nothing. He shot up from the sofa, and after a quick detour to the kitchen, headed to the shop with a full cup of coffee.

♫ ♫ ♫

An insistent nudge on Horst's elbow made his fingers skid across the computer keyboard. "What do you want, Sara?"

A glance at the wall clock provided the answer. He'd been so absorbed in generating the numerous printouts featuring different criteria that he'd lost track of time. Sara was reminding him he'd neglected to feed her. "One more report, and I'll get your food."

The soulful eyes looking at him made him feel guilty, but he pushed ahead. After a few more keystrokes, he printed the final document. He added it to his stack, which he carried back to the residence, with Sara bounding ahead. A few minutes later, he'd settled on the sofa, nursing a beer and leafing through dozens of pages spread over the coffee table. As he worked his way through the pile, his frustration grew. The same names kept reappearing—all cleared, as Sabine had so emphatically pointed out.

When he reached the report he'd run with only the criteria of the July birthdays and security clearances, he perked up. It contained a new name. His excitement vanished in an instant. A married secretary with a birthday of March 7, 1933. How in the hell did she end up on a list that was supposed to contain employees with July 26 or 27 birthdays only? Disgusted, he dropped the paper and took a big swig of beer. Either he'd made a mistake in inputting the data, or there was a bug in his program.

The offending sheet in hand, he bolted from the room. Sara gave him a curious look but stayed put. He ran the report a second time, careful to input the correct criteria. Same result. As much as he hated to admit it, that could only mean something was wrong with his program. The clock showed a quarter to ten, but there was no way he'd quit troubleshooting until he figured out what caused the error, even if it meant working through the night.

He had to find the flaw in his program so he could determine whether it affected only the one report, or whether it was systemic in nature, rendering all his reports faulty. If the latter, he would have to notify Sabine and Dorfmann. Once they learned that they couldn't rely on his program, his consulting days would be over—but there was more to it than losing business. Not only would Sabine consider him a dilettante, but he could no longer claim to have created a search method as sophisticated as any in existence. No matter what it took, he had to find the problem and fix it.

Chapter Thirty-Eight

Vienna

Vienna, Sunday, 7 August 1977

As the Ferris-wheel gondola approached the apex, Monika pressed her hands into the bench seat, readying herself for yet another descent. During the first few revolutions, she'd clenched her stomach until she managed to relax enough to enjoy the adrenalin rush of the ride down.

Günter snuggled up to her and put an arm around her waist. "I told you this would be fun."

"Maybe more fun than I . . ." The Ferris wheel slowed and then stopped, leaving them stranded at the top.

He smiled at her with those blue-gray eyes that made her knees go weak every time. "They're letting passengers off and others on. Scoot over and look."

Reluctantly, she slid to the edge of the bench and peered down the spidery web of steel cables that somehow held the giant contraption together. From this height, the people in the Prater

Amusement Park below looked like tiny specks. Steam rose from almonds roasting in the vendor stands.

She moved back and nestled her head against Günter's shoulder. He drew her close. "Thanks for agreeing to come. I know this wasn't on your must-do list for Vienna. But when I watched *The Third Man,* I knew I had to ride the Prater Ferris wheel someday."

She shuddered, recalling the movie's suspenseful scene. "The film made it look like Harry Lime was about to push his friend from the gondola. You're not harboring any thoughts like that, are you?"

Günter kissed the top of her head. "Not a chance. I want to experience more weekends like this."

"Ah yes, Vienna – the Schönbrunn Palace, the Vienna State Opera, the Spanish Riding School, the—"

"Stop!" He pinched her side. "You know exactly what—"

She brushed a strand of his dark hair off his brow and silenced him with a kiss. They'd been making love whenever they found themselves in his apartment, in the evenings, at night, upon waking in the mornings—and she wanted more. The Ferris wheel began to move, but they kept kissing until they were nearly down.

He steadied her while she climbed from the gondola. "What would you like to do next? Café Sacher or go back to the apartment?"

She checked her watch. Nibbling on pastry—even Café Sacher's world-famous *torten*—was not how she wanted to spend the afternoon before she had to catch her evening flight. "Let's go back to your place."

♫ ♫ ♫

Monika twisted one of Günter's curly chest hairs around her index finger. "Bad news, old man. Gray." She raised her head off his chest and looked up at him. "But at least, the locks on your head are still dark."

He laughed. "You like mature men, don't you?"

She pressed her naked body against his. "If you call the way you make love mature, then I'm all for it."

He caressed her side. She shivered with delight, her skin still sensitive after sex.

"Monika, would you do me a favor and keep our getting together to yourself? I don't mean to be secretive, but my work demands discretion."

She stiffened. Should she fess up?

"You haven't told anyone about coming to see me here, have you?"

She sought his eyes. "I'm sorry. I didn't realize you wanted to keep this a secret. I did let it slip to my best friend."

"Who is she?"

"What makes you so sure it's a she?" she said, trying to defuse the serious moment.

He gave an exaggerated sigh. "I give up. What's his name?"

"It *is* a she. Her name is Gisela."

"Does she work with you?"

"No." She didn't want to say more, but she felt guilty for having blabbed about him and Vienna, so she said, "She's a secretary at the Foreign Office." No need to volunteer that Gisela was the executive secretary to the minister.

"Oh, well. It's probably all right." He planted a feather kiss on her brow. "Did I tell you that I may be in Cologne this week?"

"No, you didn't." Her pulse quickened at the thought of seeing him again so soon. "Business?"

"Yes."

"When?"

"Probably midweek."

"What will you do in Cologne?"

"Attend an important meeting."

She pulled the sheet over her breasts and rolled onto her back. "You've told me you're a journalist and a writer who works for a peace organization here in Vienna. What's the name?"

"Gemeinschaft Unbegrenzt."

"But I don't really know what you do. What is this important meeting about?"

"It's kind of sensitive, and you're working for the German government." He squeezed her arm. "Ah, what the hell. The meeting is between peace groups from all over Europe. The topic is how to halt, or at least slow the pace of, West Germany's rearmament."

Monika sat up. "You're a pacifist?"

"Not to the extent that I believe force can never be justified. Certainly, Hitler had to be stopped. But what do you think about the West German government building up its forces?"

"Well, we can't really defend ourselves against the Soviets. So we need to contribute to NATO." She sank back down and stared at the ceiling. Not the type of conversation she'd envisioned for their last hour together. But he'd struck a nerve. She too had misgivings about German politics. "But maybe our role should be a little less prominent."

"I would agree, but rumor has it that the West German government is pursuing a hidden agenda."

"What do you mean?"

"There are signs pointing to a plan to beef up the German armed forces without NATO's knowledge."

"What kind of signs?"

"We have nothing concrete. I wish we could get our hands on some solid evidence."

Monika studied the white apartment ceiling, digesting Günter's comments. He seemed too grounded to be one of those conspiracy theorists. She turned and looked at him. "If you're right about our politicians harboring a secret plan, that's disturbing."

He kissed her cheek. "We seem to have more in common than I realized. You and I think alike. Now that I've bared my soul about my work, tell me what you do."

She hesitated, recalling once more the repeated admonitions not to talk about her job. But he'd been forthcoming about his, hadn't he? "I work at the Chancellery."

He sat up. "Really? What do you do there?"

"I'm a secretary."

"A secretary? You mean you take dictation and type?"

"I do some of that." The way he'd asked made her feel small. She had to set him straight. "I'm the executive secretary to the chief of the Chancellery. And I do a lot more than typing."

"I'm sorry. I didn't mean to denigrate secretaries." He kissed her. "You're too smart to do menial tasks. I bet important papers cross your desk."

She studied him. Was he pumping her for information or just curious—complimenting her? "I guess you could say that."

He rolled over and straddled her. "Well, let's not waste our last hour talking shop."

"I had no idea how quickly mature men like you can recover." She adjusted an awkward angle, pressed her pelvis up against his, then shuddered as he entered her.

♫ ♫ ♫

Though tired from the romantic Vienna weekend and nights of lovemaking, Monika was too excited to nap during the flight home. It was not until the plane prepared to land at the Cologne/Bonn airport that her pleasant thoughts turned to worries she might have said too much about her job. She shouldn't have bragged about how important a position she held. Oh well, she couldn't take it back. And Günter worked for a worthwhile cause. She could trust him, couldn't she?

Chapter Thirty-Nine

Computer Glitch

Munich, Monday, 8 August 1977

When Horst returned with Sara from their mid-morning walk, Erika Braun stopped him. "Sabine Maier called right after you left."

"Any message?"

"Just to call."

He nodded and followed Sara through the shop into the house. He'd been slouching around this morning after spending most of the weekend trying to find the bug in his program. By Sunday evening he'd given up. His system seemed to be working perfectly, passing every test he could think of. A fundamental error in his program that no test could detect, or an inexplicable anomaly? He hoped for the latter, but couldn't be sure.

He picked up the kitchen phone and stared at the receiver. What to tell Sabine? He didn't want to conceal anything or lie, but did he have to volunteer that he'd hit a snag in this one isolated case? The problem didn't seem to affect the other reports. But if he failed to disclose the glitch, was he practicing wishful thinking or even whitewashing?

To keep Sabine's trust, he'd have to be honest. He dialed the BND's number. The operator answered on the first ring, depriving him of the opportunity to change his mind. She put him on hold to the sound of some humdrum elevator music that seemed to go on forever. He resisted the temptation to hang up. Maybe Sabine had left the office or was busy.

Just when he thought he'd missed her, she answered. "Maier."

"Hi Sabine. It's Horst."

"Did you walk Sara through half of Munich?"

"Just about. Sorry it took a while to get back to you."

"Never mind. I called earlier to hear about the brilliant idea you must have had over the weekend."

He swallowed. No sense putting off the inevitable any longer. "No earthshaking insight here, but I have to tell you something that's kind of unsettling."

"Oh, oh. I don't like the sound of that."

"I spent all weekend running reports with every possible combination of criteria I could think of. There are several printouts with new names for you to check out."

"What's unsettling about that?"

"Well, that part isn't. What has me baffled is a report showing a married female with a March birthday."

"What search criteria did you use?"

"Employees regardless of marital status with a security clearance, plus July 26 and 27 birthdays."

Silence, then a huge exhale. "Are you telling me your program spit out a woman with a March birthday on a search specifying July?"

"That's exactly what I'm telling you. Listen, I checked my system every which way and I'm pretty sure it is sound. This is just one of those computer anomalies that can't be explained."

"Hmm. You're right, that is unsettling. How do we know we can rely on your other reports?"

"All I can give you is my best judgment that they are correct but I can't offer proof—"

"Do you have the printout with the married employee in front of you?"

"No, I shredded it."

"Do you recall her name, where she works?"

Horst thought for a moment. "I'd have to run it again, but I don't see the point in that. Wait a minute—I think her first name is Gisela."

"Did you say Gisela?"

"Yes."

"You don't remember the last name?"

"No, I'm sorry."

"Print out the report again. I'll be there in half an hour."

Surprised by her urgent tone, he only managed a "but" before the line went dead.

Chapter Forty

Bundeswehr

Federal Chancellery, Bonn, West Germany, Monday, 8 August 1977

Monika carried the top-secret envelope her boss had handed her to the copier. The distribution list contained three names, that of the chancellor and of the defense and foreign ministers. She removed the papers from the envelope and counted the pages. Six. As she inserted the thin stack into the document feeder, the headline caught her attention. A proposal to increase the budget of the *Bundeswehr*.

Could this be the secret plan Günter had alluded to? Neither the allied commander nor anyone else from NATO was on the distribution list. She flipped through the pages and read about the current strength of West German armed forces and equipment, and a proposed increase of ten percent. The final sheet contained a discussion of how the built-up forces would affect NATO strategy.

Monika straightened the papers for copying. Her thoughts turned to Günter's comments. She shared his concerns about the militarization of Europe, both East and West. Perhaps the peace organizations were doing the right thing. She loaded the papers and after a quick glance around, selected four copies on the keypad and pressed the start button.

Carrying the stack to her desk, she felt a pang of guilt. Günter had not asked her for any information, so why had she made an additional set? She could lose her job, maybe even her freedom. After placing the papers into folders according to the distribution list, she slid the extras into a plain envelope, which she locked in her center desk drawer. She couldn't risk taking them home but would shred them before the day was out.

Chapter Forty-One

Birthday Quandary

Munich, Monday, 8 August 1977

During the drive from Pullach, Sabine wondered whether Horst had remembered the employee's first name correctly. If so, was her last name Sturm? While not common, "Gisela" was not so unusual there couldn't be several women with that name working for the federal government. Still, when she had a hunch, Sabine always followed up, even if it appeared unlikely to lead anywhere.

Despite heavy traffic, she made it to Systems Solutions in half an hour. She screeched to a stop in the courtyard, not bothering to pull into one of the marked parking spots. She jumped from the VW and hurried toward the entrance. Before she could ring the doorbell, a buzzer sounded, and a female voice said, "Please come in, Frau Maier."

Perplexed, Sabine looked up and spotted a camera and speaker mounted above the door. An extra layer of security

Horst must have added after the break-in. She pushed the door open and greeted Erika Braun, who stopped typing.

"He's in the shop. You know the way?"

Sabine nodded and strode down the hall. She found Horst sitting in front of a computer.

He reached into a basket and held out a sheet. "Here is the printout. But I still don't understand why—?"

"Is the last name Sturm?"

He checked. "Why yes. Is this someone you've had your eye on?"

"Not exactly."

He handed her the paper. She read the scant information: Gisela Sturm, hired at the Foreign Office in 1966, worked in various secretarial positions until she was promoted to executive secretary to the foreign minister in 1974; top security clearance; born on March 7, 1933.

She looked up. "Is this all the information we have on her?"

"There should be more data in the computer, assuming the typists did their job." He pecked at the keyboard.

His typing went on and on. Various images flashed on the computer screen, but sitting behind Horst, Sabine couldn't read them. "Any luck?"

Horst kept typing. "Almost there." He finally stopped and turned around. "Watch the printer. We should have a couple of pages on Gisela Sturm in a minute or two. While we're waiting, maybe you can tell me why you're so interested in the secretary to the foreign minister."

"It's just a hunch. I met her last week when I interviewed the three secretaries. It's a long shot, especially since the computer picked her even though her birthday didn't match your search criteria. That's really puzzling."

"It's what had me tearing my hair out most of the weekend."

"There must be a reason, unless—"

"Unless my system is totally screwed up," he finished the sentence for her.

"I didn't say that, Horst."

The printer lit up and after what seemed like a long time produced one sheet, followed by a second. Sabine tore them at the perforation, kept the first and handed the other to Horst. She scanned the single-space print. More details about Sturm's career path, but nothing stood out.

She looked at Horst. "Anything noteworthy?"

He interrupted his reading. "Not so far. There are some personal details toward the end I just got to."

"May I see?"

They exchanged sheets. She sped through the personal history. Marital Status: Married, Husband Klaus; Children: Son Rainer, Age 8; Hobbies: Tennis, Hiking, Reading Mysteries.

When Sabine reached the end, she looked up. Horst finished reading a moment later. He shrugged. "Can't say that I'm any wiser."

Sabine took his sheet. There had to be something they weren't seeing. "Let's go over to the table." Once they'd settled in chairs next to each other, she said, "I want you to read both pages aloud to me."

He raised an eyebrow but started to read. She interrupted. "Go back to the beginning and read more slowly."

She hung on every word, followed the tedious work history, then the personal details.

"Married husband Klaus on May 5, 1967," Horst read.

"One year after she was hired at the Foreign Office," Sabine interjected. "Can't see any significance in that. Go on."

"Son Rainer born on July 27, 1969." Horst lowered the page. "The computer picked up the son's birthday. But why?"

Sabine stared at him. "Remember what the intercepted message said: 'The future is in your hands.' He's the future." Sabine sprang to her feet. "Your computer is smarter than we are. I could kiss it."

"Don't forget the man who developed the program."

Sabine gave Horst a feather kiss on the cheek and stepped back. "I need to call Dorfmann. Where's your phone?"

Off balance from her surprise kiss, Horst said, "Uh . . . right there." He pointed to a desk phone on the computer table.

She rushed over and Horst followed her. "Remember, it's not a secure line."

"I know, but this can't wait."

She dialed. The operator put her through to Dorfmann's secretary. After Sabine identified herself, the secretary said, "Mr. Dorfmann is out of the office."

"When will he be back?"

"Wednesday morning."

"I must talk to him right away. Can you reach him?"

"No, I'm sorry, Frau Maier, but he is traveling. I don't expect to hear from him until tomorrow. Can Frau Kraus help you?"

"*Scheiße*," Sabine muttered under her breath. She didn't like to deal with Dorfmann's deputy, but she had no choice if she wanted something done today. "Okay, can you transfer me?"

"Of course."

After a few clicks, a female voice answered, "Kraus."

Sabine started to explain the project Dorfmann had her working on when Kraus interrupted. "Herr Dorfmann has kept me informed. Do you need me to authorize something in his absence?"

Sabine took a deep breath, collecting her thoughts. "You're familiar with the text of the intercepted birthday message?"

"Yes, of course."

"We just discovered who the message was for."

"Really?"

"Yes. For Gisela Sturm. She's the foreign minister's personal secretary."

A deep intake of breath. "Are you quite sure? Do you know what you're saying?"

"Yes, I'm fully aware of the implications. I plan on leaving for Bonn right away, but I think we better have Cologne intelligence dispatch a couple of their agents to the Foreign Office immediately."

"You mean to prevent flight?"

"Yes."

"Before I can do that, you will need to give me more details. What evidence do you have?"

Sabine related the relevant contents of the computer printout, forcing herself to slow her racing mind to speak clearly, and to answer the deputy's questions.

Finally, Kraus said, "All right, I will notify the Cologne agency. When do you expect to arrive in Bonn?"

"Late afternoon, early evening at the latest."

"Great work, Frau Maier. Good luck in Bonn."

The dial tone cut off Sabine's thank you.

Horst, who'd been standing next to her, said, "I don't suppose you'd let me come to Bonn with you this time."

"Not possible."

"Could be dangerous, you know."

"I'll be careful. I'd take you with me, but it's against regulations. No private citizens on intelligence missions."

"I know. Just be sure to watch those agents from my old outfit in Cologne. Don't let them screw this up."

"Well, there's nothing I can do about that until I get there."

Horst handed her the printouts. "You might need these."

"Thank you for being so persistent. Your program may yet net us a spy or two."

"Or more. We'll celebrate when you return." He walked her out. His "be careful" followed her as she sped from the yard.

Chapter Forty-Two

Stood Up

Bonn, Monday, 8 August 1977

The moment Monika reached the entrance to Café Herbst, a distant church bell sounded the half-hour Westminster chime. Twelve-thirty on the dot, but no sign of the usually punctual Gisela. Maybe she'd gone inside. Monika caught the heavy door held open by a departing patron and entered. A large party crowded around an unstaffed wooden lectern, waiting for the hostess to seat them.

Monika slipped past the group, stepped into the dining area and surveyed the two dozen tables, most of them occupied. Conversation reverberated from the tile floor—a loud restaurant not to Monika's liking, but a favorite of Gisela's. But where was she? Monika dodged around tables, careful not to snag the low-hanging white tablecloths. Finally, she retreated to the entrance. A young hostess with short brown hair, wearing a cream-colored dress, shook her head when Monika asked whether she'd seen Frau Sturm, a regular patron.

Monika settled on a burgundy vinyl bench along the sidewall. Her watch showed 12:37. She'd grant her friend the privilege of being tardy for once. Perhaps Gisela's boss had given her a last-minute task. While waiting, Monika reflected on her Vienna weekend. Gisela would want to know everything, what she and Günter did besides make love, whether the sex was any good, what Günter was like, and on and on. Should she tell Gisela about his job, the meeting in Cologne, how she shared his skepticism about West Germany's rearmament?

A gust of wind blew in through the open door and shook Monika from her thoughts. That had to be Gisela. No, an elderly couple shuffled inside. Twelve fifty, according to the wall clock behind the hostess station. Maybe it was fast. A glance at her wristwatch dispelled that notion. Twenty minutes late. Gisela would have called the restaurant by now to let her know if and when she'd be coming. Something must be wrong.

Monika waited until the hostess returned from seating the elderly couple. "If Frau Sturm comes, please tell her I had to leave and to call me."

"She knows your—?"

"Yes."

Outside, Monika peered in both directions, then turned right and charged down the sidewalk. If she hurried, she could grab a bratwurst at a kiosk on her way back to work.

♫ ♫ ♫

Monika rode the elevator up to her office, the sausage lying heavy in her stomach. She rushed down the hall, eager to check for telephone messages. With the receptionist busy fielding calls, Monika stepped to the wall behind the desk and pulled three green slips from the cubbyhole bearing her name. One of these had to be a message from Gisela. A quick perusal dashed that hope.

Back in her office, she flung her purse onto the desk and picked up the phone. Management discouraged personal calls, but Monika rationalized that this qualified as an emergency. Gisela had never stood her up.

When the receptionist at the Foreign Office answered, Monika asked to speak with Gisela Sturm.

"She's not available. Would you like to leave a message?"

"Is she not there?"

"I'm sorry, but I can't—"

"Frau Huber, this is Monika Fuchs at the Chancellery. She was supposed to meet me for lunch but didn't show. I just want to make sure nothing's wrong."

"Sorry, Frau Fuchs, I didn't recognize your voice. Frau Sturm left the office late morning."

"Did she say where she was going?"

"No. I assumed it had something to do with a phone call."

"Do you know who called her?"

"Well, I probably shouldn't be saying anything, but I know you are best friends. The caller didn't give his name, but I'm pretty sure it was her husband."

"Did Frau Sturm seem anxious or worried to you?"

"I couldn't say. She was in a hurry, though. Didn't even wait for the elevator, but ran down the stairs."

"Thank you so much for telling me, Frau Huber."

About to hang up, Monika stopped when the receptionist spoke again, "If you reach Frau Sturm, please ask her to call me. The minister will want to know when she'll be back at the office."

"Yes, of course. I'll do that."

Monika disconnected and dialed Gisela's home number. Definitely an emergency justifying a second personal call. On the sixth ring, Klaus Sturm's voice sounded on the answering machine.

Monika drummed her fingers on the desk, waiting for the beep. "Gisela, this is Monika. Just checking to make sure you're okay. Please call me at the office as soon as you get this message."

She replaced the receiver. What could Klaus have told his wife to cause her to leave the office so abruptly? It had to be something quite serious, or Gisela would have called to cancel their lunch. Maybe their son had been in an accident. As much as she tried, Monika could not concentrate on work. The hours until quitting time seemed to drag while she waited for Gisela to call.

Not having heard from her friend, Monika left the office a few minutes early to catch the five o'clock streetcar to Gisela's apartment.

Chapter Forty-Three

Pursuit Interrupted

Munich and Bonn, Monday, 8 August 1977

Spurred on by Horst's admonition not to let the Cologne intelligence types mess things up, Sabine wove through heavy traffic on Munich's Mittlerer Ring. She repeatedly glanced at her wristwatch, praying for a less congested autobahn and for the rain clouds to disappear so she could make it to Bonn by four. Once on the A9 toward Nuremberg, she revved the engine through third gear, shifted up, and steered into the left lane to pass a column of trucks. With a clear roadway ahead, she returned to the right lane. So far, autobahn traffic was sparse. Would her luck hold all the way to Bonn?

Her stomach growled, but she had no time for lunch. Bad enough she'd have to stop for gas, and soon, according to the needle, which hovered near the gauge's empty mark. She approached a slow-moving truck and prepared to pass, but a Mercedes was coming up fast in the left lane. She stomped on the brake to slow down until the passing lane was clear. The pedal gave, traveling almost to the floor before the brakes engaged and the car slowed.

She now recalled how spongy the brakes had felt when she drove through the streets of Munich. The thought had crossed her mind to trade the VW for a BND fleet car, but she couldn't afford the extra time to drive to Pullach. Moreover, during the recent 125,000-kilometer maintenance her mechanic had assured her the brakes were good for another 10,000 kilometers.

A few raindrops splattered against the windshield. Still gaining on the truck, Sabine stepped on the brake pedal again, sending it straight to the floor. What in the hell had happened to her brakes? She turned the steering wheel to the left, but jerked it back. The Mercedes was blocking her in. Less than ten meters to the truck and closing fast. She pulled the emergency brake. The handle lifted straight up. No resistance. She let go and it flopped back down. A few more seconds and she'd slam into the rear of the truck. Fighting rising panic, she took her foot off the useless brake pedal, stepped on the clutch, and tried to shift down. The gearshift refused to go into third. Less than five meters to the truck. She clenched her jaw and pulled the knob as hard as she could. The transmission screeched as she forced the car into third gear. The VW bucked, then slowed to match the truck's speed with less than a meter to spare.

Sabine wiped sweat from her brow. The Mercedes had cleared the left lane, but she was in no mood to speed up and pass the truck. She'd rather follow at a safe distance on pavement that was beginning to turn slick under a steady drizzle. As she turned on the wipers, thoughts raced through her mind. The safest thing would be to roll to a stop on the road shoulder and signal for help. But she'd likely be stranded for some time and not reach Bonn before nightfall, if then. She'd try to make it to the next autobahn service station.

Each time she shifted gears to match the speed of the truck ahead, the gearbox screamed as if in pain. The rapid downshift earlier must have damaged the synchronization. With each successive shift, the gear knob became harder and harder to move. If the gears locked up, she'd have no way of stopping. Driving the brakeless VW much longer in the hope of reaching a service station was too risky. She decided to opt for the shoulder.

She veered over to the roadway edge. No cars were blocking the shoulder as far as she could see, but she was still going too fast. She'd have to wrestle the car into second gear, then get off the road in a hurry. Driving at a slow speed on the autobahn, even in the right-hand lane, was too dangerous. She shuddered at the prospect of getting rear-ended by a fast moving truck. Her odds of surviving such a collision in her VW were slim indeed.

Sabine grabbed the knob to jam it into second gear, but held up when she passed a road sign for *Raststätte Fürholzen Ost.* She abandoned the plan to stop roadside, betting she could make the one kilometer to the station without crashing. If she gradually reduced her speed until she reached the exit, she should be able to manage.

But why was the truck ahead pulling away all of a sudden? Preoccupied with planning her strategy for slowing down, she'd failed to notice the road's downward slope until the VW picked up speed. With her hand still on the knob, she forced it into second gear—the transmission's ear-piercing protest be damned.

Even being stuck in city traffic, it had never taken her this long to cover one measly kilometer. She did her best to ignore the blaring horns of motorists unwilling to tolerate a VW inching along, and insisting on every German's fundamental right to speed on the autobahn.

By the time she reached the exit, she had the car in first gear. She limped along the access road, thankful the rain had let up and she didn't have to negotiate a tight curve. After a hundred-meter crawl, she maneuvered past a row of cars lined up at the gas pumps. With both hands on the steering wheel, she pushed in the clutch and coasted toward a parking spot on the other side of the building. When she reached the empty space, she let out the clutch. The engine sputtered for a second or two before stalling. The VW lurched to a stop a few centimeters from the giant wall at the edge of the lot.

Sabine leaned forward, holding the steering wheel in a white-knuckle grip until the pain in her hands made her let go. Maybe the failure of the regular brakes could be attributed to an inopportune leak in the line or the master cylinder. But both systems kaput at the same time? There was only one explanation: sabotage. Someone must have tampered with the hydraulics and cut the emergency brake cable. Someone who didn't want her in Bonn; someone who wanted her dead.

She'd hunt down the saboteur and those who hired him, but that would have to wait. For now, she had to find a way to make it to Bonn. Standard procedure called for her to contact Dorfmann. He'd arrange to have her back on the road in no time, but he was out of the office. Although his deputy had been cooperative this morning, Sabine doubted Kraus would act with the same sense of urgency as Dorfmann. Her mind made up, Sabine pulled the ignition key, grabbed her purse and briefcase off the passenger seat, locked the car, and strode across the lot.

Once inside the building, she looked for a public phone and spotted several on a far wall. A burly man's voice sounded from one. She hurried to the phone farthest away from him, set down the briefcase, opened her purse and fished several coins from her pocketbook. She dropped one mark into the slot and dialed. One ring, two, three. Maybe they'd both gone to lunch.

"Systems Solutions," announced a female voice after the fourth ring.

"Frau Braun. This is Sabine Maier. I need to speak with Herr Kögler. Is he in?"

"Yes. Just a moment."

"Kögler."

Relieved to hear his voice, Sabine couldn't find the words. "Ah . . . Horst."

"Sabine. Is something wrong?"

"Yes. My VW is kaput."

"You okay?"

"I'm fine, but I'm stuck."

"Where are you?"

"Raststätte Fürholzen on A9. About 30 km north of—"

"I know where it is. Should I come——?"

"Yes, please. If you could."

"What's wrong with the VW?"

"Brakes are shot." She fed the beeping phone another coin.

"How did——?"

"I'll tell you when you get here." She hesitated. Did she dare? "Horst."

"Yes, what is it?"

"You still want to tag along to Bonn?"

"You bet. But what about your rules?"

"To hell with them."

He chuckled. "You hate useless regulations, don't you? I used to get crosswise with the bureaucrats in my old office, too. One reason I'm no longer there."

Recalling Dorfmann's heads-up about Horst being a free spirit, which had gotten him into trouble with the higher-ups at the Cologne intelligence agency, Sabine was itching to follow up, but this was not the time. "I want to hear about that, but not now. Please hurry."

"Be there in half an hour."

Sabine disconnected. After the coins dropped down the pay phone, she deposited another mark, and dialed the operator.

A few minutes later she'd arranged for her mechanic to send a tow truck. She hid the car keys under the driver floor mat and went in search of some food. Instead of her usual light lunch, she opted for the daily pork special with dumplings. Heavy, but the adrenalin rush had left her famished.

During the meal, she thought about how to justify skirting regulations. Dorfmann would want to know why she hadn't called BND headquarters for a backup. Well, she had plenty of time to think of a good answer. For now, she needed Horst to drive her to Bonn before Sturm fled, if she hadn't already.

♫ ♫ ♫

Horst kept his BMW in the autobahn passing lane during most of their four-and-a-half-hour drive to Bonn, slowing only for an occasional downpour. Sabine recounted her adventure of driving without brakes, which elicited repeated headshakes along with occasional glances of incredulity at first, then respect.

After listening to her escapade, he said, "I can't believe you made it all the way to Fürholzen without crashing. You're extremely fortunate and . . . a damned good driver."

"I'd like to think it was skill." She laughed, relieving the lingering tension. "But I'll grant you, there might have been a little luck involved."

He glanced over. "Whichever it is, I'm glad you made it."

Sabine wasn't sure how to respond. He seemed ready to cross that professional boundary between them, but she wasn't— at least not until they finished this job. Still, she was tempted to squeeze his hand resting on the gear knob.

The moment passed when he downshifted to accelerate up a hill, so she simply said, "I plan on remaining among the living, at least until I've nailed the bastard who messed up my brakes."

"You must have made a few enemies in your career. Can you think of anyone who might hate you enough to want to kill you?"

"Could be any of a handful, but as far as I know they're all still behind bars. Not that being locked up would prevent someone from . . . You know, I just can't believe that a spy I caught would plot this kind of revenge. Spies constantly live with the idea that someday, somehow, someone will blow their cover. Unless—"

"Unless the Stasi is worried about you getting too close to its network in the West," he said, giving voice to her thought. "First the break-in at my office, now your near-crash made to look like an accident."

"I hope you're right about us getting close. Let's nab Sturm and find out."

Horst stepped on the gas, barreling down the autobahn, the traffic having subsided northeast of Frankfurt. When he slowed to fall in behind cars in the passing lane, he asked, "Where do you park your VW?"

"On the street. I'm on the waiting list for a garage at my apartment building."

"I can't believe the BND has you parking your car where any thug can tamper with it. Have Dorfmann pull some strings to get you a secure garage."

"He might when he hears what happened."

Despite Horst's aggressive driving, they didn't reach Bonn until a few minutes before five. He steered the car onto damp city streets and glanced over. "Foreign Office?"

"Too late." Sabine rifled through the folder on her lap until she found the map, on which she had marked Sturm's home address. "Veil Straße 45. It's on this side of town. I'll direct you."

Ten minutes later, Horst turned into a two-lane residential street lined with apartment buildings. Had it not been for a white unmarked van and a gray Opel with black-wall tires— telltale signs of government vehicles—parked in front of a five-story building, they might have missed Sturm's address. The black numerals 45, affixed to a concrete ledge above the door, were barely visible from the street.

A few car lengths past the building, Horst pulled into a space at the curb and killed the engine. Clutching her purse and briefcase, Sabine jumped out and ran back to the building, careful to dodge a few puddles. It must have quit raining here some time ago. Once there, she pushed on the iron handle. The door didn't budge. She turned to study the names next to a row of doorbells on the concrete wall.

Horst stepped up. "Any luck?"

In her haste, she had to scan the list twice to locate the name Sturm. Apartment No. 15. She pushed the white button and waited. She fidgeted, shifting her weight from one leg to the other. What happened to the agents whose cars were in the street?

Finally, a male voice creaked from the speaker above the nameplates. "Who is it?"

"Sabine Maier, BND."

"Fourth floor." The buzzer sounded and Horst pushed in the door. They stepped into a small lobby. No elevator. Sabine charged up the stairs, Horst close behind. They were both breathing hard when they reached the fourth-floor landing. Which way? She turned left down a narrow hallway while Horst went right. She passed Apartment 13, then this side of the hall ended at No. 12.

"Over here," Horst called out. She turned back and found him standing in front of No. 15, the second apartment in the right-hand corridor. He lifted an iron doorknocker and gave her a questioning look.

She nodded.

He rapped on the door twice. After a moment, the light in the peephole darkened, then the door opened.

A young man, wire-rimmed glasses, square face, closely cropped hair, wearing a navy suit, guarded the threshold. "Credentials, please." He sounded too self-important for Sabine's taste.

Before she could fish the ID from her purse, a voice boomed from the living room. "*Guten Tag,* Frau Maier."

Surprised the agent she'd dealt with several years ago would remember her, Sabine walked over to him and extended a hand while trying to recall the graying man's name. In slacks and an open-collared shirt under a jacket, he dressed more informally than his over-eager assistant, but not as casually as Horst in his khakis.

He shook Sabine's hand. "Hans Mertens."

He must not only have noticed her failure to recall his name, but her anxious glances around the apartment as well. "The Sturms are gone."

"I was afraid of that."

"Sorry, Frau Maier, we went to the Foreign Office first. When we learned she left the office mid-morning, we got a warrant to search this place. And we've alerted law enforcement and border guards, of course."

Disappointed, Sabine turned toward Horst, then remembered she'd failed to introduce him. "Excuse my bad manners, Herr Mertens, I'd like you to meet—"

"No need for introduction. Herr Kögler and I were colleagues once." Mertens shook hands with Horst. "Don't tell me you signed on with the BND."

Sabine jumped in before Horst could respond. "Herr Kögler is working with me on this case. He's quite the computer expert, you know."

Mertens studied them both and nodded. He seemed willing to accept her response, even though it skirted his question. After introducing his assistant, he said, "I had the fingerprint experts go through the place before we touched anything. Should have a report tomorrow—expect most of the prints to match those on Gisela Sturm's security clearance. At least you'll have her husband's and son's prints."

Sabine nodded. "We appreciate your taking care of things until we got here. If you want to give us a quick tour of the apartment, we can take it from there."

"Of course." Mertens led them through the carpeted living room past a corner sofa. An imitation-wood cabinet on the far wall held a large TV, a radio, stereo, and two speakers flanking a row of books. She'd check what the Sturms were reading later.

They trudged through a kitchen large enough to accommodate a round breakfast table, then a dining room nook, a master suite, a small bedroom wallpapered with images of racecars, and an adjoining bathroom, to end up in a study with a built-in desk jutting out from the wood-paneled wall. A typewriter, a beige telephone, but no papers or personal items like photos.

Mertens pointed at the phone. "The only thing of interest we've come across so far is a phone message."

He pushed a button, and a female voice sounded. "Gisela, this is Monika. Just checking to make sure you're okay. Please call me at the office as soon as you get this message." After a beep, an electronic male voice announced, "*Montag, 14 Uhr 10.*"

"No last name, no phone number. Just a Monika calling at ten minutes after two," Mertens commented. "A friend who's worried about Gisela Sturm. If we can figure out why, maybe we can find her."

"If she's a friend, Sturm's coworkers might know her," Sabine said. "But we can't do anything about that till they come to work in the morning."

Horst opened his mouth as if about to speak, but remained mute at her headshake. He probably had the same thought as she about searching his database for a Monika, but Mertens didn't need to know that. They walked back to the living room where the young agent was still standing guard by the door.

Mertens pressed two keys into Sabine's hand. "An extra set I had made for you. The rent is paid till the end of the month, so take as long as you need to check this place over. And let me know if you want us to lend a hand. I can send over a team to do a complete search."

"That's very generous," Sabine said.

"No more turf wars like in the old days?" Horst asked.

"Believe it or not, things have changed since your time," Mertens said. "Too many intelligence failures due to a lack of coordination. Management now strongly encourages us to cooperate fully with the BND."

"Wish it had been that way when I was there," Horst said. "Not that I want to come back."

"Understood. Sounds like you found your niche in computers." Mertens pulled a card from his wallet, on which he wrote with a pen he'd produced from a jacket pocket.

He handed the card to Sabine. "Call me at home later and let me know where I can reach you. Maybe I'll have news on the Sturms." He motioned for his assistant to open the door.

When the Cologne intelligence officers entered the hall, a female voice said, "Pardon."

Sabine stepped to the open door and caught a glimpse of an attractive blonde in a business suit. The woman turned and entered the stairs to the fifth floor.

As Mertens and his assistant took the staircase down, Sabine closed the door, perplexed at the blonde's walking the fourth floor before going up to the fifth. She could think of several plausible explanations. The woman could have visited neighbors living on this floor or she might have been lost. Sabine didn't trust coincidences, but maybe she was getting paranoid, reading too much into an innocent encounter.

♫ ♫ ♫

After a brisk five-minute walk from the streetcar stop, Monika turned onto Veil Straße. Careful not to trip on the uneven sidewalk, she almost missed the white van and gray Opel parked in front of Gisela's building. Hmm. Government vehicles? She hurried to the door and reached for the Sturms' doorbell, but stopped herself. Thoughts tumbled through her mind. Gisela left her office midmorning after Klaus called her; didn't inform her boss; didn't return my call; government cars outside her building.

Still, why not ring the doorbell and see whether she answers? At that moment the sound of a bolt retracting caught her attention. The door opened a gap, which narrowed for a moment, then grew wider. An elderly man appeared across the threshold, his face straining from the effort of pulling the heavy door open.

Monika reached for the handle and pushed the door open all the way. "Let me help you."

"Thank you." The old man smiled at her, then shuffled down the sidewalk.

Shouldn't be this easy to sneak into buildings with locked front doors. She climbed to the fourth floor, two steps at a time. As she approached Apartment 15, the door opened and out stepped two men. What were they doing in the Sturm apartment? Federal agents?

Monika mumbled an apology. At that moment a slender woman in a gray, pinstriped business suit, auburn hair, appeared at the threshold. For a second, Monika considered asking about the Sturms, but then thought better of it. She turned, hurried down the hall and took the stairs to the top floor. She hoped she'd left the impression of someone who was lost.

The staircase featured a window on each floor affording a view of the front entrance below. Monika moved to the one on the top floor and looked down. After a few minutes, the two men exited the building. The young one went to the van, the older of the two to the Opel where he fumbled with something on the dashboard. Playing the radio before he drove off? Except both cars remained at the curb.

She waited. Why weren't they leaving? She was still pondering what they were up to when the man in the Opel came back to the building. He gesticulated while talking into the building intercom—with the woman in the Sturm apartment?

The man returned to his car. Neither the Opel nor the van moved.

♫ ♫ ♫

While Horst began to search the master bedroom, Sabine returned to the study. Who had tipped off the Sturms this morning? If Mertens were to be believed, they had enough time to destroy or abscond with anything that might incriminate them or leave a clue. Maybe the agents had overlooked something in their preliminary search. Before she could open the top desk drawer, the intercom buzzed.

She hurried from the study and nearly collided with Horst, who came running down the hall. Where in the hell was the—?

Horst pointed to the intercom by the front door.

She pushed the gray button. "Who is it?"

"Mertens. I have a lead for you. At five thirteen a man fitting Klaus Sturm's description bought a ticket at the Cologne train station for the transit train to Berlin."

"One ticket or three?"

"One."

"He's traveling solo?"

"Appears that way," Mertens said.

"What about his wife and son?"

"No record of them purchasing tickets."

Sabine thought for a moment. "Do the Sturms have a car?"

"Black Mercedes sedan. Bonn license plate. Border guards are on alert, but so far, no sightings."

Should she keep searching the apartment or go to the train station?

As if reading her thoughts, Mertens said, "It's only been twenty minutes since Sturm bought his ticket."

"We'll be right down." Sabine disconnected and grabbed her purse and briefcase.

She didn't need to explain anything to Horst, who'd overheard the conversation. Once downstairs, he ran for his BMW while she approached the Opel.

Mertens rolled down his window. "You're going to the train station?"

"Yes. Maybe the husband is still there. A long shot, I know, but worth a try."

"Agreed," Mertens said. "And don't worry about the apartment. I'll have it secured and send in a full search team. Can't promise the search will be tonight, but for sure in the morning."

Before she could respond, Horst drove up and opened the passenger door. She returned her attention to Mertens. "I really appreciate your—"

"Like I said, these days it's all about cooperation and coordination." He rolled up his window.

Sabine dashed around the front of the BMW, and jumped in. "How far to the Cologne train station?"

"Less than thirty kilometers." Horst stepped on the gas pedal. "Twenty minutes, maybe."

♫ ♫ ♫

When the woman she'd seen in the Sturm apartment left the building with another man, Monika opened the fifth-floor staircase window and leaned out for a better view. The woman talked to the driver of the Opel, while her companion hurried along the sidewalk to a BMW. A few moments later, the BMW made a U-turn, picked up the woman, and sped off. Monika waited for the van and Opel to follow, but they remained at the curb. Agents on a stakeout?

Not much doubt—Gisela and Klaus were in serious trouble. She needed to keep her distance and not get involved.

But how could she leave unnoticed with the agents watching the building? A movement caught her attention. The men left their vehicles, walked up to the front door, and entered the building. Monika shut the window, stepped to the staircase railing and listened. Footsteps echoed up the stairwell, grew louder, then ebbed as the men exited on the floor below. At the sound of an apartment door being opened then closed, Monika walked down the stairs, threw an anxious glance as she passed the vacant fourth floor, then ran the rest of the way down.

She kept running when she hit the sidewalk and didn't slow until she turned the corner, leaving Veil Straße behind. During the streetcar ride home, she speculated about what the Sturms might have done to warrant a search of their apartment. Perhaps Klaus had been involved in some shady deals. She didn't really know what he did for a living. If he'd been arrested, Gisela and Rainer might be at the police station. Should she go there and find out? No, she'd call Gisela's office in the morning. If Frau Huber knew something, she would tell her.

Monika had almost convinced herself that Klaus must be the one in trouble with law enforcement, when a terrible suspicion took hold of her. Gisela had access to top-secret documents at the Foreign Office. She wouldn't be the first government secretary caught passing secrets to the communists. As much as Monika tried, she could not banish the thought from her mind.

Chapter Forty-Four

German Punctuality

Cologne, West Germany, Monday 8 August 1977

A female voice boomed from loudspeakers in the Cologne train station's entry hall. "*Achtung. Transit Zug nach Berlin, Gleis Acht. Abfahrt in einer Minute. Bitte sofort einsteigen.*"

Horst and Sabine ran up the escalator, squeezing by passengers who stood on the steps. At the top landing, she grabbed his elbow. "We've got less than a minute. Track eight. Which way?"

He pointed to the far end of the terminal. Sabine charged into the throng of travelers milling about. Trying to keep up, Horst jostled a few elbows and drew stares. Unless the train was delayed they'd never make it. They were sprinting past track number six when a shrill whistle blew, doors slammed, then wheels squealed on steel tracks. By the time they reached platform eight, the red lights of the rear car were disappearing into the distance.

Hunched over, hands on thighs, Sabine muttered between gasps for air, "German trains. Always so damn punctual."

Horst drew ragged breaths, reminding him how much fitness he'd lost from his days as an agent. Out of breath—a good excuse not to respond. Whatever he said would only frustrate her more.

She straightened. "Let's find a phone."

"They're in the entry hall."

They made their way back through the crowd and rode the elevator down, this time without bumping into anyone. Horst led her to a row of phone booths between the restrooms, all occupied except one. He pulled back the accordion door, and she stepped inside. She rummaged through her purse, but quit when he handed her a few coins from his pocket. While she dialed, he took a step back and let go of the door.

The dull Plexiglas rendered Sabine a fuzzy image, but anchored in his mind were her dark eyes sparkling with energy, her auburn hair, and the figure even a gray business suit couldn't hide. He owed her privacy, no matter how much he wanted to squeeze into the booth with her. Stop the fantasies. She's right. Keep things on a professional level while we're working together. Push hard now and you'll ruin your chances for later.

Her voice drifted from the booth, but he could only catch the ebb and flow of a steady tone interspersed with excited outbursts. She might be talking to Mertens, who'd asked her to call him for news about the Sturms. No sense speculating. To distract himself, he watched travelers hurrying through the hall, trying to guess their destination.

The booth door opened, and Sabine stepped out. "Let's get the car." She strode toward the exit. "I'll explain on the way."

He fell in behind. "Where are we going?"

"I need to spend the night in Bonn and go to the Foreign Office in the morning." She stopped at the exit. "I wish you could come with me, but it's out of the question. I'll plead emergency when Dorfmann quizzes me about your presence at the Sturm apartment. But I can't possibly get away with letting a private citizen sit in on interviews at the Ministry."

Horst swallowed. "Seems to me, as a consultant, I need to have access to all the facts and evidence. And as a former agent, I'm not exactly your average private citizen."

She laid a hand on his forearm. "Sorry, Horst, but that's not going to work."

"I thought not. Worth a try, though." When she withdrew her hand after a soft squeeze, he continued, "Almost makes me wish I was still working with Mertens. Almost but not quite."

They walked to the corner of the building, crossed the street and entered the parking lot where he'd left the BMW.

On the drive back to Bonn, he asked, "Did Mertens have any news you can tell me about?"

"Look, Horst, I'm not holding back any information that's relevant to this case. Just because I can't take you along—"

"Sorry, I was off base." He stared straight ahead. "I'm just frustrated."

"I understand. Here is what Mertens told me. He'll try to contact *Bundesbahn* management and ask to have the conductor search for Klaus Sturm. But he didn't hold out much hope. Even if they locate Sturm, he doubts they'd be able to stop the train and whisk him off."

He glanced at her. "Why not?"

"I'm not sure, but I think they have Stasi personnel on those trains. If so, Sturm is safe."

"Looks like a lost cause."

"That's not all the bad news Mertens gave me," Sabine said. "Gisela is the one I'm most interested in. I believe she's the mole who passed Foreign Office documents to the East. But she and the son are gone as well. Their Mercedes passed the border at Helmstedt late this afternoon."

"That's a good three-and-a-half-hour drive from Bonn. They must have left about noon while her husband stayed behind to clear the apartment of spy toys. He probably took a cab to the train station."

"That's my guess. Mertens is checking with the taxi companies."

As they approached Bonn, Horst asked where they were staying.

Sabine cleared her throat. "Mertens is booking me a room at a hotel that's just a few minutes' walk from the Ministry."

"What about me? I thought I'd be driving you back after your interviews tomorrow."

"You're welcome to spend the night in Bonn as well. Mertens thought the hotel would have plenty of rooms since there aren't any meetings or conventions going on this week. But don't you need to get back for Sara?"

"No, I'm having a neighbor take care of her." He glanced over. When she raised her eyebrows, he added, "He only has access to the residence."

"Good to know your shop is secure." She took a deep breath. "I'd like to ask you a favor."

He didn't like the sound of that, but still he said, "Yes?"

"Would you be willing to drive back to Munich tonight after you drop me off? I want you to search your database for a Monika. It's critical we find her as soon as possible. But if you're too tired and want to wait till morning—"

"No, I can manage. But what about your ride back?"

"I'll take the train or rent a car if necessary. Dorfmann will spring for a car rental after he hears what happened to my poor VW."

"He'd better." He stopped at the first traffic light. "You have the directions?"

A few minutes later, he pulled into the circular driveway of Hotel Freiburg, a narrow high-rise of tinted glass and steel. They had a reservation in Sabine's name. After she'd checked in, Horst walked her to the elevator.

She pushed the button. "You sure you're okay driving back tonight?"

"No problem."

"If you find a Monika, please call me. Here at the hotel or at the Foreign Office in the morning." She shook his hand. "Thank you. I really appreciate all you did for me today."

The elevator opened and she entered. The door closed behind her, and Horst stood there for a moment, before walking back to the car. He was not looking forward to the five-hour drive, his only solace being that he'd earned Sabine's trust. Even if his program failed to turn up something useful, she'd know he'd given it his all. Still, he'd rather spend the evening with her than racing back down the autobahn. He thought he'd left the life of chasing elusive leads behind when he quit the Office for the Protection of the Constitution. And now he was right back to the lonely ways of an agent.

As he left the city streets behind, he told himself he was doing this for the cause of catching commie spies and their targets, but he wouldn't mind if it also impressed Agent Sabine Maier.

♫ ♫ ♫

When Horst arrived home a few minutes after midnight, Sara wagged her tail and nudged him with a cold, wet muzzle. As he stroked her soft ears, she nosed the leather leash hanging by the door and turned soulful eyes on him.

"Not tonight, Sara." Careful not to say the word "walk," whose meaning she'd figured out long ago, Horst opened the door to the backyard. With a sigh, she strolled outside. She doused her favorite corner and trotted back into the house. He then entered the shop and turned on a computer. He stroked Sara's ears until the screen lit up with the program that contained all the personnel records they'd input so far. A few keystrokes and the search for a Monika was under way.

He leaned back, and Sara nudged his elbow. Ignoring her insistent request for a walk, he rubbed her belly while waiting for the computer results. Finally, the printer sprang to life and spit out a sheet with only one name: Monika Fischer; birth date 25/03/1944; single; Federal Ministry of the Interior, 05/01/1970 – 11/02/1977.

Horst put down the paper. He'd expected more than one Monika working for the federal agencies entered in his system. Not only that, but the one produced by the program left the Interior Ministry in February. Something in the back of his mind nagged at him. The name sounded familiar. He called up her full record on the screen and scrolled down until he found the entry that explained his vague recollection: Convicted 15/04/1977 of espionage and sentenced to five years in prison. Horst now recalled the news accounts of her trial this spring for delivering state secrets to a Stasi agent.

Since Monika Fischer had just started serving her sentence, she couldn't be the one who'd left the message on the Sturm answering machine. Either Gisela's worried friend didn't work for the federal government, or he didn't have the records of the agency where she might be employed.

He turned off the computer and herded Sara back to the residence. There was nothing more he could do tonight. Maybe someone at the Foreign Office could put Sabine on the trail of Gisela's friend Monika. If not, they'd hit yet another dead end.

Chapter Forty-Five

On Monika's Trail

Bonn and Munich, Tuesday, 9 August 1977

As the fast-moving train devoured the landscape between Bonn and Munich, Sabine drummed her fingers on the shelf protruding from the window ledge. She thought about her early morning visit to the Foreign Office, which had brought her no closer to solving the mystery of Monika. The minister had been summoned to the Chancellery presumably to explain his executive secretary's disappearance and to prepare him for the anticipated grilling at the hands of the opposition party in the parliament.

None of the employees Sabine interviewed knew much about Gisela's life outside the office. She was married and had a child—that was about the extent of their collective knowledge. As befitting a spy, Gisela had kept her private life private. No one had ever heard of a Monika.

To walk off her frustration, Sabine bypassed the elevator. She made it halfway down the stairs when the secretary she'd interviewed last yelled down the staircase, "Just a moment, Frau Maier."

Sabine stopped, hopeful of a breakthrough. "Did you think of something else?" She couldn't remember the redhead's name.

"Sorry we couldn't help you, but I thought of the person who might know something about Gisela's friends."

"Who is that?"

"Our receptionist, Frau Huber."

Sabine started up the stairs. "Good, I'll come up and—"

"She's not in today. But if you go to personnel, they might tell you how to get in touch with her."

The glass door to the train compartment slid open, bringing Sabine back to the present. A portly conductor scrutinized her, the cabin's sole passenger. "Ticket, please."

Sabine fished the stub from her purse. After he'd punched it and left, her thoughts returned to the wasted morning. By pleading national security, she'd managed to worm the receptionist's home phone number out of the personnel director. He even let her use his phone. Sabine gave up after the tenth ring. Not even an answering machine to leave a message.

Her hand hurt; she must have hit the shelf. If only she'd brought something to read to distract herself. As it was, she'd worry and speculate all the way to Munich whether Horst's program might have turned up the Monika they were looking for.

♫ ♫ ♫

A guttural sound turned into ferocious barking. Horst sat straight up in bed. Sara stood at the door to the hall.

"Hush!"

Horst reached for the top nightstand drawer where he kept the Walther PPK, but a glance at the clock dissuaded him. Eight-thirty. An hour for visitors, not burglars. He never slept this late, but then he usually didn't drive past midnight and work afterwards till the wee hours. He swung his feet into the bedside slippers and shuffled to the closet to grab his robe. He eased the bedroom door open and led a growling Sara down the hall by her collar. Once they reached the kitchen, Horst commanded her to stay.

He slipped out the door to the shop and listened. The clickety-clack of typewriter keys from the reception meant Erika Braun had arrived. But Sara never barked at her, so someone must be with her. Female voices drifting into the shop validated his assumption. For a moment, he considered returning to the house to dress, but then discarded the idea. His shy days were behind him.

When he turned the corner, Erika quit typing and offered a "Good morning" that he could have sworn had a tinge of sarcasm in it.

Two BND secretaries he remembered from last week ogled his robe before returning his greeting. On the counter sat a box.

"More records?" he asked.

The senior of the two replied, "The Chancellery files you've been waiting for. Herr Dorfmann thought the two of us could enter those in a couple of hours."

"Good, let's get started." He led them into the shop and readied two computers for their input.

Upon returning to the kitchen, he found Sara stretched out on the floor, apparently assured of her master's safety. Horst started the coffeemaker and headed for the shower. Breakfast consisted of cereal and black coffee. Finally fully awake after his second cup, he felt excitement building at the prospect that the mysterious Monika might be working at the Chancellery. Slim odds, but he had nothing else to go on. He put the dishes in the sink and peeked into the shop. Eyes on the computer screens, the two secretaries let their fingers fly over the keyboards. Not wanting to distract them, Horst closed the door.

How to temper his impatience and dissipate nervous energy? Sara's silent plea for her morning walk provided the answer. Before he even made a move to grab the leash, she jumped up and wagged her tail. She never failed to sense when he'd decided to take her. Intuition, a change in his energy—whatever the cause, she picked up on it without fail.

An hour later he returned a panting Sara to the house—he'd peppered their brisk walk with a few short runs. Full of anticipation, he stepped into the shop. Finding no one there, he hurried to the reception.

"Where are the secretaries?"

Erika looked up. "They left a few minutes ago. Said to tell you the Chancellery records are in the system."

"Really?" Barely acknowledging Erika's nod, he turned on his heel.

The computer search for Monika yielded two names this time: the Monika Fischer on last night's report plus a Monika Fuchs, secretary at the Chancellery. Gisela's friend? He printed her full profile and picked up the phone. He could study the printout later. Right now he had to get hold of Sabine before she left Bonn.

Horst was all for security and privacy, but the way the Foreign Office receptionist was stonewalling reminded him all too much of his agent days.

"I'm sorry, sir, but we have no Sabine Maier here."

"I know that." He swallowed *du dummkopf.* "As I just told you, she is there interviewing some of your employees."

"Your name, sir?"

"Horst Kögler. I'm her—"

"Just a moment."

A click, then another, followed by a baritone, "Personnel. Herr . . ."

"Kögler."

"You are asking about Sabine Maier?"

"Yes. I need to talk to her right away."

"And what is your business with Frau Maier?"

Horst thought for a moment. Consultant, meaning private citizen, would get him nowhere. "I'm her colleague."

"BND?"

"Yes," he lied.

"Sorry, but Frau Maier has already left."

"How long ago?"

"You can ask her that when you see her, Herr Kögler. *Aufwiederhören.*" Click.

Horst slammed down the phone. This recalcitrant bureaucrat either hadn't gotten the message about the new policy of cooperation Mertens had spouted or the Foreign Office couldn't be bothered.

♫ ♫ ♫

Sabine called Systems Solutions from the Munich train station. Horst answered on the second ring.

After she identified herself, he said, "I tried to reach you this morning at the Foreign Office but you'd already left."

"You found a Monika?"

"Two, actually. One is Monika Fischer. She's in prison."

Sabine searched her memory. "Secretary at the Interior Ministry who passed secrets to a Stasi Romeo."

"That's the one."

"Dead end." Sabine swiped a strand of hair from her brow. "What about the other?"

"Monika Fuchs, secretary at the Chancellery."

Sabine's pulse quickened. "You have the Chancellery records?"

"Delivered this morning and entered in the system by two of Dorfmann's secretaries."

"It's about time we got those. But tell me about this Monika."

"Works for the chief of the Chancellery; has full security clearance."

"How long with the Chancellery?"

"Let me see." The sound of paper rustling came over the line. "Here it is, hired in 1965."

"Twelve years," Sabine said mostly to herself. "How old?"

"Born in forty-two."

Sabine did a quick calculation. "Thirty-five. Is she . . . ?" She couldn't compete with a departure announcement blaring from a loudspeaker above the row of public phones.

When the echo in the hall subsided, she spoke into the phone again, "Horst, can you hear me?"

"Yes, but I couldn't understand your question."

"No wonder. My eardrums were about to burst." She collected her thoughts. "I wanted to know if this Monika is married."

"She was until a few weeks ago." After a moment, Horst added, "She fits the profile, doesn't she? Divorced, right age, executive secretary to the chief of the Chancellery, security clearance. I'd be surprised if the Stasi didn't have her in its sights."

"You're right. She could be the one—Gisela's friend, and maybe more."

"You mean collaborator?" Horst asked.

"I intend to find out. But first I need to get my hands on your printout. I'm taking a taxi home. What if I stop by on my way and—?"

"I have a better idea. I'll pick you up and you can study the materials while we're having dinner somewhere."

"You don't need to—"

"But I'm dying to hear how you fared at the Foreign Office."

Sabine gave an exaggerated sigh. "Don't remind me."

"It's settled then. Meet you in front of the station in about twenty."

He hung up before she could respond. Dinner had been the furthest thing from her mind, but now she hungered for a good meal, Horst's company, and intelligence pointing the way to Gisela's friend Monika.

Chapter Forty-Six

Peace Conference

Cologne, Tuesday evening, 9 August 1977

Günter swiveled his barstool toward Hotel Solitude's entrance for the umpteenth time. The revolving door moved. This time it had to be Monika. A young couple emerged, dashing his hopes yet again. He turned back and sipped his martini.

"Expecting someone?" the bartender asked.

Günter set down his nearly empty glass. "Yes, but she's half an hour late." Could Monika have stood him up?

"Women." The bartender studied him for a moment, then leaned forward and said in a conspiratorial tone, "If you're in the mood for female company, I can arrange—"

"No, thanks, she'll be along." Lots of men paid for sex; he wasn't one of them.

"As you wish." The young man straightened. "Another martini then?"

Günter swallowed the rest of his drink and nodded. Might as well drown his sorrows. He racked his brain for anything he might have said or done that could have offended Monika or aroused her suspicion. Maybe she was having second thoughts about their romance. Not likely. Their intimacy, the way they made love, said otherwise.

His second martini arrived and he took a swig. Could the fabulous sex and the terrific way they got along be the problem? Maybe the scars from a loveless marriage made her pull back, not trusting another man, not wanting to get too close. As he took another swallow, he tried to tell himself there was a simple explanation for her no-show—traffic, an accident, working late.

His peripheral vision alerted him to a movement. He turned, bracing for another disappointment. At the sight of Monika exiting the revolving door in a cocktail dress, he tossed a ten-mark bill on the bar, jumped off his stool, and rushed into the lobby. She headed for the reception, blonde curls bouncing against her bare shoulders with every step.

"Monika, over here."

Her face lit up. She rushed to his side and hugged him. "Sorry for being so late. My boss insisted I finish a project before he agreed to give me tomorrow off." She kissed him on the cheek. "You didn't think I stood you up, did you?"

"The thought did cross my mind." With his hands on her petite waist, he held her at arm's length, forcing his gaze from the plunging décolleté to eyes warmed by her smile. "You look absolutely stunning."

She blushed. "I took the time to go home and change. No fun going on a rendezvous in office clothes, and you did say something about dinner at a fancy French restaurant."

"Yes, we have a reservation at seven thirty."

"Where is—?"

"Right here. That's why I picked this cozy little hotel."

She studied him. "You mean your meeting isn't here?"

"No. I wanted privacy. Just the two of us."

She glanced at the clock above the reception and took him by the hand. "We've got half an hour. You want to show me your room?"

Too excited to wait for the elevator, he led her up one flight of stairs and down a hallway, keys at the ready. He hardly had opened the door when she pressed her body against his and fumbled with his shirt buttons. He kicked the door shut and tore off his shirt. She kissed him hard, then stepped back and turned around. It took him a second to spot the rear zipper running down her back. A quick pull and the silky dress dropped to her ankles. She stepped out and turned back.

He was fumbling with the zipper on his khakis when she removed his hand. "Let me."

With the tender touch of teasing hands she freed him of his slacks. He guided her to the large bed as they flung their last pieces of clothing onto the carpet. Then he stopped himself. What kind of lover was he? Women wanted foreplay not a brute conquest.

As if reading his thoughts, she said, "It's okay. I'm ready." She guided him deep inside her. The sensation almost made him lose control, but somehow he managed to hang on until she climaxed. With his face pressed into the pillow, he released with one long guttural sound. He lay there motionless, waiting for his pulse to slow until Monika's gentle prodding encouraged him to roll over to the side. Lying on his back, he gazed at the ceiling and marveled at the intensity this woman elicited from him.

Monika stroked his hip. "Not bad for a quickie."

"The perfect hors d'oeuvre for a Gallic gourmet meal," he quipped.

She laughed. "I'm sure the French would approve."

♫ ♫ ♫

During their lighthearted dinner conversation Günter wondered how a woman who'd endured a rotten marriage as long as Monika had, could be so passionate a lover. She didn't strike him as the straying wife. Maybe sex had been the one positive aspect of her marriage. Well, he wasn't the first man to be puzzled by a woman. He really should broach the subject of Monika's job and explore whether she might be amenable to helping out a benevolent Vienna peace organization. Heinrich expected no less. But as much as he tried to engage his spy mode, he could not bring himself to spoil the atmosphere.

Then Monika did. She placed her fork and knife atop her empty plate and looked him in the eye. "Do you know Gisela Sturm?" Gone was the warm smile.

Where had he heard that name? "Isn't that the friend you told about our get-together in Vienna?"

She nodded without taking her eyes off him.

What had caused her sudden mood shift? "Didn't you say she works at the Foreign Office?"

"Yes."

Still perplexed as to what she might be after, he said, "Why do you ask?"

"I was just wondering whether you two might know each other."

"Never met the woman. What makes you think otherwise?"

"Some of the things she said."

Günter fought impatience. "Such as?"

"She urged me to visit you in Vienna, as if it really mattered to her." Monika lowered her gaze and played with the stem of her wineglass. "Gisela was so insistent that I see you. I didn't think much of it at the time, but now—"

"What has changed?"

Monika quit fingering her glass and looked at him. "She's disappeared."

Günter leaned forward. "Disappeared how?"

"She rushed from her office yesterday after a phone call. Didn't tell anyone where she was going. She was supposed to meet me for lunch, but didn't show."

"Are you worried something's happened to her?"

The waiter appeared, cleared the table and walked off once they'd placed their order of after-dinner cognacs.

Günter reached across the table and covered Monika's hand with his. There had to be more to this than her worrying about Gisela or she wouldn't have probed into whether he knew her. He needed to ask innocuous questions. "Does this Gisela have family?"

"A husband and a son." She hesitated, then blurted, "And they've all vanished."

"How do you know?"

"I went to their apartment. They're gone and . . ."

She withdrew her hand while the waiter served the cognacs. Anxious to hear what Monika had planned to say before the interruption, Günter ignored his drink, but when she picked up hers, he followed suit. They clinked glasses, inhaled the aroma, and sipped.

"You were about to say something about what you found at the apartment."

She studied the bulbous brandy glass, cradling it with both hands as if to warm the liquid. He thought it more likely she was contemplating whether to tell him more. Hoping she'd soon feel like filling the silence, he remained mute. Don't push, or she'll clam up.

After a long moment, she returned her gaze to him. "I'm not sure I should be telling you this, but it looked like their apartment was being searched."

"Police?"

"I don't know. Three men and a woman. Not in uniform."

Günter scooted to the edge of his chair. "You have a hunch about who they were?"

"By the vehicles in the street, I'm guessing they were some type of law enforcement."

"Do you have any idea what kind of trouble Gisela and her family might be in?"

"No, unless—"

"Yes?"

"Unless it has something to do with her job."

"You said she was a secretary at the Foreign Office?"

"Not just any secretary, but executive secretary. To the foreign minister."

Günter exhaled. "You don't think she stole—?"

"I don't know what to think. It's all so mysterious."

He once more covered her hand with his. "I'm sorry. I shouldn't jump to conclusions. Maybe there is an innocent explanation for this."

She squeezed his hand, and gazed at him. He didn't believe his own words. Gisela Sturm must have been one of Heinrich's moles. That's how he'd known about the Vienna tryst beforehand. And the Sturms apparently had plenty of warning to allow them to flee. That meant another mole had alerted them or Heinrich that West German intelligence was on their trail. What if they picked up his scent? Maybe they already had. Would Heinrich warn him in time?

"Günter, I'm sorry I brought this up. Let's drop it and enjoy our time together."

He returned her squeeze. "You're right."

But while they finished their cognacs, he couldn't stop wondering why she'd asked him whether he knew Gisela. He was glad now he hadn't pressed for details about her job at the Chancellery. Her friend's disappearance had obviously spooked her to the point she might be suspicious even of him. Good thing Heinrich had set up a cover on the off chance Monika would go so far as to check whether there really was a peace conference.

On their way to the elevator he resolved to forget about Heinrich and the Stasi. Maybe impossible, but if anyone could help him achieve that, it was the sexy woman at his side.

♫ ♫ ♫

At a feather kiss on her forehead, Monika opened her eyes. Günter, wearing a sports shirt and khakis, stood at the side of the bed. She pulled him down for a kiss on the lips, but he didn't linger.

He stepped back from the bed. "I didn't mean to wake you."

"What time is it?"

"Eight thirty."

She sat up. "I never sleep this late." She wagged a finger at him. "You shouldn't keep a girl up most of the night."

She lifted the covers, but he stopped her. "Don't get up. I'm off to the conference; should be back about four. Your turn to choose where we go for dinner."

"Wait. Where is your conference?"

He hesitated.

"It's not a secret, is it?"

"Not exactly, but we prefer to keep it quiet. And besides, you won't be able to reach me there."

"All the same, I'd like to know, just in case." She wasn't sure what she meant by that, but damn it, she wanted him to tell her.

"It's in an office complex on Lindblatt Street, about a ten-minute walk."

"What's the number?"

Günter looked at her, but didn't say anything.

Then it hit her why he was so reticent. "I understand. My job at the Chancellery—"

"I trust you, Monika, or I wouldn't have told you about the conference in the first place." He kissed her on the cheek. "If you must know, the meeting is at Lindblatt Straße 65." On his way out, he added, "Enjoy the city. See you around four."

She stared at the door long after he'd closed it behind him. His reluctance to disclose the meeting location bothered her. A legitimate reason based on secrecy imposed by the conference organizers, or Günter's personal motives? She intended to find out.

After a quick shower, Monika arrived at the hotel buffet breakfast just before it closed. With the help of the concierge's city map, Monika found her way to Lindblatt Street. She passed numerous retail shops, a department store, and several apartment buildings until she spied the numerals 65 etched into the glass door of a five-story building.

Hands on the chrome door handle, she hesitated. Günter had trusted her, and here she was checking up on him. Still, she had to satisfy herself that he'd told her the truth. She'd just make sure there was such a meeting and leave. The door opened onto a high-ceiling lobby. As she crossed the tile floor, she caught her reflection in the polished stainless-steel doors of two elevators straight ahead. To her right, a young man in a blue uniform rose from a chair behind a metal desk.

"Could you tell me where the meeting rooms are?" she asked.

His gaze traveled from her face to her breasts, where it lingered much too long, then traced her curves all the way down. "Second floor. Which meeting would you like to go to?"

At his leering and suggestive tone, Monika crossed her arms over her chest. Since she didn't want him to know she was looking for the peace conference, she groped for a plausible response.

She fashioned a smile she hoped conveyed embarrassment. "My boss only told me to attend a meeting here this morning. Is there more than one?"

The custodian gave her a skeptical look. "We have three meetings going on. Stamp collectors, sports car owners, and some kind of international conference."

Before he could ask her which one she was looking for, she quickly said, "Thank you," turned on her heel and headed for the staircase next to the elevators.

She climbed the flight of stairs, not so much to verify that the international conference was taking place, but to keep up the pretense of wanting to attend, lest the custodian grow more suspicious. From the second-floor landing, she stepped onto the taupe carpet of a long hallway leading to several meeting rooms. Not wanting to return to the lobby, she moved along the corridor in hopes of finding another exit.

On the wall by the first room hung a glass case that displayed images of vintage postal stamps. A sign on the door welcomed stamp collectors of North-Rhine Westphalia. She walked on and passed a table covered with photos of sports cars. In their midst stood a placard, on which was written in large letters, *Sportwagen Klub Köln.*

She didn't encounter anyone until she reached the third meeting room. Sitting behind a table, a gray-haired woman in a navy business suit looked up with a puzzled expression indicating surprise at facing a straggler. She fingered a folder in front of her. Monika hesitated. No doubt a list of conference attendees. Did it contain Günter's name?

Despite the attendant's stare that did not invite questions, or perhaps because of it, Monika stopped and said, "Pardon me; I'm not sure I'm in the right place. Is this the international conference?"

The woman opened the folder. "Your name?"

"Oh, you won't find me in there. I was just wondering whether you can tell me—"

"Sorry, but this meeting is by invitation only. So I need to ask you to move on."

Suppressing a tart response, Monika nodded and walked down the hall where she found a small staircase that led to an exit on a side street. On her way back to the front entrance on Lindblatt, she thought about what her visit had accomplished. While she hadn't been able to ascertain the name of the conference, she had to be satisfied with what she'd found. The secretiveness displayed by the woman stationed in front of the last room all but confirmed the meeting's nature—the international peace conference, which as Günter had said, was not for publication.

As she strolled along Lindblatt on the lookout for a promising dinner restaurant, she kept thinking about the man she was in love with. Everything he'd told her checked out. He wasn't a fraud, but worthy of her trust. And he'd never probed for details about her job at the Chancellery.

Even though he hadn't asked her to disclose information, she'd brought the illicit copy of the Bundeswehr memorandum. But now her conscience was nagging at her. She simply couldn't betray her country. Nor could she take the risk of jeopardizing her career and maybe more. She should have shredded the memo before leaving the office yesterday.

Chapter Forty-Seven

Out of Office

BND, Pullach, Wednesday, 10 August 1977

Sabine took a deep breath, then several more. She could have sworn she hadn't taken time to breathe during the rapid-fire report she'd delivered to Dorfmann for the last ten minutes. He didn't react until she told him of the failed brakes, which elicited a headshake, followed by, "You must be one hell of a driver, Frau Maier, and crazy not to pull over."

She searched his face for signs of disapproval, but his expression gave nothing away. No telling whether he thought her a failure, as she did. He poured two cups of coffee from a carafe on his credenza and offered her one. She took the hot beverage; something to slurp and hold while she waited impatiently for his response.

He took his time to drink his coffee. Finally, he set down his cup. "Do you think you could save your breakthroughs for the time I'm in the office? I'm gone for two days, and what happens? You and Kögler expose the foreign minister's secretary as a spy. You survive driving without brakes, but instead of calling the office to come to your rescue, you sweet-talk Kögler into chauffeuring you to Bonn."

She cringed at his words, expecting a reproach for having skirted regulations.

Instead, he said, "The Sturms have fled, but you've picked up a lead on a Chancellery secretary. I suggest you head for Bonn before she disappears too."

Relieved he didn't consider her incompetent, she responded, "Well, we don't know whether Monika Fuchs was in cahoots with Sturm. If she was, she'd be . . . oh no!"

"What is it?"

"When I called her office this morning, I was told she's taken the day off." Blood rushed to her cheeks. Now Dorfmann would think her an amateur for sure. "She's either gone or—"

"Did you try her home?"

"The Chancellery refused to give me her home phone number."

"Who'd you talk to?"

"Personnel."

Dorfmann shook his head. "Obstinate bureaucrats. First they drag their feet when I ask for records, and now . . ." He pushed the intercom button. "Give me the personnel director at the Chancellery right away," he directed his secretary.

He disconnected and turned toward Sabine. "I will get you that phone number." He raised his coffee cup, but set it down hard when his secretary's voice came over the intercom.

"Herr Neuhauser is on line one."

Dorfmann picked up. After a perfunctory greeting, he got straight to the point. "I need the home phone number of your employee, Monika Fuchs." After listening for a few moments, he raised his voice. "I don't care what your regulations say. This is a matter of national security. I wouldn't want to be in your shoes if another spy slips through our fingers because you stood on procedure."

A long pause, during which Sabine studied the portraits on the wall. Both the president and the chancellor of West

Germany smiled as if approving of her boss's strong-arm tactics. The sound of a pencil scribbling caught her attention.

"Thank you." Dorfmann hung up.

He tore a sheet off a notepad, handed it to her, and pushed his phone across the desk. "Call her."

She dialed, mentally composing what she would say. She needn't have bothered. At the tenth ring, Sabine shrugged and hung up.

Dorfmann pulled the phone back. "No answering machine?"

She shook her head.

"Well then, take a fleet car to Bonn and find this Monika Fuchs. I'll alert the Chancellery that you're coming. You know who to contact if you need support?"

"Yes, Agent Mertens. He's been securing the apartment."

Sabine rose and turned to leave but stopped at her boss's voice.

"Before you go, I need to remind you it's against regulations to take a private citizen on an intelligence mission."

"Kögler?"

"I can overlook him driving you, but his presence at the Sturm apartment is a serious breach of protocol."

She swallowed, considering how to respond. What the hell, why not have a little fun? "I couldn't help but overhear what you said on the phone." She tried for a mischievous grin. "Something about not caring what the regulations said."

Dorfmann stared at her. Just when she thought she'd overstepped her bounds, he broke out in a hearty laugh. "Touché. You and my wife are the only ones who can get away with talking to me like that. Now, get out of here."

She walked to the door and out of the office.

His parting words followed her down the hall. "Call me if the bureaucrats at the Chancellery give you any more trouble."

Chapter Forty-Eight

The Interrogation

West German Chancellery, Bonn, Thursday Morning, 11 August 1977

Monika rushed toward her office past the support staff cubicles. She muttered hasty good morning greetings to the few secretaries who weren't on the phone or busy typing. She always arrived for work on time, but not today. Good thing her boss was out of the office. No one questioned why she was ten minutes late. She flung her purse on the desk and made a beeline for the kitchenette. While this promised to be a slow workday, she would need the caffeine to bolster the last bit of adrenaline remaining from the hectic early morning drive from Cologne.

After a night short on sleep, she'd kissed Günter goodbye and driven back to Bonn. She arrived at her apartment with barely enough time to shed her cocktail dress, shower, throw on her charcoal business suit, and fix a piece of toast, which she swallowed while running for the 8:15 streetcar. By then Günter would have boarded his flight to Vienna. When would she see him again?

In the kitchenette, she selected the largest mug in the cupboard, poured from the coffeemaker's half-full carafe, and added cream. A few gulps and she carried the precious concoction to her office. First things first. She opened her purse to retrieve the Bundeswehr memo so she could shred it. The intercom buzzed. She dropped the purse and answered, "Fuchs."

"Neuhauser here. Frau Fuchs, please come to personnel."

"Right now?"

"Yes." Click.

She stared at her half-open purse, trying to figure out what the personnel director could possibly want. Not to inform her of a promotion or a raise; those weren't announced until year's end. Maybe a reprimand for being late. Not likely, but she'd soon find out. She snapped the purse shut and dropped it in the bottom desk drawer, which she locked. After another gulp of coffee, she headed for the staircase and walked up one floor.

Neuhauser's secretary quit typing when Monika approached. "They're expecting you in the conference room."

They? This sounded ominous. Had someone noticed she'd made an extra copy of the Bundeswehr memo? Monika nodded and strode down the corridor, her heels clicking on the floor tiles. On her way, she peeked through the conference room's interior windows. Neuhauser was talking to a woman who had her back to the hallway. Well, maybe this wasn't going to be so bad after all. Monika knocked and entered.

Neuhauser stood. "Ah, there you are. Frau Fuchs, please meet Frau Sabine Maier."

The woman swiveled her chair around, rose and extended a hand. Monika stifled a gasp. She might not have recognized her but for the pinstriped business suit. This was the slender woman with mid-length auburn hair she'd encountered at the Sturm apartment. As they shook hands, Monika looked for signs of recognition in Sabine Maier's eyes—nothing.

Neuhauser pointed to a chair on the opposite side of the table. "Frau Maier is with the BND. She's here to ask you a few questions, and I've assured her of your full cooperation."

"Of course." Monika sat facing the BND agent. Satisfaction that she'd been right about federal agents searching the Sturm apartment gave way to apprehension about what this intelligence officer wanted from her. Probably to uncover the extent of her friendship with Gisela.

On his way out, Neuhauser said, "If there's anything you need, Frau Maier, please see my secretary."

As the echo of his footsteps in the hallway grew faint, Maier opened a small notebook at her side to a page bookmarked with a pen and looked up. "What were you doing at the Sturm apartment, Frau Fuchs? You weren't lost, were you?"

Monika took a deep breath. Best to be honest. "No, I wasn't."

"You're Gisela Sturm's friend, aren't you?"

"Yes. I'd come to check on Gisela, to make sure she was all right. When I saw strangers at her apartment, I didn't know what to think. I just wanted to get away."

Maier studied her. Monika met her gaze.

"Why were you worried about Frau Sturm?"

"She was supposed to meet me for lunch, but didn't show. And I couldn't reach her at her office." Though this agent would have found out about Gisela leaving the office after her husband's phone call, Monika saw no need to volunteer that she knew, lest she'd get the receptionist in trouble.

"How long have you known Gisela Sturm?"

"Quite a while." When the agent furrowed her brow, Monika added, "Let me see, we were both new in our jobs, so I guess it must have been around 1966. Could have been '67."

After scribbling in the notebook, Maier asked, "How did you meet?"

Monika thought for a moment. "I'm not sure I can recall." She scooted her chair closer to the table. "Do you mind telling me what's happened to Gisela? Is she in trouble?"

Maier's eyes sparkled as if she appreciated Monika's diversion. "I was hoping you could shed some light on that for me. Do you know where she is?"

"I have no idea."

"But you have a guess?"

She hated to be put on the spot. How to respond without drawing suspicion? She needed time to think, time this agent wouldn't let her have. "Well, since you are an intelligence officer, I must assume you're after spies. But I can't believe Gisela would have betrayed . . . I never saw anything suspicious in her behavior."

"She ever ask you about your work?"

"Well, of course, we were chatting about office politics, problems with coworkers and bosses. I guess, you could say we were gossiping." She gave Maier a sheepish look, hoping the admission would end her prying. It didn't.

"Did you all ever discuss sensitive or secret documents crossing your desks?"

"Never. We were repeatedly admonished not to talk about that to anyone."

The agent studied her for a long moment. Apparently satisfied with her answer, she said, "I still need you to tell me how the two of you met. You said it was in 1966 or 1967. Can you relate it to a specific—?"

"Oh yes, how could I have forgotten? I'd been with the Chancellery for a few months when my boss sent me to a seminar for federal support personnel. I believe that was in June of 1966. One afternoon, I got into an interesting conversation with a secretary from the Foreign Office. We had a lot in common, and she seemed nice. So we kept in touch and became good friends."

Maier wrote in her notebook, then looked up. "How did this conversation come about? Did you approach her or did she approach you?"

Monika shrugged. "I'm not sure."

"Try to recall."

"Hmm, let me think. I believe she walked up to me during a coffee break and asked me where I was working."

Maier nodded. No doubt Gisela's making first contact fit with Maier's notion of Gisela as a spy. As much as she resisted the thought, Monika had to accept that possibility.

Maier spoke again. "Frau Fuchs, it is very important that you answer my next question truthfully."

Monika swallowed. What now?

"Have you ever given Gisela Sturm any confidential information—?"

"I already told you that I didn't." Monika stared at the agent.

"Small talk and gossip, but no secrets, is that it?"

"Yes. That's all."

"And you never suspected your friend might be involved in something . . . shall we say untoward?"

"No."

"Very well." After writing in her book, Maier leaned closer. "I must ask you some personal questions. I see from your file that you recently divorced." She paused. When Monika didn't respond, the agent continued, "You took a two-week vacation after your divorce. Where did you go?"

None of your business was what she wanted to say. But this agent likely knew the answer to her question. "Italy."

"Spent time on the beach?"

"Yes."

Maier fixed her with a stare. "Frau Fuchs, you're not doing yourself any favors by making me drag every detail out of you. I suggest it is in your best interest to fully cooperate as Herr Neuhauser has assured me you would. So where exactly did you go in Italy?"

Warning received. Did this agent suspect her of having something to do with whatever illicit activities Gisela had engaged in? One thing seemed clear: stonewall and risk losing her job. "I spent two weeks in Viareggio on the Adriatic coast and traveled around Tuscany."

"By yourself?"

Monika hesitated. Chances were this agent didn't know about Günter, but why lie? It could only get her into trouble, and she had nothing to hide. "No, I traveled with a fellow tourist."

The next half hour, Monika found herself answering the most probing questions concerning Günter. When she related how he'd rescued her from an annoying Italian on the beach, something like a smirk crossed the agent's face. It was gone so fast that Monika doubted whether it had been there at all. Maybe lack of sleep had her imagining things.

Maier finally stopped the barrage of questions, laid down her pen, and leaned back. "You look tired, Frau Fuchs. How about if we take a coffee break?"

The soft approach. The carrot following the stick. But Monika needed more caffeine, so she nodded.

Maier stood. "I'll see what I can arrange." She left the room.

Monika replayed the agent's questions in her mind. She'd asked them with a slant that seemed to cast suspicion on Günter. Monika was still debating whether she was a naïve fool who had fallen prey to yet another duplicitous man, or whether the BND agent saw treason where there was none, when Maier opened the door for Neuhauser's secretary, who was carrying a serving tray with coffee and Bundt cake.

The secretary left, and they helped themselves. Swallowing a bite, Maier looked at Monika. "Do you have feelings for Günter Freund?"

Monika tried not to tear up. "Yes, I do."

"I thought so," Maier said. "I hope I'm wrong, but my guess is that Herr Freund will ask you for information at some point."

"You mean confidential . . . ?"

Maier nodded. "Like I said, I hope it never happens, but all the signs are there that you've been targeted by the Stasi."

Monika almost choked on a mouthful of coffee. She swallowed hard. "You don't mean it."

"I'm sorry, Frau Fuchs, but you wouldn't be the first woman who's succumbed to the charms of a Stasi Romeo."

The agent's words stung. She'd suspected from time to time that Günter was too good to be true. But a communist spy? Maier's voice tore her from her thoughts.

"Here is what I need you to do, Frau Fuchs. Keep seeing Herr Freund. If he invites you back to Vienna, go. Ask to see his office there. I wish for you that you've found a true romance, a sincere relationship. Still, I want you to report the details of every meeting or phone contact. And that means immediately after. Is that clear?"

Though she felt like an underhanded snoop, Monika said, "Yes."

"And, you call me the moment he asks you for sensitive information, for secret documents." Maier fetched a card from a briefcase in the chair next to her and handed it to Monika. "The first number is my direct line. If I don't answer, call the second and tell our receptionist to track me down and give me the following message: 'The shoe has dropped.' You understand?"

Monika nodded.

"I guess that's it for today." Maier closed the notebook, stashed it along with her pen in the briefcase, and stood. She shook Monika's hand. "Thank you for cooperating. Maybe nothing will come of this." But her tone signaled she thought otherwise.

Monika stared at the door long after it had closed behind the agent. Then she leapt to her feet. The memo. She had to shred it this instant.

Chapter Forty-Nine

Empty-Handed

Stasi Headquarters, East Berlin, Thursday, 11 August 1977

Despite reading Heinrich's furrowed brow, squinting eyes, an almost imperceptible headshake, as indicating frustration or disapproval, Stefan delivered the report about his Cologne trip in a steady voice. Once finished, he readied himself for the pointed questions sure to come, but the insistent ticking of the wall clock behind him was the only sound. Stillness, except for Helga Schröder's insinuation ringing in his ears: *as long as you please him.*

Heinrich inspected the ceiling as if looking for faults in the plaster in need of repair. Finally, he lowered his gaze toward Stefan. "Do you recall what I told you when I got you out of prison?"

Not the kind of question Stefan had expected. "Do you mean what I'm supposed to do?"

"What you've *agreed* to, which is to put your skills of seduction in service of our socialist state. Does this refresh your memory?"

"Yes, General."

"You've bedded Monika Fuchs in Italy, in Vienna and now in Cologne. Is she a good lay, and more importantly, are you satisfying her?"

Stefan squirmed in his seat. True, he was following Heinrich's orders in pursuing Monika, but he'd somehow convinced himself the whole affair was not as cheap or sordid as the general's words made it sound. Not knowing what to say, he simply nodded.

"You do remember that you are fucking for the fatherland, not for yourself?"

Again Stefan nodded.

"Is that a yes?"

"Yes, General."

Heinrich flung his wire-rimmed glasses onto the desk. "I arranged a temporary office in Vienna while she was visiting. I went to the trouble of setting up a fake conference in Cologne on the off chance Monika would check up on you. And guess what? She did."

"Really?"

"Yes. I had a doorkeeper there keeping up the pretense of an ongoing meeting. That should take care of whatever suspicions Monika might have had about you. She is smarter than any of the others recruited by our Romeos, but I've got you covered."

"That's why she was quizzing me about the meeting place, but I never thought—"

"Never mind what you thought, Malik. If I'm to believe your claim that she has fallen for you and has misgivings about West German rearmament, then I have one question for you. Can you guess what that might be?"

Stefan fought to maintain his composure in the face of the general's stare and sarcasm. "You want to know why I haven't asked her for Chancellery documents or information."

"Excellent, Malik. I might be able to make a spy out of you yet." Heinrich picked up his glasses and held them in one hand. "I'm all for being cautious, but you've got a job to do. So what's your answer? Why have you come back empty-handed?"

What to tell Heinrich? Certainly not his qualms about using Monika. Then he thought of an excuse. "I was about to ask her in Cologne, but she was distraught over the disappearance of a close friend."

"Oh?"

Heinrich's expression of surprise seemed feigned, so Stefan probed a little. "Yes, her best friend disappeared under mysterious circumstances from her job as executive secretary to the foreign minister. I'm trying to think of her name." If Heinrich knew it, he was too smart to fill the pause. So Stefan said, "I believe it's Gisela Sturm. Is she one of your—?"

"Malik, I'm asking the questions here." Heinrich slid the glasses onto his nose.

"Of course, General. It's just that Monika thought Gisela might have been working for us, and she became extremely suspicious. So I didn't think it was the time to ask her for information. And I didn't even know she checked on the conference."

"Hmm. You might be right. Maybe you've got sharper instincts than I gave you credit for. But what made Monika suspect her friend?"

"She saw government agents in the Sturm apartment."

Heinrich leaned forward. "Did she make contact?"

"No, she pretended to be lost and left."

"Do you believe her?"

"Yes. I don't know why she would lie about that."

"I hope you're right," Heinrich said. "Otherwise, we can kiss the Monika Fuchs project goodbye." He rubbed his temple. "I need to give this some serious thought."

Stefan took that to mean the general would canvass his vast network of agents, informants and moles embedded in the West for any evidence that West German intelligence services had Monika Fuchs in their sights. If so, Heinrich might think it too risky to pursue Monika further. Stefan fought mixed emotions. While he wouldn't have to do more Stasi dirty work, at least for now, he'd never see Monika again.

Heinrich's voice stopped his speculations. "Don't tell me you've fallen in love with her."

Stefan scooted back in the chair, as if getting farther away would shield him from the general's penetrating stare. What kind of amateur was he, not being able to hide his feelings better?

"I can't deny that I care for her. She's attractive, intelligent and . . ." He almost blurted "a great lover," but said instead, "She's nothing like the profile portrayed in your materials of a lonely secretary with low self-esteem, desperate to catch a husband."

Heinrich cupped his chin. "Your caring for her could be a good thing, so long as it doesn't affect your judgment. It makes it easier for you to appear genuine." He stood. "That's all for now. I'll let you know whether I'm going ahead with this and if so, what your next step will be."

Stefan rose and left the office. What to do with the rest his day? He had no stomach for reading more training manuals, especially since they failed to peg Monika's character.

Helga Schröder ceased typing as he approached her desk. "Well, what exciting adventures is our secret agent off to now?"

Stefan shrugged. "Just reading boring manuals for the umpteenth time in my spacious quarters."

"It's not all romance, is it?"

The general's secretary flirting with him? He'd never have guessed after their first meeting. Keep it going. It might lead to something. "I checked the Staatsoper schedule, and Mozart is on the program in a couple of weeks."

"Which opera?"

Good, she seemed open to going. "*Die Zauberflöte*. Have you heard it on the radio?"

"Yes, but I couldn't make heads or tails of the plot, even though it's sung in German."

"It seems like a simple little singspiel with magic, but my daughter tells me it's full of Masonic symbolism. Apparently,

Mozart was a Mason." While he spoke, an idea began to form. "Traude, my daughter, has sung the soprano part in a school performance. I'll see if I can get some material about the opera from her and maybe we can study it before the performance."

.She gave him a long look. Here comes the brushoff. But no.

"Might be more interesting than what the general is having you read."

"I'll try to bring something tomorrow." He turned and walked toward his office before she could say no. While she'd not explicitly agreed, he could persuade her to go to the opera and perhaps even to get together for a study session. And things might very well progress from there.

How ironic it would be if Heinrich's secretary fit the lonely, divorced secretary touted in the Stasi materials while Monika did not.

Chapter Fifty

Gemeinschaft Unbegrenzt

Bonn and Cologne, Thursday, 11 August 1977

Having left Monika Fuchs in the conference room, Sabine Maier approached the personnel director's secretary. "I need to call my office."

The woman pointed down the hall. "There's a phone in the visitor's office. You just passed it. First one on the right."

Sabine thanked her and reversed course. She opened the door and stopped. With one foot in the hallway and the other on the threshold, she glanced back at the secretary, whose nod confirmed she was indeed in the right place. Sabine shrugged and stepped onto the plush carpeting of an office as spacious as those of the top echelon at the BND. In addition to the obligatory portraits of West Germany's chancellor and president, a photo of Cologne's skyline decorated the wallpapered room. Everything a visitor could want was there—telephone, typewriter, printer and fax. It was as if the Chancellery belonged to a government different from the one she worked for.

She closed the door, stepped to the desk and picked up the phone. The BND operator put her through to Dorfmann. He listened to her report, interrupting only with an occasional grunt. He seemed pleased with her progress, not that he bothered to lavish praise.

When she'd finished, he said, "We'll talk strategy when you get back. Give some thought to what we need to do when this Romeo asks Fuchs to spy for him." A pause. "But you didn't just call to tout your success, did you?" The ever perceptive Dorfmann was on to her yet again. "Don't tell me you want more records."

"No way. I never want to see another personnel folder. But I was wondering whether you had a contact in Vienna who could check on this supposed peace organization. I have a feeling it's a fake."

"Probably is," Dorfmann said. "Give me the details."

"Well, Fuchs could only tell me the name, Gemeinschaft Unbegrenzt, and a phone number." Sabine pulled a paper from her briefcase and read the number to Dorfmann. "She didn't have an address. Her beau discouraged her from coming to the office, so she's never seen it, if it even exists."

"Hmm. Not much to go on. But we have a good man in Vienna. I'll have him get right on it. You're driving back this afternoon?"

"After a detour to Cologne to see what I can find out about this peace conference."

"Good idea. By the time you come to work in the morning, I should know whether Gemeinschaft Unbegrenzt is real or a phantom. And I bet you there never was a peace conference this week in Cologne. But, by all means, check it out." Click.

♫ ♫ ♫

Thanks to Monika Fuchs's precise directions, Sabine found the multistory building at Lindblatt Street 65 without difficulty. She entered the lobby and headed for the custodian's desk. The young man in blue uniform matched the description

Monika had given, not only as to his appearance, but right down to his lustful stare. She could make good use of that.

Sabine tried for a suggestive smile. "I sure hope you can help me." After a furtive glance at his nametag, she added, "Herr Meisinger."

He stood. "Of course. What is it you need?"

"My colleague spoke with you on Tuesday. She told me how accommodating you were when she asked about the conferences that day. You must see so many people every day that you probably don't remember her."

"Oh, I do. She is blonde and . . ." His gaze hugged Sabine's body, as if he were recalling Monika Fuchs' voluptuous figure.

"Yes, that's her." Sabine suppressed, "you creep." Instead, she said, "My friend was too embarrassed to ask you this favor, and she is traveling today. So I volunteered to—"

"I'm at your service, Frau . . ."

Sabine picked the first name that came to mind. "Peters. Very kind of you, Herr Meisinger. You see, my friend lost her gold bracelet. She didn't notice it was missing until last night. She thinks it might have come off her wrist during the meeting here."

Meisinger came around the desk and stepped uncomfortably close. "Which meeting?"

"The international peace conference. I wonder if it might be possible for me to take a quick look." She prayed there was no meeting today. "Could you tell me which room—?"

"If the cleaning crew found something, they would have turned it in at the Lost and Found. You might check there first. It's on the third floor."

Having anticipated what he might say, Sabine responded, "My friend already called them," she lied. "No bracelet."

"That's a shame. Our people clean the rooms very thoroughly, and they are honest. Maybe your friend lost the bracelet somewhere else."

"She's quite sure she didn't. I promised her I'd search the room." She forced another smile. "With your permission, of course, Herr Meisinger."

Whether encouraged by her smile or by her use of his name, or both, he moved in closer. "It's the Westphalia Suite, third room on the second floor. There's nothing going on there today. I'd go with you, but I can't leave my post. It should be open. But you know . . ." He closed his mouth, apparently having second thoughts about volunteering information.

She fought the urge to back away. "Did you have something else, Herr Meisinger? Something about the conference?"

"Well, it's just that—"

"Yes?"

"Most everyone that morning came for the stamp collectors and car club meetings. I could have missed someone, but I recall only one person going to the peace conference. You say your colleague did?"

"Yes." Sabine kept an even voice, barely concealing her excitement at learning that the conference had most likely been a sham. But she needed to make sure. "Do you remember what the person looked like?"

Meisinger raised his thin eyebrows, probably thinking her question strange, but he answered, "Woman, probably in her fifties, gray hair, dark business suit. Why do you ask?"

Exactly how Monika had described the woman who'd shooed her away from the meeting room. Someone—the Stasi?—had made elaborate arrangements to cover the tracks of Monika's lover. The custodian's stare reminded her he expected an answer, so she told a half-truth, "I believe that's the woman who took attendance—an acquaintance of my colleague."

High time to get away from this ogler. Keep up the pretense. "My friend was right, Herr Meisinger. You have been most accommodating. I'll go ahead and look for the bracelet now. Thank you." She made for the stairs.

His voice followed her. "It's almost lunchtime. There's a cozy restaurant around the corner. When you come back down, if you're hungry . . ."

His courage seemed to have drained away. She turned back. "How thoughtful of you." Keeping in mind the side exit

Monika had mentioned, Sabine called, "I'll see you in a few minutes—with the bracelet I hope."

She struck a moderate pace walking up the stairs until she was out of his sight. Then she took two steps at a time and walked past the second-floor conference rooms. No sense searching for a bracelet that didn't exist. She hurried down the staircase to the side exit, which spared her from having to endure Meisinger's lustful eyes again.

Dorfmann had it right: there never was a Cologne peace conference. Her sympathy for Monika Fuchs gave way to worry about whether she could be relied upon to follow through with the plan. Maybe she'd already fallen for the Romeo so hard that she wouldn't give him up.

Chapter Fifty-One

The Threat

Stasi Headquarters, East Berlin, Friday, 12 August 1977

Helga Schröder ogled Stefan as he crested the top of the stairs. He looked so different from the lovers she'd taken since her divorce. Unlike their short, blond hair so typical for Germans, his was dark, long and wavy. The general must think it endeared Stefan to the ladies or he would have made him cut it. Piercing blue-gray eyes set deep in an angular face gave him a slightly wolfish look. While she preferred softer features, she wasn't the first woman who found him handsome. The detail in his file attested to that.

To protect herself from yet another affair with a Romeo, she'd been standoffish with him. No future in sleeping with men whom the general groomed to seduce West German women. But Stefan seemed different. While the others flocked to the Mediterranean beaches eager to screw for the fatherland, Stefan was a reluctant recruit. Still, he must have succeeded at bedding the Chancellery secretary or the general would not have arranged for Stefan's daughter to be admitted to Weimar's prestigious opera school.

His friendly good morning interrupted her ruminations. He carried a large plastic bag. "I brought something for you." He pulled out an LP and laid it on her desk. "My daughter gave me this."

"*Die Zauberflöte*," Helga read aloud. She scanned the names on the *Deutsche Grammophone* cover, but didn't recognize any of the artists except for Karl Böhm conducting the Berlin Philharmonic. "This was recorded in West Berlin. How did your daughter—?"

"I don't know, but I think it's all right. Traude tells me it's her favorite performance, and she's never heard a better Mozart tenor."

Helga read, "Fritz Wunderlich. Hmm, name doesn't ring a bell, but if your daughter thinks he's great . . ." Embarrassed how quickly her resolve to keep her distance had evaporated, she let her voice trail off.

Stefan filled the gap. "The LP just has the highlights, but I also brought a synopsis and the libretto." He handed her the bag. "All I know about this opera is what Traude told me. How about we study it together?"

Say yes and risk another messy affair. Brush him off? Before she could make up her mind, the intercom sounded.

"Frau Schröder," Heinrich's voice boomed. "Has Malik come in yet?"

"Yes, General."

"Have him come to my office." Click.

She motioned toward the door. "You heard the general."

Stefan pointed to the LP. "You might want to put this away; keep this opera thing between us."

"Good idea."

By the time he disappeared into Heinrich's office she'd slid the record into the bag and stashed it among the files in the credenza behind her desk. She hadn't explicitly agreed to meet with him and could always say no later, though the prospect of attending the opera with him excited her.

♫ ♫ ♫

Not a minute had passed since Heinrich sent for Stefan when he entered and sat. Maybe his Romeo-in-training was still too green to get the job done, but short of aborting the Fuchs mission, Heinrich had no reasonable alternative. He'd spent all of yesterday canvassing his assets in the West. None had picked up any information suggesting that the West German intelligence services were keeping an eye on Monika Fuchs. Even if his agents had missed something, Heinrich decided to go ahead. Losing an inexperienced Romeo was worth the risk.

Stefan shifted in his chair, apparently uneasy at Heinrich looking him up and down. Handsome face, broad shoulders, athletic build—no mystery why the ladies found him attractive. What a shame if he got caught and spent years behind West German bars. Heinrich pulled himself together. He couldn't afford that kind of thinking. Time to give Stefan his marching orders.

"You'll have another go at Monika Fuchs."

Stefan gave a slight nod. Was he pleased to be able to see Monika again? Maybe he just tried to look agreeable since he didn't have a choice.

Heinrich continued, "You're passenger Kurt Thiessen on a Monday morning flight to Vienna. Frau Schröder has a passport for you. Then as Günter Freund you'll board an afternoon flight to the Cologne/Bonn airport."

At Stefan's quizzical expression, Heinrich explained, "Just a precaution. I don't want to leave any trace of Freund's flight having originated anywhere but in Vienna. Certainly not in East Berlin. You understand?"

"Yes, General. But what do I tell Monika?"

"That you're on temporary assignment to Bonn from Gemeinschaft Unbegrenzt to check on rumors of West German rearmament. You've already laid the groundwork for that with Fuchs during your Vienna tryst, haven't you?"

"Yes."

"Good, then you'll be ready to do some real spywork. No more pussyfooting around. Probe what she knows about rearmament. Has she seen documents? Tell her she's helping world peace by giving information to the altruistic society you're working for. You know about pillow talk."

At Stefan's meek nod, Heinrich said, "Is that a yes?"

"Yes, sir."

"I'll give you a week. If I don't have something in hand by then . . ." Heinrich paused to give Stefan's imagination a chance to speculate. "Well, I don't think I have to spell the consequences out for you, do I?"

"No, General."

Just to be sure Stefan got the message, Heinrich said, "I look forward to watching your daughter perform at the Staatsoper Unter den Linden in a few years."

Stefan's slight frown signaled the threat had hit home.

"Questions?"

Stefan shook his head.

"You remember what you learned about tradecraft, how to use the dead drops, how to transmit?"

"Yes, General."

"Then see Frau Schröder for your travel papers." Heinrich rose, walked around the desk, and waited for Stefan to stand before shaking his hand. "Good luck. I'm counting on you to do your job."

"Yes, General."

After Stefan had left, Heinrich wondered whether his threat had been explicit enough to propel this Romeo to do his level best to turn Monika Fuchs into an informant—the goal Heinrich had been coveting for longer than he could remember.

♫ ♫ ♫

As he closed the door behind him, Stefan could hardly contain his rage at the general holding Traude's career hostage to her father's performance.

Apparently it showed, because Helga said, "You look upset. Bad assignment?"

He took a deep breath, then another, trying to let the anger pass. "It's not the assignment, but . . ." Did he really want to level with her? "I'd rather not bother you with my personal problems."

She gave an almost imperceptible nod. "I understand."

Maybe he was reading too much into her tone, but it suggested she didn't buy his excuse. His mind churned. How he hated being the general's minion, doing his dirty work. He had to find a way out, but how?

"I have your travel papers ready."

At the sound of Helga's voice an idea from the previous day resurfaced. If anyone had any dirt on the general, it would be Helga Schröder. He dutifully signed the documents she put in front of him and pocketed the money she gave him.

"Not counting?" she asked.

"No. You wouldn't lead me astray, would you?" When she didn't respond, he continued, "Since I'll be off Monday morning, how about we do that study session this weekend?"

She held his gaze for a long moment. He braced himself for a brushoff, but then her face relaxed. "Friday nights I usually have dinner at *Freier Genosse* around the corner. Maybe you could join me there to look over the opera materials."

Her words caught him off guard.

She took his hesitation the wrong way. "You have other plans?"

He regained his composure. "No, I don't. But Freier Genosse might not be the best place to talk about our opera adventure."

She slapped her forehead. "Too close to the office, of course. We're likely to run into a colleague or two there. And we can't leave together." She grabbed a pen, wrote on a notepad, and tore off a sheet, which she handed to him. "A more private restaurant. See you there at six."

She returned to her typing.

Note and travel papers in hand, Stefan walked toward his office. Something in Helga's demeanor told him learning about *The Magic Flute* might not be the sole reason she'd agreed to meet with him.

Chapter Fifty-Two

Elusive Strategy

BND, Pullach, Friday, 12 August 1977

In one hand a coffee cup filled to the brim, in the other her briefcase, Sabine navigated through Dorfmann's open office door. He'd summoned her the moment she arrived this morning. Good thing she'd spent the thirty-minute drive to work formulating what she needed to tell him. While following his invitation to take a chair, she gauged his mood. The good-morning greeting had been friendly enough, and he was not frowning.

After depositing her briefcase on the carpet and her cup on a desk pullout, she readied herself for the barrage of questions that was sure to come. He remained uncharacteristically quiet, and that unnerved her. The calm before the storm? She held his gaze.

Finally, he spoke. "Remember what I told you when I hired you?"

Surprised, she had to think for a moment. Which of the many pointers he'd given could he possibly be referring to?

The corners of his mouth turned upward. He seemed to enjoy her bemusement. "I'm talking about how important it is for us in the intelligence business to take failures and successes in stride. Ring a bell?"

She had a vague recollection. "You mean how we have to plug away, never mind the stumbles and wild-goose chases we're going to have?"

"Exactly."

What was he driving at?

As if reading her thoughts, he said, "You're wondering how this relates to your pursuit of Romeos? Well, it does. Let me recount our missteps to this point."

What a great boss, sharing responsibility for her lack of success.

Using his fingers for emphasis, Dorfmann rattled off things gone wrong. "First, we can't figure out how to use Rasterfahndung to track down spies. Second, we unmask three Stasi agents, but manage to arrest only two. Third, we let the entire Sturm family slip through our fingers even though you and Kögler did a great job blowing their cover."

At least he finished the list of failures with praise. But, still perplexed where he was going with this, she said, "Enough blunders to call into question whether we will ever manage to break up the network of Stasi spies and informants in the West."

"That may be overly ambitious. Inflicting serious damage on their assets is probably the most we can hope for." He cupped his chin. "So here is where we are. Our man in Vienna confirmed that Gemeinschaft Unbegrenzt is a phantom."

Though she'd expected as much, she asked, "He's sure?"

"Yes. No listing in the phone book or anywhere else. His contacts in city government assured him there is no evidence such an organization ever existed."

"What about the phone number Monika Fuchs gave me?"

"We've tracked it to an apartment block about one kilometer from the Prater. Our man called the number from a public phone and hung up when he reached an answering machine. Let's hope that won't tip off the Stasi, if that's who's picking up messages. No one has gone in or out of the place since yesterday."

"So Monika's beau doesn't live there, and he works for a nonexistent peace organization." She scooted forward and put a hand on Dorfmann's desk. "And you were right, of course. There never was a peace conference." She reported what she found at the Cologne office building. He seemed to get a kick out of her description of the lusty custodian.

"So we've established this Günter Freund is a fraud," Dorfmann said matter-of-factly, as if proclaiming a scientific principle.

"I suppose this gets us back to your point. After all the dead ends we've endured, we may have finally picked up the scent of a Stasi Romeo." She was proud of herself for following his example of using we instead of singling herself out for recognition.

"And this time we are not going to let him get away." Dorfmann leaned forward. "Knowing you, Frau Maier, you've already worked out a plan."

"Tentative, subject to your approval, of course."

"Let's hear what you've got in mind."

"We could arrest him as soon as he shows his face. That would send one more spy to prison, but I think we should shoot for more."

Dorfmann raised his eyebrows. "You mean turn him?"

"Exactly."

"I'm not sure we can take the risk of yet another Stasi spy escaping."

"It's a risk I'd be willing to take."

"I appreciate your offer to assume full responsibility, Frau Maier, but it's not your individual risk. You're not the only one whose career is in jeopardy if I don't have him arrested the first chance we get."

"Sorry, I didn't mean—"

He put up a hand. "Enough said. Let's discuss strategy. How did you leave things with Monika Fuchs?"

"She is to report every contact with him, and she promised to call me immediately if he asks her for information or documents."

"Do you trust her?"

"Not enough to rely on her promise alone. I'd like to ask Mertens to have his people keep an eye on her."

"Hmm. Has he been cooperative?"

"Yes, very much so."

"Even when Kögler was with you in the Sturm apartment?"

She furrowed her brow. "Why do you ask? Is there bad blood between them?"

"Well, they had their issues when they were colleagues. That's all I can say. Ask Kögler. Maybe he'll tell you. As far as Mertens, let me know if you need me to lean on him or his superiors to assure full cooperation."

"I will, but I don't expect that'll be necessary. He's been extremely accommodating."

"Good. So enlighten me on your plan."

She rested her elbows on his desk. "Rather than wait on Günter Freund prodding Monika to spy for him, I want to move things along. Catch him red-handed and soon."

"Lay a trap?"

"Yes."

"This better be good, Frau Maier."

He leaned back and studied the ceiling while she laid out her scheme.

Chapter Fifty-Three

Intimate Undercover

East Berlin, Friday, 12 August 1977

A few minutes past five, Stefan closed the door to his office, relieved he wouldn't be confined in the claustrophobic space for a week, maybe longer if he could persuade Monika to hand over sensitive Chancellery documents. As he walked down the hall, his thoughts turned from Monika in distant Bonn to the intriguing rendezvous awaiting him this evening. Full of anticipation, he rounded the corner and stopped. He'd intended to ask Helga Schröder for directions, but she wasn't at her desk.

Could she be in the general's office? He didn't dare knock on the door to find out. The black vinyl cover over her typewriter told him she must have left already —to meet him or to avoid telling him she'd changed her mind? Quit worrying about being stood up and go to the restaurant. But first he had to figure out where it was. He fished the paper Helga had given him from his shirt pocket. *Gasthof Zum Feierabend,* Zwickauer Straße 35. No phone number. For a moment, he considered looking for a phone book, but he couldn't risk Heinrich catching him rummaging through his secretary's desk.

He went back to his office—so much for not having to endure this closet for a week. He pulled a city map from a drawer and spread it across the empty desktop. After consulting the street index, he located Zwickauer Straße. Clear across town. Two underground rides away. He pocketed the map, ran from the office and down the stairs. If he missed her because he was late, he'd never know whether she'd been there and left, or whether she'd had second thoughts and reneged altogether.

♫ ♫ ♫

Finding Zum Feierabend turned out to be easier than he'd expected. The name and the silhouette of a person lifting a wineglass were stenciled into a copper sign dangling from a curved metal hook. Stefan pushed open the heavy wooden door and entered a sizable foyer. A young hostess and a middle-aged man wearing a toque and a white apron huddled around a desk at the far end. No patrons waiting on a Friday after work? Something was amiss. Maybe Helga had chosen this place because it wasn't very popular.

As Stefan approached, the chef said, "I'm sorry, sir, but our power went out this afternoon. The kitchen is closed, but we are serving drinks in the bar. Or, if you prefer, there is a nice restaurant down the street."

Stefan checked the clock on the wall. Seven minutes to six. He could use a drink, but he'd better wait for Helga. "I'm supposed to meet someone here."

"Pardon me, sir, but I believe your companion is seated in the bar," the hostess said. "She mentioned a gentleman might be looking for her. This way, please."

Stefan followed the woman through a vacant dining area. Her ill-fitting brown uniform hid any assets she might possess. She led him into a carpeted room that featured a long bar and half a dozen small tables, most of which were occupied by patrons who must have opted for a liquid dinner. If it hadn't been for the short, brown hair and the round face, he might not have recognized Helga sitting at a corner table. She stood and waved. Gone was the business suit, replaced by a form-fitting flowery dress that revealed ample cleavage.

His surprise must have been obvious. As they sat, she said, "The general left the office this afternoon. So I took off early and went home to change."

"I wish I could have too." He made a dismissive gesture toward his charcoal suit. "As you can see, I came straight from the office."

She pointed to a glass of red wine. "I hope you don't mind, but I ordered this for you." She raised the half-empty glass in front of her. "Cheers."

He took a sip. Not bad for a German red, though he preferred the French varieties when he could get them. "How did you know I'm not a beer drinker?"

"Easy. You're the refined type, Herr Malik."

He lowered his voice, even though no one was sitting at the table next to them. "You've been around spies so long, something had to rub off."

"Probably true, but I must confess your file contains a few hints of your drinking habits."

"You've read my file and you still want to go to the opera with me?" He paused, wondering if he dared. What the hell, why not? "Since you know all the sordid details of my life, I think it only appropriate you call me Stefan outside the office . . . and if I may call you Helga?"

She raised her glass. "Agreed." They clinked glasses and drank.

"Did you bring the synopsis and libretto I gave you?" he asked.

"*Ach, Scheiße!* I must have left them at home. But you know this place isn't very conducive to carrying on a deep discussion about opera. And I'm sorry about the closed kitchen. Are you hungry?"

"Not very." He didn't want to give her a reason to cut the evening short, so he quickly added, "Though I could eat a bite later, if you're up for going somewhere else. The chef recommended a restaurant down the street."

She gazed at him. Was she looking for a way to call it a day? Finally, she said, "I made a mess of things, forgetting to bring the opera stuff, picking a restaurant without food. So let's finish our drinks and go to my apartment. It's a ten-minute walk. We can play your daughter's record while you fix dinner."

"You know I like to cook?"

"It's all in your file."

"Why am I not surprised?" He swallowed the rest of his drink.

♫ ♫ ♫

Before dipping below the horizon, the sun peeked through clouds that had brought a light shower earlier in the day. During their leisurely stroll on damp sidewalks, Stefan kept wondering whether Helga's failure to bring the opera materials had been deliberate. Maybe he was reading too much into her inviting him to her place. Wouldn't be the first time he'd misread a woman's intentions. Still, she'd ditched her drab office garb for a sexy dress, and she looked fabulous in it.

An image of Monika flashed into his mind. Why did he have to complicate matters by developing feelings for her?

"You're awfully quiet, Stefan."

"Sorry, I'm just enjoying this pleasant evening. How far to your place?"

Helga pointed to a six-story building across the street. "We're there."

The closer they got, the more impressed Stefan became. Unlike his dreary apartment complex with its gray mortar flaking in large patches, this building seemed well maintained. A Stasi general's secretary obviously had more pull with the party functionaries than a lowly writer.

As they entered, he took little comfort in the fact that this place, like his, lacked an elevator. They trudged up the wooden stairs to the top floor. She unlocked the door to an apartment quite a bit larger than his. A small hall led into a carpeted living room furnished with a sofa, two armchairs, a bookcase, and a console that held a radio, a phonograph, and a small television.

If he'd had any doubts about whether her apartment was more upscale than his, they vanished at the sight of a small dining area off the kitchen. He pictured the table and chairs crowding his living room. Hers were out of the way in their own little niche.

As she led him into the small kitchen, he asked in a low voice, "Is it safe to talk?"

She nodded. "No bugs."

"You know how to sweep—?"

"I've learned a few things in my years with the Stasi."

She opened a cupboard. "Pick out something for dinner. I'm getting kind of hungry. I'll put on the record and open a bottle while you cook."

"Pasta all right?"

"Yes," she said. "It'll go great with my red wine."

He was once again speculating whether reading Traude's materials had been a pretext to lure him to her place, when she said, "We can study your daughter's articles over dinner."

He loosened his tie, undid the top button of his white shirt, set a large pot of water on the gas stove, and turned up the burner. To the sound of Mozart, he sliced bread and searched the pantry for a suitable sauce. Humming along with the music, he waited until the water came to a rolling boil before dropping in spaghetti. Helga set the table and read out loud the song titles on the record's cover each time a new musical number started. At the tenor's first aria, Stefan strolled into the living room. They both stood motionless, listening.

At the aria's end, he asked, "Who is the tenor?"

Helga picked up the cover. "Fritz Wunderlich. He's fabulous."

"Just like Traude said." He went back to the kitchen to stir the spaghetti whirling in the bubbling water.

Helga announced the next character with a snicker, "Queen of the night."

But they both listened awestruck to the soprano's coloratura fireworks. By the time the bass descended to his low notes, they were eating. She pronounced the meal delicious, apologizing for not having any Parmesan—the store had run out.

After the last note had faded and the phonograph needle had lifted off the record, Helga stood. "Delicious meal and heavenly music. You did the cooking; I'll clear the dishes so we can study the materials. Though I'm not sure how much focus I have left after three glasses of wine."

Ignoring her protest, Stefan carried his plate and silverware to the kitchen and dropped them into the soapy water she'd run in the sink. As she submerged her dishes, their hands touched briefly. Before he could catch her eye, she stepped aside.

Conflicting emotions surfaced again. *She's interested in more than opera, fool. She's attractive, and I need to get some dirt on Heinrich.* He recalled a scene from one of his favorite movies. Anthony Quinn in *Zorba the Greek* telling Alan Bates, "God has a very big heart, but there is one sin He will not forgive. If a woman calls a man to her bed and he will not go."

Besides, he couldn't realistically expect to have a true relationship with Monika. She'd never forgive his deception, even though he'd been blackmailed by the Stasi. Why agonize over something unattainable? He wanted to sleep with Helga, whether or not she had dirt on Heinrich.

♫ ♫ ♫

While she laid Traude's materials between the half-full wineglasses on the table, Helga asked herself why she'd pretended to have forgotten them and why she'd suggested they have dinner here. The obvious answer—she wanted romance. *He was handsome, charming, and irresistible, but he'd slept with an array of women, some married, and now Heinrich had him seducing West German secretaries. Still, Stefan was not crass like so many of the others who'd paraded through the general's office over the years. But what about her resolve never to become involved again with another Romeo, to spare herself the regret she felt after each of the previous affairs?*

Stefan returned from the kitchen. "I don't know about you, Helga, but having listened to the record and your reading from the cover is all the information I need. But if you want to go over Traude's—"

"No need to. The program at the performance will have the synopsis, won't it?"

"Yes." He played with the stem of his glass. "Helga, I feel I'm at an extreme disadvantage."

"Oh?" What was he leading up to?

"You know everything about my personal life, and I know nothing about you, other than that you work for the general. Please tell me a little bit about yourself."

To gain time to think, she drank some wine. Did Heinrich know about her indiscretions with previous Romeos? Not from her, but some men liked to boast about sex, real or imagined. But even if he knew or suspected, he surely wouldn't have told Stefan. She certainly wouldn't. Although she periodically swept the apartment for bugs, none had ever turned up. Still, one could never be sure. So she put the record back on.

When the overture sounded, she scooted her chair next to Stefan's and said, "I got pregnant when I was nineteen, married the father, shouldn't have, divorced him after ten miserable years; my daughter is the only good thing to come out of the whole affair."

"She's not living with you?"

She shook her head. "Beate is majoring in science at Weimar University. She wants to become a doctor. Maybe she and your daughter will meet there."

"They're quite the opposites—left-brain scientist versus right-brain artist. Be interesting to listen in on a conversation between the two." Stefan sported a mischievous grin. "Any serious relationships since your divorce?" When she shot him a look, he said, "You know about my love life."

"Nice try, *Herr Spion*. I don't talk out of school like so many of your gender are prone to." She'd fended that off well, but now what—send him home or see where the evening might lead?

She was still on the fence, when Stefan said, "Forgive me. I had no business prying. It's just that I feel vulnerable, with you knowing about all my sexual exploits."

"I have no problem with consensual encounters, which yours were." She sought his eyes. "Just don't forsake your principles when you do the general's bidding."

He furrowed his brow. "You know I have no real choice?"

She nodded. "Rummelsburg Prison for you and no opera career for Traude."

He looked grim. Should she risk sharing her secret with him? An easier decision than she'd imagined. She would let him in on at least part of what she'd gathered over the years for her protection. "Stefan, I might be able to give you a choice."

"You *what?*" He leaned in.

"Put on your spy hat and tell me whether you've noticed anything unusual about the general."

Stefan stared at her, first blankly, then he raised his eyebrows. "You mean his looking at magazines he doesn't want anyone else to know about? Pornography?"

"Yes, but a certain kind." She enjoyed keeping Stefan guessing. "What else?"

"I thought it strange that he has no family photos on his desk." Stefan cupped his chin. "Oh, I see. He's gay, isn't he?"

"Excellent, Mr. Spy."

"That's why he's been ogling me. But I don't see how knowing that will help me, since homosexuality is legal."

"Don't be naïve, Stefan. You don't buy the official party line, do you?" She paused, considering whether she was taking too big a risk speaking so freely. Too late to pull back now, and Stefan's file showed him to be the antithesis of an informant.

She continued, "On the surface, the Stasi tolerates homosexuals. In reality, they monitor them and repress them. Woe to regime opponents who happen to be gay."

"I see your point. That explains the number of homosexuals languishing at Rummelsburg. But surely, a Stasi general like Heinrich could get away with it."

"In most cases, yes."

Stefan laid his hand over hers resting on the table. "You know something that . . . ?"

Her decision made, she took him by the hand and led him to the bedroom. To the tenor's mellow voice, she undid his tie, unbuttoned his starched shirt, and dropped both to the floor. He flicked the straps of her dress off her shoulder, freeing her breasts, caressing them. They playfully undressed each other. She pulled him down onto the hard mattress, kissing, groping. He kept teasing, but she could wait no longer, and guided him deep inside her.

♫ ♫ ♫

In the quiet apartment, the last note of Mozart's opera having sounded long ago, Helga nestled against Stefan's naked body. He was breathing deeply, dozing after they'd made love a second time. It had been too long since she had a man, and she might never have another one like Stefan. Fortunately, she had a way to keep him interested. Monday, he'd be off to woo Monika Fuchs, but this weekend he was hers, and if she intrigued him by disclosing bits and pieces of Heinrich's exploits, she might have Stefan back after the Bonn assignment.

Chapter Fifty-Four

Free Spirit

Munich, Saturday, 13 August 1977

Sabine muted the opera highlights record and strode toward the ringing telephone. Either Dorfmann bugging her on a Saturday afternoon, or more likely, Mother calling to chat.

She answered on the fourth ring. "Maier."

"Hello Sabine. It's Horst. I hope you don't mind my calling you on a weekend."

Her heart jumped at the sound of his baritone, but she kept her voice even. "That's quite all right. You have another breakthrough?"

A long pause, then a hesitant, "Actually, this isn't about business. I was wondering whether I could persuade you to hit the tennis ball this afternoon." Before she could respond, he quickly added, "I have a five-o'clock court time, but my partner isn't feeling well. I was about to cancel the court, but then I remembered your mentioning that you play."

On the verge of saying no, she recalled Dorfmann's comment about Horst being a free spirit. This might be her chance to dig a little, find out what caused his departure from the Office for the Protection of the Constitution.

Horst's voice interrupted her thoughts. "Sorry to spring this on you at the last minute."

"I don't mind." She gazed at the sun breaking through clouds that had brought morning showers. "Are the courts dry?"

"They will be by five."

"You know I haven't played in years, but if you're up for watching me shake off some rust, I'm game." No need to tell him she was the number two singles player on her university team.

"Great. You know where the tennis club in Schwabing is?"

"Yes."

"See you there." He hung up, not giving her a chance to reconsider.

In search of her tennis gear, she headed for the hall closet. Racquet and shoes should be no problem, but could she still squeeze her thirty-seven-year-old body into one of the outfits she'd worn in her mid-twenties?

♫ ♫ ♫

Her auburn hair gathered in a ponytail by a red rubber band, Sabine followed Horst to court seven. Its smooth red clay attested to an attentive groundskeeper. While upscale, the club was not so stodgy as to require all-white attire like Wimbledon. She'd found a pair of tan shorts and an off-white shirt in her closet that still fit. Horst looked handsome in navy shorts and a white shirt that set off his olive complexion and dark hair.

She felt his gaze travel from her to the Dunlop Maxply racquet she was freeing from its wood press.

When he took the green cover off an oversize metal racquet, she asked, "Is that the new Prince Classic?"

"Yes. Aluminum frame. I've only had it for a few weeks. The large sweet spot has drastically improved my game." He pointed to her wooden stick. "The pro shop has a few demos. You want me to look for a Prince racquet in your grip size?"

"No thanks. I'm used to my trusty Dunlop. Maybe after we play for a while, you'll let me hit a few balls with yours, though. I'm curious what it feels like."

He nodded and opened a Slazenger can. Out tumbled three yellow balls.

She picked up one. "Shows you how long it's been for me. Never played with anything but white balls."

During warmup, she assessed his strokes. Good topspin forehand, but like most club players, he had a weak slice-backhand. She guessed he must have picked up the game later in life. She could teach him how to come over the top of the ball, but she resisted the urge to give instructions he hadn't asked for. While rusty, her strokes were coming back—the advantage of having learned the game at a young age. She likened it to what they said about riding a bike—once you learned, you never forgot.

After retrieving a ball by the fence, Horst walked up to the net. "You up for playing a set?"

Not wanting to show him up, she said, "I'm okay with just rallying. Get more exercise that way." He looked disappointed, so she added, "But I'll play if you want."

"Yes, let's." He spun his racquet.

She called up, but the logo on the grip was upside down, and he chose to serve. She netted the first return and hit the second wide. She'd not shaken off the rust entirely. But she drove the next ball deep to the baseline. It landed right at his feet, causing him to miss. From then on, her instincts from college play resurfaced—gauging the flight of the ball, taking little steps to reach the perfect hitting spot, guiding the racquet on the proper swing path, imparting different kinds of spin. A rush of adrenaline reminded her how much fun the game could be.

Horst's athleticism made up for what he lacked in stroke production. He was a remarkably consistent intermediate. Of course, her keeping the ball in play by hitting to him instead of running him side to side, helped. She wouldn't embarrass him by going for winners, but neither would she concede points.

When the ball climbed up the net cord, hung suspended, then dribbled over to Horst's side to give her the set at 6:2, she raised her hand in the apologetic gesture customary among tennis players. But as they shook hands, she said, "It's my clean living."

He laughed. "I bet."

They grabbed two water bottles from a courtside cooler and settled on a bench.

"If this is how you play when you're rusty, I can't imagine what you're like at the top of your game." He dabbed pearls of sweat from his brow. "And I know you were playing down."

She took several hefty swallows of the cold water, before responding. "I probably should have told you that I played on the college varsity team. You did very well."

"I appreciate that. How about we rally some more? I've been taking a few lessons, but if you have any tips on how I can improve, please speak up."

"It would help if you watched the ball instead of me," she teased.

It took him a moment to catch on. "You can't blame me for being captivated by your smooth strokes."

Enough flirting. So she said, "Seriously, there is one part of your game that could stand improvement."

"My backhand," he blurted.

"Exactly. Your slice is pretty good, but it's a defensive shot. If you want to be more aggressive, you need to develop a topspin backhand." She stood. "Come on, I'll show you."

For the next several minutes, she adjusted his backhand stance and his grip. When he faced the net, she admonished, "Pretend you're wearing a T-shirt with a slogan on the back. Turn far enough so your opponent can read it."

After practicing a few swings, he said, "I'm not sure I'm doing it right. Can you guide me?"

Though she suspected committing the stroke to muscle memory might not be the sole reason he asked for a hands-on demonstration, she took hold of his racquet-arm. The touch stirred feelings in her she hadn't experienced in a long time. It was all she could do to keep her hand steady and move his forearm through the low-to-high swing path required for generating topspin.

The moment they completed the motion, she released his arm and hurried to the far side of the court. "Let's rally some more. I'll hit to your backhand, and I want to see nothing but topspin shots coming back."

After numerous mishits, Horst started to get the hang of it, but to make his shot more penetrating would require countless hours of practice. Before she could stop herself, she offered to hit with him again. He enthusiastically accepted.

When she tried his aluminum racquet, she sailed several balls long until she compensated for the racquet's extra power. No doubt, the stick had a larger sweet spot than her Dunlop. If she took up the game again, she'd have to own one of these.

As they rested on the bench, she asked, "How long have you been playing?"

"About ten years, off and on. But I didn't play regularly until after I left Cologne and started my own business here."

The opening she'd been waiting for. "What made you leave Cologne?"

He replaced the balls in the Slazenger can and slid the Prince Classic into its cover. Instead of answering, he deflected her question with one of his own. "What has Dorfmann told you?"

"He warned me that you're a free spirit who somehow upset the Cologne bureaucrats. But he wouldn't give any details. Told me to ask you, which is what I'm doing. But it's none of my business, so I understand if you don't want to talk about it."

"It *is* your business, Sabine. We're working together, so I want to earn your trust. And once we're finished hunting Stasi Romeos, I was hoping we could see each other socially. But you know that."

She held his gaze. "Yes, I do. But you have my trust already. You don't owe me an explanation."

He stood and offered his hand to pull her up from the bench. "They have a good restaurant. Let's have some drinks and dinner and I'll tell you the sordid story of my demise as an intelligence officer."

She took his hand, and carrying their tennis gear, they strolled toward the clubhouse.

♫ ♫ ♫

After taking a hefty swallow, Horst set down his half-liter mug. "Nothing like a good beer after exercise."

Sabine lifted her small glass of *Hofbräu*. "Agreed."

"While we're waiting on dinner, I might as well get started." Horst wiped foam from his upper lip. "You understand that I can't divulge any case specifics."

She nodded, eager to learn more.

"I really enjoyed my job until my boss was promoted. They replaced him with a paranoid bureaucrat consumed with covering his ass. He insisted on petty details to no purpose. As you can tell, I didn't much care for him, and the feeling was mutual."

Talking about his lousy boss seemed to weigh on him. As he took a swig of beer, she said, "That sounds awful. It makes me appreciate working for Dorfmann even more. Of course, he could be promoted tomorrow and I might end up with a boss like yours." She grinned. "Maybe I ought to screw up this assignment just enough to make sure he doesn't get kicked upstairs."

Her comment pulled Horst out of his pensive mood. "You've had better ideas, Sabine. Anyway, back then I was working on tracking Red Army Faction terrorists we thought were in the Frankfurt area. The new department head didn't trust me, so he assigned a second agent to the mission. I was not to do anything on my own. You'll never guess who he saddled me with."

"How in the world would I . . ." Then she recalled Dorfmann's probing about their encounter in the Sturm apartment. "Hans Mertens."

Horst's jaw dropped. "None other. Did Dorfmann tell you?"

"Only that you were colleagues."

"Hmm. Well, I had nothing against Mertens. He seemed capable, but he too was a stickler for detail. Anyway, late one afternoon I received a Rasterfahndung report that singled out customers paying their utility bill in cash—one of the criteria fed into the computer to identify terrorists."

"That's what gave Dorfmann the idea of using Rasterfahndung for catching Stasi spies, but I persuaded him it wouldn't work. Please go on."

"A Frankfurt apartment listed in the report caught my attention. Both Mertens and my boss had already left for the day. Maybe I should have tried to reach one of them at home, but I decided this couldn't wait. Terrorists don't stay in one place too long. So I alerted the Federal Criminal Police. Asked them to have a squad meet me at the Frankfurt address, but to wait till I got there."

He took a drink.

"Let me guess. The police beat you there and didn't wait."

Horst set down the mug hard. "You got that right. Took me two hours from Cologne. They only had half an hour coming from Wiesbaden."

She leaned forward. "And?"

"Three RAF terrorists, heavily armed. I arrived at the tail end of a shootout. One officer severely wounded; all three terrorists dead."

"Did the policeman survive?"

"Yes. As far as I know, he made a full recovery and is back on the force."

"So your quick action eliminated three terrorists."

He shrugged. "My boss didn't see it that way. He blamed me for the botched operation. Said if I'd notified him first, we could have caught the terrorists alive, kept the officer safe, and picked up some fresh intelligence."

"*Quatsch!*" she exclaimed, causing several heads in the dining room to turn.

"A load of nonsense for sure, but an expedient pretext for my boss to demote me. Long story short, he had Mertens take my position and relegated me to a desk job. I resigned the next day."

"Do you regret leaving?"

"Not in the least. Truth be told, I'd received a few reproaches from my first boss for skirting regulations. I've always been a bit of a rebel—a contrarian."

"That's why Dorfmann called you a free spirit. Thank you for telling me."

"I wanted you to know I didn't do anything unethical. And it all turned out for the best. I found my niche in a business that'll take off in the coming years. Mark my words."

"I for one am glad you came to Munich."

He smiled. "So am I."

Chapter Fifty-Five

Pillow Talk

East Berlin, Sunday, 14 August 1977

Stefan kept his eyes shut against the morning light, afraid if he opened them, the tranquil feeling in his limbs would dissipate. Nor did he want to disturb Helga's deep breathing. The rhythmic sound of light rain falling on Berlin throughout the night had been perfect for lovemaking. Helga couldn't seem to get enough; she'd awakened him from a slumber during the last two nights. Sex-starved from not having had a lover in a while? Not that he'd ask her.

He'd left her apartment late Saturday morning to run errands and to get a start on packing for his trip to Bonn. He returned in the evening to candles illuminating a table set for dinner and to the pleasant smell of roasting meat and onions.

She greeted him with a long kiss, but slipped from his embrace at a sizzling sound from the kitchen. "Oh, the *rostbraten!*"

Now as he lay there in bed, he conjured up the aroma and the taste of the tender meat. In addition to the spacious apartment, fringe benefits for the personal secretary of a Stasi spymaster apparently included cuts of meat usually reserved for party functionaries. The drizzle turned into a morning downpour, and the sound of tires splashing on wet pavement filtered through the tilted window. When Helga stirred, he opened his eyes. The sheet outlined the mounds of her breasts.

"Enjoying the view?" she asked in a sleepy voice.

Good thing his blushing days were behind him. "Immensely."

She snuggled up to him. "That's good. Did you get enough last night?"

"You nearly wore me out."

She punched his side. "I might have believed that before I read your file."

"All right, Helga. You know everything about my sex life, but you've been skirting my questions about yours. How about baring your soul?"

She gave an exaggerated sigh. "What do you want to know?"

"I'm not your first Romeo, am I?"

"No, but you might be my last."

"Why do you say that?"

"I swore after the last one I'd never get involved with another. Too messy. Not that I expected a meaningful relationship, mind you. I'm okay with great sex, just like we're having, even as a *quid pro quo*."

She'd seen through him.

While he considered how to respond, she laid her head on his chest. "I have no illusions, Stefan. You want information and I'm willing to give it as long as we're having fun together. A fair bargain, if you ask me."

He nuzzled her crown, thinking of a comeback. "I don't blame you for being suspicious, Helga, but believe me I wanted to sleep with you the first time I laid eyes on you. But I'm not saying I wouldn't appreciate whatever you can do to help me pry loose the general's grip on me."

She snickered. "Very smooth. You almost had me convinced, but no one could ever accuse me of naiveté. You can't work for the Stasi as long as I have without developing a healthy dose of suspicion. Not to worry. Your secretary in Bonn is not going to be as jaded as I am."

Stefan reflected on the irony of Heinrich encouraging him to use pillow talk for wresting secrets from Monika. If he only knew his secretary was talking in bed with his newest Romeo. The thought triggered a question. "Do you think the general knows about your affairs?"

After a slight hesitation, she said, "Not from me. But one of the Romeos might have boasted. You know how some men are."

He wondered how many Romeos had found their way into her bed, but asked instead, "You did say your apartment is clean?"

"That's right. No bugs."

Time to steer the conversation to what he needed to learn. "Do you have more on Heinrich than his being gay—something I could use to get out?"

She wrapped the bedsheet around herself and sat up. "Maybe."

Fighting irritation at her equivocation, he asked in a steady voice, "*Maybe* you have something, or *maybe* what you have isn't good enough?"

"I don't mean to be coy, Stefan. Whether the information I've come by will set you free depends on how you use it."

He propped himself up on his elbows. "Try me."

She turned to face him and moved her hand down his abdomen. "All in good time, my Romeo. First, let's make sure you're in shape for your Bonn assignment." When the bedsheet tented, she said, "It looks like you're ready."

She threw off the sheet and straddled him. He raised his pelvis and entered her, meeting her thrust for thrust.

♫ ♫ ♫

Famished after their early morning romp, Stefan devoured the pancakes and sausages Helga had whipped up for breakfast. He stacked their plates, empty except for pools of sausage grease and syrup, and carried them to the kitchen. The green robe Helga had found for him in a closet must have belonged to someone with a wide girth. Careful not to trip in his bare feet on the hem dragging on the kitchen tile, Stefan returned to the table. Drinking coffee, Helga shifted in her chair. She wore a fitted black nightgown that accentuated her full hips and shapely bosom.

He let his gaze wander up to her round face and tousled brown hair. "So, will you enlighten me on what Heinrich has been up to?"

"Ah, yes. The *quid pro quo*. You already know about his looking at photos of men wearing nothing but jock straps. Their muscles are so overdone." She shuddered. "They disgust me."

"Do you know where he gets those magazines?"

"No."

"Does he act on his desires?"

"You bet he does."

Stefan scooted forward. "Tell me."

"He goes to bars where homosexuals hang out."

"How do you know this?"

"Not from personal visits, believe me." She drank more coffee, testing his patience. "One of the Romeos liked to drink when he wasn't on assignment. I always made sure to have a good supply of beer and schnapps on hand."

Stefan suppressed a grin at the thought of Helga having made a similar swap with someone else—liquor and most likely sex in exchange for information about her boss's indiscretions. Could this be the agent who crashed his car into a ditch in the wee hours of the morning? If he'd heard the name, he couldn't recall, and Helga would not want to reveal her lover's identity.

He asked, "So what did you learn after you loosened the boozer's tongue?"

She gazed out the window that afforded a view of low-hanging clouds swirling around the apartment complex across the street.

After a long moment, she turned back. "What did I learn? Something quite disturbing. Turns out my friend went to gay bars looking for action."

"Are you saying he's—?"

"Bisexual. I had a funny feeling about him. Should have trusted my instincts. I'm pretty open-minded, but I didn't want to risk catching some dreaded venereal disease."

So she cut off the sex, Stefan thought, but he said, "A multidimensional Romeo."

"You could say that. I don't think the general knows he has an agent who could seduce either gender."

"Let me guess. On one of his jaunts he ran into Heinrich."

"Not ran into exactly. One glimpse of the general and my . . . friend bolted."

Fighting disappointment at the meager news, Stefan said, "So that's all you know about your boss's escapades?"

"Hardly."

He raised his eyebrows. "There's more?"

"My friend kept watch outside. After some time, the general emerged and hurried down the sidewalk. Our Romeo was about to give up, when a young man exited the bar and lingered. Within a few minutes, a Wartburg sedan came rumbling around the corner and stopped a few meters past the bar. The passenger door swung open, and the car's interior light illuminated Heinrich's face for the few seconds it took the man to jump in and slam the door."

"Hmm. Heinrich canvassing a gay hangout for romantic prospects. Is this the only pickup your friend witnessed?"

"Far from it. He wanted to collect as much dirt as he could on the general, just in case he ever found himself in a tight spot. He discovered which establishments Heinrich frequented, and he claimed to have photos of the general and a few of his paramours."

Stefan leaned forward onto the table, causing his cup to tip in its saucer. "You've seen the pictures?"

"No."

"Did he say what they show?"

"Only that they left no doubt what the general and his partners were doing."

"Taken at Heinrich's house?"

"He didn't say."

Stefan sought her eyes. "Any chance you'll tell me this Romeo's name?"

"We'll see after you return from Bonn."

Chapter Fifty-Six

The Bonn Assignment

Bonn, Monday and Tuesday, 15-16 August 1977

Thanks to the complicated flight arrangements Heinrich had insisted on, Günter didn't reach his Bonn hotel until evening. He bypassed the check-in line and dialed Monika's number from a lobby phone. After a dozen rings, he hung up. The clock above the reception desk showed six thirty. Could she still be at work? No way to find out. Contacting her at the Chancellery was out of the question.

Judging from the lengthy queue, Hotel Freiburg was popular with business travelers and tourists alike. With rooms in high demand, he hoped Helga's skills extended beyond the bedroom.

"You'll be staying with us for a week, Herr Freund?" the brunette in blue uniform asked.

He nodded. "What checkout date do you have?"

She gave him a curious look. "Sunday, August 21. Isn't that what you reserved?"

"Yes, just wanting to make sure." True to his word, Heinrich had given him exactly one week to deliver.

His room on the seventh floor turned out to be rather plain. Was the Stasi scrimping, or trying to foster the image of their Romeo working for a low-budget Vienna peace organization? He heaved his suitcase onto the bed, but instead of unpacking, tried Monika's number again. Still no answer. Where in the hell was she? Then he caught himself and scoffed at the ridiculous expectation of her sitting by the phone waiting for his call. So much for the romantic dinner he'd envisioned for his first night in Bonn.

Every so often, he stopped unpacking to dial Monika's number. With every unanswered call his speculations meandered from her enjoying after-work drinks with colleagues, to having gone to a movie, to being out on a date.

He couldn't fathom her becoming involved with someone just days after their Cologne tryst. She'd fallen for him, hadn't she? Or was his male ego deceiving him? An attractive blonde divorcee could always draw a suitor or two. He still hadn't come to grips with how he felt about her having an admirer, when she answered his nine-o'clock phone call.

He said, "*Guten Abend*, Monika."

"Günter?"

"Yes, it's me. I've been trying to reach you all evening."

"I just got home from a long day at the office. We're swamped. Is something wrong?"

"No, nothing's wrong. You won't believe this. I'm on temporary assignment to Bonn."

"Oh, really."

Günter held the phone off to the side for a moment, studying its speaker. Could it have distorted her expression so it didn't convey the surprise he'd expected to hear in her voice? He pressed the handset back to his ear. "Aren't you excited?"

"Yes, of course."

"Would you like me to come over?"

A pause. "Sorry, I'm just too tired, Günter. How about we meet for lunch tomorrow?"

He swallowed his disappointment. "That'd be great. Where?"

"Café Herbst. Twelve thirty."

Long after he'd written down the directions and they'd said their goodbyes, he stared at the phone on the nightstand. The Monika he knew would have asked him over no matter how tired she was.

♫ ♫ ♫

Günter exited the streetcar and crossed over to the sidewalk. He stopped and peered up at the noontime sun obscured by a thin cloud cover. By the time he'd determined that east lay to his left, a business type jostled his elbow with a briefcase. Instead of apologizing, the man hurried past muttering something about blocking the sidewalk. Günter set off in the opposite direction. Monika had told him he'd find Café Herbst a few hundred meters east of the streetcar stop.

As he fell in with the throng of pedestrians moving along the sidewalk, he replayed last night's phone conversation in his mind. Did Monika really work late yesterday or had she found someone else? Maybe she'd asked him to lunch for the sole purpose of saying goodbye.

He'd told Heinrich the truth about having developed feelings for her. While his stomach churned at the thought of losing her, his intellect counseled thoughtful consideration. Going their separate ways might be for the best. He could end his deception and perhaps maintain or regain the principles Helga had seen in him. A breakup would hurt, but who said doing the right thing was supposed to be easy?

Even better, her ditching him for another could give him the perfect excuse for failing to turn her into a traitor. The Stasi avoided targeting secretaries who were in a relationship as too risky. That's why the general had gone to great lengths to ensure Monika remained unattached until he could send a Romeo to Italy. If Monika had a new beau, Heinrich might just give up on her and maybe even discharge him as an incompetent Romeo. But expecting the general to let him return to his private life was wishful thinking. Most likely, he'd end up back in prison and

Traude's voice studies would come to an abrupt halt. No matter what happened with Monika, Günter vowed to get more dirt on the general by staying on Helga's good side.

He was still sorting his emotions when Monika walked up to him from the café entrance and gave him a feather kiss on the cheek.

He reached for the door, but she stopped him. "There's at least a thirty-minute wait and I have to be back at the office by one thirty. I had no idea they'd be this busy. How would you feel about walking me back to the Chancellery and grabbing bratwurst on the way?"

Not the sit-down lunch he'd imagined. "Sure."

Purse slung over her shoulder, she took him by the hand and led him through the crowd. The congested sidewalk made it impossible to put his arm around her waist or to carry on a conversation, other than professing his delight at meeting up so soon again. After passing numerous shops and restaurants, they stopped at a sidewalk stand and ordered bratwurst and cola. Standing, they ate from paper plates.

With no one else on their side of the cart, Monika said between juicy bratwurst bites, "I can't believe you're actually here. What is this temporary assignment?"

He gave the answer Heinrich had rehearsed him on. "Gemeinschaft Unbegrenzt received an anonymous tip that the West German government is accelerating its covert rearmament plan. You recall us discussing it in Vienna?"

"I remember."

"My boss sent me here to gather whatever intelligence I can. What better place than Bonn to dig up some hard evidence." He took a chewy bite and chased the food with cola. He would need to be more explicit if he wanted her to help him, but this was not the right time.

"You're in a hotel?"

"Yes."

"How long are you staying?"

"Not sure, but I'd say at least a week."

"That's wonderful. I told you they're working me to death, but my evenings are yours, if you like."

"Of course, I like, silly." After wiping juice off his lips with a paper napkin, he kissed her cheek. She leaned into him for a moment, but then pulled back.

They tossed their empty plates and Styrofoam cups into a large trash can and resumed their walk. This time he kept an arm around her waist. While she didn't resist, she didn't seem exactly responsive.

When the Chancellery came in sight, she stopped and faced him. "I should make it home by seven. Want to come by then?"

"Yes."

"You remember my address?"

"Of course."

"What's your hotel in case I need to call you?"

"Hotel Freiburg."

She laid a hand on his forearm. "And I want to ask you a favor."

"What is that?"

"I'm sure I won't feel like cooking. Can you bring a carryout dinner--a roasted chicken or pizza or whatever looks good to you?"

"Be glad to."

"Great. I'll supply the wine and I'll have a surprise for you."

He imagined a black, sexy negligee. "What kind of surprise?"

"It wouldn't be one if I told you, would it?"

"I suppose not, but a hint would be nice."

"Something that might put you on the right track." She kissed him on the mouth for only a moment, then turned away and strode off in the direction of the Chancellery. She called over her shoulder. "See you at seven."

Long after she'd disappeared, he remained at the same spot, transfixed. Had she just offered to help him gather intelligence? As executive secretary to the chief of the

Chancellery, she'd definitely have access to highly classified documents. Secrets could be there for the asking, but he'd better ask soon or Heinrich would have his hide.

Chapter Fifty-Seven

No Time to Linger

Bonn, Tuesday, 16 August 1977

Monika made it to her apartment a few minutes before seven. She dropped her briefcase on the small desk in the bedroom, kicked off her high heels and slipped into a pair of comfortable loafers. About to trade her pinstriped business suit for something casual, she changed her mind. Office garb would be better suited for what she'd agreed to do this evening.

To fortify herself for the task ahead, she started for the kitchen to open a bottle of wine, but stopped at the sight of the briefcase on the desk. She spun its combination lock, overshooting two of the four numbers. A few deep breaths and she'd calmed enough to select the right combination, retrieve a business-size envelope from inside, and set the case on the floor.

She slid the envelope under a stack of papers in the desk's top drawer, but even as she shut it, she scanned the room for a better place to stash it in case she was the target of a trap. Tape the envelope to the back of a drawer or to the bottom of the mattress, or stash it behind pillows on the top closet shelf? No, none of these would elude a professional for long. In fact, no place in her apartment was safe.

Now she needed that glass of wine. Uncorking a bottle of Beaujolais in the kitchen, pouring herself a glass, and taking a quick gulp would have relaxed her if she'd only been able to quit thinking about that stupid envelope. She was raising her glass when the perfect hiding place came to her.

She set down the glass, returned to the bedroom, and pulled the envelope from the desk drawer. She slid it inside a larger one, which she addressed to herself and sealed. She rummaged through the desk until she found a roll of adhesive tape. Envelope and tape in hand, she was rushing into the hall when the doorbell sounded. She froze for an instant, then yanked the mail-chute cover open. A few seconds, and she'd taped the large envelope to the inside. If someone surprised her, she could launch it down to the basement and reclaim it when the mailroom opened in the morning.

She tossed the tape onto the bedroom desk and hurried to the front door. A quick look through the peephole, and she opened.

After a moment's hesitation, Günter handed her a bouquet of red roses. "You did say seven?"

"Yes. I haven't had time to shed my office clothes." She smelled the roses. "Ah, lovely." She wagged a finger. "Thank you, but you shouldn't have. Please come in."

He carried a pizza box across the threshold, keeping it at arm's length from his navy blazer and tan slacks. His wavy, dark hair, the easy smile playing in his blue-gray eyes reminded her why'd she'd fallen for him. She turned away, lest she lose her resolve.

"Where do you want the pizza?"

"Kitchen." She led him across the Persian carpet covering most of the hardwood living room floor. Along with the cream-colored sofa and the stereo, the rug was one of the few nice things she'd managed to salvage during the divorce.

In the kitchen, she pointed to the small table opposite the sink and stove. While Günter set the carton next to the bottle of wine and her half-full glass, she reached on tiptoe for a vase on an upper shelf.

As she placed the bouquet on the table, Günter flipped open the carton, revealing a large, round pizza sliced into eight pieces. "I took a guess that you like pepperoni and mushroom."

"An excellent guess." Even though food was the last thing her knotted stomach desired, she added, "Smells good."

To deflate lingering tension, she busied herself with silverware and plates and a wineglass for him. "I don't have any Austrian or German wine, just Beaujolais. I hope that's all right."

"Oh yes. That's a special treat we don't normally . . . I mean, I usually choose German and Austrian varieties."

A special treat for whom? East Germans? She joined him at the table and filled his glass. "I'm surprised you wouldn't find Beaujolais in Vienna," she said with as innocent a tone as she could muster.

"It's just that my neighborhood store carries hardly any French wines." He took a sip. "Very smooth. I like it."

Good recovery on his part. She'd better ease up, or he might wonder if she was on to him. "I understand. I buy this Beaujolais in a store near the office that specializes in French varieties."

He nodded and grabbed a slice of pizza, but before eating, he fixed his warm gaze on her. "I know it's only been a week, but I really missed you."

To gain time to think how to respond, she forced herself to take a bite. "I still can't believe you're here in Bonn."

He stopped eating. "You seem distant, Monika. Is something wrong?"

"I'm sorry, Günter. I'm just overwhelmed with work." His doubtful look told her she needed to be more convincing. "It has nothing to do with you," she lied.

"Are you sure?"

Good thing she'd rehearsed. She covered his hand with hers. "I told you my evenings were yours, but I'm afraid not until later in the week. My boss asked me to come in early tomorrow. And I'm just worn out. If I don't get a good night's sleep, I can't function at the office, and I won't be fit company. I have to turn in early tonight. I hope you'll understand." She didn't avert her eyes like someone making up an excuse, but held his gaze the whole time.

Still, he didn't seem convinced. "You're sure there's nothing wrong between us?"

"Absolutely. More pizza?"

He ate another slice while she picked at hers. To steel herself, she gulped more Beaujolais. She wanted so much to believe Günter was genuine and not the Stasi Romeo the BND suspected him to be. Even if he was a commie spy, she felt sure he had feelings for her. He couldn't possibly fake such passion, could he?

Besides, could she really trust the government? Enough secret documents had crossed her desk to shake her belief in the total veracity of the federal government's pronouncements. Still, Sabine Maier had briefed her, presenting compelling evidence that Gemeinschaft Unbegrenzt didn't exist and that there never had been a Cologne peace conference. Even if the agent had exaggerated, she couldn't have invented all of it, unless this whole thing was a trap. Monika didn't know whom she could trust—the government or Günter, if that was even his real name.

He pushed back his empty plate, interrupting her musings. While she stacked her plate on top of his and closed the carton on half a pizza, she made up her mind.

"I do care about you and your cause, Günter. And I'm going to prove it to you."

"How—?"

"I'm going to give you something to help your peace organization. Be right back." She rose and walked through the living room into the hall. She peeled the large envelope off the chute wall and tore it open. After retrieving its contents, she tossed the ripped envelope onto the bedroom desk and headed back, but hesitated out of Günter's sight. She took a deep breath and went on, casting her lot irrevocably with the government.

She eased back onto the chair and slid the business-size envelope across the kitchen table. "Take a look."

He peeled back the flap and pulled out several sheets stapled together and read, "A memorandum proposing to increase the budget of the Bundeswehr." He lowered the memo. "Is this classified?"

She nodded. "Go on." She reached for her glass. Careful, she'd better slow down.

He read for a minute, then looked up. "There is more to this than West Germany wanting to beef up its armed forces, isn't there?"

"Yes, evidence of the covert rearmament plan your organization sent you here to uncover. Look at the distribution list."

"The chancellor, defense minister, and foreign minister. Hmm, no one from NATO."

"Nor the allied commander," Monika added.

He started to read again, but she interrupted. "Not here. I've been on pins and needles just having this in my apartment. You can take it with you, but you have to promise me you won't reveal where you got it. I cut out a couple of phrases to make sure the memo can't be traced to me. If it is, I'll not only lose my job, but . . . well, you know what. So I need your word you won't tell a soul how you came by this."

He raised his hand. "I swear. Thank you, Monika. You've done a good deed."

"I hope it helps your cause. I wish you could stay, Günter, but I just can't have the memo in the apartment a moment longer. Please understand."

"I suppose I better go, but that doesn't mean I like it." He stuffed the memo back in the envelope.

She walked him to the door and kissed him on the cheek. "I'll call you tomorrow and let you know when I'm free."

He gave her a goodbye hug and slipped out.

As she closed and locked the door behind him, guilt assaulted her. Hoping she'd made the right choice, she headed for the kitchen in search of the Beaujolais.

♫ ♫ ♫

Günter rode the elevator down in a daze. Feelings of confusion over the abrupt way Monika had dismissed him rivaled his elation over his good fortune at getting his hands on the memo. It had been almost too easy. Upon leaving the building, he peered up and down the street, checking entrances to shops, restaurants and office buildings. All quiet. On his way to the streetcar stop, he continually scanned his surroundings. No sign of anyone following.

He should go straight to the dead drop in the park, but no way would he deliver the document to Heinrich without having read it all the way through. And if it contained information he could put to good use later, he should keep a copy, too. His mind made up, he slipped the envelope into his inside pocket and took the streetcar back to his hotel.

After one more look around, he entered the lobby of Hotel Freiburg. The bar looked inviting, and he certainly could use a drink. But he was eager to read the memo and flashing it in a public place was not a good idea. So he collected his key at the front desk and ran up three flights of stairs to his room. Anticipation, excitement and adrenalin caused him to fumble with the key until he finally managed to insert it in the lock and push open the door.

He flipped the light switch. A shove sent him staggering forward. The door banged shut behind him. As he squinted against the bright overhead lights, a female voice came from a corner of the room.

"Good evening Herr Freund. I think it's time we had a chat."

Chapter Fifty-Eight

An Early Night

Stasi Headquarters, East Berlin, Wednesday, 17 August 1977

Heinrich had barely exchanged good morning greetings with Helga Schröder when she handed him a sealed envelope bearing his name. "This was delivered a few minutes ago."

"Well, it's about time . . ." He stopped himself. This had better be a transmission from Stefan.

"Is there something I can help with, General?"

Schröder's solicitous tone and her expression of undue interest put him off. Though the purpose of Stefan's Bonn mission would not be a secret to her, the details were none of her business.

"No." Having sounded gruffer than he'd intended, he added, "I'll let you know after I take a look at this."

Eager to read the message in private, he went to his office, dropped his briefcase on the desk, and ripped open the envelope. A transmission from the operative he had tasked with keeping an eye on Stefan. According to the time stamp, it was received at one fifteen this morning.

His eyes flew over the cryptic message. It took a second, slower reading, to decipher the meaning.

Stefan left Monika's apartment at 8:15 Tuesday evening. He slipped an envelope into his jacket and returned to his hotel. He stayed in, at least until midnight when the operative broke off the surveillance.

Heinrich flung the paper onto the desk and slumped into his chair, digesting the disturbing news. Stefan had not spent the night at Monika's.

Either the romance had worn off or his Romeo had gotten cold feet, or God forbid, he had developed scruples. More likely, Monika had dumped him, though that seemed inconsistent with her giving him an envelope, which surely didn't contain a love note or a *kuchen* recipe. Maybe she'd sent him away with incriminating material she was afraid to keep in her apartment. The thought buoyed Heinrich's spirits, but only for an instant. If she'd entrusted him with state secrets, he should have put them in the dead drop immediately. No report from either him or the agent responsible for pickup meant he had not done so. What the hell was Stefan up to? He'd been in Bonn more than two days and had yet to make contact.

Heinrich read the transmission once more, hoping to wring additional meaning from the text. To no avail. He crumpled the paper and dropped it back on the desk. He considered his options. Having the agent responsible for collecting materials from the dead drop make contact with Stefan was out of the question. Heinrich held to one of tradecraft's central tenets: operatives communicating through a dead drop must not know one another and should never see one another. He would not deviate from that ironclad policy. Nor did he want to blow the cover of the agent he had tasked with shadowing Stefan.

Perhaps the delinquent Romeo would respond to an order to report immediately. With that thought in mind, Heinrich wrote *Sofort Bericht erstatten* on a notepad. He tore off the sheet, folded it in half, and slid it into an envelope, which he addressed to *Knast*. He congratulated himself for having assigned Stefan the perfect code name for radio transmissions—an unequivocal reminder to his Romeo to perform or he'd find himself back in the can. About to buzz his secretary, Heinrich withdrew the finger poised over the intercom button. Chances were she knew the code name. He grabbed a large envelope, slid the smaller one inside, sealed it, and called Schröder.

After she'd gone to the radio department, Heinrich sat back. He'd give Stefan until the end of the day to report. But planning ahead, Heinrich opened the wall safe and searched through the list of assets in the West for the best man to make contact with his errant Romeo should he fail to comply with his order. He couldn't use the one who'd bungled the break-in, nor the one who'd sabotaged the brakes of the BND agent's VW.

Not to worry, he had plenty of operatives to choose from.

Chapter Fifty-Nine

The Dead Drop

Bonn, Wednesday, 17 August 1977

Having walked the aisles of Hotel Freiburg's gift shop twice, Günter approached the clerk at the cash register. "Pardon, where do you keep the chewing gum?"

The young woman shook her head. "I just sold the last package, but I expect a delivery shortly."

Günter stared at her. Shortage of supplies was commonplace for the socialist economy back home, but here in capitalist West Germany?

He must have looked perplexed as the woman added, "The salesman was due here this morning. If you want to come back in an hour or so, I'm sure I'll have some then."

Time was something he didn't have. "Thank you." He left the shop and the hotel.

Hurrying along the sidewalk in search of a place likely to sell gum, he chided himself for not having bought some yesterday. But then, Monika's delivery had taken him by complete surprise, to say nothing of the reception committee in his hotel room.

A neon sign ahead caught his attention. *Fam. Müller Lebensmittel.* He entered the small family grocer's store and made his way past fruits and vegetables toward a rack with candy bars. The chewing gum had to be close by—sure enough, he found it on the next shelf over. Not one to chew gum, he searched among the selection for a flavor he could stand. A few minutes later, he exited the store with a package of spearmint in his jacket pocket.

After a short ride on Stadtbahn line 66, he emerged from the underground *Universität/Markt* station onto a cobblestone sidewalk and found himself in a green oasis in the center of Bonn. A city map nestled against the envelope in his inside jacket pocket, but he had no need for it, since Heinrich had briefed him on the layout in minute detail. He took the footpath that meandered eastward through the park. Leaves of the plane and beech trees populating *Hofgarten* rustled in the breeze, and an occasional gust of wind tousled his hair.

He counted the benches—all empty due to the overcast, windy day, until he reached the sixth, on which lounged a bearded man in a rumpled overcoat. Throwing breadcrumbs from a brown paper bag to a flock of fluttering pigeons and sparrows, the man paid him no attention, and Günter moved past without making eye contact.

At the seventh bench, he slowed his steps and peered hard, seeking the oak tree captured in Heinrich's photos. Beech and plane trees but no oak as far as the eye could see. The directions he'd committed to memory would get him there, but a furtive glance over his shoulder convinced him he couldn't take the risk. The man feeding the birds from a seemingly bottomless bag was a mere fifty meters away. A BND operative, a Stasi agent, or a private citizen?

Günter opted for being extra cautious by biding his time until the bird nut left. He walked on, picking up his pace. Might as well get some exercise in the fresh air. Every so often, he slowed, admiring an unusual tree or the graceful trios of light globes sitting high on steel lampposts alongside the path. After fifteen minutes, he turned around. The man should have run out of breadcrumbs by now.

He cut his pace and peered ahead. His luck was changing. No sign of the bird-feeding man down the path and bench seven still stood empty. As Günter broke into a fast walk, a young couple came strolling hand in hand from the opposite direction. They stopped by the bench, eyeing it as if contemplating a cozy snuggle there. Before they could sit, he flopped down on the wooden slats, not caring how rude he appeared. He caught a look passing between them before they moved on. He wondered whether they might settle on the next bench. They kept going, but his gaze remained fixed on the woman's shapely butt in tight jeans until the couple disappeared around a bend.

Back to the task. With no one else approaching, he headed into the woods in a northerly direction, counting his steps as he went. Before he reached the magic number of eighty-seven, he identified the gnarled oak by the pictures in Heinrich's portfolio. The tree had not one but three trunks, intertwining like lovers engaged in a ménage à trois. What was the matter with him? First, he'd lusted after the woman with the eye-catching butt, and now his mind likened an oak tree to eccentric sexual behavior. He must be sex-starved, and he blamed Monika for being so standoffish lately.

A headshake, and he snapped out of it. He circled the tree until he spotted a narrow gap between the trunks. After checking his surroundings, he stepped across the thick roots and squeezed through the small opening into a cramped space. Not seeing well in the dim enclosure, he straightened and promptly hit his head. He stooped, but then a movement startled him. Just as he thought snake, a squirrel dashed past him.

Musky smell assaulted his nostrils as he searched for a hollow space. With his pupils not yet adjusted to the dim light, he kept turning while examining the three trunks centimeter by centimeter. There it was: a cave-like depression by his left thigh. Unable to lean forward in the confined space, he lowered himself by bending his knees in a yoga pose. He fingered the envelope in his breast jacket pocket, separated it from the city map by feel, and pulled it out. One more maneuver and his job was done, or so he thought. The damn thing refused to go all the way into the depression. No matter how remote the possibility, he couldn't risk that someone might stumble upon this hideout. He retrieved the envelope. To check on the obstruction, he did a deeper knee bend, ignoring his burning thigh muscles.

He should have brought a flashlight, but by now, his pupils had adjusted enough to permit a decent look inside the depression. He almost broke out in laughter at the sight of a pile of nuts filling half the chamber. A provident squirrel was getting an early start on planning for the cold season. He scooped up a handful of nuts and dropped them on the ground. Although winter was months away, he almost felt guilty for depriving the squirrel of its stash. Now the envelope slid far enough inside that only its front edge remained visible.

He stuck his head outside and scanned the area. Still no one around. He climbed out, brushed soil off his jacket and trousers, and headed back to the path. The sound of voices brought him to a halt. A woman and a man had taken the bench and were carrying on a lively conversation. Too many Germans who weren't working and could afford to while away their hours in the park. Nothing about this mission was easy, but there was no point getting frustrated. Careful not to step on loose twigs, he resumed his walk, changing directions to connect with the path out of the benchwarmers' sight.

He gained the footpath and hurried back to the entrance. With his luck, he expected a horde of passengers milling about the underground exit. He was half-right. Although travelers emerged from the station, no one hung around the posts displaying the train schedule. Finally, no complications.

He started across the cobblestone pavement toward blue U-signs marking the Stadtbahn station. While waiting for a silver coupe turning from a side street onto *Am Hofgarten*, he fished the chewing gum from his jacket pocket, unwrapped two strips, and put them in his mouth. The spearmint tasted refreshing. He stepped up to the underground signs held up by three steel posts. A bicycle chained to the front post obscured part of the train schedule displayed in a rectangular yellow box. He bent forward, pretending to study the schedule while in fact scrutinizing the rear post facing the side street.

When a woman walked up, he moved aside, letting her peek at the schedule. She hurried off, apparently in pursuit of her soon-to-arrive train. Before anyone else approached, Günter extracted the gum from his mouth and stuck it high on the rear post.

Mission accomplished, he went back to the station. He was tempted to stay around despite Heinrich's order to leave immediately after he had given the dead-drop signal. The general hadn't said why he needed to clear out, but Günter had a good idea what the reason was.

No matter. He was pretty sure other eyes would be watching.

Chapter Sixty

The Stakeout

Hofgarten Park, Bonn, Wednesday, 17 August 1977

Sabine emerged from the *Universität/Markt* underground station and lingered on the cobblestone sidewalk while pedestrians hurried past. After a moment, she walked straight ahead, away from Hofgarten Park, and entered a lot in front of a church whose steeple stretched high toward the overcast sky. She headed for a white Volkswagen van stationed close to the park, right next to a large no-parking sign. *Stadtbahn Bonn* was painted in blue cursive letters on the vehicle's side panel.

Before she could knock, the side door slid open. With a firm grip, Mertens pulled her inside and shut the door. He indicated a young man sitting in front of a black-and-white video screen. "You remember my assistant, Jörg Eck?"

"Of course." How could she forget the overeager agent who'd attempted to vet her at the Sturm apartment before Mertens intervened? She said, *"Guten Tag."*

Eck nodded at her, then returned his attention to the monitor. With his body in the way, she couldn't make out the image.

Mertens pointed to a swivel stool next to Eck. "Have a look."

She sat. Now she had a clear view of the cobblestone promenade, the underground station, and the U-signs displayed on the screen.

When Mertens settled on a stool by her side, she asked, "How long have you been watching?"

"Since eleven." He pulled his gaze from the monitor and turned toward her. "What took you so long?"

"Sorry, but my boss kept me on the phone, quizzing me on every minute detail about the setup."

Mertens chuckled. "Yes, that's the Dorfmann I know."

The screen showed people leaving and entering the Stadtbahn station. "I haven't missed anything, have I?"

"Only our Romeo making his drop."

"He's gone already?"

Mertens nodded. "Stuck the chewing gum on the rear post of the underground sign and took off."

"Everything go as planned?"

He gave her a sheepish look. "Actually, we had a little excitement, but—"

At a knock on the chassis, Mertens jumped off his stool and slid the van's side door half open.

A policeman poked in his head. "Your Stadtbahn credentials, please."

An awkward pause, then Mertens said, "Ah, officer. We're not actually with the city rail system. But we—"

"I thought so. You're in a no-parking zone." He pulled a ticket book from his uniform breast pocket.

"Wait a minute, officer." Mertens stuck his credentials under the policeman's nose. "We're engaged in an undercover operation that involves national security." He softened his tone. "Your thoroughness is to be commended, but we must get back to our observation before the suspect slips away. We'd appreciate your discretion."

The police officer tipped his cap. "Sorry for disturbing you, sir. Please carry on." He withdrew just as the van door slammed shut.

Mertens turned back. "German police. So thorough, so conscientious . . ."

"And so meddling," Sabine finished his sentence. "But tell me about the excitement you—"

Eck's urgent voice reverberated through the van, "Likely courier approaching."

Sabine and Mertens crowded around as he pointed at an image on the black-and-white screen. A man Sabine judged to be in his early thirties with short hair parted on the side, wearing a herringbone jacket and plain slacks, moved across the cobblestones. On his way to the U-signs, he kept glancing around. When he faced the van, Eck pressed a button, unleashing a series of camera clicks.

Sabine took in the broad face, the slim body—not bad looking for a carrier. Surely, the Stasi didn't use Romeos for dead-drop pickups. The young man waited while an elderly woman checked the timetable. When she left, he leaned forward. He seemed fascinated with the table in front of him, as if train schedules made for the most interesting reading in the world. As best as she could tell, he didn't check the posts for gum.

He quit his perusal and joined a throng of passengers hurrying toward the station. Mertens shot Sabine a questioning look. She held her breath, anticipating the man's descent into the underground station, but he veered off at the last minute and took the path into Hofgarten Park.

"If he looked for the gum, I sure couldn't tell," Mertens said. "I bet he's the carrier, and skilled at that. We should know soon."

"Are you monitoring the oak tree?"

"No good way of doing so without scaring off the spook."

"But you have agents patrolling the park?"

"Of course."

Tension-filled silence pervaded the van's interior, the labored breathing of Mertens being the only sound. All three stared at the monitor even though its range didn't include the park.

Static crackled from a speaker, interrupting their wait. A female voice cut through, "Subject off the path."

Mertens reached for a console on the shelf and pushed a button. "Advise when pickup is complete."

"Okay." Static followed by silence.

Mertens explained, "Message from our lovebirds strolling through the park."

After another seemingly endless wait, the female spoke again. Sabine strained to understand her whisper. "Cargo on its way."

When the man appeared on the screen, Eck activated the camera again. The shutter didn't stop clicking until the subject disappeared down the station entrance. After a few seconds, a man moved across the cobblestones and entered the station.

"Our tail?" Sabine asked.

Mertens nodded. "And we have a female agent stationed on the platform." He then clapped Eck on the back. "Good job."

He turned back to Sabine. "First step accomplished. We'll check the photos against our database. Stop by my office later for your set."

"I will, but I'd still like to know what the excitement was about."

"Oh, yes. We had our agent positioned too close. Freund got spooked and kept on walking. But it all worked out. We pulled our man and Freund made the drop."

"He must know we're watching him."

"I suppose he didn't want to take any chances." Mertens scrunched up his face. "But the way he kept his wits about him by moving on makes me question his story of being a novice, a reluctant Romeo pressed into service by General Heinrich."

"You think Stefan Malik a/k/a Günter Freund could be a plant?"

"I wouldn't put it past the Stasi spymaster to concoct a reluctant spy, who only pretends we've turned him."

She wrinkled her brow at the thought the Stasi might be playing them. "We could have a comrade on our hands—a true believer . . . a Red Romeo."

Mertens shrugged. "We'll just have to see what he brings us, but it won't be easy to tell the difference between disinformation and real intelligence." He looked her in the eye. "I trust we made the right decision to let him go. Once he's back in East Germany—"

"He'll come through for us." She hoped she sounded more convinced than she felt. She'd persuaded Dorfmann to approve her plan. Günter Freund couldn't be a fake, or her career would be stuck in neutral, and she could kiss the promotion Dorfmann had promised goodbye.

Mertens slid back the side door. "So far so good."

As she stepped down, she knew he shared her worries about the several obstacles ahead. For the BND to succeed, the Stasi spymaster had to buy his Romeo's surprising success in obtaining the Bundeswehr memo. And Günter Freund's conversion to double agent had to be genuine. He could simply reveal that his cover had been blown and remain in East Germany. In that case, she'd have to do a lot of explaining as to why she'd let a Stasi Romeo get away.

Chapter Sixty-One

Inexcusable Delay

Stasi Headquarters, East Berlin, Wednesday, 17 August 1977

Heinrich shoved the magazine into a desk drawer. Nothing could take his mind off the Bonn dead drop, not even pictures of men in jock straps flexing their muscular bodies. He walked to the window and gazed down on Ruschestraße. Pedestrians hurried along the sidewalk, perhaps intent on reaching home before nightfall. Exhaust fumes from sputtering Trabant and Wartburg sedans spiraled in the twilight.

He turned away from the window. The agent must have missed the transit train in Cologne, scheduled to arrive in East Berlin over an hour ago. Otherwise, the packet would have been delivered by now. Heinrich rued having stayed at the office hours past quitting time. No point wasting any more of the evening. He locked his desk, grabbed his uniform jacket off the coatrack, slipped into it, and headed for the door.

Passing Schröder's vacant workstation, he stopped at the sound of footfalls and labored breathing. A few seconds later,

Lieutenant Gruber lugged his stocky frame from the staircase onto the tile floor of the reception area.

His fleshy face red from exhaustion, he took several ragged breaths and handed over an envelope. "I'm glad I caught you, General."

"What took you so long?"

"I'm sorry, sir, but the transit train was delayed at the border. There were several passengers without proper papers." He took another deep breath. "Then I had to wait until the restroom was free before I could pull the materials from the hiding place. I got here as fast as I could."

Heinrich grunted. "I wish everyone around here was as dedicated, Lieutenant."

"Thank you, General." Gruber turned and walked down the stairs.

Heinrich went back to his office. As much as he wanted to rip into the envelope, he took the time to grab the silver letter opener from a pencil holder on his desk. Careful not to damage the contents, he slid the opener along the flap and pulled out a stapled document. So focused was he on reading the memo that he almost missed the seat of his chair as he lowered himself.

Proposal to increase the budget of the Bundeswehr. On the face of it, nothing to get excited about. He'd gotten his hands on West German military budgets before. He speed-read through the six-page document. When he reached the last page, eager anticipation gave way to disappointment. What was he missing? He flipped back to the front. Of course. No one from NATO on the distribution list. He must be tired to have overlooked something so obvious—clear evidence of West Germany's secret plan to beef up its armed forces without NATO's knowledge.

His threats had finally borne fruit; Stefan Malik had delivered valuable intelligence. This called for a little celebration. He dropped the papers on the desk and fumbled for keys in his trouser pocket. A few moments later, he'd unlocked the credenza cabinet and poured schnapps into a shot glass. He downed the liquid in one big gulp and shivered. The burning sensation traveled down his throat, jolted his stomach, and spread relaxation into every cell.

He had a good idea how Stasi chief Mielke and party chief Honeker would use this intelligence. They would love nothing better than to instigate a political firestorm by exposing the West Germans' covert militarization efforts. The resulting rift and distrust between West Germany and its allies might last for years, even decades. All good for East Germany.

Heinrich took a second drink. The schnapps shook loose worries he'd been subconsciously suppressing. Monika Fuchs could turn out to be his most valuable asset yet in the West. She had to have access to documents showing the inner workings of the Chancellery. But feeding intelligence gathered from the memo to the Western media could very well finger her as the source of the leak. He couldn't take that risk, but convincing his higher-ups to forgo the public relations coup would be a huge challenge. He could picture them reading with glee newspaper headlines that screamed outrage at West Germany's betrayal. Maybe he'd keep the memo to himself for now and see what else Stefan might weasel out of Monika.

Keeping intelligence from Mielke and Honeker was dangerous. To fortify himself, he had a third glass of schnapps. With the drink came suspicion. Why had Stefan delayed putting the memo in the dead drop? His explanation had better be damn good. In no mood to wait, Heinrich wrote the code words *Heimat Sofort* on his notepad, commanding Stefan's immediate return. He put the schnapps and glass away and picked up the recall order.

Now, what to do with the Bundeswehr memorandum? Normal procedure called for locking it in his desk, but wanting to pore over the memo this evening, he stuck it in the inside breast pocket of his uniform. As Stasi lieutenant general and head of foreign intelligence, he could ignore the rules when he deemed it necessary. Who would dare question him?

The order for Stefan's return in his hand, he rushed from the office. On his way to the radio department that should still be staffed at this hour, something besides Stefan's inexcusable delay worried him: the relative ease with which his novice Romeo had coaxed the memo out of Monika. Experience had taught Heinrich to be wary of affairs that went as smoothly as this one apparently had.

It took the brisk walk in fresh air to bring clarity. Not only did he need to grill Stefan, but first thing in the morning, he'd question the one person who would know better than anyone whether it was plausible that Monika would betray her country and risk her freedom for love.

Chapter Sixty-Two

The Pretense

Bonn, Wednesday, 17 August 1977

Monika dropped the dinner dishes into hot, soapy water and snatched the brush from its holder by the kitchen sink. How could she have been so naïve as to miss so many red flags and fall for a Stasi Romeo? It all started with the staged fight on the Viareggio beach when the handsome German who saved her just happened to love opera as much as she did. Then the ever-so-thoughtful man wooed her by taking her not only to the Puccini Festival but by fulfilling her lifelong dream of attending the Arena di Verona. Yet, he didn't seem to know much about *Aïda*, an opera so popular that even philistines were familiar with the story and the musical highlights.

She should have listened to her instincts. He was too good to be true. Had her broken marriage left her vulnerable, desperate for a considerate companion, and Günter just filled the void? He seemed the exact opposite of her abusive ex. Or had the fantastic sex blinded her to the subtle warning signs?

The loud clinking of plates startled her back to the present. Her hand ached from clutching the brush as if it were to blame for her predicament. The reddened skin of her arms and hands meant she must have been working over the dishes for some time—a wonder her intense scrubbing didn't break anything. She took a deep breath. No point in taking her anger out on the dishes. She rinsed the plates and silverware and set them on the drainboard.

She settled on the living room sofa with her second glass of wine. A buzz might make the rest of the evening tolerable. She thought about playing one of her opera records, but that would create the wrong mood. She turned on the television. The *Tagesschau* aired the usual fare of politicians' shenanigans and the crime du jour, one reason she made it a point never to watch the evening news.

No sooner had she turned down the sound than came the dreaded knock. She jumped up, almost spilling her wine as she set the glass on the coffee table. A quick look through the peephole, and she opened the door.

Clad in a maroon sport shirt and khakis, Günter stood in the hallway. "I brought a few necessities."

He brushed at a strand of his wavy dark hair in a vain attempt to sweep it off his forehead. As he shifted from one leg to the other, he moved a small duffel bag from hand to hand. His blue-gray eyes studied her.

Gone was the self-assured man she'd fallen in love with, but he'd find no sympathy here. She was much too angry to feel sorry for him. She averted her eyes and with a wave of her hand gestured him inside.

He set his bag on the carpet and gave her a questioning look. "Where—?"

"Settle on the sofa. That's where you'll be sleeping."

He shrugged and pointed to the glass on the table. "I should have brought some wine. Do you mind if I have some of yours?"

She saw no point in refusing him a drink, but no way would she serve him. "Bottle's in the kitchen; you know where to find a glass."

Left alone, she paced the living room. As much as she wanted to have it out with him, she would not let him see how much he had hurt her. An argument wouldn't resolve anything, but only increase her pain.

He returned from the kitchen with a full glass of red wine and took up his seat on the couch. "Monika, please let me explain—"

"What's there to explain?" She stared him down. Before she could help herself, she vented. "You're a goddam spy. You came on to me, pretended to love me, all so you could get me to spy for your commie masters. Tell me, how many others have you fucked for your fatherland?"

As if disconnected from her conscious thoughts, her fingers holding the wineglass twitched, urging her to dowse him.

His calm voice brought her back. "Monika, listen to me. I'm not trying to excuse my behavior. And I don't blame you for setting me up. After what I did to you, you had every right to turn me in to the BND."

"You got that right." She kept staring at him. "I may have to pretend we're still a couple to protect your cover, but that's it. It's over between us. You might be good at faking *Herr Spion*, but I don't like it one bit. If my job weren't on the line, there's no way you'd be here."

"Please hear me out. I never wanted to be a Stasi Romeo."

She held his gaze. He was a smooth talker, perhaps adding one more lie to the many tales he'd concocted to beguile her. But with his cover blown, to what purpose? He could no longer harm her. She turned off the television.

Arms crossed over her chest, she lowered herself onto the far edge of the sofa. "Make it short."

While he spoke of prison, General Heinrich, and his daughter, Traude, she studied him, looking for hints of yet another tall tale. He maintained eye contact throughout. As much as she didn't want to believe his story, she had to admit it rang true. No one would invent such an incredible tale and expect to be believed.

Still, she held onto a healthy dose of suspicion. Although he had claimed she'd been his first assignment, she asked nevertheless, "How many others have you seduced?"

"Zero." He took a big swig, as if washing down the unpleasantness, then faced her. "Monika, I've had my share of sexual partners, all East German women. That's why Heinrich picked me to do his dirty work. But I have never pretended love to . . ." He held up a hand, fending off her attempted protest. "I admit, I pretended at the beginning with you, but you must surely know that my feelings for you became real."

"No, I don't know that, and after all that's happened, I don't see how I could ever trust you again." She dropped her arms to her lap. "What am I saying? That's no longer relevant. Looks to me like you have little choice but to keep spying, and who knows, you might even become enthralled with the game of deception."

"Never." He waved his hand in protest. "I swear to you, Monika, there hasn't been anyone else in the West, and there never will be."

"How can you be so sure? Are you ready to rot in an East German prison cell?"

"Definitely not, but I think I have a way out."

"You *what?*"

"I can't say any more. But with any luck, my daughter and I will be in West Germany before long."

How could he be so confident about escaping from the GDR? He must have agreed to become a double agent for the BND to stay out of jail, but if the Stasi found out, he would be shot.

Her pulse raced. "What if the Stasi knows your cover has been blown?"

"I'll have to take my chances." He played with the stem of his glass. "I can't imagine you contacting the Stasi, and it's very much in the BND's interest to keep it quiet."

She put down her glass. "You can't defect, because you're worried what the Stasi will do to your daughter."

He nodded.

"And you have to do whatever the BND says, don't you?"

He looked away. "You'll be pleased to know that we won't have to keep up this charade for the rest of this week."

"Aren't you here till Sunday?"

"No, I've been ordered to return home early. I'm taking the morning transit train from Cologne."

"But the charade isn't over, is it? Your spymaster is going to send you back to coax more state secrets out of me."

He shrugged. "If I can convince him that you're crazy about me."

She drank some wine to sort conflicting emotions, not sure what would be worse—to keep up the pretense of romance or to never see him again. She tightened her jaw, banishing those thoughts.

Before she could change her mind, she picked up her glass and headed for the bedroom. "I'll do some reading in bed."

His voice followed her. "Thank you for hearing me out, Monika."

Closing the bedroom door, she wasn't sure whether to root for him and his daughter to make it to the West or to wipe his memory from her mind so she could get on with her life.

Chapter Sixty-Three

Monika's Friend

Stasi Headquarters, East Berlin, Thursday, 18 August 1977

Looking ahead to a busy Thursday morning, General Heinrich stepped from the staircase and approached Helga Schröder. She stopped typing and wished him a friendly good morning.

He reciprocated and said, "Check whether Gisela Sturm is back from vacation. If she is, I want to see her right away. And bring coffee."

"Yes, sir." She picked up the phone.

Heinrich had hardly hung up his uniform jacket on the coatrack when Schröder knocked on the half-open door and entered his office with a serving tray. "I brought a carafe and an extra cup for Frau Sturm. She's on her way."

"Good thinking." He indicated an empty desk surface. "Just leave it there."

She set down the tray and picked up the carafe.

"Thank you, Frau Schröder. I'll take it from here. Please leave the door open."

Heinrich was still doctoring his coffee with milk and sugar when Gisela Sturm entered the office and took a visitor's chair. They exchanged good morning greetings, and he offered her coffee. While she helped herself, he studied her. She looked different. Her makeup left something to be desired, and the hair color he'd found so attractive when he debriefed her and husband Klaus upon their hasty return from Bonn, now looked faded. The roots showed signs of gray. Maybe she couldn't find coloring in East Berlin to her liking, or she was depressed about leaving the good life in Bonn after so many years. She should count herself lucky to have made it out of West Germany just before the BND could arrest her.

He waited until she set her cup on the desk pullout before he spoke. "I've gone over my notes from our debriefing session last week, and there's an area I need to explore with you further."

"Of course, General."

"You know Monika Fuchs better than anyone. I'm going to tell you how she has turned over a top-secret document to our novice Romeo. Then I want your opinion whether anything rings false."

Without identifying its content, he proceeded to describe how Stefan had come by the Bundeswehr memo. She listened attentively to his account. After he finished, he asked, "Given what you know about Monika's character, her politics, do you find it credible that she'd betray her country like that?"

"I'm not sure, General. The way you described it, the whole thing seems a little smooth. But then, Monika was hopelessly in love. Your Romeo might be new, but he appears to be very good."

Just what he didn't need—a nonanswer. Heinrich leaned forward. "Are you saying it's possible Monika did this on her own out of pure love?"

"I have to say it's possible, General. You targeted her at the perfect time when she was the most vulnerable. Coming off a divorce from a real jerk who treated her like crap, she fell hard for this Romeo of yours."

Maybe he'd underestimated Stefan. Still, he couldn't shake the feeling that something didn't add up. "And there's nothing that would make you suspicious?"

She lowered her gaze and shifted in her chair. After a long moment, she looked up. "You taught me to always be suspicious, sir. But from what you've told me, I can't point to anything that would make me question Monika's action. As you know, things occasionally do go smoothly in the spy trade. That doesn't mean the operation wasn't legitimate."

She was echoing his thoughts; he wouldn't get any more useful information from her. He stood. "Thank you, Frau Sturm."

As she walked out, Heinrich sank back into his chair. He was no further along than before. Maybe he was too suspicious, inventing problems. Still, he would pursue this until totally satisfied Stefan Malik's delivery was a genuine coup.

With that thought, he pressed the intercom button. "Frau Schröder, has Malik come in yet?"

"A few minutes ago."

"Send him in."

He disconnected, cutting off her response.

Chapter Sixty-Four

The Suspicion

Stasi Headquarters, East Berlin, Thursday 18 August 1977

Stefan shot Helga a questioning look as he passed her desk. Her slight headshake signaled he'd likely face a general not in the best of moods. After perfunctory greetings, Heinrich pointed to a chair. Stefan took a seat right in front of a coffee tray on the desk, but the general didn't offer him any.

"How did you get Monika to hand over the memo?" Heinrich asked.

"When I saw her last Monday, I gave her the spiel you instructed me on—my temporary Bonn assignment to uncover evidence of—"

"I know the spiel I gave you, Malik. Just tell what you did to convince her to give you the memo."

Stefan swallowed. "After I told Monika why I'd come to Bonn, she hinted she might be able to put me on the right track."

"Did she say how?"

"No, but I was hoping she was referring to information she might be willing to let me have."

"But you didn't see her that evening?"

Stefan shook his head.

"Why not? Wasn't she eager to jump in the sack after she hadn't seen you for quite some time?"

"She was tired from doing overtime at the Chancellery. She told me to come to her apartment the next evening."

"Tuesday?"

"Yes. I had just arrived at her place that night when she handed me the memo. She told me it was the right thing for her to pass it on to my peace organization."

"You read it?"

"Before I could, she pointed to the distribution list. No one from NATO was listed."

"Did you sleep with her?"

That question Stefan had expected. "No, she was too anxious to get the memo out of her apartment. So she told me to leave and she'd see me the next day."

"Why was she so anxious?" Heinrich asked.

"Maybe the enormity of what she'd done had started to sink in."

He held the general's stare, anticipating the next round of questions. They'd be more probing and harder to answer. He could only hope the BND rehearsals had been on point.

"So you left her apartment at what time?"

"About eight."

"What did you do with the memo?"

"Took it back to my hotel."

Heinrich leaned forward. "Why didn't you deposit it in the dead drop immediately?"

"I thought about it, but decided I'd never find the place in the dark. So I waited till morning."

"But by the time you did, it was late Wednesday morning. Why all that delay, Malik? If you have a good explanation for that, I'd like to hear it."

Stefan knew he was on shaky ground. He answered in a steady voice. "Because I had trouble finding chewing gum. The shop at the hotel was completely out. I had to go to a family grocery store for it. The Stadtbahn ride to the park went okay, but I had to wait for an old man feeding birds to leave before I could approach the right bench." He stopped, too much explanation and the general might suspect he was covering up.

Heinrich broke off his stare and sat back. Stefan felt the heavy silence, punctuated by the insistent ticking of the wall clock behind him. Had he sounded convincing? The general's expression gave him no clue.

"Did you read the memo?"

Stefan gave the only answer the general would believe. "Yes."

"Why?"

"Curious what it contained and why Monika was so worried about giving it up."

Stefan expected a rebuff, but his answer didn't seem to have made the general angry.

"You spent Thursday night at Monika's apartment?"

"Yes."

"Sleep with her?"

"Yes," Stefan lied.

"Did she say any more about the memo or what else she might have to give you?"

"She just wanted to talk about our relationship." Stefan collected his thoughts, recalling what the BND coached him to say to entice Heinrich to send him back to Bonn. "But I pressed her a little, and she hinted she might have other documents of interest to my organization."

Heinrich leaned forward. "Did she say what kind of documents?"

"No. I tried to dig, but she shut me down, insisting we talk about personal stuff.

"Just pillow talk and screwing, is that it?"

"Yes, General"

Another long pause. Stefan expected another barrage of questions, but to his surprise Heinrich dismissed him.

"That'll be all. I know where to find you if I have something else."

Closing the door behind him, Stefan felt he'd passed the first test. The BND had prepared him well for this round. He'd worry about the next one when it came.

"Everything okay?" Helga asked in a low voice.

"I think so."

"See you at seven?" she whispered.

He nodded.

♬♬♬

Stefan gazed at the white ceiling of Helga's bedroom, luxuriating in afterglow as his heartbeat slowed. He treasured sex for its own sake, even when it lacked the emotional attachment that pervaded his lovemaking with Monika. He was a bit confused as to which he preferred, probably both if he were honest with himself.

Helga snuggled up. "Daydreaming?"

He grunted.

"Sex leaving you speechless, I see. Not good for a Romeo."

He interlaced his fingers with hers. "The way you make love is just too good for words, Helga."

She squeezed his hand. "And I'd say Heinrich found himself his best Romeo yet. I take it he was pleased with your performance?"

"You couldn't tell it by the way he grilled me this morning."

"Oh?"

"I guess he was surprised that I managed to deliver so soon after I got to Bonn." Stefan kept his eyes on the ceiling. The general probably thought his performance was too good to be true, but there was no need to share his suspicion with Helga.

"He doesn't know what he has in you."

Stefan suppressed a chuckle at the thought of how true Helga's statement was, on more than one level. Time to probe a little. "Speaking of the general, I was wondering whether you might be willing to give me the name of the Romeo who has the photos of Heinrich and his lovers."

Helga withdrew her hand. "The *quid pro quo*."

"I'm sorry, but I really need—"

She put her hand on his lips. "It's all right. The Romeo is Uli Borst. He's recovering from a car accident. Last I heard, he's been released from the hospital." She played with his chest hair. "Tell you what. We do another romp like we just had, and you'll leave here with his address and phone number."

Chapter Sixty-Five

Conflicted

Munich, Friday 19 August 1977

Sabine took Horst by the hand and led him through the throng of patrons streaming across the Max-Joseph-Platz toward the National Theater. "I wouldn't want you to get lost in the crowd."

He squeezed her hand. "Not a chance. I have the tickets."

"That's what worries me. What if you have second thoughts and leave me hanging?"

"Very funny." He put his arm around her waist and gently guided her inside the opera house.

Not that she needed guiding—she'd been to more Bavarian State Opera performances than she could count on two hands—but she slowed her steps, luxuriating in his touch. The wide range of opera patrons' dress continually amazed her: tuxedos and evening gowns for the older generation; cocktail dresses and suits for the in-between ages; T-shirts and jeans for students.

Horst pointed out a young man in jeans. "And I thought I might be underdressed."

She regarded his open-collared blue shirt and khakis. "Well, we don't exactly match, but you're okay. The most important thing is to be comfortable so you can enjoy the opera."

She wore her favorite evening gown, a strapless style made of burgundy silk-like material that showed off her figure—perfect for this balmy evening. She'd almost turned down Horst's invitation. Now she was glad she hadn't. He was good company and since his consulting role was nearing its end, she felt freer to socialize. Besides, the opera might take her mind off worrying whether she'd done the right thing in letting Stefan return to East Germany. She couldn't decide which she would dread more in case he betrayed her—having her career come to a screeching halt or having been played for a fool.

Horst's voice cut through her bleak thoughts. "You look stunning, Sabine."

"Thank you." She once again took his hand and led him to the near side of the checkroom where a middle-aged man was selling programs.

Horst reached for his wallet, but she stopped him. "You bought the tickets; I'll get the program."

She exchanged a five-mark coin from her purse for the glossy booklet, which she handed to Horst. "I'm glad you took my advice to heart and chose an Italian opera, and one of my favorites at that."

He looked at the program. "*La Traviata.* You've seen it before?"

"Several times, but I never get tired of it. You'll find Verdi's music much more accessible than Wagner's."

"I sure hope so."

"And I brought plenty of tissues."

"You mean you cry even though you already know what's going to happen?"

"Like a baby; every time." She gave him a mischievous look. "I brought enough tissues for two."

He laughed. "Are men allowed to cry at the opera?"

"You might be surprised what Verdi does to you."

"My Italian is a bit rusty."

"Not to worry. Even if you don't pick up all the words, you'll get the drift just from the music . . . unless you have a heart of stone and no soul." She took him by the elbow. "And there's a detailed synopsis in the program. Let's find our seats so you can read it."

"No champagne?"

"Maybe during intermission."

♫ ♫ ♫

Surrounded by patrons milling about the foyer during intermission, Sabine and Horst clinked glasses and sipped champagne. Invariably, the buzz from the myriad conversations filling the hall excited Sabine, as she imagined the variety of opinions ranging from gushing admiration to critical analysis. But this evening she was mostly interested in Horst's reaction. She set her glass on the small shelf to the side of the checkroom that remained largely empty; hardly anyone had bothered with coats on this warm August evening.

"Well, Horst. What do you think so far?"

"I like it."

She furrowed her brow. "Like—is that all? Is the opera not speaking to you?"

He touched her forearm. "Oh, but it is. The drinking song and the soprano's high notes—the music is glorious, and the story heartrending."

"But?"

He set his champagne glass next to hers, apparently searching for the right words. "My heart aches for Violetta having to endure the hypocrisy of nineteenth century Parisian society, but I have a hard time accepting her capitulation."

"You mean agreeing to give up Alfredo, because she's a courtesan who sullies his family's honor."

"Exactly."

Sabine nodded. "You've put your finger on a delicate issue. I can give you a couple of reasons." Chimes rang throughout the house. "Remind me to talk about it later."

They finished their drinks and joined the crowd filing into the auditorium for the final two acts.

♫ ♫ ♫

During the drive home, Sabine and Horst conversed about the opera, their favorite parts, and which singers they liked best. The time flew and before she knew it, Horst steered his BMW into a vacant curbside space in front of her apartment.

He looked around. "Where is your VW?"

"Still in the shop. I'm driving a company car." She pointed to a row of garages. "It's parked safely off the street."

"Good. Glad to see Dorfmann came through for you."

Horst kept the engine running. Either he had no interest in prolonging the evening, or he was just plain considerate, not wanting to pressure her to invite him up. She couldn't imagine him being blasé about their relationship, so she chose to believe in his thoughtfulness. But what did she feel? Invite him in or not?

His voice cut through her thoughts. "I forgot to remind you to finish what you were saying when the chimes interrupted."

"Ah, yes. What might explain Violetta's sacrifice."

She studied his face in the faint light of the streetlamp, looking for clues. Had he really forgotten, or was he looking to continue the conversation elsewhere, like in her apartment? It didn't take a sharp mind to discern how passionate she was about opera and that she liked to talk about it. His expression gave nothing away.

What the hell, she was a big girl. And Horst was no Stasi Romeo like Stefan, who'd seduced Monika by pretending to love opera. "Would you like to come up for a glass of wine?"

"That sounds great." He shut off the engine and hurried around the car to open the passenger door.

She suppressed a snicker. So much for his being blasé.

They took the elevator to her seventh-floor apartment, which he'd not seen earlier when she'd met him downstairs.

She let him in. "Just a one bedroom, nothing fancy."

"But look at that stereo and the speakers. That's where you get your opera fix."

"Beats watching TV." She indicated the sofa. "Make yourself comfortable. You prefer red or white?"

"Whatever's open."

A few minutes later, she set two glasses of *Spätburgunder* on the coffee table and settled on the sofa next to him. "Better fortify yourself. When I get to talking about opera, there's no stopping me. Raise your hand if I'm boring you."

He raised his glass. "I'm ready for the onslaught, Sabine."

She lost herself in his smile that must have pierced many a woman's heart. Why was he still unattached? None of her business. "All right, you questioned why Violetta would let herself be pressured to give up the love of her life, all so Alfredo's sister could make an advantageous marriage. I grant you that is hard to swallow for a modern audience."

To gather her thoughts, Sabine drank some wine. "The first thing is to transport yourself back to the middle of the nineteenth century and its rigid societal power structure."

"Meaning men have all the power, women none," he interjected.

"Not only that, but the hypocrisy. Men of means were expected to take mistresses, but their playthings became outcasts."

"That still doesn't explain why—"

"What do you think Violetta, the fallen woman, feels? No matter how much she tells herself she's worthy of Alfredo's love, she is haunted by her past. And Alfredo's father skillfully exploits her feelings of guilt and shame."

He raised a hand.

"Am I boring you already?"

"Heavens no. This is fascinating. I just wanted to point out an inconsistency. Violetta's caving seems out of character for the strong, independent woman we've grown to admire."

"I'm impressed. You really immersed yourself in the drama. I agree that she is strong, but her character is more complex. You have to allow for the shame and guilt she feels.

But, we could argue this point until the cows come home and never resolve the conflict. And do you know what makes the opera so poignant?"

He shook his head.

"Giuseppina Strepponi, Verdi's wife, suffered the same hypocritical treatment by the citizens of his home town, Busetto, because she had two illegitimate children before she met Verdi."

He took a drink. When he set his glass down, she laid her hand on top of his. "Look, Horst, you have a logical mind. The most important point about appreciating opera is this: switch your mind from analytical to creative. You can't comb through opera plots with a magnifying glass and not find a logical flaw or two. Instead, let your soul experience the heightened emotions of the music. There's no other art form that . . ."

She withdrew her hand. Her cheeks burning, she took a big gulp of *Spätburgunder*. "I'm sorry. I sound like a preacher."

"Not at all, Sabine. I love your passion and enthusiasm. They make you even more beautiful than—"

She leaned forward and shut him up with a kiss. After an initial hesitation—she'd surprised herself as much as him—he responded enthusiastically. Then another kiss, even more passionate. When they came up for air, he caressed her cheeks, her neck, her bare shoulders, first with his fingertips, then with his lips. Her pulse raced. She took a deep ragged breath. His hand drifted downward, lightly caressing her breast, and she stiffened.

He noticed and sat back.

"Oh, Horst. I don't mean to be a tease, but could we take things a little slower?"

"Of course. I want you to be certain."

She gave him a chaste kiss on the cheek. He was the most sensitive man she'd met in a long time. "Thank you for being so understanding. You must know how strongly I'm drawn to you."

She nestled against him, and he held her close. The silent embrace felt comforting.

Horst broke the spell. "What about those tennis lessons you've been promising me?"

"*Lessons?* I said I would hit with you and maybe give you a pointer or two."

"Why don't I reserve a court for tomorrow morning and we'll have a nice lunch at the club afterward?"

"Deal. Sounds like a fun way to spend Saturday."

Still holding each other, they drank some wine. She set down her empty glass. "So tell me, did Verdi turn you into an opera fan?"

"That will take more than one visit to the opera house, but I must admit your enthusiasm is catching. There is still hope, so don't give up on this philistine quite yet."

He returned his empty glass to the coffee table and stood. "It's getting late. I'd best be going."

She walked him to the door, and they kissed again.

"I'll call you with the court time," he said and slipped out.

She refilled her glass. Would he think her a prude? This was 1977 Germany, the sexual revolution of the sixties still lingering, birth-control pills everywhere. Still, she longed for a meaningful relationship, as he had professed he wanted. Give it time. It will happen or it won't.

The magnificent music and stimulating conversation had banished all thoughts of Stefan's potential betrayal. Tomorrow, she could pick up the worry beads again, but tonight she'd think about Horst.

Chapter Sixty-Six

Disgruntled

East Berlin, Saturday, 20 August 1977

Low morning clouds hovered over Alexanderplatz, threatening rain. Stefan Malik carried the day's edition of *Neues Deutschland* prominently in his left hand, just as Uli Borst had instructed him during yesterday's phone conversation. Convincing the star Romeo to meet with him had been no easy task. Not only had Helga come through by giving him Borst's address and phone number, but she'd tipped him off to a small restaurant a few blocks from her apartment, whose lobby phone was unlikely to be bugged by the Stasi.

Since he couldn't be sure about Borst's phone, Stefan had talked in circumspect terms after the man answered. "A friend of yours suggested I contact you."

"And who are you?"

"A friend of your friend. She thought I'd love some of your visual art."

"You're an art collector?" Borst obviously knew the drill of speaking in code.

"I'm always interested in pieces that can help me." Afraid Borst might hang up, Stefan asked, "Could you meet—?"

"What number are you calling from?"

Stefan read off the lobby's phone number.

"Stay there." Click.

Stefan guarded the sole phone in the lobby, at one time waving away a woman carrying a shopping bag. "Pardon, but I'm waiting on an urgent call."

She shrugged and walked on.

When the wait stretched to over five minutes, Stefan began to wonder. Borst hadn't expressly said he would call. He'd give him another five and either redial or set out for his address.

Finally, the phone rang. Stefan picked up. "Hello."

"Your name?"

Stefan recognized the voice from earlier. "Are you in a safe—?"

"Yes."

"I'm Stefan Malik."

"Ah, yes. I've heard about you. The journalist, pressed into service at the last minute for the Fuchs mission that was supposed to be mine."

"Sorry about your accident. Are you back at work?"

"Ha!" A sneer. "Not on your life. I've been pushed aside."

Stefan's pulse quickened. A disgruntled Borst might be more cooperative. "Sorry to hear that. Have you recovered from your injuries?"

"More or less. But enough about me. I assume our mutual friend is Helga?"

"Yes."

"She's something, isn't she? One of the better lays I've had. Too bad she . . ." His voice turned gruff. "She mentioned photos?"

"Yes."

A deep exhale came over the line. "I wish I'd kept my mouth shut. Must have had too much of her schnapps." Another exhale. "What are the photos to you?"

"I'd like to tell you in person."

"Why would I—?"

"Exact a little revenge while helping a fellow Romeo." If the prospect of getting even didn't persuade him, Stefan was ready to play his trump card—homosexuality—though he'd rather hold it in reserve.

"Hmm. You're not as green as I suspected."

A backhanded compliment, but would he agree to meet?

"Did Helga give you my address too?"

"Yes."

Borst snickered. "You must be good. She told me I was the last goddamn Romeo she'd take up with. Now you've got me curious what she sees in you."

"You want me to come to your place?" Stefan said.

"Hell no! Maybe you're not so smart after all." A short pause, then Borst said, "Alexanderplatz, ten, tomorrow morning, *Neues Deutschland*, left hand."

Stefan replaced the receiver, silencing the dial tone.

Raindrops on his face tore Stefan from his thoughts about yesterday's phone conversation. He'd circled Alexanderplatz twice. Either Borst wasn't going to show, or he'd been watching. Couldn't blame him for being extra cautious. If the roles were reversed, Stefan would do the same. So he kept walking.

He hadn't brought an umbrella, and the paper started to get damp. No big loss. He'd scanned the headlines when he bought it at a kiosk—the usual propaganda: workers exceeding their goals under the party's plan-du-jour; unemployment lines in the West; triumphs of East German swimmers at the European championships in Sweden. He almost felt ashamed that a few of his articles had been published by the party's propaganda mouthpiece.

A man in his thirties clad in a dark polyester suit, stepped from an entryway. "Stefan?"

"Yes."

"Follow me, but not too close."

At about one meter seventy-five, he was more than ten centimeters shorter than Stefan. Hard to believe Uli Borst was, or had been, one of Heinrich's top Romeos. His charm and charisma must be considerable to compensate for the man's rather ordinary looks. The recent stint in intensive care had left his face pale and drawn, though his brown hair must have started to thin long before the accident.

Borst charged down the uncrowded sidewalk—the weather had kept many Berliners at home—not bothering to open his umbrella to fend off occasional raindrops. As instructed, Stefan followed at a distance. Borst took the first street to the right. Stefan did the same, but the Romeo had vanished. Panicked, he rushed to the next corner, and exhaled at the sight of his man a few meters down an isolated side street.

When Stefan caught up, Borst indicated a wastepaper basket fastened to a lamppost. "You can throw your newspaper away now, unless you . . ."

Ever the cautious spy, Borst didn't finish, lest Stefan turned out to be a party sympathizer, even though his quest for the Heinrich photos dispelled that notion.

"I don't enjoy reading propaganda any more than you, Herr Borst." With no other witnesses around, Stefan threw *Neues Deutschland* into the basket with gusto.

Borst grinned. "Call me Uli. So what do you want with the photos?"

"To buy my freedom."

"The general's got a hold over you?"

Stefan related how Heinrich had recruited him from prison, threatened to throw him back in the slammer—he omitted any reference to the queers—and put an end to Traude's career.

"Looks like you're in big trouble. But give me one good reason why I should risk my neck for you."

The dreaded question. Stefan could only hope his answer wouldn't be too far off the mark. "Because after your accident the general parked you on a dead-end track. As you said, you've been pushed aside. Remember what I told you on the phone: this could be your chance to get even, exact a little revenge."

Uli regarded him for a long moment. His expression gave nothing away. "Nice try, but I'm not buying. I'm not looking for revenge. I'm saving those pictures for a rainy day, as a bargaining chip to save my own skin."

Stefan had anticipated his response. Time to use what leverage he had. "Do you really have a choice? Look Uli, I know about your persuasion."

"That's a skillful threat delivery." Uli pressed his finger into Stefan's chest, hard. "But it won't fly. You know damn well homosexuality is legal here."

Stefan took a step back. "Legal on paper maybe, but not in practice. Or have you forgotten the many gays locked up at Rummelsburg?"

"But I'm in good company, don't you agree? What do you think Heinrich will do when I tell him you threatened to expose the trait he and I share?"

Stefan fought to keep his composure. He had to try once more. "Look, no one but the three of us ever needs to know about you and the photos. I bet you have multiple prints. I'll take one set. I won't use them unless I have to, and I will always insist that I took them. You have my word on that."

"Helga really screwed me, didn't she? Well, both of you can go to hell!" Uli clenched his jaw. "You can stick your word right up your ass, and I dare you to mention photos to Heinrich. If he comes after me, I promise the two of you will go down with me."

"But—"

"The answer is no. No pictures. Ever." Uli stepped into the street, then turned back. "And I'll give you a tip you don't deserve. If you're thinking about defecting, better watch yourself; there's a highly placed mole in one of the West German intelligence outfits who feeds Heinrich inside information."

"Do you know . . . ?"

His question hung in the air. Uli was already halfway down the street, sheets of rain careening off his open umbrella.

Back to square one. Stefan pulled up his collar and headed back to Alexanderplatz. As if to mock him, rain pelted his cheeks and stung his eyes.

Chapter Sixty-Seven

Voice Studies

Weimar, Sunday, 21 August 1977

When the train gradually slowed at the outskirts of Leipzig, the young couple sitting across from Stefan quit holding hands and stared out the window. They'd been regaling him with their weekend adventures in Berlin. The station came into view and they stood. Being at least a head taller than the young man, Stefan pulled their two suitcases down from the overhead storage where he had deposited them when they joined him in the compartment in Berlin.

They thanked him and exited as soon as the train screeched to a halt. With no one left to distract him, Stefan brooded about yesterday's ill-fated meeting. Not only had his quest for the Heinrich photos been a colossal failure, but Borst had threatened him. What if the disgraced Romeo tried to win back Heinrich's favor by blabbing Stefan might have thoughts of defecting? Helga felt certain that he wouldn't, so long as they kept his sexual preference a secret. True, she knew Uli much better than he, but just because she'd slept with him didn't mean she could predict what he might do.

A whistle blew, doors clanged shut, and creaking steel wheels fought inertia. The sounds tore Stefan from his ruminations, but not for long. Without the photos, he had to find another way to throw off Heinrich's yoke, but no matter how hard he racked his brain, nothing came to him. He gazed out the window as the last houses of Leipzig disappeared in the distance. The sun broke through the clouds, causing steam to rise from fields still damp from yesterday's showers.

By the time the train rolled into the Weimar station, Stefan had turned his focus to the purpose of his visit. He hoped his skills of persuasion wouldn't fail him as they had yesterday. Briefcase in hand, he moved onto the top step of the exit and scanned the crowd on the platform for curly red hair. As soon as he spotted Traude, he disembarked and rushed toward her. In jeans rolled up at the ankles, jogging shoes, and T-shirt, she looked nothing like a serious opera student, but then this was the weekend. She could pass for one of those sloppily dressed teenagers he'd seen in the West, which might prove beneficial for what he had in mind.

He extended a hand, which she ignored, giving him a hug. Surprised by the warm welcome, he hesitated before holding her in the rare embrace, his briefcase dangling awkwardly from his hand on her back. Glad to see him after four weeks, or expressing her gratitude for whatever role she imagined he might have played in her admission to the prestigious conservatory?

He released her. "How is school?"

"Hard, but so far I'm keeping up. But the way you sounded on the phone, I'm guessing you didn't come just to check on how my studies are going."

"Well, I do want to hear about your courses, your professors, and to see where you live. But you're right, there is something extremely important I need to discuss with you. Do you know a place where we can talk in private?"

"Park an der Ilm is about a kilometer and a half from the train station, and it's a beautiful day for a walk."

He responded by nudging her elbow, and they joined the passengers moving toward the terminal. On the way to the park, she told him about her classes, the professors she liked and the ones she detested.

As they settled on an empty park bench, Traude pointed into the distance. "Goethe's garden house is that way. I read that he had some say in styling this park like an English landscape garden back in 1778. You don't have to walk far in Weimar to stumble across history. But you didn't come all the way from Berlin to hear about landscaping or history."

Stefan scanned the surroundings. On the bench to the right sat a middle-aged man in a brown suit; his head buried in a magazine, he seemed oblivious to the green oasis around him. An elderly man in baggy pants and a plaid long-sleeve shirt slouched on the bench to the left, tossing seeds from a plastic bag to a collection of sparrows and blackbirds.

Stefan clutched his briefcase and stood. "You want to show me Goethe's garden house?"

Traude looked up, her expression a question mark, then she rose and tucked her arm in his. She had understood—even park benches offered no refuge from sophisticated listening devices. He might be paranoid, but he wouldn't put it past the Stasi to have planted a bug in the branch of the maple tree overhanging their bench.

After they passed the man engrossed in his reading, Traude asked, "So what is so extremely important?"

Stefan took a deep breath. Where to start? He'd mulled over on the train what to tell her. Enough to persuade her, but not one word more. The less she knew, the safer she would be if questioned by the Stasi, whose harsh interrogation methods broke anyone down, no matter how tough. He shuddered at the thought of her facing General Heinrich.

"Remember our conversation at Café Franken in Berlin?"

"That was over four weeks ago, but I do recall your mysterious comment about traveling to the West and that you wouldn't tell me who you're working for. But I figured it had to be the government, or you'd never be allowed to mingle with capitalists. So what are you doing for our great socialist state?"

He waited to respond until they were out of earshot of a couple sitting on a bench along the footpath. "I'd rather not give you specifics, Traude. The less you know about my job, the better off you are. Let me just say I am forced to do some things you'd find despicable."

She freed her arm from his and stopped. "What things? Forced how and by whom?"

"If I don't follow orders, I'll be back in Rummelsburg Prison or—"

"You've been in jail? What did you do to—?"

"Absolutely nothing. I was framed. Part of a plan to coerce me into service I'd be refusing if I had a choice. You have to believe me." He resumed walking and she followed.

"You still haven't told me who is coercing you into doing what, but I can guess. You're an informant for the Stasi."

"Not an informant."

She grabbed his forearm. "Don't tell me you're a goddamn spy!"

"Traude, listen to me. I came here to warn you. It's not just my life that's on the line."

She had stopped walking. "What are you saying?"

He turned to face her. "I have to get out as soon as I can find a way."

"You mean defect?"

"If I can."

She stared at him, hard. "And leave me behind in this socialist paradise? Well, at least I'll have my voice studies to keep me sane."

A couple of men walked past, giving them curious looks for standing in the middle of the path.

Stefan nudged Traude's elbow. "Let's keep moving. We don't want to draw attention."

While they strolled in silence, Stefan summoned his courage. He dreaded what he needed to tell her, but it had to be done. "Traude, listen to me. If I quit doing the Stasi's dirty work, you won't be allowed to pursue an opera career here."

She stopped again, but he gripped her arm and pulled her along. "Keep walking."

After a few steps, she matched his pace and shook off his hand. "Now I understand. I was admitted to the voice program not on merit, but because of your connections."

She started to tear up, and Stefan laid his arm around her shoulder, gently guiding her along the path. She was right, of course, but there was no need to cause her even more pain.

This called for a little white lie. "It is true that the school gave your application favorable consideration, but it was made clear to me that you would not be admitted unless you were qualified."

She turned her face and studied him. Hoping he'd sounded sincere, he wiped a tear off her cheek and squeezed her shoulder. "You have the voice and the talent, and don't let anyone tell you different, not even your mother."

Traude shrugged. "She thinks I'm wasting my life pursuing a fantasy. Study something practical, is what she's told me more than once. I hate to think she's right. I can already hear her I told you so when they give me the boot here after you've disappeared."

"It won't come to that. There is a way for you to . . ."

He stopped speaking when they came upon several pedestrians walking across a grassy field toward a gray-mortared house beyond a hedge. High treetops towered over the small residence, dwarfing its steep gable.

"Is that Goethe's garden house?"

"Yes, do you want to see if we can go inside?"

"Another time, perhaps. We have too much to discuss today. So let's head back."

She nodded and they turned around. "You were talking about a way—"

"Yes. You can pursue your dream, but not here in Weimar."

She frowned. "Are you saying I should run away with you?"

"Leave, yes, but not with me."

"How in the world could I possibly get out? I'd give just about anything to follow my passion, but I don't want to get shot while climbing over the Wall. And even if I made it, who's to say I'd have any chance of getting into an opera school in the West?"

"I'm the one to say so, Traude."

"How can you be so sure?"

"Because you have what it takes, and I can arrange a spot for you. All you have to do is pass another audition." No need telling her he still needed to negotiate the terms with the BND, but he was determined that she'd be given the opportunity. "Let's slow down. What I need to tell you is going to take some time."

They assumed a leisurely stroll like a couple admiring the beauty of the park. He told her she could leave East Germany without having to scale the Wall. She pressed for specifics, but he dodged her questions, assuring her he would tell her what she needed to know when the time came. Not that he had worked out the details for himself at this point.

She remained silent for a long time after he'd finished speaking. Finally, she said, "I'll have to think about that, Dad. You know what they do to defectors they catch."

"Yes, I do, and I would never propose anything that would put you at great risk. I expect to be sent back to the West soon, and I should know more after I get back. I'll ask you to keep an open mind until then."

She looked him in the eye. "All right. I can do that."

"Do you want to walk back to the train station with me?"

"Yes, of course."

"Good. I need to get a couple of details from you as we walk."

"Such as?"

"Your dress and shoe sizes."

She scrunched her face into a quizzical expression. "What on earth for? You're buying me presents with your huge salary?"

He laughed. "Something like that."

She started to rattle off numbers, but he stopped her and pointed ahead. "Wait till we're in the station where I can have you write them down for me."

They crossed the street and entered the terminal. He moved to a vacant ticket booth, far away from the only one open on this Sunday. Resting his briefcase on the counter, he spun the combination lock and pulled out a pen and notepad. After Traude had scribbled some figures on the paper, he put the pad and pen back in the case and scrambled the combination.

"When does your train leave?" she asked.

He checked the huge terminal clock. "Ten minutes."

"I'll see you off."

The train pulled in just as they reached the platform. He still had a few minutes before he needed to board. A strained silence fell between them. He hated goodbyes for their awkwardness, though he thought they were always harder on the one remaining behind.

"Thank you for coming, Dad." She reached into her purse. "Oh, I almost forgot. The school took pictures of the students for a directory. I thought you might like one of me." She handed him a glossy photo showing off her freckled face.

"Very thoughtful. My pictures of you are a couple years old." He realized this headshot was ideally suited for the purpose he had in mind, but he didn't give voice to his thought. Much too early to mention it to her.

So he said, "Please think about what I told you."

"I will."

He embraced her. "When I come back, I'll have more details for you. And not a word to anyone."

She kissed his cheek. "Please be careful, whatever they're making you do."

"I'm sorry I didn't have time to see where you live."

He gave her a squeeze, let her go, and boarded the train. He found an empty compartment from which he could see her standing on the platform. A piercing whistle, slamming doors, and the train began to move. He peered at the slight figure waving at him until the image faded in the distance.

Had he sounded too optimistic, giving her false hope? Whatever it took, he had to come through for her.

Chapter Sixty-Eight

The Lure

Stasi Headquarters, Monday, 22 August 1977

Stefan lingered in the underground station long enough to give Helga a head start. She had insisted they not arrive at the office together. As he joined the early morning pedestrians striding down Normannenstraße toward the Stasi headquarters, he came to appreciate her caution. Even though a chance encounter on the way to the office wouldn't be so unusual as to raise suspicion, they couldn't afford to give the slightest hint that they might have set out together from her apartment this morning.

She entered Building 15, and he followed at a safe distance. By the time he reached Heinrich's reception area, she had already laid the black typewriter cover on the credenza. She lowered herself into her chair. Her drab office clothes—a loose fitting plaid jacket and a black skirt extending below her knees—gave no indication of the sexy woman they concealed.

"*Guten Morgen,* Frau Schröder," he said with enthusiasm, as if he hadn't seen her since work on Friday. "Did you have a pleasant weekend?"

A smile warmed her eyes. "Not bad. I've had worse."

Before he could retort, the intercom buzzed.

She picked up. "Yes, sir." She listened while looking at Stefan. "Yes, sir, he's here." A moment later, she said, "Right away, sir." She switched off and nodded toward the general's office. "He's expecting you."

Stefan glanced at his watch. Whatever Heinrich might berate him for, today at least it wouldn't be for tardiness. He knocked on the door and entered at the general's loud "*Herein.*"

Heinrich pointed to a chair and greeted him with the friendliest good morning Stefan could remember. Maybe no rebuke this morning.

The general slurped some coffee and set his mug on his desk next to a tape recorder. "Listen to the message your new girlfriend left on the Vienna apartment answering machine." He punched a button.

"*Hallo* Günter. This is Monika. Did you have a safe trip home? I'm calling to tell you that I'm still thinking about our last night together. I know, it's only been three days, but I already miss you terribly. I wish I could come to visit you in Vienna, but these days I even have to go to the office for a few hours on Saturdays. Can you believe that?"

During a momentary pause in the recording, Stefan appreciated how Monika managed to convey genuine frustration. What an actress!

"I have a present for you, but you'll have to come back to Bonn to get it. You remember what I told you. Well, I got it. So hurry back. I love you."

After a click, a mechanical male voice announced, "*Sonntag, 15 Uhr 30.*"

Heinrich turned off the recorder. "What is this present she's referring to?"

Stefan reeled off what Sabine Maier had drilled into him. "Monika was hoping she could get her hands on high-level correspondence that might shed some light on Bonn's covert plans."

"Meaning what?"

"She wouldn't give details. I don't know if she was being coy or didn't know for sure herself. I assumed she was referring to something related to rearmament, to communications at the top level of the Chancellery."

Heinrich pushed the recorder aside. "The chancellor?"

"Possibly."

"But she didn't say who the correspondence might be with?"

"No, sir."

As the general leaned back, Stefan wondered whether Sabine's lure was too obscure to hook Heinrich. Maybe it should have been a bit more explicit. The longer the general remained silent, the more worried Stefan grew. He clenched his jaw.

Finally, Heinrich spoke. "Well, this sounds awfully good, perhaps too good."

Stefan gripped the edge of his seat.

After another long pause, Heinrich said, "But we can't afford not to check it out. You're going back to Bonn in the morning."

"Yes, sir," Stefan said, trying to convey apprehension in lieu of the relief he felt.

"And I promised you a promotion if you performed to my expectations. For a newbie you've done pretty well, except for the delay in making the dead drop. I convinced Mielke to authorize your promotion to *Hauptmann*. With that comes a nice raise. What do you say to that?"

"Thank you, General. I appreciate it."

Heinrich stood, reached across the desk and shook Stefan's hand. "Congratulations. Keep up the good work and there'll be more rewards. I'll have Frau Schröder get your travel papers ready for tomorrow. Good luck."

Stefan walked to the door. Helga could tell him what a captain was paid, but she might be miffed at his being sent back to Bonn so soon.

Chapter Sixty-Nine

Women's Clothes

Bonn, Tuesday, 23 August 1977

Engrossed in studying the material she and Dorfmann had prepared for Günter's second dead drop, Sabine startled at the ring of her private phone line. Aside from a select group of agents, only Monika and Stefan, alias Günter, knew this number.

"*Hallo.*" She never answered the line with her name.

Static mingled with background noise, echoing as if in a huge hall. A female voice broadcast over a loudspeaker, "*Lufthansa Flug Nummer 2547 nach Köln*—a male voice drowned out the rest of the flight departure announcement—*Heute Nachmittag.*" Click.

Sabine disconnected and buzzed her secretary. "Please call Lufthansa and find out what time flight 2547 arrives in Cologne this afternoon."

She then called Dorfmann on the intercom. "The Stasi is biting on Monika's phone message," she told him. "I just heard from our man. I'm leaving for Bonn to meet him there this afternoon. Could you call Mertens and have him arrange adjacent rooms for us at Hotel Freiburg?"

"Which name are you using?"

She opened her purse, unzipped the inside pocket and pulled out a couple of identity cards. The one on top would do. "Petra Resnick." She spelled the last name.

"I'll take care of it. You sure Günter is returning to the same hotel?"

"I have to rely on him to follow instructions. God knows, I drilled into him enough times to name a hotel only if it was not the Freiburg."

"And you're satisfied with the papers for the dead drop?"

"I think so. Actual correspondence that won't do much damage plus embellishments to convince the Stasi that Monika thought it would benefit Günter's peace organization."

"Report to me when you can and . . ." Dorfmann's tone turned lighthearted, ". . . don't even think about taking Horst along."

He hung up before she could think of a response. His using Horst Kögler's first name meant he was aware their professional relationship had morphed into the personal. No time to worry about that now. She put away the IDs, dropped the documents into her briefcase, shut it, and left her office.

As she passed the support staff cubicles, her secretary stepped into the hallway. "Lufthansa Flight 2547 from Vienna is scheduled to arrive in Cologne at two forty this afternoon."

Sabine thanked her and made for the staircase. She should have prepared for Günter's early return to Bonn by keeping an overnight case at the office. Now she had to stop at home and pack. But no matter how much she pushed the sluggish BND fleet car, she couldn't possibly reach Bonn before Günter. If only she could ask Horst to race his BMW down the autobahn with her buckled in the passenger seat. She bounded down the stairs, admonishing herself to quit fantasizing.

♫ ♫ ♫

Sabine entered Hotel Freiburg and surveyed the lobby, which was populated by patrons getting an early start on cocktail hour. She headed for the reception desk, but slowed when a movement caught her eye. A young man at the bar lowered his newspaper and gave a slight nod—Mertens' assistant, signaling that the room arrangements had been made. She resisted walking over to ask him whether Günter Freund had already checked in. She'd find out soon enough.

The brunette reception clerk greeted her with a friendly, "*Guten Tag*, Frau Resnick," and handed her a key. "Suite 2500."

What had possessed Mertens to arrange for a suite? Her surprise must have shown. "You'll have to use your key to access our restricted twenty-fifth floor," the clerk said with emphasis, as if initiating her into an exclusive society. "Enjoy our executive suite." If that weren't enough, she added in a conspiratorial tone, "Your party has already checked in."

My god, did the clerk suspect Frau Resnick had come for a tryst? Not a bad cover, actually. Still, she'd give Mertens a hard time about his weird sense of humor. She thanked the woman and headed for the elevators, ignoring the clerk's overly solicitous wishes for a pleasant stay. After a smooth ride to the top floor, Sabine stepped into a carpeted hallway. A door directly across from the elevator displayed the number 2500 in bronze.

Curious what comforts the hotel suite might have to offer and eager to make contact with Günter, Sabine unlocked the door and entered, only to stop after a step or two. She dropped her luggage and briefcase onto the carpet.

A glass of beer in hand, Günter rose from a leather sofa spanning a corner of the spacious living room. "Come on in, Frau . . . Resnick, is it? I made myself comfortable while I waited. I hope you don't mind. This is quite the place." He pointed toward a counter separating the room from the kitchen. "You'll find beer and wine in there, if you'd like to join me."

"Not now." Time to assert control. "Where is *your* room?"

"This way." He led her past the kitchen through a connecting door into a large room with a double bed, a table and two chairs. The bathroom featured a shower tub. "Not as fancy as yours, but better than what goes for a nice hotel room in East Berlin."

He gazed at her with his blue-gray eyes. With his wavy dark hair, a lean body clad in a blue open-collared shirt and crisp tan slacks, he could turn a woman's head. No mystery why Monika had fallen for him.

She reined in her thoughts. "We've got a lot to talk about. Let's get started."

They went back to her room. The bottles protruding from a wine rack on the kitchen counter looked inviting, but she needed to keep the meeting strictly business. Perhaps sensing her thoughts, he gulped the rest of his beer and set the glass on the counter. While he sat on the sofa, she picked up her briefcase where she had left it and joined him.

She opened the case and laid a folder on the coffee table. "Monika's phone message obviously worked since Heinrich sent you, but did he have any hesitation?"

"He quizzed me about what Monika might be referring to. I gave him the answers we rehearsed."

"And?"

"He said something like this sounded almost too good."

She leaned forward, pressing her hands onto the top of the folder. "But he still had you come?"

"He apparently thought the promised materials justified taking a risk. I suspect he's not losing any sleep over the possibility that his new Romeo might be caught."

Sabine chuckled. "From what we know about Heinrich, he's one hell of a spymaster, but I'd be surprised if his job description included compassion for his Romeos." She turned serious. "Do you have anything new to report?"

"I believe Heinrich has placed a mole in one of your intelligence services."

"What makes you think so?"

"He seems to have a knack for getting blown agents out."

"How do you know about that?"

"The Romeo assigned to Monika absconded to the East right after he'd been exposed. That's how I ended up with the job. I'm pretty sure I was Heinrich's second or third choice."

"That's one case," Sabine said. "You said 'agents.' Who else?"

"Let me think." Günter studied the beige carpet as if it held the answer. "There were others." He returned his gaze to her. "I heard a Foreign Office secretary and her family were recalled just before the West Germans could arrest them."

Sabine pondered how the Sturms' flight bore the hallmarks of a tipoff. To test Günter's knowledge, she asked, "Do you know the secretary's name?"

"Only her first name, Gisela. Wasn't she Monika's friend?"

"Not much of a friend, I'd say." Sabine had been suspecting for some time that Heinrich had infiltrated one of their intelligence agencies. Maybe even the BND. How else to explain the high number of arrests of West Germany's foreign agents?

She probed, "Is that all you know about Heinrich's mole?"

"I'm afraid so."

"Nothing that would indicate which agency might have been infiltrated?"

"Sorry, but I don't have anything concrete."

She searched his expression for the slightest hint of obfuscation, but he gave nothing away. Either he'd told her all he knew, or he'd quickly become a seasoned agent.

So she said, "Well, can you guess what I want you to do after you return to East Berlin?"

"Find out what I can about the mole?"

"Exactly. Get as much detail as possible. Something to help us identify the mole or at least the agency. You understand?"

"It won't be easy, but I'll try."

"Tradecraft isn't supposed to be easy." She slid the folder across the table. "This is for your second dead drop. Same procedure as last time. You spend the night at Monika's. In case the Stasi is watching you, keep the folder hidden on your way to her apartment. When you leave there in the morning, have it visible before tucking it away, but don't make a show of it; nothing too obvious. You with me?"

He nodded.

"Tomorrow, go straight to the dead drop from Monika's." She reached into the briefcase and handed him a pack of chewing gum. "I don't want any delay this time."

"You think of everything, don't you?" He dropped the gum in his shirt pocket.

"That's my job. Any questions?"

"Not about what you're having me do. But I have a couple things I need to ask of you."

She leaned back, wondering what he could possibly want.

"I'll be right back." He stood and carried the folder into his room.

What was he up to?

Günter returned, clutching an envelope as if it contained a prized possession. He sat and after a slight hesitation handed it over.

She felt his eyes upon her while she peeled back the flap and pulled out two black-and-white photos. "You and your daughter?"

"Yes."

Although she had an inkling what the pictures were for, she asked, "What do you want me to do with these?"

"A passport for Traude and one for me."

"You don't ask much, do you?"

"I've agreed to do everything you've asked on the condition you would help me with my daughter. If I'm unable to defect or if the Stasi catches me, she'll be dismissed from the Weimar conservatory and God only knows what else they might do to her. I must get Traude out as soon as possible."

What could she tell him? She fiddled with the photos in front of her. Finally, she said, "We stand by our promise to do what we can for your daughter. But unless you have her climbing over the Wall, she'll need more than a West German passport. Do you know what I'm talking about?"

"I do. She must have a visa. She obviously can't apply for the authorization to enter the GDR like a bona fide West German citizen. So you'll have to forge both the passport and the visa stamp, but I bet this won't be the first time for your outfit. You can arrange that for Traude and me before I go back tomorrow, can't you?" He'd kept his eyes on her the whole time.

"Her passport needs to have more than one stamp: a visa to enter the GDR given at the border and a stamp by the *Volkspolizei* granting permission to leave by a certain date. I'd be lying if I told you that we've not done that before, but we limit it to special cases. The papers have to be just about perfect to pass muster with your comrades at the border. The guards screw up, and they're in serious trouble with the Stasi."

Günter leaned so hard on the table that it tilted. "So, you can have those for me tomorrow?"

"I'll see what I can do, at least for your daughter. But as long as Heinrich thinks Monika is feeding you state secrets, you can travel here."

"I want the papers for me as well, just in case. If Heinrich's mole learns about me, I might have to run at a moment's notice, and I sure as hell don't want to try my luck at the Wall."

He had a point. Still, she didn't want to lose the rare double agent she'd managed to plant inside the Stasi. She'd best be noncommittal. "Well, I'll think about it, and you think about how to convince us you won't just leave as soon as you have the papers." Before he could raise objections, she quickly added, "You need to head over to Monika's."

"Before I go, I'd like to ask your advice."

"About what?"

"Where's a good place in this town to shop for women's clothes?"

"Not for you, I take it?"

He raised a hand in mock protest. "No, I'm not into crossdressing."

"For your daughter, then?"

He nodded.

"What exactly are you looking for?"

"Either a dress or a blouse and skirt, and a pair of shoes."

"Just so she'll have Western clothes?"

"I figured they might help her pretend to be a West German tourist departing the GDR."

Great foresight. Her appreciation of Günter grew. Maybe she was prejudiced, but as a typical male, he'd be clueless as to how to shop for a young woman's clothes.

Before she could stop herself, she blurted, "I have some free time tomorrow. If you'd like, I can get those for you. If you trust my judgment, that is."

"Absolutely. I'll reimburse you tomorrow."

She looked at the black-and-white photo. "Curly hair. What color is it?"

"Red."

"Hmm, I should be able to find something that'll suit her. Do you have her sizes?"

Without a word, he handed her a crumpled-up sheet from his shirt pocket. She straightened it and studied the numbers. Even during her college days, she hadn't worn clothes that small. She looked up. "Are you sure of these?"

"That's her handwriting."

"You think she's cut out for an opera career?"

"Never been surer of anything in my life. I grant you, she doesn't fit the stereotype of rotund soprano, but you'll be amazed at her glorious voice, never mind how slim she is."

"That I'm looking forward to hearing." She smiled. "But I bet she won't be singing Wagner anytime soon."

"Probably not."

She checked her watch. "It's time for you to pay Monika a visit."

He shrugged. "I can hardly wait to spend another night on the couch. I'm up for a lot of things, but platonic relationships with beautiful women are not among them." He stood. "Until tomorrow." He walked through the connecting door and drew it closed behind him.

Now was the time for a glass of wine. She headed for the kitchen, opened a bottle of Beaujolais with a corkscrew she found in a drawer, poured a glass and took a gulp. She relished the soothing sensation of red wine traveling to her stomach, but relaxation would not come.

Her mind churned. How in the hell was she going to get fake passports with visas by tomorrow? Should she even try? It would be next to impossible, unless . . .

She took a hefty gulp, set down the glass and reached for the phone.

Chapter Seventy

Travel Papers

Bonn, Wednesday, 24 August 1977

Sabine entered Suite 2500, deposited a large plastic bag on the coffee table, and set her briefcase on the carpet. She shouldn't have volunteered to do Günter's shopping, not with the extra time she had to spend at the Office for the Protection of the Constitution in Cologne. After she'd called Mertens yesterday afternoon, he'd worked a small miracle in having his experts produce the travel papers in record time. On the upside, the Cologne department store had a bigger selection and better prices than what she could have found in Bonn.

She knocked on the connecting door. "Günter?"

A few seconds, a clicking sound, and the door swung open. Günter crossed the threshold, clad in the same blue shirt and tan slacks he'd worn yesterday. They settled on the corner sofa.

Even though she already knew the answer, she asked, "Did you make the dead drop?" No need to let on that Mertens' people had observed him.

"Yes." He regarded the shopping bag on the coffee table. "For Traude?"

She reached inside, pulled out a sizable box, and lifted its cover. "Take a look."

He leaned forward and ran his fingers over the teal dress. "The color should go great with her red hair. Is that real silk?"

"It's *Kunstseide,* made to look and feel like natural silk. Do you want to see the style?"

He shook his head. "No need. I'd rather see it on Traude."

She folded back part of the teal dress to reveal the one underneath. "What about this color?"

He gave her a quizzical look. "You got more than one dress?"

"I couldn't resist. They were on sale, and I thought both would look great on your daughter. Pistachio green with dark-blue pinstripes should be nice with her hair color, too."

"I'll let you know after I . . . but what am I saying? You can judge for yourself when she's safely over here." He turned his gaze from the dresses to her. "Which reminds me, do you have the travel papers?"

"Before we get to that, I also bought a blouse, a skirt, and shoes, of course. She needs to have at least a smattering of West German clothes in her suitcase." She reached into the bag. "Would you like to see?"

"I'm sure they're fine. What I really want to know is what you've done about passports and visas."

"Fair enough."

After putting the box back in the shopping bag, she picked her briefcase off the carpet and opened it on her lap. She unfastened the inside accordion pocket, took out two passports, and handed one to Günter.

He opened it, turned a few pages and read. After a moment, he looked up. "Maria Weber; Traude should have no trouble remembering that."

"That's the easy part. We've made up a background sheet about Maria Weber, where she lives, who her parents are, where she studies, who the relatives are she visited in the GDR, and so on. I'll go over it with you in a minute. You'll have to recite Maria Weber's background to your daughter from memory. So, you're not leaving here until I'm satisfied that you've retained every last detail."

"Not a problem."

"She won't have much time. The visa stamp granting her permission to leave the GDR is only good through Sunday."

He nodded. "The sooner she gets out, the better." He pointed to the passport in Sabine's hand. "Is that mine?"

"Yes, but before I give it to you, we need to have a clear understanding."

"About what?"

"Don't even think about defecting until you've gathered enough information on that mole for us to identify him or her, unless, of course, your cover is blown. You understand?"

"Yes."

"Did you think of something that'll assure us you won't fly the coop as soon as you have these papers?"

"I don't know what I can tell you."

Time to apply pressure. She held up the passport. "Well, I thought of something. If you abscond without doing what you've agreed to, we will have you prosecuted for espionage. Our courts might be more lenient than yours, but a conviction as a commie spy will net you a chunk of time behind bars. Granted, our prisons are luxurious compared to the torture palaces in the GDR, but I don't think you want to spend your best years in the slammer bereft of female company."

He flinched. The threat hit home.

"Are we clear then?"

"You've made your point. I will do all I can to find out about Heinrich's mole."

"Good." She handed him his passport.

He studied it. "Harald Lang. Not a bad name, either. But why is my visa stamp for thirty days?"

"We want to give you as much time as possible to identify the mole, but a visa longer than thirty days would raise suspicion."

"What if I can't get the information in a month?"

"Then we'll entice Heinrich to send you over for more state secrets. At that time we'll assess what to do about new travel papers." She thought for a moment. "Can you get the papers and your daughter's clothes through the controls at the East Berlin Schönefeld airport?"

"Shouldn't be a problem when I show them my ID. I still can't believe Heinrich made me a Stasi captain."

"Then let's study the backgrounds of two upstanding, if fictitious, West German citizens." She retrieved two sheets from her briefcase and gave him one. "First, read about Maria Weber. Let me know when you're ready for me to quiz you. Then we'll do the same thing with Harald Lang."

He nodded and began to read.

Almost two hours later, Günter had answered all of the background questions to Sabine's satisfaction. She went to the kitchen, poured two glasses from an open bottle of Beaujolais, and carried them to the coffee table. She raised her glass. "To a successful mission."

After they drank, she said, "That's it then."

"Not quite. I can only persuade Traude to defect by convincing her that she'll be able to continue her voice studies. I want her admitted to a topnotch conservatory in the West."

"What you're asking is impossible for me to—"

"I have to be sure Traude can pursue her career. That's the most important thing, after her safety, of course."

Sabine held his gaze. He really wasn't in a position to bargain. If he didn't perform, his daughter would remain in the GDR. And if the Stasi arrested him, her voice studies at Weimar would come to a sudden end. Still, without him, she might never learn the identity of Heinrich's mole.

"Look, I cannot guarantee that Traude will be accepted at one of our opera schools. What I can promise is this: I will use what connection I have to arrange an audition for her. She'll be given a fair chance. If what you've said about her talent is true, she should have no trouble being admitted to a first-rate conservatory. Agreed?"

He hesitated, then nodded. "Okay."

"Good. And I promise to meet your daughter the moment she sets foot on West German soil. I stuck a train ticket for Maria Weber in the back of her passport. It's for Friday morning's Interzonenzug from Weimar to Frankfurt. She'll cross the border at Gerstungen, and I want her to get off the train at the first station in West Germany. That's at Bebra, Hesse. Are you with me?"

"Yes."

Sabine retrieved a notebook from her briefcase, flipped through it until she found what she was looking for. She pointed to a pad and pencil by the phone on a side table near Günter. Before she could make the request, he handed them to her.

She copied the number from her notebook, tore off the sheet and gave it to him. "This is a West Berlin telephone number. Call it and leave a message that will tell me whether your daughter will be on the Friday interzonal train, or if she's coming later or not at all. Memorize the number and the exact words for the different messages I'm about to give you."

When Sabine was satisfied that Günter had understood her instructions, she said, "It's time for you to head for the airport."

"Before I go, I need to pay you for the clothes and shoes. What do I owe you?"

"Never mind. I'll have the agency reimburse me. I've expensed similar items before."

"Very well." He walked through the connecting door. She followed, carrying the shopping bag, then returned to her suite and waited.

A few minutes later, he reappeared with a suitcase. "Thank you for agreeing to help Traude."

She rose from the sofa and shook his hand. "One last thing. Repeat everything I've told you to yourself on your flight home and be sure to test your daughter's retention. She must be able to recite Maria Weber's background to border guards without the slightest hesitation. Let's hope they don't try to match up the visa stamps with a nonexistent permit to enter the GDR. You might alert her to have a fallback plan ready in case of that."

"What kind of plan?"

"You're the spy. You think of something."

"Thanks for the confidence." He opened the door and on his way to the elevator said over his shoulder. "*Auf Wiedersehen.*"

Chapter Seventy-One

Helga's Intuition

East Berlin, Wednesday, 24 August 1977

Helga tensed at the sound of the doorbell. She put down the romance novel she'd been reading since dinner and checked her wristwatch. Ten o'clock. Unannounced visits at odd hours usually spelled trouble. Heaven knows, she'd read countless accounts of Stasi operatives dragging East German citizens from their homes at all hours of night for interrogations. Had someone found out she'd been feeding information to Stefan?

She jumped up from the sofa and approached the door. If only it had a peephole! "Who is it?"

"Stefan."

She unlocked and opened the door.

"Sorry for dropping by at this hour."

She pulled him inside, shut the door and kissed him. "I'm glad it's you, Stefan."

"Why, who'd you expect?"

"Not a soul, and that's what had me worried. You should know as well as anyone what a late-night knock on the door could mean. I thought you'd be in Bonn all week. Did something go wrong?"

"Not really." His tone and his clenched jaw said otherwise.

"That didn't sound convincing. You seem stressed out. Let's see what we can do to take your mind off whatever's troubling you."

She took him by the hand and led him to the bedroom.

♫ ♫ ♫

Helga woke at the sound of Stefan's agitated voice.

"Traude . . ." He tossed, his words becoming unintelligible.

The red digits on the alarm clock showed 11:17. She'd drifted off into the blessed slumber that followed good sex, but now she was wide awake.

Stefan once again called out, "Traude, please—"

She poked his side. He opened his eyes. "Was I snoring?"

"No, but you're talking to your daughter in your sleep, and none too quietly."

"Sorry."

She felt for his hand and intertwined her fingers with his. "It's all right, but now that we're both awake, why don't you tell me what's making you so anxious about Traude?"

The room grew quiet for several seconds. Then he turned toward her. "I don't want to involve you any more deeply in my affairs."

"Hmm, interesting choice of phrase."

"Oh, I didn't mean—"

"Relax, I'm messing with you. But I do want to know what's troubling you about your daughter."

He took a deep breath. "I'm worried what will happen to her when—"

"When you defect?"

"Or when I'm caught," he added.

"But if you're arrested in the West, you'll be a hero here and the general will make sure your daughter is taken care of."

"I know that."

"So why are you worrying about Traude?" She'd hardly voiced the question when the answer hit her. "You're afraid of being caught here, aren't you?"

She strained to read his expression by the alarm clock's faint light, but he turned his face toward the ceiling. With their fingers still entwined, he gave her a squeeze, as if to confirm her supposition. "Let's just say I'm a doting father who worries too much."

"You don't sound real, Stefan. There's more to it."

He faced her. "You are right. If Uli Borst rats to the general that I might defect, I'll be rotting in a cell and Traude's career will be over. I have to get her out of East Germany, or I'll be stuck here forever."

"You know what will happen to her if she's caught. Maybe you ought to shelve your plan to defect."

"No, I can't go on with the deception, the double life."

He sounded sincere. As much as she wanted to, she couldn't hold him back. He'd either make it to the West or be arrested here. How could she help him and his daughter without endangering herself any more than she already had? She'd hired on with the Stasi not for ideological reasons but for the steady paycheck and the fringe benefits that came with the position of a general's secretary. If she were caught in bed with a traitor—

Stefan's voice interrupted her thoughts. "I'm not going to ask Traude to take unnecessary risks. What I have in mind . . . but it's best that you don't know. I'll catch a train to Weimar right after work tomorrow."

"You don't mean it." But the firm set of his chin, visible even in the dim light, showed just how serious he was. Maybe she could talk him out of it. "Unless there is an overnight train, you won't make it back to work Friday morning. Why don't you go Saturday? I can drive you then and visit Beate while you see your daughter."

"You have a car?"

She nodded. "Just a Trabi, but it'll get us there."

He remained silent. Just when she thought he'd agree, he said, "Thank you, but I can't wait till Saturday. I have to go tomorrow evening."

She looked at the wall, torn between letting him fend for himself and offering more help. What the hell, she'd already entangled herself. One more step wouldn't make much difference. "All right. Tomorrow, you come here straight from the office, and I'll drive you."

He hesitated. "Would it be too much to ask you to pick me up at my apartment? I'll have to take a few things."

"Okay."

"Thank you, Helga. I'll give you directions tomorrow."

"It's settled then."

He propped himself up on his elbows. "There's something else that worries me. What if the mole Uli Borst warned me about learns of my plan to defect? I must find something that'll finger him, or at least the agency he's infiltrated before he can alert Heinrich."

"What makes you think it's a *him?*" As soon the words left her mouth, she regretted them.

"Do you know something that . . . are you saying it's a woman?"

"I'm not sure what I'm saying. It's just a guess."

He squeezed her hand, hard. "Tell me. Let me judge whether there's something to your guess."

"Take it easy!"

He loosened his grip. "Sorry, I'm just excited at the thought of getting a lead on the mole."

"It's all right." Should she say more? To gain time to think, she teased, "I'm glad you're not this rough during sex."

Her attempt at banter fell flat, drawing a serious response. "Please forgive me. I didn't mean to—"

"Apology accepted." Her mind made up, she said, "Here is what I know. There's been a rumor going around for some time about a high-placed mole in one of the West German intelligence services. That's what Uli Borst was referring to."

"Do you think he knows who the mole is?"

"I bet he's just going by the rumor."

"But you have something that points to a woman?"

She turned onto her back. The faint light from the alarm clock reflected on the far wall. What to say that didn't sound far-fetched, the fanciful imagination of an overly suspicious Stasi secretary? She gazed into the darkness looking for the right words. Stefan kept silent, probably figuring she'd answer him eventually.

She faced him. "You've heard about the Foreign Service secretary fleeing Bonn just before the West Germans could arrest her as a Stasi spy?"

"Yes, Monika's friend. Gisela . . ."

"Gisela Sturm. Someone tipped her off just in time."

"And you know who?"

"No, but after Gisela returned, I overheard Heinrich talking to Lieutenant Gruber about a woman with an autistic daughter. The general sounded pleased with himself, as if he'd scored a real coup. He was even more pompous than usual. I might be making a connection where there is none, but I have a hunch that the general was referring to his highly placed mole—the one Uli Borst warned you about. I'm quite sure we don't have a female employee with a disabled child, but I don't know all of the domestic informers who report to Heinrich, so the description might fit one of them."

Stefan scooted closer. "Why do you think it's someone in the West?"

"The timing of Heinrich's comment, coming right after Gisela's narrow escape. It made me think he might have been referring to the mole who tipped her off. I could be way off base."

"Don't sell yourself short, Helga. Trust your intuition." He kissed her forehead. "Thank you for telling me."

"Promise me, whatever you do with the information, you didn't hear it from me."

"You have my word."

"Does Heinrich know you came back early?"

"No."

"He doesn't like surprises. I hope you have a good explanation."

"I've thought of something to tell him tomorrow." He gazed toward the alarm clock. "It already is tomorrow. We should get some sleep."

She curled her body close. "I have a better idea."

Chapter Seventy-Two

Insubordinate

Stasi Headquarters, Thursday, 25 August 1977

General Heinrich crested the staircase, ready to receive his secretary's morning greeting, but the black cover over her typewriter meant she hadn't arrived yet. According to the wall clock behind her desk, she had five minutes before the eight-thirty starting time. He couldn't recall her ever being late. Most mornings, she greeted him with a freshly brewed cup of coffee. Not that he needed caffeine to jump-start his day. He'd awakened early, excited at the prospect of presenting Stasi Chief Mielke the dead-drop materials he'd received yesterday afternoon. His threats to jail Stefan Malik and end his daughter's career were bearing fruit: his newest Romeo was performing beyond expectations.

Keeping his office door open, Heinrich walked to his desk, dropped his briefcase on the credenza, and stepped to the wall safe. A few spins of the dial and he held in his hand correspondence between German Chancellor Helmut Schmidt and U.S. President Jimmy Carter. Yesterday's read-through had not yielded any bombshells, but the fact that Monika Fuchs had access to communications between the heads of state promised riches of intelligence that were sure to exceed anything he could have hoped for.

He'd begun a more thorough reading when Helga Schröder entered. She bid him good morning and set a full cup of coffee on the desk. Eager to resume his study, he muttered, "*Danke*" and lowered his gaze.

"Pardon me, General, but Herr Malik would like to see you."

He stared at her. "What did you say?"

"Herr Malik—"

"But he's in Bonn."

She hesitated, apparently loath to contradict him, then blurted, "He came back . . . I mean he arrived at the office a few minutes ago."

Trying not to appear dumbfounded, he commanded, "Well then, send him in."

She turned on her heel and left.

While he waited for Stefan, Heinrich tried in vain to resume his study of the materials in front of him. He wondered what might have possessed his Romeo to return early. Had he run into difficulties after making the drop?

Following a half-hearted knock on the open door, Stefan took a few tentative steps into the room. "*Guten Morgen, Herr General.*"

"Have a seat. Did something go wrong in Bonn?"

Stefan sat. "No, General."

Heinrich glared at him. "What were your orders?"

Stefan fidgeted in his seat. "To stay in Bonn till the end of the week."

"And do what?"

"Get as much material from Monika as I could."

"Good, you remember my orders. So why didn't you follow them?"

"I felt under observation and thought it wise to come back after I made the dead drop."

Could the operative he'd tasked with keeping an eye on Stefan have been so amateurish as to let himself be detected?

"You *felt* you were being observed? What the hell is that supposed to mean? A spy acts based on intelligence and evidence, not on some vague feelings. What signs did you pick up that someone might be following you?"

"I saw the same man twice. First when I went to Monika's apartment and again on my way back to the hotel."

"Describe him."

Stefan scooted forward. "He kept his distance. I'd say rather tall, probably in his forties, in a dark suit."

The description didn't fit his operative who was in his thirties and of average height. Maybe Stefan was imagining things. "And it didn't occur to you to radio me for instructions instead of panicking and running home?"

"I'm sorry, General, but I thought—"

"Never mind what you thought. I don't need to tell you the penalty for insubordination." He paused to let the threat sink in. "It's your good fortune that you delivered some decent material. I assume you read it."

"Just enough to make sure it contained worthwhile intelligence. When I saw it was correspondence between Chancellor Schmidt and President Carter, I knew Monika had given me something good."

Heinrich leaned back. Stefan's admission that he'd looked at the materials rang true. As he weighed what to do with his Romeo, he wondered who could have tailed Stefan. What if the tall man worked for West German intelligence? Heinrich resolved to canvass his assets in the West. Surely, his mole could find out whether Stefan and Monika were under observation.

He caught Stefan stifling a yawn. "Not getting enough sleep?"

"I'm sorry, General, but I didn't make it home till late last night."

"Very well, that'll be all for now. Close the door behind you."

He waited until Stefan had left to compose a radio message to a number of informants and his mole. If he received confirmation that Western intelligence had Stefan and Monika in its sights, should he send his Romeo back to Bonn anyway?

The decision could wait. For now, he needed to evaluate the latest dead-drop documents. He could already picture Mielke smiling while reading Chancellor Schmidt's and President Carter's mail.

But first things first. He sealed the envelope containing his radio transmission and buzzed Helga Schröder.

Chapter Seventy-Three

Launching Traude

Weimar, Thursday, 25 August 1977

Helga stopped the car in front of the Weimar train station and turned toward Stefan. "Should I wait until you can make sure she's here?"

"Very thoughtful of you, but not necessary. Traude promised to come, and she's always true to her word." He opened the passenger door, stepped out, and grabbed his briefcase and the shopping bag off the rear seat. "Thank you for driving all this way."

"No big deal. Only three hours and daylight most of the way."

"I can spell you on the way back, if you like."

"We'll see. How much time do you need?"

"No more than an hour. But we can be longer if that's not enough time for your visit with Beate."

She checked her watch. "It's a quarter to nine. I'll pick you up at ten."

"Okay." Holding the case and bag in one hand, he shut the door with the other.

A grinding gearshift, a cloud of exhaust fumes, and the Trabi lumbered down the street. As the taillights grew dimmer, Stefan entered the station. A neon sign, *Zum Durstigen Reisenden*, drew him to the far end of the entrance hall. Thirsty Traveler—a fitting name for a train-station bar, and certainly better than the usual monikers extolling the virtues of socialism.

Elongated planters with flowering bushes encircled a patio that held half a dozen small tables. Traude waved from the far corner. A better choice than inside the bar, but still no guarantee the Stasi wouldn't be listening.

As he walked up, she rose and hugged him. He leaned his case and bag against a table leg and sat.

She raised a mug and pointed to one in front of him. "I took a guess you'd be thirsty after your travel."

He lifted his mug and they drank.

"What did you bring—?"

He put up a hand. "Tell me about your studies."

She understood and changed the subject, talking about her classes, her apartment, and Weimar.

They gulped down the last of their beers. After paying, Stefan said, "I enjoy watching the trains coming and going. Are you up for strolling?"

"I'd love to." Her tone of voice conveyed enthusiasm that couldn't escape anyone who might be listening.

Picking up his belongings, Stefan led the way down the sparsely populated hall. There weren't too many trains arriving or departing at this late hour.

Traude slipped her arm through his. "Now you can tell me what's in your shopping bag."

"Two dresses, a blouse, a skirt, and a pair of shoes."

"From your trip to the West?"

He nodded. "I hope you'll like them."

She tugged at his elbow. "You didn't buy these merely for my enjoyment, did you?"

"I'd be lying if I said I did. Let's keep strolling while I tell you my plan." She didn't need to know that Sabine had a large part in devising the scheme.

"But—"

"Please hear me out. When I'm done, you can make up your mind whether you want to pursue your dream in the West. If I can't convince you that you should leave, then . . ." He didn't want to think about the consequences if she decided to stay in East Germany.

"And the Western clothes are part of the plan?"

"Yes, you'll have to assume the identity of a West German returning from a visit to relatives in Weimar. If you agree to go along, I will give you the particulars on her background. We don't have much time, so listen well."

While they moved down the departure hall, he detailed how she could escape to West Germany. She interrupted every so often to ask for clarification.

When she'd run out of questions, he said, "What do you say? Is it a go?"

She held his gaze. "You're forced to do the Stasi's dirty work as long as I'm here, aren't you?"

As much as he wanted to persuade her to leave, he couldn't bring himself to insist that she defect for his sake.

He grabbed her arm. "You must decide on what's best for you and not what might happen to me."

"What about Mom? I might never see her again."

Even though he'd expected her to agonize over leaving her mother behind, he groped for a response that wouldn't sound feeble. "I know you love your mother despite her nagging you about your career choice, but there comes a time when it's right to break away from your parents, and leaving for university is a natural way to do it."

"But I couldn't return home for a visit between semesters like my classmates. As far as our regime is concerned, I'd be in a foreign country, never to set foot in East Germany again."

He released his grip. "I can't argue that. You have a tough choice to make. I would never ask you to consider leaving if I didn't believe with all my heart that it will give you the chance to fulfill your dream, to lead the life you are destined for."

He paused, not sure whether to voice what was on his mind. She might as well know. "And there's no guarantee that I'll make it out. Even if I never see you again, I will picture you on an opera stage somewhere in the world. For your dream to come true, you have to leave the GDR."

"I never realized how much you love me, Dad. I love you back, but I'm going to have to think about it."

"There's no time, Traude. The exit visa you'll use expires midnight Sunday. And I have a ticket for you on tomorrow morning's interzonal train from Weimar to Frankfurt." Seeing her questioning look, he added, "*Frankfurt am Main* not *Frankfurt an der Oder*. You have to make up your mind now."

A whistle sounded nearby. Traude turned, seemingly engrossed in watching the diesel locomotive pull out of the station. Was she looking for a way to let him down gently? Finally, she faced him. "All right, I'll chance it."

He studied her expression, looking for clues as to whether she truly believed she had a better future in the West, or whether her father's dilemma had influenced her decision. He couldn't tell which it was. He kissed her forehead and she hugged him. They held one another for a long while.

She stepped back. "How am I going to break the news to Mom?"

"You can't. She's a true believer. To her, the party propaganda is gospel. Call her if you must, but for God's sake, don't mention our plan."

Traude scrunched up her face. "But I can't just leave without saying goodbye."

"You must. Tell her whatever you like, but say nothing that'll give her the idea she may not see you for a long time. Who knows what she might do if she has even a whiff that you're about to defect."

"I suppose you're right, but I still need to call her."

"Just be careful what you say. Don't give us away." Afraid she might change her mind, Stefan handed her the bag and stepped to an empty bench, which he used as support to open his briefcase.

He retrieved the passport he needed and handed it to her. "Meet Maria Weber."

She opened it and flipped through the pages. "I don't believe this. How did you manage to—?"

"Never mind that. Don't lose the train ticket. It's in the back of the passport."

He shut the case, took her by the elbow and pointed to the platform straight ahead. "Let's walk down here while I give you Maria's background. Interrupt me if something is not clear. You must remember every detail."

She slipped the passport into a jeans pocket and they resumed their stroll. After he'd finished, he asked her to repeat to him all she'd learned about Maria Weber. He only had to correct her a few times.

Satisfied with her level of retention, he led her back to the entry hall. He glanced at the wall clock. Five minutes past ten. "I've got to go." He gave her another embrace. "Remember what I've told you and you'll do fine."

She teared up. "Thank you for everything, Dad."

One last kiss on her cheek, and he pulled away. "I can't wait to see you wear those dresses over there."

He turned and headed toward the exit, hoping that he'd done right by Traude. When he passed a row of pay phones, he inserted a few coins in one and dialed the number Sabine had given him.

On the fourth ring, a computer generated male voice announced, "Please leave your message."

Stefan hesitated, wondering whether he'd remembered the number correctly. Of course, he had. The lack of identification as to person or entity was to be expected. He said, "Shipment to arrive as scheduled," hung up and left the station.

He found Helga's gray Trabi idling out front and jumped in. As she drove off, he asked, "How was your visit with Beate?"

"Short but good." She looked over. "But more importantly, how did you do with Traude?"

Chapter Seventy-Four

The Confirmation

Munich, Thursday, 25 August 1977

At the sound of the ringing telephone, Sabine rinsed her mouth, dropped the toothbrush and padded down the hall as fast as her slippers would allow. Ten fifteen at night. This had better be important.

She flopped her pajama-clad body onto the living-room sofa and picked up. "Hello."

"Frau Maier?" a low male voice inquired.

"Yes."

"Our machine just received the message you're looking for."

"What is it?"

"Shipment to arrive as scheduled."

"Thank you." She disconnected.

So Stefan had convinced his daughter to flee. Sabine fought mixed emotions, admonishing herself to feel compassion for the young woman whose ambitions were subject to the whim of an oppressive regime. Toe the party line and you survived, but God help you if you bucked the trend and dared to question anything.

Under different circumstances, Sabine would have been the first to cheer Traude's escape. But not now. As long as his daughter remained in the GDR, Stefan would be tethered there, focused on identifying Heinrich's mole. Once Traude made it safely to the West, he might well follow suit. Sabine's only leverage to prevent that was her threat to have him prosecuted as a Stasi spy, a card she didn't want to play unless she absolutely had to.

Moreover, getting the daughter settled would divert Sabine's attention from handling Stefan as a double agent. She shrugged. Whatever. The plan had been set in motion.

Shaking off her negative thoughts, Sabine picked up the receiver and dialed. She wouldn't have dared to call anyone but Horst at this hour. He answered on the first ring.

"Sitting by the phone expecting your girlfriend to call?" she teased.

"Yes, and she did, didn't she?"

Sabine laughed and could feel herself blushing. "You're too quick, Horst."

"I have to be to keep up with you. What's new? Feeling like a late-night chat?"

"No, I risked tearing you out of bed to let you know that I can't see you tomorrow evening."

A pause. "What's happened?"

"I'm leaving town early in the morning, and even if I'm back by evening, I'll be preoccupied with . . ." Not for him to know.

"I suppose that's all you can tell me."

"Yes, it is. Sorry, I was so looking forward to our—"

"No need to apologize, Sabine. I understand. That's the life of an intelligence officer. I remember it well, and I don't miss it."

"I'll call when I'm free."

"Please do. And stay out of trouble."

"Sweet dreams," she said and hung up.

As she headed for the bedroom, she added breaking her date with Horst to her regrets about Traude's flight. Oh well, instead of feeling sorry for herself, she needed to get a good night's sleep to be ready for early morning travel.

Chapter Seventy-Five

The Border Crossing

Weimar and Gerstungen, Thuringia, Friday, 26 August 1977

Traude kept her eyes shut against the early-morning daylight, but travel nerves and worries about what lay ahead thwarted her attempt to doze a few more minutes. She gave up and rolled out of bed. She'd stayed up past midnight to pack and spent a short night chasing elusive sleep.

She trudged to the bathroom for a shower. As she turned her face into the stream of hot water, realization hit that she'd packed her East German favorites—the wrong clothes for this trip. Fortunately, she had several hours this morning to repack.

She washed her hair, toweled off, and brushed her teeth. A few minutes later, she carried her makeup case and pajamas into the bedroom. After putting on the panties, bra and stockings she'd laid out on top of the dresser, she turned toward the closet for the big decision: which of the two dresses should she wear? She slipped them off their hangers and ran her fingers over the smooth material that felt like silk. *Kunstseide* like that couldn't be had in all of East Germany, not even by the wives of party bosses.

She shook her head at her silliness. What did it matter which one she chose? As she put on the teal one, she wondered how her father had managed to pick two dresses that complimented her red hair and pale complexion. Maybe he had help from the woman who was supposed to meet her. The thought catapulted her into action.

She lifted the small suitcase off the closet floor, laid it on the bed and opened it. She must have been tired last night not to have thought through what type of clothes Maria Weber was likely to have in her luggage. Certainly not all those garments that screamed *Made in the German Democratic Republic.*

She spread the contents of the case over the bedcover. True, she couldn't avoid taking a few East German clothes, but she'd better be smart about it. She picked out several articles of clothing she'd bought in Weimar. A few were brand new, others she'd worn once or twice.

After half an hour of agonizing over what to take, she closed the suitcase and slipped her feet into the low-heel black pumps. Even though they were the right size, they pinched her feet, but the leather would soften with wear.

She glanced at her watch. Seven twenty. A few more minutes and she'd have to make the call if she wanted to catch Mom before she left for the office. As she chewed on a slice of dark bread laden with butter and strawberry marmalade, Traude pondered how to say goodbye to her mother without tipping her off. When she couldn't put the call off any longer, she picked up the kitchen phone and dialed.

"Is anything wrong?" Ortrud sounded surprised at the early morning call.

"No, everything's fine. I just had a little time before class, and I thought I'd call."

"Do you need some money?"

"No, I just felt like saying hello."

"Well, that's a nice change."

Traude swallowed a tart response to her mother's reminder that most of her calls home had been to ask for something. There was no need to rub it in, especially not during their last conversation for a long time. Of course, Ortrud didn't know, and Traude couldn't tell her.

In as even a voice as she could muster, Traude said, "I know you need to leave for work. I just wanted to let you know how much I appreciate all you've done for me, Mom. I didn't realize it until after I left home."

If it hadn't been for the total silence, Traude could have sworn Ortrud had dropped the phone. She couldn't recall her mother ever having been speechless.

Finally, an uncertain high voice came over the line, "That's the nicest thing you've ever said to me, Traude."

"I've been too self-absorbed to thank you before."

"You know you're always welcome back home if that voice study doesn't work out. I can get you in the business course at Humboldt University."

"Yes, Mother. You've told me more than once." Traude unclenched her jaw. She didn't want to end the conversation feeling resentful. So she said, "I just wanted to tell you that . . . I . . . that I'm fine."

"I'm glad to hear. I do need to go. Let's talk again soon when we have more time to chat. Goodbye."

"*Tschüs, Mutti.*" She replaced the receiver, regretting that she hadn't said *I love you.* She may never have another chance. At least, she'd managed to say goodbye without letting on that she was about to abscond.

When she closed the door to her apartment a few minutes later, it felt like locking away the first eighteen years of her life. Before she could change her mind, she carried her small suitcase down two flights of stairs and stepped out into a mild morning. The sun peeked from behind scattered clouds left after an overnight rain. With a stiff breeze at her back, she joined the pedestrians on the sidewalk. A brisk five-minute walk brought her to the Weimar train station.

The wait for the interzonal train's arrival seemed endless. The one time she could have used a crowd to let her blend in, only a handful of passengers were milling about on the platform. When a man in uniform passed by, she met his gaze, recalling her father's admonition not to appear timid or afraid. A horn sounded and the train pulled into the station. Snorting like a weary rhinoceros, the diesel locomotive ground to a halt. A smattering of travelers left the train and headed for the terminal.

Suitcase in one hand and purse in the other, Traude climbed on board. She passed up several compartments until she found an empty one. After storing her case in the overhead luggage rack, she sat by the window and surveyed the platform, alert to any hint of trouble. All seemed normal, but she couldn't relax, silently imploring the engineer to hit the throttle. Finally, the whistle blew and the train began to move. When the station became a blurry dot in the distance, she released a long breath she'd been holding without realizing it. So far so good.

The bumpy ride over uneven tracks matched her inner turmoil about forsaking the only country she'd ever known. True, she had little future in the GDR repressive police state, but still she felt guilty about running away without having given her mother a proper goodbye. It was not until after they passed Eisenach that her qualms gave way to worries about what awaited her at the border, now only a short ride away.

As the train rolled through the last few kilometers of the East German countryside, she shifted her focus to the woman she needed to inhabit in a few minutes. She'd hardly finished her silent review of Maria Weber's background when squeaking brakes foretold their arrival at the border station.

A peek out the window of the slowing train afforded her a view of the sign *Gerstungen* in front of an imposing complex that encompassed three buildings. The yellow façade and the curved red-tile roof projected benevolence, but Traude knew better. No sooner had they come to a stop than a horde of uniformed men fell upon the train.

Doors opened with successive bangs that echoed down the platform. Then the door to her compartment slid back and a middle-aged man in a gray uniform stepped inside.

"*Guten Tag.* Papers please."

She handed him the passport. He turned a page or two, then alternated his gaze between the document and her. She met his scrutiny with a faint smile, secure in the knowledge that she could pass the comparison with the passport picture. Apparently concluding he had a match, the man flipped through the document. Unfamiliar with uniforms, she hoped he was a border guard and not a Stasi officer.

"What was the purpose of your visit, Frau Weber?" His tone was firm, though not menacing.

"I attended my uncle's funeral."

"Where?"

"In Weimar." She answered in an even voice, resisting the temptation to point out that he damn well knew from the stamp in the passport.

"Your uncle's name?"

"Hermann Metzger." Good thing her father had anticipated the question. He'd also assured her the guards would have difficulty verifying the information since the Weimar phone book listed half a dozen men by that name.

"Your mother's name?"

"Ulrike Weber."

He frowned. "Her maiden name?"

"Sorry. Her maiden name is Metzger. He was her only brother."

The guard, if that's what he was, showed no reaction. He turned a passport-page. "Where do you live?"

Recalling her father's instructions, she said, "Stuttgart."

"What do you do there?"

"I'm a student."

"Studying what?"

Her father had rightly warned her how inquisitive the border guards could be. "I'm a voice studies major at the Stuttgart opera school."

"You don't have a Swabian accent."

"I'm from Frankfurt. That's where I'm headed to visit my parents before the semester starts next week."

As soon as the last phrase escaped her mouth, she wished she could take it back. Father had told her more than once only to answer what was asked and not to volunteer information. But he'd crammed so much detail into her that something had to slip out, and it had. Surely, such a tiny mistake wouldn't matter.

"You just told me that your semester hasn't started yet." The guard stepped closer, towering over her. "So why did you take the train to Weimar from Stuttgart instead of Frankfurt?"

Her stomach tightened. The plan had her leave at a different border station from the one she supposedly had entered to keep the guards from trying to match up the visa with her nonexistent permission to enter. Coming through the Probstzella border station signaled to the guard that she must have taken the interzonal train either from Stuttgart or Munich. Because of her slip of the tongue, the scheme now backfired. She started to get up, groping for a plausible response that would get her out of the difficulty of her own making.

He put up a hand. "Please remain seated."

She sat back down, knowing what to say now. "I was in Stuttgart looking for an apartment."

He studied her for a long moment. "Did you find something?"

"Yes."

"You care to give me the address?"

"Heilbronner Straße 47."

The guard produced a pen and a small notebook from his uniform breast pocket. "And your parents' address in Frankfurt?

"Veil Weg 5. That's in Bad Homburg, north of Frankfurt."

He scribbled. Surely, he wouldn't have time or take the trouble to check. She hoped both addresses were real, but she didn't know.

He put away his pen and notebook. "Please accompany me to the customs building and wait there."

"Is there a problem?"

"Not if Probstzella has your permit to enter the GDR on file."

She felt blood rushing to her face. What could she do to prevent him from contacting the other border station?

He pointed to the overhead luggage rack. "Please bring your suitcase."

She stood, half expecting him to help her. Instead, he slid open the door and waited. Was he playing the authority card or simply observing procedures that prohibited guards from assisting West German travelers? She lowered the case, grabbed her purse and moved past him onto the gangway. At least he took the case while she climbed down from the wagon, but handed it right back the moment she stepped onto the platform.

Purse slung over her shoulder and suitcase in hand, she hurried after him, her feet aching. But pinching shoes were the least of her problems. They moved down the platform, eerily deserted, save for a handful of uniformed men carrying rifles. Was she the only passenger being escorted to customs control?

The guard headed in the direction of a multistory building, whose upper two levels featured huge windows overlooking the tracks. He walked past the sign, *Pass- und Zollkontrolle,* and opened the door to a low-slung structure that abutted the apparent observation post. Two officers at a reception desk looked up. He nodded in their direction and led her down a concrete corridor with heavy steel doors on both sides, all closed. Their steps echoed in the bare hall. He motioned her into a windowless room barely large enough to hold a metal desk, a vinyl recliner on one side and a wooden chair on the other.

"Put your suitcase on the desk and wait here."

He left little doubt which chair was hers. The door slammed shut. Had he locked her in? The high-pitched hum of a single fluorescent ceiling bulb further frayed her nerves. She heaved the case onto the desk and, resisting the urge to pace, sat on the edge of the hard seat. For all she knew, the room was under surveillance, and she didn't want anyone to see how nervous and worried she was.

What would happen to her when the guards couldn't find a permit for Maria Weber to enter the GDR? She should never have agreed to her father's hare-brained scheme. Dismissal from the Weimar opera program now seemed inconsequential compared to the years in prison awaiting her. Well, if she wasn't willing to risk jail in order to fulfill her dream, she didn't deserve a career. The plan would have worked but for this suspicious guard. Who would have thought one border station would check with the other? In retrospect, she should have been ready for it. Germans were nothing if not sticklers for detail, even anal-retentive.

The door flew open and the guard entered. He seemed more frustrated than angry. What had he found out?

"Open your suitcase."

She unlatched the locks and lifted the cover, exposing a lavender nightgown and crimson panties, from which she'd cut out the labels. For all this male guard knew, they were from West Germany. She'd packed them on top, hoping an embarrassed male guard would refrain from digging deeper. No such luck.

"Put those on the table."

She complied, exposing a black dress.

"For the funeral?"

"Yes."

He examined the material. "That's not from West Germany, is it?"

No doubt, the shoddy quality gave it away, but she wasn't about to say that. "No, I forgot to bring something to wear at the funeral. So my aunt bought this for me."

He picked up the dress, laid it aside, and turned his attention to the next layer of clothes—all East German except for the blouse and skirt Father had brought her. "Why do you have so many clothes from the GDR?"

"I didn't bring a whole lot with me, so I bought these in Weimar. I only wore the jeans and a couple of shirts. The rest are brand new." How glad she was to have repacked this morning!

"And you want to take them with you?" He didn't quite manage to hide his incredulity.

"They'll remind me of my family here."

He shrugged as if dumbfounded as to why a West German woman would choose to wear clothes of such inferior quality, but that was not a sentiment an East German border guard would dare express. She reached for the top of the suitcase, hoping he'd let her close it, but he would have none of it.

"Keep unpacking."

She removed the East German clothes and exposed her makeup case, stockings, slips and a bunch of knickknacks, but he zeroed in on the shopping bag.

"What do you have there?"

"A new dress I took to East Germany with me. It's similar to the one I'm wearing."

He gazed at her teal dress as if noticing it for the first time, then returned his attention to the bag and read aloud, "*Kaufhof Preiswert, Köln.*" He pointed. "Open it."

She hesitated, thinking she might have discovered the diversion that could save her. Father had said she might have to improvise. She pulled the pistachio-green dress with dark-blue pin stripes from the bag and held it against her figure.

Eyes widening, the guard took a step back and looked her up and down. She began to feel uncomfortable, wondering whether he was staring at the dress or her body, when he asked, "What material is that?"

"*Kunstseide.*"

"And you bought it at a Cologne department store?"

"Yes."

He kept ogling the garment. After a long moment, he said, "Not the kind of dress we . . . well, repack your suitcase."

She folded the dress, ready to put it back in the shopping bag, but the way he kept staring gave her an idea. You're an artist, she told herself. Follow your intuition.

She placed the garment on top of the suitcase and faced him. "You know, I don't really need two dresses. I'm a student who'll be wearing jeans and T-shirts for the next four years. Do you by chance have a relative or close friend this dress might fit?"

He narrowed his eyes. "Then tell me why you brought two dresses if you only need one."

Nothing escaped this man, but she had the answer. "I brought it as a present for my cousin, but it didn't fit her, and she didn't like it."

"She didn't *like* it?"

He obviously fancied it. He took a step back, opened the door, and peered down the hall. Was he going to turn her in for attempted bribery?

"Put your belongings back and come with me."

Trying to keep her hands from shaking, she repacked the suitcase, closed the lid, and followed him to the end of the corridor. He eased open a steel door, peeked, then motioned her forward. She found herself in a courtyard with a few concrete tables and benches. They had the place to themselves, but lunchtime couldn't be too far off.

He shut the door. "Probstzella couldn't find your permission to enter the GDR. Why do you suppose that is?"

She held his gaze. It took her a moment to respond. "They must have misfiled it."

He looked around, then continued in a low voice, "My daughter Agnes is about your height, but maybe not quite as slim."

Traude opened the case on the nearest table and pulled out the dress. "There's plenty of material to be let out."

His eyes darted between her and the dress, back and forth. She tried hard to think of what else she could say, when he gave a slight nod.

She closed the suitcase, and folded the garment. He scooped it up and stashed it inside his uniform jacket. Then he pulled her passport from a pocket and carried it to the table. He produced a stamp from another pocket and punched it down on the paper. She might never hear a sweeter sound.

"Your exit visa, Frau Weber. I'll take you back to the train."

Traude stared at the visa stamp showing her departing Gerstungen on 26 August 1977, 11:52. She dropped the passport in her purse, picked up her suitcase, and followed him to the platform as if in a trance. They stepped aside as an officer with a firm grip on an elderly man's elbow pushed past them. An arrest? Traude shuddered—how close she had come to suffering a similar fate!

Once at the car, she climbed the steps. The guard handed the suitcase up to her. "Have a pleasant trip home."

In a daze, she went back to her compartment. Perched by the window, she watched the guard return to the customs building. Had he suspected something and traded the dress for his silence? She would never know.

No matter now, she'd made a narrow escape. With luck, she would be in West Germany in a few minutes, but the train remained stationary. What was taking so long? Were they interrogating others in the customs building?

How fortuitous that Father had bought her two dresses. Without the second one, she might be—

A whistle interrupted her thoughts. She never imagined she'd find such a shrill sound so pleasing. Doors banged shut and the train started to move.

What awaited her in the West? She'd find out soon enough, but she wasn't quite there yet.

Chapter Seventy-Six

The Ex

Stasi Headquarters, Friday, 26 August 1977

Helga stuffed her purse into the credenza and pushed the chair up to her desk, ready to tackle the tasks left undone when she'd gone to lunch. Before she could grab the top document in the in-box, Lieutenant Gruber entered the reception area. A woman in a brown business suit followed close behind. Short red hair, freckled face, rotund figure, probably late thirties—her face contorted, as if she were in agony.

"We need to see General Heinrich." Gruber spoke with inflated self-importance.

She'd never liked this brownnoser, so she said with satisfaction, "The general gave strict orders not to be disturbed this afternoon."

Gruber took a step back. The woman opened her mouth to say something, but he raised a hand and shushed her. "I'll handle this." He glared at Helga. "I suggest you buzz the general and tell him I have someone here with vital information he needs now, before it's too late. I wouldn't want to be in your shoes, if we miss catching . . . uh . . . let me just say, the general would not look kindly on your obstructing us."

She couldn't afford to ignore this officious bureaucrat's threat. "All right, I'll interrupt him." She asked the woman, "What is your name?"

Before Gruber could stop her, she blurted, "Ortrud Malik."

Helga turned toward the intercom, hoping her expression didn't betray the shock she'd felt at hearing the woman's name. What in the hell did Stefan's ex have to tell Heinrich? For sure, nothing good for Stefan or his daughter.

Heinrich answered on the fifth ring. "I thought I told you not to bother me."

"I'm sorry, General, but Lieutenant Gruber is here with Frau Malik. He insists that they must see you."

"Did you say *Malik?*"

"Yes."

"Send them in and hold my calls."

The door had barely closed on the general's visitors when Helga leapt to her feet and rushed down the hall. She knocked on Stefan's door, praying he'd returned from lunch. Not waiting for a response, she pushed into the tiny room—vacant. She hurried back and almost collided with Stefan coming up the stairs.

He did an exaggerated sidestep. "What's so urgent that you're running me over?"

She caught her breath. "You have to get out of here."

"I don't understand."

"Your ex is in with the general."

Stefan grabbed her arm. "You're sure?"

"If her name is Ortrud, I am."

"What in the hell could she . . . she must have found out what Traude was up to. *Verdammt,* I asked her to be careful when she talked to her mother." He let go of Helga's arm.

"Could your daughter have said her defecting was your doing?"

He shrugged. "I don't know. She could've let something slip."

"If she did, Heinrich will have your ass. Go to my apartment. It should be safe, at least for a while. You know where I keep the spare key. I'll see you there after work." Stefan stared past her, as if she weren't there. When he didn't move, she said, "Do you hear me? Go, *now!*"

His eyes refocused on her. He seemed to shake off a daze. "You're right, but first I need to get a few things from my place."

"Make it fast before the general sends his goon squad there."

He squeezed her hand. "I don't know how to thank you."

"Go!"

He turned and ran down the stairs.

♫ ♫ ♫

Heinrich pushed aside the file he'd been working on and eyed Stefan's ex-wife as she entered with Gruber. He thought her reasonably attractive even with a few extra pounds on a figure that might once have been called voluptuous. She gave him a limp handshake and settled on a visitor's chair.

Gruber took the other. "Sorry for barging in on you, General, but I thought you needed to hear what Frau Malik has to say."

Heinrich turned toward her—a woman in obvious distress. "Does this concern your former husband?"

"I believe it does."

"What made you come to us?"

"I guessed he was involved with the Stasi somehow."

"Did he tell you that?"

"No. We haven't spoken in years. I just heard about his foreign travels and figured he had to be working for the government."

Heinrich thought about asking her how she'd learned about her ex's travels, but decided against it. Most likely, Stefan had told his daughter who'd let it slip to her mother. Instead, he said, "What do you want to tell us?"

"I fear my daughter plans to leave. Maybe she already has."

Heinrich leaned forward. "You mean defect?"

She nodded.

"What makes you think so?" Even as he asked the question, he hoped she was a distraught woman imagining things. If not, he'd just lost one of the main holds he had over Stefan.

"My ex-husband got her into the opera program at Weimar. I've tried to persuade her for years to study something practical instead of pursuing the pipe dream of an opera career, but she wouldn't listen." She sighed.

Heinrich wanted to shout, *get to the point, woman,* but he said, "We're familiar with her studies. Just tell me what you know about her wanting to leave."

Ortrud scooted to the edge of her chair. "Traude called me early this morning."

His patience began to wear thin. "And?"

"You have to understand she only calls when she needs something. This time she just wanted to chat, and the way she talked . . . well, it felt like she was saying goodbye. So I tried to call her from the office. I'm a secretary at the Humboldt University admissions office."

Heinrich nodded as if he didn't already know where Stefan's ex was working. He prodded her on, "But you couldn't reach her?"

"No, she didn't answer. So I called the school. They put me through to the professor whose class she was supposed to be attending this morning. She didn't show." Ortrud raised her voice. "That's not like Traude. She is so responsible."

Heinrich gazed at her. What to make of this? A doting mother inventing problems or something more? "And you think your ex-husband has something to do with this?"

"Yes, I do. He encouraged Traude's aspirations to become an opera singer against my advice, and I wouldn't put it past him to have planted the idea in her mind she'd be better off studying in the West."

As much as Ortrud's ramblings sounded like the far-fetched imaginings of a resentful ex-spouse, Heinrich couldn't ignore them. Was there any reality to what she was saying?

He stood. "Thank you for coming forward, Frau Malik. I will look into this."

Reluctantly, she got up. "Please find my daughter and stop her."

A mother so distraught at the thought of losing her daughter, she probably hadn't thought through what might happen to Traude if she were caught trying to defect. Not that he would enlighten her. He said, "If you'll excuse me, I will get right on it before it's too late."

He nodded at Gruber, who took the hint and led Ortrud Malik from the office.

As soon as they were gone, he buzzed Helga. "Have Stefan come to my office immediately."

"I'm sorry, sir, but Herr Malik just left."

"When do you expect him back?"

"I don't know."

"Did he say where he was going?"

"He left in such a hurry, I only picked up that he had some kind of an emergency."

"Did he mention his daughter?"

"Not that I heard, General."

"Call me as soon as he's back." About to disconnect, he thought of something else. "And get our man in Weimar on the line."

While waiting for the phone call, Heinrich retrieved Stefan's file from the safe, flipping pages until he found the information on Traude. He composed a message alerting the border stations to watch for a slender eighteen-year-old woman with curly red hair, to apprehend her and notify him. He wrote *extremely urgent* at the top of the paper and carried it out to Helga, who was on the phone.

She covered the receiver. "Colonel Heydt from Weimar for you."

"Put him on hold. I'll pick up in my office."

"The general will be right with you, Colonel." She pressed the hold button.

Heinrich handed her the message. He hadn't taken the time to seal it. Every second counted. "Have the radio department send this urgent message immediately to all border stations."

He hurried back to his office, gave the man in Weimar the information he needed to check on Traude Malik's whereabouts, ordered him to report back, and ended the call. He resisted the temptation to unlock the credenza drawer where he kept the schnapps. What a hell of a day this was turning out to be. He hoped Stefan had bolted from the office to get his daughter out of some difficulty—the most logical explanation for his sudden disappearance.

He was still clinging to that hope when Helga, back from the radio department, put through a call from the Gerstungen border station.

An anxious male voice came over the line. "General, a redhead fitting your description came through here just before noon."

"And you let her pass?"

"Uh . . . yes. She had a West German passport with all the requisite visas."

"Under what name?"

"I'm sorry, General, but the guard who checked her papers can't recall the name."

"Well, if he does, call me." Heinrich hung up.

How in hell did Traude get her hands on a forged West German passport with all the required visas? The most likely scenario: Stefan had somehow arranged for it. But how? Heinrich did not dare contemplate the unthinkable. If his Romeo had sold out to the other side, then the intelligence that seemed like such a coup—

An urgent knock on the door, and Helga carried in an envelope. He tore it from her hand. From the radio department. He ripped it open before she was halfway out the door.

A transmission from his mole, Bohrer: *Monika Fuchs and Günter Freund under observation. Forged West German passports with visas issued on 24 August for Maria Weber and Harald Lang. Given to Freund.*

Heinrich dropped the paper and slammed his fist on the desk. He'd never been double-crossed before, and this by a novice Romeo! He grabbed the notepad and feverishly wrote a description of Stefan, possibly traveling with a West German passport in the name of Harald Lang.

With no time to lose, he stormed from the office and handed the note to Helga. "Go back to the radio department. This is to be sent to all border stations immediately."

She headed for the stairs.

♫♫♫

On her way down, Helga peeked at Heinrich's message. What she read jolted her. She tripped, barely catching herself on the banister. So Stefan planned to abscond with a West German passport issued to a Harald Lang. He couldn't have procured the forged document without substantial help. Had he signed on with western intelligence? Heinrich probably thought so, judging by his urgency in notifying the border stations.

She exited the building and pulled up her jacket collar against a light drizzle. A dreary day, and not just because of the weather. She had too much to do to go back for an umbrella. She set out for the radio department, but halfway up the street, she took a detour. Around the corner stood a public phone booth, empty thank God. She pushed in the accordion glass door, stepped inside and dropped a twenty-pfennig coin in the slot as the door swished closed.

With her index finger poised over the dial, she racked her brain for Stefan's number, but she couldn't recall it. She took a deep breath, then another, and voilà, the number came to her. She had to disconnect twice before her trembling fingers managed to turn the dial to the correct number. She listened. Would he be home already? Would he pick up?

She'd lost count of the number of rings when he answered, "*Hallo.*"

His phone would likely be bugged, so instead of identifying herself, she said, "Please bring Harald Lang's items."

She listened into the silence. Would he understand? If she had to be more specific, anyone listening might be able to identify her.

Finally, Stefan said, "*In Ordnung.*"

She hung up. His okay meant he'd understood. She pulled open the door, got out and resumed her trek to the radio department. With the borders on the alert, Stefan could no longer make it through with the Harald Lang passport. Part of her wanted him to stay, but another part fervently hoped he had a backup plan.

Chapter Seventy-Seven

The Debriefing

Bebra, Hesse, Friday, 26 August 1977

Sabine alternated between glancing at her watch and peering into the distance toward the point where the two rails converged. Owing to East Germany's painstaking border controls, interzonal trains were notoriously late, but at twenty minutes past due, she started to worry. Mertens had assured her that the forgeries produced at the Cologne office were first rate. She would have preferred to use the expert at BND, whose documents had always passed muster with the GDR border guards, but there had been no time.

She recalled the portrait picture—curly hair, a freckled face, probing eyes. But what had stayed with Sabine was the young woman's determined expression. Then a vision of Traude in handcuffs flashed through her mind. She shook her head, dispelling the image.

Twenty-three minutes past schedule now. She searched the horizon for signs of an approaching train. Nothing. A low hum drew her attention to the tracks. They were vibrating. A diesel locomotive appeared in the distance. A whistle blew, the train rolled into the station and stopped. A conductor stepped from the first car and walked the length of the platform.

Standing near the exit stairs, Sabine shifted from one leg to the other, ready to scrutinize anyone getting off, but no one did. Surely, not all passengers were bound for Frankfurt. What happened to—?

The door of the last car flew open with a bang. The conductor stepped to the exit stairs, reached up and took a suitcase from a passenger who stepped down. Sabine narrowed her eyes and stared, but all she could see was the conductor's back. Finally, he moved aside, revealing a slight woman. Suitcase in hand, she peered up and down the platform before heading toward the terminal. Sabine's heart jumped at the sight of red hair and a teal dress. The plan had worked!

The conductor climbed back on board, blew his whistle and the train pulled away from the station with all passengers still on board. All, save Maria Weber.

Sabine stepped into the middle of the platform where she could be seen. Stefan's daughter approached, studying her with uncertain eyes.

"*Willkommen*, Traude. I'm Sabine Maier."

Traude set down the suitcase and shook Sabine's hand. "*Danke*, Frau Maier." She teared up. "I can't belief I made it."

"Please call me Sabine. The dress looks fabulous on you, and I bet the pistachio-green does too."

"I don't know. I never got the chance to wear it."

"You don't have it any longer?"

"No. I gave it to a border guard for his daughter. It may have bought my freedom."

Sabine stared at her, itching to find out more, but this was not the time. "You must tell me about your escape over lunch." She picked up the suitcase.

Traude hesitated. "I'm sorry, but I have no money. My father didn't give me any West marks, and smuggling out East German currency seemed too dangerous."

"That's okay. Lunch is on me, and I'll have some money for you later."

With Traude following close behind, Sabine carried the case down the stairs and made for her car parked a few meters from the station. After storing the suitcase in the trunk, she pointed to a half-timbered house down the street. "The restaurant is over there."

As they strolled along the sidewalk, Traude asked, "Did you help my father pick out the shoes and clothes for me?"

"Yes. I figured that was too important a task to leave to a man."

Traude grinned.

Sabine gave her a smile, pleased that she'd put at ease the woman who'd just risked her life escaping from the GDR. When they reached a copper sign engraved in cursive script, *Zum Ochsen,* Sabine opened the beveled-glass door into a smoke-filled room. Most of the patrons occupying the dozen tables appeared to be enjoying an after-lunch cigarette or cigar. Smokers still ruled German society. Traude coughed and took one hesitant step. Sabine considered looking for another restaurant when a portly woman wearing a checkered apron approached and grabbed two menus from a wooden box.

"*Guten Tag.*" She must have noticed Sabine's expression, as she added, "Would you prefer our nonsmoking dining room?"

"*Ja, bitte.*"

Taking a few shallow breaths, Sabine followed the innkeeper down a narrow hall that led into a room barely large enough to accommodate four tables, all unoccupied. They settled on a small table by the window and studied the menu in silence until a waitress appeared. Traude ordered *Sauerbraten mit Knödel.* Thinking red meat and dumplings too heavy, Sabine opted for trout with wild rice. Though she had a three-hour drive ahead, she ordered a glass of Riesling and encouraged Traude to select an appropriate red wine.

A few minutes later, the waitress brought Sabine's white wine and a glass of *Trollinger.* Little did Traude know, she'd be spending time in Swabia where Trollinger reigned as the national drink.

Sabine raised her glass. "Congratulations on making it to the West. I expect you're anxious about what awaits you here. Don't worry. We . . . I promised your father to take good care of you."

Traude picked up her glass. "Thank you."

After they sipped, Sabine said, "I'm dying to know how the other dress bought your freedom."

As if a plug had been pulled from a dammed-up place inside Traude, the words tumbled from her mouth. Sabine only interrupted the intense recounting a few times to ask for clarification.

When Traude had finished, Sabine said, "You are a very brave young woman. And to think so fast on your feet. I'm glad I bought two dresses, even though I only get to see you in one."

"A dress for my freedom. A bargain I'd make every time."

The waitress carried two plates into the dining room and served them. Between bites, Sabine began to debrief Traude. "What has your father told you about me?"

"Only that you would meet me and take me to my new home. Can you tell me where—?"

"I will in a moment, but first I need to ask you a few more questions. Do you know what your father does?"

"He's involved with the Stasi somehow. Is he a spy?"

Sabine ignored the question. "What did he tell you?"

"Only that he's forced to do despicable things."

"Do you know what he meant by that?"

"No, he never explained. Is he spying for the Stasi or for whoever you work for?"

Sabine placed her fork and knife on top of her half-empty plate, contemplating her response. What to tell Stefan's daughter? Enough to reassure her but no more.

She waited until Traude finished her meal. "The Stasi coerced your father into spying. After we caught him, he agreed to gather intelligence for us."

"So you work for West German intelligence?"

Sabine hesitated, but there was little point denying what Traude had already surmised. "Yes. Rest assured, we will help your father escape."

The waitress cleared the plates. When they were alone once more, Traude asked, "When will he come?"

"As soon as he's fingered a Stasi informer for us. Did he by chance say anything to you about that?"

Traude shook her head.

Sabine studied her, looking for signs of evasion. "This is really important. Please try to think of anything he might have said about an informer or a mole in the West. Any offhand remark, a slip of the tongue, could be crucial. The sooner we learn who this mole might be, the sooner can we get your father out."

Traude held her gaze. "I'm sorry, but he never said anything about an informer or a . . . what did you call it?"

"A mole."

"No, I've not heard him use that term."

Sabine grimaced, almost wishing Stefan had let something slip, but apparently, he'd been tightlipped even with his own daughter. "If something occurs to you, no matter how insignificant it might seem, be sure and tell me. You'll have plenty of time to think during the three-hour drive ahead of us."

Traude fidgeted. "Where are you taking me?"

"The place where you supposedly boarded the interzonal train to East Germany."

"Stuttgart?"

"Yes. Do you know anything about the town?"

"Home of Mercedes and Porsche, and apparently a conservatory."

"With a first-rate opera school."

Traude scooted forward. "I'll be admitted there?"

"After you pass an audition, which should be no problem if you have half the talent your father claims." Sabine lifted her glass. "Let's finish up. I have to get you settled in Stuttgart."

As if on cue, the waitress appeared with the check and Sabine paid with cash. After a visit to the restroom, they walked back to the car.

On the way, Traude asked, "How long until I can audition?"

Sabine waited to respond until she started the engine and put the car into first gear. "I've arranged a special audition for you this Sunday." She looked over. "Two days is enough time for you to prepare, isn't it?"

"If I'm allowed to sing what I performed at my audition in Weimar."

Sabine let out the clutch and accelerated. "If it got you admitted to Weimar, it should be good enough for Stuttgart."

Chapter Seventy-Eight

Opera Tickets

East Berlin, Friday Evening, 26 August 1977

Please bring Harald Lang's items. Helga's parting words stayed with Stefan during his crosstown bus ride. There was no mistaking the meaning: Heinrich had learned of the forged West German passports, but from whom? Certainly not from Sabine. She was too invested in unearthing Heinrich's mole. Who else but a Stasi operative who infiltrated West German intelligence could have alerted the general to the forgeries within two days?

Stefan grabbed his duffel bag and got off the bus. On his walk to Helga's place, he recalled her guess that the mole could be a woman with an autistic daughter. If so, which of the three West German intelligence agencies had she penetrated? The question occupied his mind during the three-block walk to the apartment building. He found the entrance unlocked as Helga had told him he would.

He entered, crossed the foyer, and walked down a flight of stairs to the basement. At the flip of a wall switch, a bank of fluorescent lightbulbs flickered on with a hum, illuminating a row of small storage compartments along a brick wall. All of them were locked, including number 27 assigned to Helga, but that did not concern him. A musty smell assaulted his nostrils as he moved to the far end of the dank cellar. He set down the duffel bag, turned around and listened. No sound. He removed the loose brick Helga had shown him, took a key from the niche, and replaced the brick. Anyone discovering the hiding place wouldn't know which storage compartment or which apartment door the unmarked key would open.

After turning off the lights, he carried his bag up to the foyer. With no one in sight, he climbed the stairs to the sixth-floor apartment. On his way up, he wondered once again where the general could have placed his mole. Only after he caught his breath at the top landing, did a possible answer come to him. The speed with which Heinrich had been tipped off suggested that either his informant worked at Sabine's shop, the BND, or at the agency in Cologne that produced the forgeries.

A woman with an autistic daughter might be enough information for Sabine to identify her, but he wouldn't divulge this intelligence until Traude was taken care of. At the thought of his daughter, he fumbled with the key. Had she made it across the border before Heinrich could alert the guards to detain a Maria Weber? He couldn't find out until he made contact with the BND unless Helga had heard something, but she wouldn't be home for several more hours.

After a steadying breath, he managed to unlock the door and step into the living room. He set the duffel on a chair in the breakfast nook and tossed the key onto the kitchen counter. He needed a stiff drink, but all he could find was an open bottle of red wine.

He filled a glass to the brim and took a healthy swig. No way around it, he had to leave the GDR, and fast. Heinrich would have his henchmen combing East Berlin, all of East Germany even, searching for his traitorous Romeo. Escape as Harald Lang was now impossible. At the thought, he set down his glass and stepped to the chair holding the duffel bag. He dug out the passport from an inside pocket and carried it back to the kitchen.

A quick search through drawers and cabinets yielded a stainless steel pot, tongs and hot pads. He lit a burner on the gas stove and held the passport over the flame. He moved the document around until a singe on a corner grew and the entire document caught fire. Smoke filled the kitchen as he dropped the burning passport into the steel pot. Luckily, the apartment did not have smoke alarms. He opened windows in the kitchen and living room.

Back in the kitchen, he found burnt pages smoldering in the bottom of the pot. He stirred the remains with the tongs, turning what little was left of the document into a heap of ashes. While he waited for the remaining sparks to extinguish, he took a few gulps of wine. Then he dumped the cold ashes into the wastebasket below the sink, pulled out the plastic liner and twisted it closed.

He grabbed the key off the counter, carried the bag from the apartment, down the stairs, and out of the building. He walked to one corner. Nothing but a dirt path that dead-ended after a few meters. He moved to the other side and found five large garbage bins lined up along a wooden fence. He heaved the sack into the first container and returned to the apartment.

Despite the open windows, the place still smelled of smoke. Maybe by the time Helga came home, the odor would have dissipated. He stepped to the open living room window and stared at the gray façade of an apartment building across the street. He should have had a plan B at the ready, but he didn't. Short of climbing the Wall, he couldn't think of a way to leave the workers' paradise. Well, he had a few hours until Helga's arrival to come up with something.

♫ ♫ ♫

A key scraping in the lock interrupted Stefan's thoughts. The door swung inward, admitting Helga clad in her tan business suit. Her severe expression softened when she caught sight of him. "You made it."

He hugged her. "Thank you for alerting me."

She kissed him on the cheek, slipped from his embrace, and wrinkled her nose. "Did you burn something?"

"Harald Lang's passport."

"Do you have a backup plan?"

He shook his head. "I'm working on it."

"Are you thinking about going over the Wall?"

"Not if I can help it."

"I might be able to—"

"You have an idea?"

She pointed to his drink on the coffee table. "Pour me a glass of wine and we'll talk."

After swallowing the last of the red wine, he carried his glass to the kitchen but stopped short at the sight of the bottle on the counter. Only now did he remember finishing it while racking his brain for a solution to his predicament. He stared at the empty wine rack. "*Verdammt!*"

Helga came into the kitchen. "What's the matter?"

"I'm afraid I drank all of your wine."

"You didn't." She opened the refrigerator and produced a bottle. "I like this one better than the red anyway." The corners of her mouth turned upward. "And there's another chilled one should we need it while we brainstorm."

He read the label, "*Weißburgunder,*" then uncorked the bottle and poured the golden liquid into two glasses Helga was holding. They settled on the sofa and sipped the white burgundy. He let his gaze travel from her face down the length of the formless costume she had to wear at the office, imagining the shapely body that lay underneath.

She laid a hand on his thigh. "Later, Stefan. First, let's talk about how we can get you out of here. You know I don't really want you to leave, don't you?"

He put his arm around her shoulder and held her tight. "Any chance of your coming with me?"

"Oh, Stefan." She kissed him. "I wish I could, but I won't leave Beate."

"I understand. I wouldn't either in your situation, but I don't have a choice. And I hope Traude is safely in the West. You didn't hear anything about an arrest at the border?"

"No. You should have seen how angry Heinrich was after he took the call from the Gerstungen border station. Traude must have passed through just before his alert reached them."

Stefan exhaled. "I hope you're right. But how did Heinrich find out about Harald Lang?"

"Radio transmission."

"From his mole?"

"Probably."

While Helga drank, Stefan said, "You hinted at a plan that didn't involve my climbing over the Wall."

She set down her glass, hard. "I did no such thing."

He furrowed his brow. "Were you putting me on?"

"No, you didn't let me finish. I do have an idea. It's not foolproof, but I believe it's relatively safe." She covered his hand on the sofa with hers. "But it does mean going over the Wall."

"Please tell me you're not serious. Do you know how many have died trying?" Not waiting for her to respond, he blurted, "I'd have to make it past a signal fence, a hundred-meter death strip between the two walls, watchtower strobe lights, and German shepherds. And if the guards haven't shot me by then, I'd have to climb up three and half meters of border wall and go over the barbed wire on top. It's impossible."

"Most places yes, but—"

"You know where I could get through?"

She nodded. "There's a section between Checkpoint Charlie and Prinzenstraße."

"In the wall?"

"On the GDR side. It needs repair. And the barbed wire is loose in a few places."

"Really?" He sat up. "But how do I know they won't repair them any minute?"

"I have the latest word."

"From?"

"From a memo sent to Heinrich this week. I've learned they won't start repairs until Monday morning."

"Are you sure?"

"The one thing I'm sure of is this—you must act fast."

"The signal fence could give me away."

"It's not working. But you have only so much time before they fix that too."

"What about those high concrete blocks on the border wall?"

"That section of the Wall is still original, but they'll start upgrading to new concrete blocks very soon." She scooted forward. "Be aware of the raked sand in the death strip."

"So the authorities can keep track of intruders by their footprints," he said.

"That's one purpose, but more diabolical, it lets officers see whether a guard neglected his duty."

"You mean, failed to shoot a trespasser?"

"Exactly."

"Shoddy barbed wire on the border wall won't do me any good if I don't get there, will it? Even if I clear the first wall and the signal fence without alerting the guards, I'll make for easy target practice in the death strip."

Helga laid a hand on his forearm. "I didn't say it would be easy, but if you go at night you can time the watchtower strobe lights. And the good news is, there are no dogs there yet."

To gain time to digest the information, Stefan took a big gulp, then another. "Thank you, Helga. I'll have to mull this over."

"Well, don't take too long. Remember, the window closes Monday. And your risk of getting caught goes up with each day you remain in the GDR."

"You're right. I don't have a backup plan, but going over the Wall?" He stared out the window, in search of a better idea. But nothing came to him.

He turned back to Helga and squeezed her hand. "Seems I've run out of options. I can't stay. I can't put you at greater risk, and if Heinrich catches me, he'll have me shot. I'll be lucky, if he doesn't have me tortured first. But if what you say is true, I might have a decent chance of making it. I just have to take the risk. I'll go for it."

"When?"

Stefan thought for a moment. "Tomorrow."

"I suppose that's for the best." Helga's voice quivered. "I was so looking forward to your taking me to the opera tomorrow evening."

"But I am."

"No, I don't want you to risk your life just to keep your promise."

"The Staatsoper is the last place the Stasi will be looking for me."

He rose, walked to the breakfast nook, rummaged through his duffel bag until he found what he was looking for, and returned to Helga. "Here are the tickets to *Die Zauberflöte*. You and I will be there for the seven-thirty curtain. I have something in mind for later."

She gave him a quizzical look. "Meaning?"

"I'll tell you what. Let's scour your fridge for something to eat. You open that second bottle of Weißburgunder, and I'll tell you over dinner about my plan for our night at the opera."

Chapter Seventy-Nine

Die Zauberflöte

Staatsoper Unter den Linden, East Berlin, Saturday Evening, 27 August 1977

Helga drove the Trabant sedan into the parking lot close to the Staatsoper. A white-haired man in a green uniform exited a booth and approached the car. The driver's wet window squeaked as she rolled it down. She gave the attendant five marks, took the ticket, drove to the end of the lot and parked.

She turned toward Stefan, checking again the fit of the herringbone jacket, black shirt and trousers she'd purchased for him. Since he couldn't risk leaving the apartment, she had spent most of the morning filling his extensive shopping list and the car now held everything he needed for his escape.

During the afternoon, they had made love with urgency—their last chance for intimacy. Satiated, Helga held Stefan tight, imagining it might prevent him from leaving. The rhythmic sound of soft summer rain drifted through the cracked bedroom window, as if to soothe her. She wanted the time to slow, but instead it accelerated.

They spent the twenty-minute drive from her apartment in silence. She couldn't think of anything to say that wouldn't sound trite. He kept fidgeting, scanning the streets.

Helga turned off the engine. Stefan checked the rear seat, probably making sure that nothing was missing. The car locked, they moved across the lot toward Unter den Linden. During a lull in the traffic, they crossed the wide boulevard in the twilight, and joined the throng of patrons streaming into the theater. Evening gowns dominated, but quite a few women wore summer dresses like Helga. She would not stand out.

Even though the opera house was the least likely place the Stasi might look for Stefan, they took no chances. He stayed close to her side, away from the usher tearing tickets, and they went straight to their seats some twenty rows from the stage. Since the theater had been rebuilt after the war, she'd expected a modern interior instead of rococo style. This had to be the original design going back two centuries.

Stefan pulled Helga's seat down. "Sorry, but these were the best available."

Given what awaited him, how could he possibly worry about their seats? "Don't be silly. These are fine." She touched his arm. "Let's hope this performance is good enough to distract us."

"I'm going to pretend the soprano role is sung by Traude. We're far enough from the stage that I can hold onto that illusion."

They stood to let several patrons pass to the center of the row. Before long, the theater filled up. The lights dimmed and muted conversations stopped. Applause greeted the conductor taking the podium. She'd heard the overture numerous times on the radio. But on this day, the beautiful melodies couldn't dispel her worries about Stefan. Maybe he'd noticed, because he took her hand.

As much as she tried to focus on the stage, especially when the tenor sang the aria she recalled from Stefan's album, she couldn't help but scan the audience for anything out of the ordinary. No uniforms in sight, but that didn't mean Stasi informers weren't there. Still, no one seemed to be watching her and Stefan; all eyes were glued to the stage. She forced herself to quit turning around, lest she'd call attention to herself.

The queen of the night's coloratura fireworks and the ensuing thunderous applause drew her attention back to the opera. Each time thoughts of the real world intruded, Helga pushed them away.

Finally, the curtain closed on the first act and the lights went up. Stefan stood and took her by the hand. There was no time to lose; the intermission lasted only forty minutes. They squeezed by seated patrons and elbowed through the crowd to the exit.

They made it to the car in less than two minutes. Out of sight of the ticket booth, Stefan jumped into the rear seat where he took off his jacket and shoes. She started the engine. He pulled out the new hiking boots from beneath the passenger seat and put them on. Then he grabbed the gray anorak off the backseat and came around to the front. She let out the clutch the moment he climbed into the passenger seat and pulled from the lot onto Unter den Linden.

Helga resisted the temptation to floor the gas pedal. With the light evening traffic, she'd make the drop-off point easily within the time frame they'd calculated. Nor could she afford to draw the attention of police by speeding. A few hundred meters before Friedrichstraße and Checkpoint Charlie, she made a left turn onto a residential street.

Cars were parked along the right side of the road, but there was no traffic. Her mouth dry, she swallowed. How could she possibly locate the next turn by the dim streetlights? She stared straight ahead. It started to rain again, and she turned on the wipers.

Stefan asked, "What are we looking for?"

"Graulengasse."

Helga kept the Trabi in second gear. Each time she slowed at a side street, Stefan shook his head, and she drove on.

Her heart sank at the sight of a traffic light a short distance ahead. That had to be the Prinzenstraße intersection. They'd gone too far.

She rolled to a stop, debating whether to turn around.

Stefan pointed to a sign. "Graulengasse."

She made a sharp right into an alley barely wide enough for the Trabi. Wooden fences lined both sides, shielding from view what lay beyond. After a minute's drive, they came to a wall blocking the way. A dead end.

Helga cut the headlights. She grabbed the flashlight from the glove box and stepped from the idling car. Stefan put on his anorak. She moved the light beam along the wall until it illuminated a pile of bricks lying on the ground. The memo was right: part of the wall had crumbled.

Helga turned toward Stefan coming up behind her. "This is the place."

He hugged her.

She wanted to hold his embrace forever, but she released him. "You must go."

"I'll never forget you, Helga, and what you did for me."

She kissed him, then drew back. She reminded him yet again, "Don't take any chances. See if you can get through the signal fence without cutting it, just in case it's actually working. And you know how to cross the death strip."

"Yes." He sounded determined.

"You'll make it." Maybe he actually would. Helga pointed the beam at a spot above the pile of bricks. "It's low enough for you to make it over. I'm with you all the way, Stefan. Good luck."

He kissed her forehead, then stepped on the heap of bricks and pulled himself up to the top.

For the briefest moment, he looked back. "Thank you. Take good care."

She said, "*Auf Wiedersehen*," but he had already dropped to the other side and slipped into the darkness. Out of her life. Maybe forever.

Tears mixed with raindrops on her cheeks. Sadness was one thing, but she would not give in to self-pity. Nor could she afford to linger if she wanted to keep her alibi intact. She had to be back at the theater before the intermission ended.

Helga jumped into the car, the flashlight on her lap. She put the Trabi in reverse and after several passes back and forth turned around in the tight space. She eased the car down the narrow alley, the high fence her guide in the darkness.

Before venturing out into the street, she stopped and peered in both directions. Deserted. She turned on the headlights and stepped on the gas as soon as she hit the pavement. Fifteen minutes to make the eight-minute drive, find a parking spot and reach her seat.

♫ ♫ ♫

Rain-soaked grass squished with every step Stefan took. What would Heinrich do to Helga if he discovered her role in the escape? Stefan shuddered. It was out of his control. He couldn't turn back. But he could make sure she hadn't risked her freedom in vain. He had to make it to the West. Not just for himself and Traude, but also for Helga. He owed her that.

Stefan tried to get his bearings, but his eyes hadn't yet fully adjusted to the darkness. How far did the grassy field under his feet stretch before he'd reach the first obstacle? Too risky to go on until he could see the lay of the land. He stopped and pulled a pair of stiff working gloves from an anorak pocket. He slipped them on and waited, resisting the urge to rush.

After a few minutes that felt like hours, his surroundings began to take shape. Low-slung structures abutted the field on both sides—probably commercial buildings. If houses or apartments had once stood here, the regime would have leveled them. Back in the early days, residents living next to the border had jumped from windows and gone over the Wall.

Stefan ventured forward, alternating between watching the uneven ground and peering ahead. Beams of light jerked across the horizon reminiscent of lightning before thunder. He would have gladly chosen a thunderstorm, no matter how violent, over these watchtower strobe lights. Stefan pressed on until he nearly stumbled into a fence. About two meters high, no barbed wire. He couldn't detect any electrical leads, but this had to be the signal fence. Keeping Helga's admonition in mind not to cut it unless he had to, Stefan walked down one side then the other, looking for any place to squeeze through without making contact. There was none.

He stepped back and looked around. There had to be something that would allow him to jump over the fence without touching—branches, discarded tires, or other trash. Stefan walked a circle and returned, deflated. Either no one ever came here or the border patrol kept the place free of anything that could be used to hurdle the fence. He would have to cast his fate with the memo. If it was wrong and the fence actually worked . . . well, there was no point in dwelling on the consequences.

Stefan unzipped an anorak side pocket, took out a pair of wire cutters and stepped to the fence. With the blades hovering above a knee-high wire, he took a deep breath, then cut in one swift motion.

He listened for the slightest noise.

Soft rain falling to the ground was the only sound. Of course, the alarm might be silent. Stefan waited a minute or two, looking for signs that the guards had been alerted. All remained quiet.

He went to work, feverishly cutting away the bottom part of the fence. He put the wire cutters back in his pocket, then dropped down and crawled through, arms and head leading the way.

Once on the other side, Stefan got to his feet and brushed off wet clumps of grass. Again, he listened. Nothing but falling rain. He pushed forward. A few steps and his shoes sank into sand. No sooner had the thought of death strip entered his mind than a strobe light came his way. He dropped to the ground. The beam crept closer. He held his breath. The shaft of light hovered over an area no more than a few meters away. A few seconds, and it swooped off to the side. He exhaled.

Helga had said to time the strobe lights, but he couldn't read his watch in the dark. Back on his feet, he moved straight ahead while silently counting seconds. His grip soles clung to the wet sand with every step. He'd barely counted to sixty when the beam moved toward him. Lying flat on his stomach, he kept his face down lest it reflect the light passing over him. Sweat formed on his forehead and pooled in his armpits. Having to wear an anorak on a muggy night like this didn't help, nor did the knot in his stomach.

No sirens blasted as the light swept past. Stefan jumped up and continued his trudge through the death strip, reaching the Wall just before the light came around again. This time he pressed his body against the foot of the Wall and remained immobile. The slightest movement and the guards would detect him, even with decreased visibility in the rain.

The strobe light moved on. Stefan stood and ran his fingers along the Wall until he felt a brick jutting out. He anchored his right leg onto the foothold, dug his left leg into a small recess and pushed himself up. As he reached for the top, his soles slipped on the wet brick. The rain came down harder.

He clawed at the wall, desperate to steady himself. Before he could, the strobe light closed in. He let go and tumbled down. Pain shot through his left calf. A pulled muscle, that was all. He flattened himself against the foot of the Wall.

Stefan scrambled to his feet as soon as the light beam had passed. The left leg hurt, but he could put weight on it. He had sixty seconds at most to make it over. Using the same footholds, he climbed high enough to reach for the top of the Wall. Something sharp pricked his fingers through the glove. Stefan gritted his teeth and pulled himself up, straight into a section of barbed wire. But it was loose, just as Helga had said.

As he pushed the wire off to one side, it ripped a hole in his pants and slashed his thigh. Blood trickled down his leg. He moved across the top only to have glass shards pierce his skin, right through his pants and gloves. Wincing in pain, he began to scoot and roll toward the west rim when the strobe light blinded him.

Stefan raised an arm, trying to shield his eyes. Voices, then gunshots. Bullets whizzed past. His left shoulder exploded with searing pain. He slumped onto the glass shards on top of the Wall. The pop of gunfire rang in his ears. He crawled across the shards toward the far edge. Deep barks sounded below. The guard dogs! Then an urgent voice pierced his semiconscious state. He plummeted into darkness.

♫ ♫ ♫

Driving along Unter den Linden, Helga turned the windshield wipers on high and looked for a curbside space. She couldn't risk drawing the parking attendant's attention by returning to the same lot. The next one was close to a ten-minute-walk from the theater—ten minutes she didn't have. She slowed, looking for an open spot big enough for her Trabi, but the cars were parked tight, leaving barely enough room for pedestrians to slip through. She passed the opera house. What now? Try the next side street. Just then a black Wartburg sedan pulled out not ten meters ahead. She stepped on the gas and claimed the vacant space

She turned off the engine and exhaled. How fortuitous—had someone left the opera early? She could only hope Stefan would have similar luck. The spot was so close to the theater she didn't even grab her umbrella. She rushed toward the entrance, huddling against the rain. She was a few meters away when a distant noise brought her up short. She stopped. Thunder? Successive popping sounds dispelled that notion. These were gunshots coming from the direction of the Wall.

Stefan shot? Please no. The plan couldn't have failed; he must have made it. It had to be something else, but even if it wasn't, there was nothing she could do for him now. Rain pelted her cheeks as if to remind her to go inside. Watching an opera while her lover could be lying dead at the foot of the Wall felt like sacrilege. But her getting caught wouldn't help him, to say nothing of what the general would do to her.

Flickering house lights signaled the end of the intermission. Being the last one to return, she had to squeeze by the half dozen patrons in her row, hoping they didn't notice her damp dress. She slumped into her seat and wiped a few drops from her brow as the lights dimmed. As much as she tried to focus on the stage, she could not. She should have stuck to her vow to never get involved with another Romeo. Great sex had turned into something more, at least for her. She hadn't planned on falling in love, but absent that, she wouldn't have taken the huge risk of helping Stefan escape.

The masonic themes of the opera reminded her of religion. She hadn't seen the inside of a church for as long as she could remember, but this might be the right time to pray for Stefan—either for his good fortune in the West or for his soul. She wouldn't know which prayer to say until she walked into the Stasi headquarters Monday morning.

Chapter Eighty

East or West?

Berlin, Saturday Evening, 27 August 1977

There was that insistent voice again. "Rudi, *zurück!*"

Stefan opened his eyes to a fuzzy image. He blinked, trying to focus. His vision cleared enough to take in a large muzzle. After a quick sniff, the dog obeyed the command and drew back. Helga must have been wrong about this section of the border not being patrolled by German shepherds. But why hadn't they attacked before he made it to the Wall? The dog's handler, a border guard or a *Volkspolizist*, would slap handcuffs on him any second now.

"Where are you hurting?"

A compassionate East German guard or police officer? Stefan peered in the direction of the voice. A bearded young man stepped closer. No uniform, but civilian clothes—a raincoat, jeans, jogging shoes. A wonderful sight.

"Where am I?" Stefan asked.

"West Berlin. You're safe. Rudy barked when he spotted you on top of the Wall and I yelled at you to jump, but I wasn't sure you could hear me over the gunshots. Tell me where you're hurting."

"Uh . . ." He wanted to say everywhere, but croaked, "Shot in the left shoulder. Pulled a calf muscle."

"Your shirt and pants are bloody."

"From glass shards." He had actually made it over the Wall, and mostly alive. If he could have reached the man, Stefan would have kissed him, beard and all.

The rain had stopped. Stefan started to push himself up onto his elbows, but slumped back down from the pain in his shoulder. He took a deep breath. Leaning on his right side, he managed to sit.

"I'll call an ambulance."

"No."

Stefan rolled onto his side, trying to get up. The dog watched, but kept his distance.

The man took hold of Stefan's right arm and pulled him onto unsteady feet. "Can you walk?"

"I think so."

"I live right around the corner. I'll drive you to the nearest hospital."

With the man supporting his right elbow, Stefan limped along the sidewalk, putting as little weight as possible on the injured leg. Apparently sensing they were in a hurry, the dog trotted to the next corner and waited. When they caught up, he bounded ahead to an apartment building down the street.

As they followed, the man said, "I'm Franz Selig. What's your name?"

"I'm . . ." Stefan almost blurted the cover he'd used in the West. "Stefan Malik. I don't know how to thank you."

"Don't worry about that."

Stefan resisted the temptation to ask what could have possessed the man to come out to the Wall on a rainy night. He was just thankful he had.

As if reading his thoughts, Franz said, "You're probably wondering why we're out in this weather. Rudi loves to be walked in the rain, and I'm glad he pestered me this evening."

They found the dog guarding the entrance to a multistory building, but Franz led Stefan past to a row of garages. He stopped at the second one. Stefan leaned against the sidewall while Franz unlocked the door and lifted it, exposing the rear end of a black Mercedes station wagon. He raised the tailgate and tossed his raincoat onto the rubber cargo mat. Rudi came running and jumped in.

With the dog settled in the back, Franz opened the passenger door, but before Stefan could get in, he said, "Wait just a moment."

He stepped to a wall shelf and returned with a beach towel, which he spread over the seat. "I hope you don't mind, but these leather seats—"

"I understand."

After easing Stefan into the seat, Franz circled the rear of the car and a moment later climbed behind the steering wheel. He started the engine, flipped on the headlights and backed out. He closed the garage and drove down the deserted residential street. Rudi stuck his wet muzzle into Stefan's neck until Franz ordered him to lie down. After several turns, they reached an avenue with busy evening traffic that commanded the driver's full attention.

Stopped at a red light, Franz faced Stefan. "May I ask what made you so desperate that you'd risk your life by going over the Wall?"

"I had to get out or I'd be rotting in a Stasi prison."

"Why is the regime after you?"

"I'm a journalist. One of my articles must have offended a party functionary."

"Easy to do over there." After a quick glance at the light, Franz said, "So I take it you're not a secret agent like the one in John LeCarré's *The Spy Who Came in from the Cold.*"

Stefan shifted in his seat to keep the pressure off his injured shoulder and to consider his response. What if the man's presence at the Wall was no coincidence? He shook off the paranoia and responded in an even voice, "Heavens no."

The light turned green, and Franz drove on. "I didn't think so, or you would have had an agent waiting to meet you, and not a crazy Berliner walking his dog." He chuckled. "Of course, back in the sixties when the LeCarré novel takes place, escape was much easier. Now with two walls—I don't know how you made it."

No way would he volunteer the intelligence that had helped, lest he get Helga into serious difficulty. "Lucky, I guess."

"And brave." Franz glanced over. "How are you holding up?"

"I'm okay."

"Good." He pointed to a well-lit complex just ahead. "We're almost there."

He pulled into a parking space next to the emergency entrance, shut off the engine and helped Stefan from the car. The bleeding had mostly stopped, and the towel showed only a few isolated smears. Rudi had been quiet, curled up in the rear cargo compartment. Franz commanded him to stay and locked the Mercedes.

Favoring his injured leg, Stefan followed Franz to the hospital entrance, its glass door swishing open to admit them. They passed a dozen chairs, half of them occupied, and stepped to a desk.

The female clerk looked up. "What are we seeing you for?"

Stefan hesitated, not sure what to tell her. "Cuts from glass shards, leg and shoulder injuries."

She squinted, maybe thinking she had a bar-fight victim on her hands. If so, he'd not find much sympathy here. Still, she must have noticed his bloodstained clothing. "Are you in severe pain?"

"Not severe, no."

She handed him a clipboard with several forms and a pen. "Please fill these out."

Franz walked him back to an empty chair. "Would you like for me to stay?"

"No, thank you. I'll be all right."

Franz shook his hand. "Good luck, and welcome to the West." He nodded in the direction of the clerk. "You'll have to endure some bureaucracy, but they should take good care of you."

He turned to leave, but stopped. "Oh, I forgot to ask you whether you have somewhere to go after you get out. Any relatives or friends I can notify?"

The question jogged Stefan's memory. He should have thought of this earlier. "Yes, there is someone I would like you to call."

He tore a corner off the top sheet on the clipboard and wrote down his name and the Berlin phone number Sabine had him memorize. "If you get an answering machine, just leave a message that I'm at this hospital."

"Okay. Is there something else you need?"

Stefan handed him the pen and the clipboard. "I'd like to have your address and phone number, so I can thank you properly after they stitch me back together and I get settled."

No need to tell him that he'd have Sabine check out this Good Samaritan. Maybe he'd become overly suspicious during the last few weeks, but there was no harm in making sure that Franz's being at the Wall at the right time was mere happenstance.

"Be glad to." Franz scribbled and handed the clipboard back. "Call me if I can help in any way. All the best to you."

"Thank you. And please, make the call as soon as you get home."

"Of course." With that, Franz walked out the door.

Stefan turned his attention to the forms. It took him a good twenty minutes to fill them out, leaving many spaces blank. Though of no use to the hospital, he did write down his East Berlin address, but he had no answer to the questions regarding insurance.

The clerk leafed through the forms, her expression becoming increasingly puzzled. "You come from East Germany?"

"Yes."

"How did you . . .?" She stopped herself. "Do you have any identification?"

Stefan pulled his ID card from an inside anorak pocket and handed it to her. She compared it to the address he'd written down, and gave it back.

"Please take a seat. I'll get you to a doctor as soon as I can."

He limped back to a chair. She picked up the phone and spoke in a hushed voice. Was she calling the physician or the immigration authorities? If the latter, he'd have to stonewall them until Sabine arrived, which would be in the morning at the earliest, and then only if Franz made the call tonight.

Chapter Eighty-One

The Mole

Munich, Saturday Evening, 27 August 1977

Too worked up from the hectic events of the last two days to sleep, Sabine settled on her sofa with a glass of red wine. She'd spent most of the drive to Stuttgart debriefing Traude before giving up in frustration. Stefan hadn't told his daughter anything of significance. By now, Traude was probably sound asleep in her room at the Hotel Königshof, dreaming of her audition tomorrow.

Sabine leaned back. She'd kept the promise she gave Stefan to take care of his daughter. Would he keep his and dig up intelligence on the mole? She was reaching for her glass again when the phone rang. Apprehensive about a ten-thirty Saturday night call, she picked up.

She'd barely said hello when the same voice who'd alerted her to Traude's escape inquired whether she was Sabine Maier.

After she confirmed, the man said, "We received a message a few minutes ago from a Franz Selig. He took Stefan

Malik to the emergency room at Städtisches Krankenhaus Charlottenburg this evening."

Sabine swallowed. "What for?"

"He didn't say."

She thought for a moment. "Charlottenburg City Hospital; that's in *West* Berlin, isn't it?"

"Yes."

"Did the caller leave a phone number?"

"No, but he said Stefan could use some new clothes, that his shirt and pants were torn and bloody, and then he hung up."

"Thank you." Sabine disconnected.

She stared at the far wall, trying to make sense of the message. Stefan must have made a run for it when the guards realized the passport was forged. His injuries couldn't be life threatening or the caller wouldn't have bothered to ask for clothes. Why had Stefan chosen to flee now? She hoped that meant he'd collected the intelligence she'd asked for and not that he'd been exposed. Or he could have just been scared and reneged on his promise to find out about the mole.

She broke off her speculations, opened the phone book and looked up Air France. She began dialing, then stopped when she remembered the clothes. Good luck on finding a department store open on the weekend in Germany. He'd just have to wait until Monday morning.

Then a thought came to her. Did she dare? Of course, she did. She dialed Horst's number. With her index finger poised over the hook ready to disconnect, she counted the rings. Either he was out on the town or sound asleep.

He answered on the fifth ring. "Systems Solutions."

"Good evening, Horst. Did I wake you?"

"No, I was just reading in bed, hoping for another late-night call from my girlfriend."

She laughed. "Your wish has come true."

"You want to make up for our missed Friday night date?"

"I'd like to, but I can't. I have to catch an early morning flight to Berlin, and I have a strange request."

Horst didn't miss a beat. "What could be more exciting than a strange request from an attractive intelligence agent? Let's hear it."

She hesitated. "You wouldn't have an extra shirt and pants I could borrow?"

Silence. She'd stumped him, but not for long. "Yes, I do, unless it's for a boyfriend fallen on hard times."

Ever the smart ass. "No, nothing like that."

"Let me guess—you can't tell me. What makes you think my clothes will fit this mysterious stranger?"

"He's slim like you, but a couple centimeters taller. Close enough in an emergency."

"Okay, I'll pick out a few things. When do you want—?"

"I'll stop by on my way to the airport in the morning. It'll be early, so get some sleep. I really appreciate this, Horst."

"Anything to help out my favorite secret agent. See you in the morning."

"Good night." She hung up and called Air France.

♫ ♫ ♫

West Berlin, Sunday morning, 28 August 1977

The taxi stopped in front of a multistory yellow-brick building ornamented with oriels and turrets. Sabine leaned forward. "You're sure this is the hospital?"

The cabbie looked at her through the rearview mirror and shrugged. "I know, it looks more like a nineteenth-century villa, but this is Städtisches Krankenhaus Charlottenburg."

She handed him twenty marks, grabbed her suitcase and stepped onto the curb. The taxi sped off, as if the driver wanted to make sure she wouldn't reconsider her generous tip. She entered the building, crossed a small lobby and approached a young woman sitting behind a large desk.

"Where is Stefan Malik's room, please?"

The clerk made no move to open the thick book in front of her. "Visiting hours are not until two."

"I need to speak with your supervisor."

Sabine's resolute tone had the desired effect. The clerk shot up from her chair and disappeared into a corner office.

Sabine set down her suitcase, then turned the book around and opened it. She flipped through several pages until she came to August 27. Only three patients had been admitted last night. Stefan was in Room 327. Leaving the book the way she'd found it, she carried her suitcase to the flight of stairs across the way.

As she reached the first landing, a man's voice drifted up, "Where is she?"

"I'm sorry, sir. She must have left," the clerk answered.

Sabine bounded up the stairs and opened the door to the third-floor station guarding the junction of two corridors. Several nurses and a man in a white coat were busying themselves behind the counter. With no numbers on the wall to guide her, Sabine took a guess and walked down the left hallway. She passed Room 310. When the numbers became lower, she turned back, but before she could gain the opposite corridor, a man stepped from the station. The nametag on the lapel of his white coat displayed *Prof. Dr. Hallmann.*

Blue eyes studied her through rimless glasses. "You look like you're lost." He didn't sound at all like the bureaucratic clerk in the lobby.

Sabine pointed down the hall. "Is this the way to Room 327?"

He nodded. "Did reception admit you outside visiting hours?"

Many German professionals were enamored of their titles, so she said, "*Herr Professor Doktor,* I'm not here on an ordinary visit."

His benevolent smile told her he'd seen through her attempt to stroke his ego. "And what is the nature of your visit that makes it . . . out of the ordinary?"

Not wanting to disclose her profession unless absolutely necessary, she said, "It's a sensitive matter." Before he could probe further, she asked, "Are you treating Herr Malik?"

"Yes."

"What is his condition?"

"I'm sorry, Frau . . . ?"

"Sabine Maier."

"I will need to know your relationship to the patient before I can divulge medical information."

She produced her BND ID from a coat pocket. The doctor studied it, raising his eyebrows. "I see. Herr Malik listed an East Berlin address on the emergency room admittance form, but he has refused to answer any questions about his status. He's obviously an East German refugee. We were planning on calling the immigration authorities on Monday."

She put her ID away. "Please don't. That's my business. Now can you tell me his condition?"

"Of course. He suffered a gunshot to the left shoulder, but the bullet went straight through. A flesh wound that should heal over time. He has a pulled muscle in the left calf and some deep cuts on his legs, arms and torso."

Sabine exhaled. "Nothing life threatening, I take it?"

"No. I should be able to discharge him by the end of the week."

"How did he get the cuts?"

He stepped closer and said in a conspiratorial tone, "I'm guessing they're from glass shards on top of the Wall. The comrades will go to any length to protect their populace from our decadent society in the West, won't they?"

She nodded while digesting the news. What had made Stefan risk his life? Why had he not used the forged passport?

Doctor Hallmann interrupted her thoughts. "I'm glad you're here. It'll save us a lot of trouble dealing with immigration." He pointed down the hall. "He's in a private room, third on the right. I'll be around if you need me." He went back to the station.

Eager to check Stefan's condition and to have her pressing questions answered, Sabine hurried to Room 327. She knocked on the half-open door and entered. A bed with side rails filled most of the small room.

Reclined against a pillow, Stefan cocked his head toward her. "There you are. I wasn't sure Selig would make the call."

"I got the message late last night and took the first flight this morning."

She studied his bandaged left shoulder partly covered by a sleeveless white hospital gown, but before she could ask him about his injuries, he said, "Did Traude make it?"

"Yes."

"How is she?"

"She's fine. I took care of her, just as I said I would."

He propped himself up on his unbandaged right side. "Where is she?"

Sabine set down the briefcase and took the chair. "All in good time. First, you need to answer my questions, Stefan."

"Fair enough. You want to know why I ran so soon, why I went over the Wall, and whether I have any information about Heinrich's mole."

"That'll do for starters, but maybe in reverse order."

"Well, the bad news is that the mole must have tipped off Heinrich to the forged documents. You say Traude made it across the border in time?"

"Yes, she's safe and sound. But what did you do with your passport?"

"I burned it. That left me with little choice but to go over the Wall."

Sabine shook her head. "I can't believe you'd even try."

"I decided the risk of getting shot by the border guards beat being tortured to death by the Stasi."

"And you actually made it."

"I had good intelligence on a place where the Wall could be breached."

"How did you find out about that?"

"A reliable source."

"But who?"

He studied her for a long moment. "I can't say. If it gets back to the mole, my helper's life will be worthless. But I will tell you how I managed to escape."

Sabine listened intently to the incredible tale, interrupting only now and then to ask a clarifying question.

After he'd finished, she said, "You realize you're part of only a handful who've made it over the Wall alive in recent years, though you've obviously paid a price. Are you in pain?"

He shrugged. "I'll live. The nurses were trying to sedate me, but I refused. So they gave me over-the-counter pain pills. I have to be alert so you can walk me out of here. I can't wait to see Traude."

"The doctor said not before the end of the week."

"You've got to get me out of this place long before then. A little pain and a bum shoulder aren't enough to keep me in bed."

"We'll see about that, but please, do you have anything on the mole?"

"That's the good news. I believe I can help you identify the one who's been feeding Heinrich intelligence."

She scooted forward. "What do you have?"

"Well, first of all, I think you need to look at your outfit and the Cologne agency."

"What makes you think he's there?"

"Because of how quickly Heinrich was tipped off to the forgeries. The leak must have come either from the Cologne office that produced the documents or from your shop, from someone who's in the loop."

"Is that all?"

"Far from it. But before we go any further with this, I want to know where Traude will be studying."

Sabine stood and towered over him. "Listen, Stefan. You're not in a position to negotiate. I've kept my promise and arranged a special audition for your daughter. It's at five this afternoon."

"Where? I have to be there."

"First you divulge every last detail you've learned about the mole. If you don't, there will be no audition today, or ever. And our deal of immunity for you is off. Do you understand me?" She sat back down.

He leaned into his pillow. "All right, here's what I know about the mole; just get me to that audition."

She stared at him. "You're in no condition to—"

"You let me worry about that. If I can walk out of here, do I have your word that you will get me to Traude's audition?"

She sighed. "All right. Now, who's the mole?"

"My source thinks Heinrich gets his information from a woman with an autistic daughter. You'll have to take it from there."

Sabine sprang from the chair, knocking it over. "*Scheiße!* I can't believe it." She stepped across the fallen chair. "I've got to make a phone call." With that, she bolted from the room.

♫ ♫ ♫

Propped up by the pillow, Stefan peered through the doorway into the hall. Sabine's extreme reaction had caught him by surprise. He thought his information might give her a lead on possibilities, but he had no idea she'd be able to identify the mole based solely on an autistic daughter.

The minutes passed and he grew worried. He prided himself on being able to read women, and Sabine struck him as someone who would keep her word. Maybe he'd been a fool to trust her.

Just then, she burst into the room. Her flushed face, her excitement, made her even more attractive. Not that he had any designs on her. Helga and Monika were still too fresh in his mind.

"You know who the mole is?"

She nodded. "If your source is right, I'm afraid so."

"Care to tell me?" he asked, knowing full well she wouldn't.

"I don't think so, *Herr Spion.*" She gave him a quizzical look. "Let's see if you're as tough as you claim." She opened the suitcase. "Your savior—and I do want you tell me more about this Franz Selig—he left a message that you needed clothes."

She showed him a pair of pants and a shirt. "These are not new, but they should do for now. And there are socks and briefs in the suitcase if you need them."

"How in the world did you manage to get men's clothes on a weekend?" He thought he detected a slight blush. "I see, keeping spares for overnight guests."

"Very funny, Herr Romeo. Now put on these clothes before the good doctor shows up and locks us in."

"Are we leaving this minute?"

"As soon as you're decent. Your flight to Stuttgart departs in an hour."

Chapter Eighty-Two

The Audition

Stuttgart, Sunday afternoon, 28 August 1977

Favoring his left leg, Stefan carried the suitcase Sabine had left him to the reception at Hotel Königshof. She'd paid for his flight and given him a hundred marks. The BND would take care of his hotel bill and wire money on Monday so he could shop for a new wardrobe. But he'd also smuggled out his stash of West marks left from his trips to Bonn. Helga might have suspected, but she never said a word.

He told the shapely blonde behind the desk his name. After a quick glance at the bandage the short-sleeved shirt didn't quite cover, she flipped through a file and pulled a card.

"Welcome Herr Malik. Your registration has already been taken care of." She handed him a key and pointed to a bank of elevators across the lobby. "You're in Room 715."

Sabine must have made the arrangements while he was in the air. The clerk hadn't even asked for an identity card or passport.

When he didn't move, the woman said, "Is there something else I can assist you with Herr Malik?"

"Uh . . . yes." The wall clock above the reception showed four thirty—half an hour until Traude's audition. "How far is it to the conservatory?"

Her blank look told him she was not into classical music or opera.

"Do you have an address?"

"It's on Urbansplatz."

Her face lit up. "Yes, of course." She pulled a sheet from a drawer, made a few marks with a red pen, and turned the street map around. "We are here. You go through the park into the underpass. When you come up on the other side of Konrad-Adenauer-Straße, walk up the side street by the Staatsgalerie to Urbansplatz." She pointed to a red circle. "I marked it for you. Shouldn't take you more than fifteen minutes."

Twenty with a sore calf, he thought. He thanked her and bent down to pick up the suitcase when his eyes fell on his hiking boots. Sabine hadn't brought him street shoes. If he had to go to the audition looking like a farmer, he would, but maybe . . .

He glanced at the clerk's nametag, *Heidi Sommer.* "Frau Sommer, do you have a lost-and-found department?"

"Yes."

"I'm in kind of a bind. All I have with me are boots, and I'm going to a function for which I need regular shoes. Could I look to see if someone might have left a pair that would fit me? I'd be glad to return them tomorrow or to pay for them."

She frowned. "We usually give access only to guests who've lost something."

Well, she'd said usually, meaning he might be able to persuade her to make an exception. He smiled at her. "I'm sorry to impose on you like this, but you see my daughter is auditioning at the conservatory in half an hour. It's her lifelong dream to sing opera. I have to be there to support her, but I'm afraid they might not let me in with these boots."

She held his gaze. "I'd like to help you, but I could get in trouble—"

"It'll only take a minute, but I understand if you need to check with your manager."

"He's not in." Her face relaxed. "Okay, but let's be quick."

He took in her tight skirt and long legs as he followed her to an office by the end of the counter. A few minutes later, he entered his room in black dress shoes that were a size too large. He thought about her parting words that she would see him tomorrow. Only to remind him when to return the shoes? He could never be entirely sure of a woman's intentions, especially one as attractive as Heidi Sommer. And no wedding band graced her finger.

He dropped the suitcase and the boots onto the carpet and went into the bathroom. A shower would take too long, especially having to be careful not to get the bandage wet, so he freshened up by washing his hands and face, then rode the elevator down. Heidi had resumed her position behind the counter.

He nodded at her and started toward the front door when she called out, "Herr Malik, the exit to the park is the other way."

He turned around, mouthed a quick "*Danke*" and made for the rear door. While sore, his left leg wasn't painful and didn't slow him as much as he thought it would. During the walk, his thoughts shifted from Heidi to Traude, imagining her surprise at seeing her father. Unless Sabine had contacted her, Traude would think him still in East Berlin doing the Stasi's dirty work.

He arrived at the conservatory a few minutes past five. A young man in uniform stepped from behind a small desk. "May I help you?"

"I'm here for my daughter's audition. Can you direct me to—?"

"You must have the wrong date. The school is closed on Sundays."

"It's by special arrangement. Her audition is today at five, and I'm already late."

The guard studied him, probably assessing whether he had a nut on his hands. "I'm sorry, sir, but I can't let you wander around in the school while it's closed."

So much for East Germany having a monopoly on bureaucracy. Keeping anger out of his voice as much as he could, Stefan said, "My daughter is auditioning right now, and you need to tell me which room."

"I just started my shift, and no one said anything about an audition." The guard hesitated, then stepped to the desk and picked up the phone. "I'll see what I can find out."

He sounded less sure of himself. Maybe the man was human after all. He dialed, then listened.

After what must have been half a dozen rings, he hung up and shrugged. "No one's up there."

"Can you call a different extension?"

"All right, I'll give it a try, but I'm not likely to reach anyone."

While the guard dialed anew, Stefan eyed the staircase across the way. If he didn't have a sore leg and a bum shoulder, he'd make a run for it. He couldn't bear the thought of having to miss Traude's career-defining moment, all because no one had bothered to inform the guard.

He had to think of a way to see her perform. But for now, he'd pray someone in a room upstairs would answer the damn phone.

♫ ♫ ♫

Traude stepped onto the stage of the small auditorium and turned to face the three professors sitting in the front row below. The man in charge fit the stereotype with his unruly white mane and beard. He wore a pinstriped suit, a white shirt and a red tie, as if the audition were a long-planned formal occasion instead of having been hastily arranged. In contrast, his younger male colleague was in jeans and a T-shirt. The woman with the short-cut brown hair that made her look younger than she might be, had opted for a white blouse covering her flat chest and a pair of black trousers.

The sixtyish professor spoke. "Frau Malik, I hope you have several pieces ready." He nodded to the woman sitting at the piano on the stage. "Frau Wendlich has brought a wide selection of arias, but she might not have your first or second choice."

Traude swallowed hard. What if she had none of her favorites?

"So what is your first selection?" the professor asked.

"The 'Vilja Lied.'"

The pianist shuffled through a stack of booklets. Surely, she had the soprano showpiece aria from *The Merry Widow*. Finally, the woman nodded and began to play. Traude had practiced this poignant aria more times than she could remember. She carried the high notes easily and infused the melody with the haunting beauty it required. After she finished, she studied the listeners' expressions, looking for the slightest indication of approval or disapproval. All three remained stone-faced.

The young professor said, "That's certainly a beautiful operetta aria, but I'd like to hear you sing opera. Do you have something that is not in German?"

He'd sounded encouraging, but Traude tried not to read too much into his tone of voice. "Yes, I have several pieces in Italian and French." She thought for a moment. Did she dare sing one of the daunting Verdi arias from *La Traviata?*

She felt in good voice. "I'd like to sing 'Sempre libera,' if the music is available. While the pianist pulled the booklet from her pile and put it on the piano stand, Traude thought she detected all three professors raising their eyebrows. Surprise at her foolishness in attempting such a fiendishly difficult piece? Anticipation of how she would do? Admiration of her courage? Perhaps all three.

The beginning was easy enough, but ascending to the coloratura passage had undone many a soprano. Just when Traude reached the critical part, the door of the auditorium opened and in walked—could that be—her father? As hard as she tried to keep her focus, she couldn't, and she broke off. The professors stared, as if pitying her. But when she gasped and peered past them, all three turned in unison.

Stefan waved as if apologizing for the interruption and slid into a back row seat. The old professor asked, "Who are you?"

"Stefan Malik, Traude's father. I thought you'd been told that I'd be coming, and I'm sorry for being late. Please don't hold it against my daughter. She had no idea I'd fled East Germany."

Traude headed for the stairs leading down from the stage. Audition or not, she wanted to embrace her father, but he said, "Please, go on. I came to hear you sing, Traude."

"You risked your life to attend your daughter's audition?" The female professor sounded incredulous. "I bet you have quite a story to tell, but another time. Today we must decide whether to admit your daughter to the opera school." She turned and faced Traude. "Please start 'Sempre libera' from the beginning."

The second time through, Traude did not hesitate when she reached the high notes, but sailed through the coloratura passage in good form, or at least she thought so.

While she was catching her breath after the final note, the younger male professor said, "You obviously have the high notes. So I'm going to ask you to sing something that's more in the mezzo range. Do you have anything like that in your repertoire?"

Traude nodded. "I'd like to sing '*Mon coeur s'ouvre à ta voix*.'" She hoped the pianist had brought the *Samson and Dalilah* score.

Back when Traude was unsure whether she was a mezzo or a soprano, she had sung the most seductive aria in all of opera in several student performances. Frau Wendlich put the booklet on the piano and started to play.

Traude infused the opening lines with the sensuousness they demanded. "My heart opens to your voice like the flowers open to the kisses of the dawn." She hoped her French diction wouldn't offend the professors' ears.

Dalilah's impassioned plea for Samson's tenderness faded and the auditorium fell silent—whether in appreciation of

Camille Saint-Saëns' lyrical music, her rendition, or the professors' search for the words to tell her she'd failed, Traude couldn't tell. Well, she'd given it her best shot, and if that wasn't good enough, so be it. She was free in the West and so was her father, and if an opera career eluded her, she'd cope.

The senior professor said, "You can go and say hello to your father, while the three of us confer."

Traude rushed to the rear and embraced Stefan. "I can't believe you're here. How did you . . . what did you do to your shoulder?"

"Shh," he shushed her. "My story can wait. You sang beautifully and I'm so grateful that I could be here to witness it."

"Frau Malik." The senior professor's voice sounded from the front. "Would you and your father join us?"

She took Stefan by the hand. Being reunited with him in the West now trumped her ambition for an operatic career. But the professors' smiles told her she'd passed the audition.

The white-haired professor said, "Our semester starts tomorrow. Report to the registrar at nine in the morning. Congratulations and welcome." He shook her hand, as did the other two.

"Let's enjoy what's left of the weekend." With that, the senior professor dismissed her.

She followed her father from the auditorium, unsure whether her feet were touching the ground.

Chapter Eighty-Three

The Trap

Pullach, Tuesday, 30 August 1977

"She's not falling for our trap." Dorfmann quit peering out the Volkswagen bus and turned toward Sabine. "This is the way to her apartment."

Sabine held his gaze. She'd persuaded her boss to let her generate a fictitious intelligence report. If the black Mercedes ahead was really carrying the mole home, she either didn't consider the information urgent or figured it was bogus. The tail they had on her all day Monday had not turned up anything suspicious. They needed to catch her red-handed. The tip from an unknown Stasi source about a woman caring for an autistic daughter was not enough for an arrest. They had to have evidence of her actually contacting the Stasi.

The light turned red before they could follow the Mercedes through the intersection. "*Verdammt!*" Dorfmann slammed his fist into the rear seat. "Call the backup," he told Sabine.

She spoke into the microphone. "We've lost her. Are you—?"

"We're on her," a male voice responded.

"Where is she going?"

"So far, looks like her regular route home."

Dorfmann cut in. "Let us know if she deviates."

Their light turned green and the VW driver gave them an over-the-shoulder look that said where to now?

Dorfmann pointed ahead. "You know where she lives. Keep going."

They were halfway down the street when an urgent voice came over the radio. "She just pushed through another signal, but we stayed right behind. She changed her route."

"To where?" Sabine asked.

"She's on B11."

"Don't lose her. Let us know as soon as she exits," Dorfmann said and motioned the VW bus driver to turn left at the next intersection.

She was just following the practice agents use to shake a potential tail, Sabine told herself. They'd kept a safe distance, and both the VW and the backup team's Opel were nongovernment vehicles, making them less suspicious.

They'd hardly made it to B11 when the backup commando reported, "She's heading west toward Neuried. Cancel that. She just made a right turn. That's the way to Forstenrieder Park."

Sabine's pulse quickened. Dorfmann raised his eyebrows. He didn't speak, but she knew he shared her thoughts. The mole wasn't going to the green oasis to relax or to feed the birds. Dorfmann instructed the driver to take the quickest route to the park.

A few minutes later, the radio voice announced, "Suspect parked at Stäblistraße. She's getting out of car with something in her hand that looks like . . . uh . . . it's a book. We're taking pictures. She's heading into the park."

"Stay put," Dorfmann commanded. "We're almost there."

The VW driver passed the backup team's white Opel and pulled into a spot at the curb several car lengths short of the Mercedes. Sabine raised the binoculars to her eyes. Despite the warm evening, the park was almost empty. Maybe because of the dinner hour or maybe the mole had selected this spot for its remoteness. Perhaps both.

"Do you see her?" Dorfmann asked.

Sabine tensed at the apprehension in his voice. "Yes."

"Well, what in the hell is she doing?"

"She's stopping at the second bench . . . looking around . . . sitting down . . . letting a couple stroll by . . . opening her book."

Dorfmann scoffed. "Don't tell me she's come to the park for a relaxing evening read."

"Not likely, boss."

Sabine kept watching. The woman seemed engrossed in her read, turning pages. Either they'd been wrong about her, or she was playing it cool. Sabine's arms grew heavy, but she would not lower the binoculars.

"Anything new?" Dorfmann asked.

"No, she's reading . . . but wait, she's—"

"What?"

"Looks like she's fiddling with something on the bench." Sabine squinted. "She laid down the book and . . . crap, she just turned her body so I can't see what she's doing." She lowered the glasses and gave Dorfmann a questioning look.

He shook his head. "Let's give her a chance to leave a signal for the courier. I'd like to get both of them."

Sabine resumed her watch. The woman, still in her office garb of a navy business suit, was coming back down the path, but instead of going to the Mercedes, she veered off toward a metal wastepaper basket affixed to a light pole. Tossing the book? No, she produced chalk from a coat pocket and ran it along the side of the basket, leaving a white mark.

Dorfmann grabbed the microphone. "Meet us at the Mercedes."

"*Sofort,*" came the response.

Dorfmann jumped from the VW bus. Sabine ran alongside him, the two men from the backup team close behind. They'd enlisted an officer from the Federal Criminal Police, the only one among them authorized to carry a gun.

As they closed in, the woman whirled around. Her panicked expression said she recognized them.

"*Guten Abend,* Frau Kraus," Dorfmann said to his deputy. "Reading something interesting on this lovely evening in the park?"

Kraus slumped against the fender. The book and car keys fell from her hands onto the asphalt. A shadow of resignation passed over her face.

The young BND agent picked up the book and the keys and started to hand them to Dorfmann, who waved him off. "Keep those for now, and hold Frau Kraus here, while Sabine and I take a look at the bench."

Sabine could hardly keep up with Dorfmann striding down the path. They waited until a man walking his dog passed before examining the wooden bench, supported by metal posts. None of the slats appeared to be loose. Sabine poked around one end, trying to lift one board after another, while Dorfmann did the same on the opposite side. They worked their way to the center. Nothing gave way.

They stood back, studying every square centimeter. The hiding place, if there was one, had to be somewhere else. They circled the bench, examining the metal posts. Still no luck. Then Sabine's shoe caught on something. She looked down at a metal plate screwed into the concrete slab that supported the bench. The tip of her shoe had dislodged the plate a tiny bit. She bent down and rotated the loose plate, laying bare a recess that held an envelope.

She handed it to Dorfmann. "It's sealed."

He ripped it open, read and nodded. "It's your doctored report all right."

He slid the envelope into a coat pocket and produced a sealed one containing the identical document of disinformation. He placed it in the cubbyhole and rotated the plate back in place.

He waved Sabine on. "We've got all the proof we need. Let's take Kraus to the office and grill her. Prepare for a long night. For once, we're one step ahead of the Stasi spymaster."

Sabine followed him down the path. "What about the courier?"

"We'll have the backup team keep an eye out for now. As soon as we get to the office, you arrange for around-the-clock surveillance." He stopped, causing her to run into him. "Great work, Sabine. Just remember to trade your VW for the Mercedes we talked about after I get you that promotion."

She smiled, but all she could think about were the many agents Dorfmann's deputy must have betrayed over the years. Her anger grew as she remembered her phone call asking Kraus to send the Cologne agents to arrest the Sturms. A mystery no more who had tipped them off in time to flee.

Chapter Eighty-Four

Trust

Stuttgart, Saturday, 3 September 1977

Traude pulled Stefan along the path of Höhenpark Killesberg. "Look at these begonias and busy lizzics—yellow, white, pink, fuchsia. I loved the park in Weimar, but it has nothing like this sea of colors."

Stefan nodded, trying hard to keep his focus on the beautiful surroundings, but he could only think of one thing: would Monika show? After he'd told Traude the despicable things he'd had to do for the Stasi, she shocked him by insisting that he call Monika. "You had no choice, *Vati*. And you did it for me."

He'd resisted at first. Monika would probably hate him forever, but he'd regret it for the rest of his life if he didn't at least try to make up for what he'd done. By Thursday, he'd summoned enough courage to make the call.

When she answered, Stefan spoke fast as if that would prevent her from hanging up. Tripping over his words, he'd started to explain how he had fled when she interrupted.

"Sabine told me about your escape. You no longer have to do the Stasi's dirty work and your daughter is studying at the Stuttgart opera school. I wish both of you all the best—"

"Please hear me out, Monika."

"What else is there to say?"

"I'd like to tell you in person. What if I come to Bonn this weekend?"

Silence. He anticipated the dreaded dial tone, but she said, "Only if you bring your daughter."

Stefan swallowed, trying to understand why Monika wanted to meet Traude. Perhaps to act as a safety blanket, a chaperone of sorts. Or to let her know how shabbily her father had behaved?

"Well, what do you say?" Monika prodded.

"I don't think she can get away. She's spending every waking hour on her music studies." An idea came to him. "But I've persuaded her to take off a few hours on Saturday. We're going to the Killesberg. It's supposed to be one of the most beautiful parks in all of Germany. Why don't you come to Stuttgart and join us? You and Traude have a lot in common, and I'd enjoy listening to the two of you talking opera."

"I'll think about it. What's your phone number?"

"I'm staying at the Hotel Königshof, Room 715." He picked up the hotel notepad from the nightstand and gave her the phone number and address.

"I'll call you tomorrow." Click.

He didn't mention the conversation to Traude, because he might never hear from Monika again. But early Friday morning, call she did. No less surprising was Traude's enthusiastic agreement to meet the woman her father had romanced for the Stasi.

"Dad, you're not even looking at the flowers." Traude's voice brought him back. "Don't worry, she will come."

"I hope you're right." He checked his watch. "Time to meet her for lunch."

They made it to the restaurant with a few minutes to spare. The hostess assured them she could seat them as soon as their party arrived. Traude took a seat on the bench in the lobby while Stefan stepped out into the mild afternoon and paced. He peered in all directions, scanning the strolling visitors. Each time he spotted blonde hair, he took a step forward, only to stop in disappointment.

At ten after one, he joined Traude inside. "Let's get a table. Looks like it'll be just the two of us."

Resigned to having been stood up, he followed the hostess leading them through the dining room to a corner table. The menu items swam before his eyes. Food was the last thing he wanted. The waitress took their beverage orders, a *Dinkelacker* beer for him and a bottle of mineral water for Traude.

While they waited for their drinks, Traude said, "Maybe she was delayed."

"Could be." He tried to sound hopeful.

The waitress served his beer, and he took a hefty swallow. Not having studied the menu, he ordered the daily special of *rostbraten mit spätzle,* a typical Swabian dish. Traude did likewise.

Determined not to feel sorry for himself, he lifted his glass and waited for Traude to raise hers. "Let's be grateful for our freedom and for your opportunity to pursue your life-long dream."

Traude nodded and they drank. He put down his glass, but Traude held hers in midair while staring toward the entrance. He turned and stifled a gasp at the sight of Monika zigzagging around chairs and tables. Her blonde curls bobbing, she rushed toward them. The way her flowery summer dress showed off her figure nearly took his breath away.

He jumped up, wanting to hug her, but she kept her distance, offering her hand. As they shook, she said, "I apologize for being late."

"We're so glad you came. Please meet my daughter, Traude."

After their handshake, all three sat and Stefan waved the waitress over for another order of the daily special and a Dinkelacker. Overcome by gratitude at being with his two favorite women, Stefan grappled for a conversation starter.

Monika beat him to it as she said to Traude, "I understand you've been admitted to the conservatory here."

That's all it took and the two of them were off talking about opera. Having regained his appetite, Stefan listened throughout the meal to the lively exchange about their beloved art form. Whenever they ventured into musical terms that didn't interest him, he found himself admiring their unmitigated passion.

Once, his thoughts drifted to Helga. If not for her, he wouldn't be here. And no matter how hard Sabine and her superiors pushed, he would never betray Helga. Would he ever see her again? Only if there came a day when East Germans could travel freely.

"Where are you, Dad?" Traude's voice cut short his ruminations.

"Sorry, I was just thinking about the person who made it possible for me to make it over the Wall."

"I want you to tell me about your hair-raising escape," Monika said. She faced Traude. "But I understand if you don't care to listen to the story you've probably heard more than once."

Traude shook her head. "Actually, I'm dying to ride the chairlift while you two catch up."

Stefan reached across the table and squeezed Traude's hand. At that moment, the server brought the check and Stefan paid. On the way out, he suggested they meet at the main entrance at five, but Monika insisted on four o'clock since she had a four-hour drive back to Bonn. So much for his hope, however faint, that she might spend the night.

After Traude took off, Stefan pointed in the opposite direction. "This way to the *Tal der Rosen*. While we walk, I'll tell you all about my narrow escape and the Good Samaritan who found me crumpled at the foot of the Wall."

Halfway through his account, he stopped speaking when they reached the valley of roses. Monika stepped off the trail, smelling the blooms that came in all colors, red, yellow, white, purple—thousands and thousands of them. Stefan resisted the temptation to break off a red rose for her. Too many visitors and park employees around, and too dramatic a gesture. It might put her off, given that their relationship—if one even existed—remained on a shaky footing.

Monika returned to the path. "Sorry, I couldn't resist those beautiful roses. Please go on with your story."

By the time they settled on a bench facing the water lily pond, he'd given her a full report, save for Helga's role. Like Sabine before her, Monika asked how he'd learned of the vulnerable section of the Wall.

"I may not be a professional spy, but my time with the Stasi taught me how to ferret out secret information."

She gave him a quizzical look that said she knew he wasn't giving her the full picture, but she didn't press for details. Instead, she asked, "How is your shoulder?"

"Should be as good as new in a few weeks."

"And what are you going to do with yourself while Traude studies?"

"I'm hoping for an offer from a certain national news magazine to work in its Stuttgart bureau. Sabine arranged the job interview—my reward for keeping my end of the bargain helping her catch the Stasi mole in her agency."

"Won't you miss the excitement of playing Romeo, romancing government secretaries?"

He tried to read her expression, looking for signs of mockery, disdain or just good-natured teasing, but before he could, she turned toward the pond. Finding it impossible to determine her intentions from her profile, he too gazed at the lilies floating on the calm water. The image soothed him.

He took a deep breath. Still keeping his eyes on the pond, he said, "Monika, my feelings for you were . . . are real. Won't you give me a chance to prove it?"

She likewise stared straight ahead. "I don't know that I'll ever be able to trust you again. I know you were forced, but still—"

"All I'm asking is a chance to make up for what I did. To make amends."

"And just how do you propose to do that?"

"One visit at a time. Judge me by my deeds, not my words."

She faced him. "If we get together at all, it'll be on my terms."

"Deal," he said. Not that he had any other option. He'd accept whatever conditions she imposed.

"Good." She gave him a half smile. "First rule: you don't call me; I'll call you."

Though he couldn't imagine himself sitting by the phone waiting for a woman's call, he said, "Agreed."

"All right then. Let's enjoy the scenery for a little while before we meet up with your daughter."

He checked his watch. "A few more minutes and we need to go. The park has a small-gauge train with a steam locomotive. If you like, we can ride it back to the main entrance."

"Fun."

He chose to interpret her smile as meaning he'd taken a baby step towards possible redemption, but the annals of history overflowed with examples of men who'd misread women's intentions.

Chapter Eighty-Five

Consultant or Not?

Munich, Saturday, 3 September 1977

Early Saturday evening and Sabine had Systems Solutions's courtyard all to herself. She parked close to the door and tossed her cap onto the passenger seat. She ran a comb through her windblown hair, grabbed the straw-covered bottle of Chianti, and climbed from the car. Normally, she wouldn't close the top on a mild evening with no rain forecast, but the weather could change by morning.

She removed the rear cover and had the folded top halfway up when Horst's voice bellowed over the courtyard, "I don't believe it—a silver 280SL. Did you rob a bank or have you found a rich boyfriend I should know about?" Arms crossed, he stood below the Systems Solutions sign and smiled. Dark hair, olive complexion—God, he was handsome.

But she couldn't let him get away with a smart-ass remark like that. "Well, there's something to be said for an older man of means who likes to spoil his woman."

Horst laughed. "Touché." He walked over and helped her fasten the top. "I'm envious. Looks like more fun than my BMW. But how did you—?"

She opened the door. "Have a look."

As he sank into the driver's seat, she explained, "It's two years old. My mechanic sold it to me after giving me the bad news it would cost too much to fix the transmission on my poor old VW. This beauty was his wife's car, but she's expecting their first child. So the two-seater convertible had to go."

Horst ran his fingers over the dashboard, the gearshift, the leather seats, as if caressing a lover. "I hope he made you a good deal."

"He did, but I still had to splurge, counting on Dorfmann putting me in for a promotion and a healthy raise."

"He'd better, after all you've accomplished." Horst let go of the steering wheel, stepped out and eased the door closed.

She handed him the Chianti. "To go with the Italian dinner you promised."

He waved her on. "A culinary feast is waiting."

A tail-wagging Sara and a soprano-tenor duet greeted her in the living room. Sabine stroked the Great Dane's soft, floppy ears.

"Very thoughtful of you, Horst, to put on opera for me."

"I thought it a fitting theme for the evening, and I've been listening to a lot of opera this week while you were busy chasing your mole and debriefing your Romeo. You know, of course, what this is from."

"Third act of *La Bohème*. Probably the most performed opera of all time."

He furrowed his brow. "Does that mean you've seen it all you want?"

"Of course not. I could never grow tired of the glorious music. Why?"

"Just curious."

She felt sure there was more to it than idle curiosity, but she let it go. He pulled the Chianti's cork and, bottle in hand, led her into the dining room. The ambience brought her up short—

soft candlelight, fine china plates and serving dishes on a crisp white tablecloth.

Horst poured the wine into crystal glasses and pointed to the nearby chair. "Come on, I've never seen you shy before."

She sat. "I had no idea you were such a romantic."

He settled next to her and raised his glass. "A special occasion that calls for a celebration. You turned a Romeo, you caught the mole, you're getting a promotion, and best of all, you can spend a little more time with me. At least until your next big case."

She lifted her glass. "And here's to you and your computer program that put us on the right trail."

After they drank, she asked, "So what kind of gourmet meal did you prepare for the occasion?"

He couldn't hide his sheepish expression as he uncovered one serving dish after another. "Sorry to disappoint you, Sabine, but cooking is not my forte. So we'll be dining on veal scaloppini, angel hair pasta, garlic bread, and Caesar salad from your favorite Schwabing restaurant."

"You ordered this from Trattoria Bel Canto?"

He nodded. "*Guten Appetit.*"

During their meal, Horst got up a few times to change the record. After putting the final side on the turntable, he turned down the sound and asked, "Did you find out who sabotaged the brakes on your VW?"

"Not yet, but the order must have come from the Stasi spymaster." Careful to reveal neither name nor gender, Sabine said, "The mole has been cooperating, hoping for a lenient sentence. We've already arrested several Stasi informants, and the mole admitted to having tipped off the Sturms."

Horst held up his fork. "Didn't you call Dorfmann's deputy from my shop and ask her to dispatch the Cologne agents to the Sturm apartment?"

"So what?"

"I'm just connecting the dots. As far as I'm concerned, you haven't told me a thing."

He'd put two and two together. She should have known better than to volunteer information to someone schooled in tradecraft.

As the final note of the opera sounded, Horst slid an envelope across the table. "A surprise for you."

She fished out two opera tickets. "*La Bohème* at the Bavarian State Opera. You sneak."

"I thought I'd made a mistake when you said how often it is performed."

She reached across the table and covered his hand with hers. "Thank you. You'll love it."

"So you'll go with me?"

"Wouldn't miss it for the world."

She withdrew her hand, and he cleared the table. "The dessert is in the freezer."

"What are you serving?"

"Spumoni. Would you like some now?"

She finished her wine. "Maybe later. If you're up for walking off the rich food, let's take Sara."

At the sound of her name, the dog jumped to her feet and came running. Horst fastened the lead on her collar and the three of them strolled out into the balmy evening.

A few minutes into the walk, Sabine said, "I almost forgot to give you the good news. Dorfmann is asking for your final bill."

Horst pulled Sara to a stop. "So my consulting services are no longer required. Why is that good news?"

"I must say, for a former intelligence officer, you're a little dense." She nudged him. "We're no longer working together. Get it?"

He took her hand in his. "No more constraints."

When they returned to his courtyard, he said, "There's something else I'd like to know, if you're allowed to say. Who broke into my shop and what were they after?"

"The mole alerted the Stasi to your consulting. We've arrested the two burglars. They were after your computer program and they were planning on installing a bug."

"Good thing Sara woke me and we scared them off."

Back inside, Sara went straight to her water bowl.

"You ready for spumoni now?"

Sabine shook her head. "Still too full. But about that break-in—you never did tell me what you grabbed to chase away the burglars."

"You don't forget much, do you?"

"It's a requirement for doing my job well. So tell me, where do you keep your gun?"

"In my nightstand."

"Show me."

He gave a quizzical look, but led her to the bedroom. "I keep it over—"

She shut him up with a long kiss. Coming up for air, she gazed into his eyes. "Seems like we left something unfinished after *La Traviata* last week."

He unbuttoned her blouse while she tore at his shirt. Shedding trousers and skirt, they tumbled onto the bed.

♫ ♫ ♫

Sabine stirred at a shrill ring. Instinctively, she fumbled for her phone on the nightstand, except she wasn't in her apartment. She squinted against the sunrays spilling into Horst's bedroom.

"Systems Solutions." Horst's voice barely penetrated her stupor.

She wondered who could be calling on a Sunday morning. Tired from a night short on sleep, she let her eyelids close, but her ears remained on alert as she strained to hear.

Judging from Horst's responses, the caller was giving him instructions. A business call on the weekend?

Before she could drift off, Horst nudged her. "You'll never guess who that was." He paused to make sure he had her full attention. "That was your boss."

She opened her eyes. "Dorfmann?"

"None other."

"What possessed him to bother you on a Sunday morning?"

"There's been a security breach at the Chancellery. He's on the trail of another Romeo, and he's putting me back on the consultant payroll. He said if I talked with you to have you call him at home right away."

She sat straight up. "Do you think he knows I'm here?"

Horst shrugged. "He might suspect."

"Must be damned urgent for him to bother me on a weekend. *Scheiße!* I have to get home and call him."

She leaped out of bed and almost tripped over the clothes that were still strewn across the carpet from last night.

As she zipped up her skirt and buttoned her blouse, Horst said, "I can't really afford to turn him down. Having the government as a steady client is my best shot at Systems Solutions really taking off."

She bent over and kissed him on the forehead. "I understand."

"I'm not sure what this means for us, but after last night, I thought we might . . ."

Before he could find the right words, she shot back, "We'll just have to see."

Then she stepped around a sleeping Sara and charged from the bedroom.

♫ ♫ ♫ THE END ♫ ♫ ♫

Dear Reader:

Thank you for reading my book. If you enjoyed it, won't you please take a moment to leave me a review at your favorite retailer?

Thanks!
Peter Bernhardt

About the Author:

As I approached my prime, I developed the powerful urge to write thrillers. My wife harbored the absurd suspicion midlife crisis had struck, because I was bound in those days to courtroom and desk at the U.S. Attorney's Office. So my dream remained just that for a long time. As soon as I retired, though, we moved to Arizona and I took things in hand by enrolling in a workshop for wannabe authors. German is my native tongue, not English, and my experience as an author consisted of the publication of a couple of student papers and law journal articles, plus cranking out numberless legal pleadings and briefs. What was I thinking?

The workshop was a bust, but it did push me into tackling my first book, *The Stasi File – Opera and Espionage: A Deadly Combination,* in which, following the age-old advice to "write what you know," I wove together the unlikely combination of a German upbringing, a lifelong love of opera and my experiences as an attorney. After a beginning that seemed to take forever, I was surprised when the challenge of creating characters and building a plot that was real and intriguing started to take over my waking hours, and a few sleeping ones too.

My skill and talent developed quickly, but there were many times they seemed almost superfluous--I was too busy holding on tight as "my" characters and their actions took over and went their own ways, leaving me to serve as their scribe and menial servant. What a journey!

Connect with Me:

https://www.facebook.com/peter.bernhardt.583
https://twitter.com/@sedonawriter
http://sedonauthor.com
http://sedonaauthor.blogspot.com
https://www.smashwords.com/profile/view/sedonawriter

Other Books by Peter Bernhardt:

1. *The Stasi File: Opera and Espionage—A Deadly Combination.* An American lawyer and his former lover, an Italian opera diva, are drawn into an assassination plot by a Stasi General desperate to prevent the collapse of the East German police state after the fall of the Berlin Wall. Read chapter 1 on page 490.

2. *Kiss of the Shaman's Daughter,* features *The Stasi File* protagonists, Rolf Keller and Sylvia Mazzoni in their next adventure in Santa Fe, New Mexico, where they are pressed into searching for a missing archaeologist. They not only encounter ruthless antiquities traffickers, but find their fates intertwined with that of a shaman's daughter, who centuries earlier played a crucial role in the Pueblo Indian Revolt that drove the Spanish from New Mexico.

The Stasi File

Chapter One

Sylvia Mazzoni stepped out the stage door of the Big House, the locals' name for the Stuttgart Opera Theater. In her blue jeans and sweatshirt, she looked more like a member of the cleaning crew than a soprano leaving a rehearsal called solely on her account. She took several deep breaths, releasing the lingering tension with each exhalation. A gust of November wind whipped the trees around, causing shadows to thrust and parry in the dusky Schlossgarten Park. She shivered, pulled a long wool scarf from her shoulder bag, and wrapped it, Pavarotti style, around her throat. Anything to protect The Voice. She removed her hair clasp to allow heavy, dark tresses to cascade around her shoulders.

The music director had engaged her for two performances as Micaëla in *Carmen* after seeing her in the part at the regional opera in Ulm. She had done well this evening, but would she pass the real test tomorrow? Her debut at the renowned Stuttgart Opera could make or break her career. If she failed to impress, she'd be relegated once again to bit parts in provincial houses. She vowed not to let that happen. She had worked too hard for too long to fail now.

The park adjoining the theater, brimming with life all day, was deserted. Sylvia thought of waiting for a colleague to accompany her, but eager to catch the next streetcar, she ignored her intuition and stepped onto the cobblestone promenade along the lake. A glimmer of city lights filtered through the bare branches of giant oaks and sycamores. Dim sidewalk lamps cast long, crooked fingers across the dark water. To shake the foreboding image, she looked for the soft ripples that would precede swimming mallards and swans, but it was late even for them.

Sylvia peered up the dark path. A few meters ahead, the desiccated leaves of a giant poplar rustled in the night air. From there it was only a few minutes to the shopping arcade and the streetcar stop. She pressed on.

A burly man came around the bend, his right hand tucked inside the front of his leather jacket. Startled, Sylvia felt an adrenaline rush. She clutched her umbrella and stepped to her right to give him a wide berth. Out of the corner of her eye she caught a sudden movement, a lunge toward her. She spun around. Glinting metal ripped through her sweatshirt and slashed her left upper arm. She winced with pain as she jammed the metal tip of the umbrella as hard as she could into the attacker's chest. He grunted. The impact jarred the umbrella from her hand and sent it clattering to the ground. Warm liquid trickled down her arm. Sylvia staggered onto the damp lawn. She fought to regain her balance but slipped and fell hard.

Frantic, she looked for the umbrella, but it had rolled down the path, beyond her reach. Get up, she exhorted herself in a panic, but too late. The towering figure came at her again. Heart thudding, Sylvia skidded backwards on the grass. She heard herself scream, "Help, help . . . help me!"

The man drew back the knife and slashed downward again. She rolled. Her face, covered by her tangled hair, flattened against the wet ground. She clawed the hair aside and saw the knife plunge to its hilt into the earth, at the spot where she had been a second ago.

"Damn you, traitor!"

She'd heard that guttural voice before. She raised her head and found herself staring into hate-filled eyes. Could it be . . . ? Before she finished the thought, his massive body crushed her, knocking the breath out of her. She opened her mouth to cry again for help, but could only spit blades of grass. Cold fingers dug beneath her scarf and closed around her throat. Muscular thighs straddled her hips, pinning her so that struggle was useless. She brought her hands up, trying to loosen his grip, but the vise only tightened.

"Ple . . ." Sylvia's voice trailed off in a gurgle, her trachea compressed in his grasp. Blood rushed in her ears. The man's menacing face became a distorted blur. Panicked, she fought for a breath. Her limbs went numb. Darkness swallowed her.

Then a sharp thump penetrated the void. Dead weight slumped against her chest. The vise at her neck loosened.

She gulped for air, fighting the crushing weight. One small breath came, then another. She opened her eyes. The attacker's face pressed at an unnatural angle against her chest. Blood trickled from the man's slack mouth. Repulsed, she pushed the stubbly face away and struggled to shove the corpse aside. It tipped for a moment, then rolled back on top of her. She shuddered.

Sylvia took several more ragged breaths, gathering her strength, but before she could make another attempt, someone lifted the body off her. Her chest heaved with relief.

"Frau Mazzoni, are you all right?"

She stared at the man. Then she recognized Intelligence Officer Dieter Schmidt.

"Herr Schmidt. What are you—?"

"You're safe now." He took her right arm to help her sit up, then pointed at the blood-soaked clothing on the other. "Can you move your arm?"

Sylvia gingerly lifted her left arm. The pain was tolerable. The sweatshirt's damp sleeve clung to the wound, stemming the blood flow. "I guess it's okay."

"Good." He motioned toward the lifeless body lying in the grass next to her. "Do you know him?"

She forced herself to look. "He's with . . ." She took a deep breath. "He was with the RAF. Manfred Klau, a friend of Horst." She shivered. For years she had looked over her shoulder expecting the Red Army Faction terrorists to come for her. They never had. Why now, twelve years later, just when she'd begun to think she was safe from their revenge?

Schmidt nodded. "I was afraid of that." He bent down and felt for a pulse. After a few seconds he said, "His terrorist days are over."

Sylvia stared at Schmidt. "Did you shoot him?"

He steadied her on her feet. "We'll talk about this later. You have to get away from here now—before the police arrive."

He scrutinized her face. "Can you make it back to your hotel by yourself?"

In a daze, she nodded.

"I have to take care of things here, but I'll check on you as soon as I can." He collected her bag and umbrella and thrust them toward her. "Frau Mazzoni, not a word about this to anyone. Go. Now!"

Sylvia stumbled in the direction of the shopping arcade.

Made in the USA
Charleston, SC
09 February 2016